the MATING GAME

MELISSA SNARK

The Mating Game

Series: Sassafras Shifters

ISBN: 978-1-942193-40-1 (paperback)

COPYRIGHT © 2021 by Melissa Snark

Nordic Lights Press. Second Edition.

Publishing History

First Scarlet Rose Edition, 2014; Print ISBN 978-1-62830-378-0; Digital ISBN 978-1-62830-379-7.

Cover design by Jacqueline Sweet Design

Contact Information:

Email: admin@nordiclightspress.com

Nordic Lights Press

PO Box 323

Anacortes, WA 98221

Published in the United States of America.

ACKNOWLEDGMENTS

To my friend and reader Jess Kisia, thank you all your support and feedback.

To my editor Write Now Creative, many thanks.

To my line editor and fellow author, Nicole Zoltack, thank you so much for all your hard work and support.

To my fabulous fans, thank you for your readership and support.

TRIGGERS

Mentions of past mental and physical abuse.
Adult language and subject matter.
Fantasy violence.

BOOK DESCRIPTION

Two dominant male wolves must enter a romantic competition for mating rights with the alpha female. The winner will claim The Heart of the Iron Stone Pack and take the throne to rule as the Wolf King.

Single mother Theresa Russo struggles to protect her only child in a treacherous world full of dangerous lies and even more startling truths. She has a secret crush on her best friend, but their romance is forbidden. No one must know, no one must suspect, until everything changes. Unexpectedly, Theresa discovers that she commands the wolf magic touch needed to heal the broken pack.

The current overbearing alpha male rules with an iron fist and encourages rivalry within the pack. He has the power to force Theresa into an arranged marriage. Need rules her body as she comes into heat, but how can she choose only one mate when her body craves both the virile beta and the man she loves?

Zachary Hunter will do anything to claim his fated mate, anything except killing his friend. Robert Blane is just as determined to ascend to alpha. Both their beasts howl to mark her flesh and bond with her soul, but only one can survive to claim her forever.

With enemies circling, they must fight for the pack, and a future together.

Note to readers:
The Mating Game was previously published with The Wild Rose Press Digital ISBN 978-1-62830-379-7. This edition has been extensively revised and includes new scenes. The Mating Game has sizzling-hot, sexy shenanigans and a Happily Ever After ending.

CHAPTER ONE

A two-story bungalow in Iron Stone, Nevada - Sierra Nevada mountains – Saturday morning

Bright and early, Theresa Russo opened her front door to discover Zachary Hunter clad in a bright orange dress on her porch. The loose bodice fell low on his chest, displaying dark blond curls and showcasing his broad shoulders and powerful torso. The lacy hemline stopped above the knees, revealing his muscular calves, strong ankles, and shapely feet.

It was unusual attire for a dominant male werewolf.

For the longest moment, neither of them spoke a word. Theresa stared with her mouth hanging open. Pleasure shone on Zach's handsome face, and he gestured *ta-dah* like a stage magician.

Unable to resist, Theresa stepped closer and sniffed, seeking to satisfy the impulses of her she-wolf. Zach's earthy scent flooded her nostrils—masculine and potent—inciting the heated ache of arousal between her thighs. She licked her lips, hoping that drool hadn't dribbled down her chin. Her gaze tracked downward, irresistibly drawn to his spectacular physique, admiring everything but his choice of attire. Her heart throbbed, and who could blame her?

"My eyes are up here, love," Zach quipped in a crisp English accent. He stroked the underside of her chin with a long, elegant finger. His teasing touch sent shivers coursing through her.

"Oh, right. Sorry." A flush warmed her skin.

Reluctantly, Theresa forced her roaming eyes upward, away from his buff chest, striving to remember that she and Zach didn't play like that. The man was many things to her—best friend, confidant, and protector. He fixed leaky faucets and kept her old car running, but of all the roles he played, he remained "lover" only in her dreams.

"Good morning, Theresa." His tone was incredibly dry. No doubt, the irony of his predicament had not escaped him.

"Good morning, Zach." Theresa struggled to

keep a straight face out of respect for Zach's status. He far outranked her within the pack's hierarchy. Repressing her mirth proved impossible; however, she held a hand to her mouth to hide a sassy smile.

"Are you laughing at me, pet?" Zach cocked his head, and silken bangs fell across his forehead. His blue eyes twinkled, and the corners of his sensual mouth quirked. He had an aristocratic brow, an angular nose, and high cheekbones set in an oblong face.

"Oh, yes. God, I'm so sorry." Laughter overwhelmed her until she felt ready to burst. Her abdominal muscles ached. She flipped her long, curly black hair forward to conceal her expression.

"Go on. Look your fill." Zach spread his arms in a display of self-mockery, causing that ludicrous skirt to rise, revealing masculine knees and athletic thighs. "Get it out of your system once and for all."

"Thank you, but I think I've teased you enough for one day."

Belatedly, Theresa noticed his disheveled appearance. He had a five o'clock shadow at eight a.m. A scruffy beard covered his square jaw and throat. His shoulder-length, golden-blond hair was a tangled mess about his striking features.

Out of concern, she asked, "Are you going to tell me how you wound up on my front porch in a dress?"

Zach sighed. "I went running in the woods last night to clear my head."

Theresa arched a brow. "Writer's block again?"

Suddenly serious, he rubbed his jaw. "I haven't written a word in days."

The man had a talent for gross exaggeration, so Theresa mentally revised the time frame to twenty-four hours and the word count to less than a page.

She cooed her sympathy. "You poor thing. It must be so hard on you."

He snorted. "You've no idea."

"Zach, you're a bestselling author. Can't you afford to take a break from cranking out the murder mysteries? At least until you get your mojo back?"

"I've got a deadline, love. My editor is an absolute slave driver. That's why I'm in this state." He indicated his flamboyant apparel with a flourish.

She rolled her eyes. "Of course. Your editor made you run through the forest in an orange dress. Makes perfect sense. I'm sorry I asked."

He frowned. "I was running on four legs, love, not two. You know that."

"Of course I do, but you didn't expect anything but a hard time showing up here in that." She gave him a quick up-down.

Zach chuckled. "Not really. To make a long story short, I left my possessions in a hunter's blind, but when I returned, my clothing was gone."

"Did someone find your clothes?" she asked with a worried frown.

Such a minor thing might result in unforeseen troubles for the pack. As a rule, the local werewolves went to great lengths to conceal their presence from the human population. Ordinary people in the small Nevada town of Iron Stone remained blithely unaware of the wolves living amongst them.

"Not someone. Something," Zach said. "Raccoons, three of the scrotty little sods. They ripped my clothes to shreds and dredged the creek with my shoes."

"Oh, no!" Laughter again threatened to split her sides. She pressed her hands to her ribcage and gasped for breath. "Did you eat them?"

"No." Zach looked miserable for the admission. "It was a mum and two kits. I didn't have the heart."

Theresa touched his hand. "You're a good man, Zachary Hunter."

"Thanks, but I'd rather be a clothed man," Zach said. "I stole this getup off a laundry line in the Widow Crawley's yard."

"For shame! Stealing from a little old lady."

Zach rolled his shoulders to add emphasis to the voluminous dress. "Not so little."

She poked him in the ribs. "You're so bad."

"Can I come in, or are you going to force me to beg?" Zach sounded exasperated.

"I don't know. What if Isabel sees you looking like this? Whatever will my daughter think?" With a welcoming sweep of her arm, she stepped back to allow him entry.

"Then I'll have two of you laughing at me," Zach said tartly. Crossing the threshold, he stepped into the foyer of her small two-bedroom bungalow. He moved with primal grace, befitting his long limbs and muscular physique.

Poetry had never seen a lovelier motion.

"Boy, you can say that again. Orange is all wrong for your complexion. It makes your calves look fat." Theresa glanced outside just to be sure that something weirder wasn't following on his heels then closed the door.

"Never mind my calves." Zach stopped near the base of the staircase and rested an arm on the railing. He twisted his hips, causing the billowing skirt to flare. "I'm convinced this monstrosity makes my arse look fat. What do you think?"

Following his invitation, Theresa had no other choice than to look. Her gaze swept all six-foot-plus of him, lingering over his muscular shoulder blades. Unfortunately, the horror of a dress concealed his tight backside. Fortunately, Theresa knew his body well enough to fill in the blanks with a fantasy.

"Oh, yeah. Your ass has never looked bigger." Her gaze dropped to the floor where his muddy feet had left tracks on the tile. Her wolf surfaced, and a growl of displeasure rolled from her throat. "Zach, your feet are filthy. Don't you dare walk another step!"

Zach swung back to Theresa with an unrepentant grin. "Yes, ma'am."

"Stay put." Theresa rushed from the room and returned in a flash with a bar of soap, a tub of warm water, and towels. She placed her palm against Zach's chest and pushed him toward the stairs. "Sit."

Theresa sank to her knees before him and placed the tub on the floor. Obediently, he planted his backside on a step. Sharp tension reverberated in the air along with a sudden spike in musky pheromones.

"Theresa?" His deep voice contained a distinct note of confusion.

"Yes, Zach?" Theresa infused her reply with innocence, pretending not to understand. Deep down, however, she derived satisfaction from the subtle evidence of his arousal. It didn't hurt to remind Zach now and then that Theresa was a woman as well as his friend. He might regard her with nothing more than brotherly affection, but that wasn't how she felt about him at all.

"Nothing." His gruff tone said the exact opposite.

Theresa glanced down to hide her smile. She

leaned forward and sniffed, drinking in his aroma, an irresistible combination of untamed wilderness and virile male wolf.

"It's bad enough my neighbors might have seen you prancing down the street in that eyesore, but I'm not going to have you tracking mud through my house." Theresa took his left ankle between her hands. "Lift."

He complied, and she lowered his foot into the warm water. Zach remained still but alert as Theresa set about scrubbing his dirty toes with a small bar of soap. Energy thrummed through his body, and his uncharacteristic silence worried her. Typically, the vivacious Brit cracked jokes a mile a minute.

His calves were muscular and covered in a layer of blond hair. Theresa ran her fingernails across his instep, and his foot jerked. He stifled a sound somewhere between a gasp and a grunt and cleared his throat at the end.

Theresa looked up with a small smile playing on her lips. "Zach, are you ticklish?"

"Don't be absurd." In his denial, Zach sounded even more like a proper aristocrat than usual.

To prove a point, Theresa ran her fingernails across his instep, tickling sensitive skin. His foot jumped again, and her smile called him a liar.

"Stop that." Chuckling, Zach leaned back on his elbows against the stairs, exposing his throat. A guttural groan escaped him when she ran her hands over his ankle to lift it from the water. He indulged in physical pleasure with a hedonistic freedom that she secretly envied.

Theresa hid behind a curtain of black hair, hoping to disguise the intense satisfaction she took from the simple act of touching him. Heat radiated from his skin, a scalding contrast to the cool morning air. Her hungry gaze roamed over his bare flesh, and her fingers itched to explore.

The man had a superb physique defined by exquisite details—sinew beneath tanned skin. Not a spare ounce of body fat marred his granite form. He was a magnificent male animal. She wanted to see all of him, but she was hesitant to act on her desires.

Naughty thoughts filled her head. The bunched material of the skirt had hit the point of no return. The knowledge that she was mere inches from uncovering *all* of Zach's masculine glory sent shivers along her spine. More than anything, she longed to shove that ridiculous skirt into his lap and wrap her mouth around his cock. Envisioning it, she licked her lips with the tip of her tongue, and her mouth watered for the taste of his flesh.

How would he react if she did?

Fear of rejection kept her from acting on her fantasies. She massaged Zach's calves, digging her fingers into the corded muscles, and he gave a throaty moan.

"Ah, that's it, love," he rumbled. "This is seventh heaven."

"Like that, do you?" she teased, playing with the hemline of the silly dress. Her pulse pounded beneath her breast. She stole a glance up, and her breathing hitched.

Zach was watching her with his wolf in his gaze. He flashed a wicked smile that left her quivering. "There are no words for how much I'm enjoying this."

"Zach," Theresa whispered, gnawing her lower lip.

Desire urged her to keep going, but self-doubt held her back. As a divorced single mother, she wasn't a virgin; however, her sexual experience was limited, and her marriage had been an abysmal disaster. If she couldn't please an abusive jerk like her ex, then how could she ever hope to satisfy a man like Zach?

Zach stirred as though sensing her reservations. "It's your choice, Theresa," he said softly. "If you don't want me, then just say so. I'll always respect no."

Hastily, Theresa averted her gaze, but her gut wrenched when she glimpsed the way Zach's mouth curled in disappointment before she looked away.

Tears stung her eyes because she wanted him so much she ached inside. The sad truth, she was a coward, and she hated herself for it.

"Theresa, did I do something wrong?" Zach asked. A husky timbre threaded his voice, so full of confusion and hurt, and she felt awful.

"No, of course not. Nothing's wrong," she lied, staring down.

He sighed long and low. "Where are you, love? What're you thinking?"

"Nothing. Sorry. I was thinking about washing the kitchen floor." She sprang to her feet and retreated to the bathroom. "Hold on while I grab a towel."

"Right." Zach's clipped tone conveyed his skepticism, and his gaze bored a hole in the back of her head.

Of course, he must've smelled her arousal. A heartthrob like Zach must be used to being the center of female attention.

Theresa endured a stab of jealousy when she thought about other women fawning over him. She snatched a clean bath towel from the downstairs bathroom. The break gave her the breathing space she needed to recover a semblance of composure. Upon her return, she treated Zach like a piece of silver as she polished his feet.

He stayed stoic, patiently enduring.

Task complete, she gathered the tub and towel in her arms. "I'm just going to put this stuff in the laundry room. I'll be right back."

Silence greeted her announcement. Inwardly cringing, Theresa hurried off. It made her ill to consider that this encounter would go down as a lost opportunity she would regret for the rest of her life.

CHAPTER TWO

In the utility room, Theresa emptied the tub and tossed the dirty towel into the washer. She drew several deep breaths, striving for calm, and splashed her face with cold water. Once she could think straight, she returned to the front entryway.

Zach was loitering on the stairs.

"You still have a change of clothes here," she said. "They're hanging in the downstairs closet."

"Back in a sec." He surged upright and departed in a flash of orange.

Downtrodden and defeated, Theresa headed into the kitchen. When Zach returned a few minutes later, he wore his usual attire—a rugby jersey with tight-fitting blue jeans and white athletic shoes. He carried a crumpled orange ball under his arm.

"Would you like for me to make sure that finds its way back to Widow Crawley's laundry line?" Theresa held out her hand.

"Yes, thank you," Zach said with such marked relief that she snickered. He passed her the bundle, and she set it aside to deal with later.

"I'll wash it first." Theresa regarded Zach with fond amusement. "Hungry?"

Zach nodded. "I'm peckish."

"I only have bacon and eggs." Anxiety crept into her voice.

Theresa would never begrudge Zach a meal, but a male wolf his size could easily break her food budget. She didn't worry about herself, but she had to place the interests of her daughter first.

Unfortunately, Zach perceived too much and understood her precarious finances too well. He leaned in. "Theresa, I won't ever allow you or Isabel to go hungry."

A blush suffused her cheeks. "I know that."

Zach's hand brushed her arm. "Coffee?"

She shook her head, grateful for the diversion. "No coffee. I'm out. Is tea okay?"

"Tea will be splendid. Thank you."

"I'll get some."

Before she reached the pantry, Zach caught the

inside of her elbow. Theresa stopped in her tracks, responding to the implicit command of a dominant wolf.

"Theresa, has Antonio shorted you on child support again?" he asked.

Theresa's neck and ears burned with shame. She despised admitting her money problems to Zach. However, it did no good to lie to him or deny it. One way or another, he would figure out the truth.

"Antonio is a week late," she admitted. "He says business at the shop has been bad, but rent is due this Friday. The landlord said that if the payment is late again, he'll evict us."

"Let me give you the money," he said.

Theresa had to refuse. Standing on her own two feet was a matter of pride. "No, thank you. It's kind of you to offer, and I appreciate it, but I can't take money from you."

His flinty stare conveyed his displeasure. "You and Isabel shouldn't be made to suffer because Antonio is a deadbeat dad. I'll speak with him."

"No, it's okay. I can handle my ex-husband."

Zach's jaw clenched. "I want to help. Why won't you let me?"

Theresa flushed with anger, and her tone grew sharp. "You're my best friend, but this isn't any of your business."

Zach tilted his head at her open show of

defiance. The sparkle in his eyes and the flash of his teeth conveyed his approval. "All right. It's your call."

Theresa stared at him in disbelief. "That was too easy."

Zach offered a bland smile but made no reply. His silence ended the conversation, and the clatter of feet descending the stairs made it impossible for her to say anything else.

Just then, Isabel, Theresa's five-year-old daughter, burst into the room. A miniature version of her mother, Isabel had a cascade of corkscrew curls that reached the middle of her back. She radiated beauty and warmth.

"Mama!" Isabel called out in greeting.

"Good morning, Isabel. How did you sleep?" Theresa welcomed her daughter with open arms and a smile.

Isabel flew into her mother's embrace. "Okay. I had a nightmare about a bad fairy."

"Why was the fairy bad?" Theresa released the girl and returned to making tea.

"It just was." Isabel's gaze fell on Zach, and her entire face lit up. She headed straight for him at full speed. "Zach!"

"Pixie, look at you! You're ten times prettier than the last time I saw you!" Zach caught Isabel up and spun the giggling girl around. He deposited her on one of the four oak chairs around the small kitchen table and took the seat beside her.

"What would you like for breakfast?" Theresa asked.

"Scrambled eggs!" Isabel said.

While Theresa prepared breakfast, Isabel regaled Zach with tales of kindergarten and imaginary garden fairies. As Theresa listened in on their conversation, she couldn't help reflecting on how Zach paid more attention to Isabel than the girl had ever received from her biological father.

Stop it. That's petty and spiteful, Theresa scolded herself. *Not to mention dangerous.* As much as she dreamed of being a happy family, it was the sort of fantasy that could only end in disappointment. Zach far outranked her within the pack hierarchy. She might as well reach for the stars. If she weren't careful, her schoolgirl crush would lead to a broken heart.

"Here you go." Theresa placed a plate before Isabel and another containing ten times as much food in front of Zach.

He inhaled with an appreciative gleam in his eyes. "Thank you."

"You're welcome." Theresa tingled with pleasure. Nothing made her happier than taking care of him, especially when it meant earning his admiration. She had so few opportunities to impress him.

Carrying a plate for herself, Theresa sat across from her daughter. Isabel dominated the conversation until Zach cleared his throat. He pinned Theresa with his gaze and said, "I've been talking with Adam...."

Theresa tensed at the mention of the Wolf King's name. She strove to sound unconcerned when she asked, "What about?"

"Adam is talking about resigning as pack leader. He and Becky want to retire and do some traveling."

"I haven't heard anything like that." Theresa stiffened with sudden concern.

The Wolf King, also known as the Alpha, was the all-powerful leader of the Iron Stone wolves. Adam Teller was stern and autocratic. He gave orders and expected blind obedience. Despite his authoritarian tendencies, Adam and his wife, Becky, were a vast improvement over Mitch Zanatos, the abusive bully who had ruled before. Zanatos had scarred every wolf in the entire pack—emotionally and spiritually. His reign of tyranny had shattered the mystical bond that had once united them all.

Theresa still woke up sweating and shaking from nightmares.

Zach shrugged. "It's not official. Yet."

"Adam is going to leave us?" Isabel asked.

"Adam was never meant to be a long-term solution," Zach explained. "He's sixty-six."

"That's old." Isabel scrunched her nose.

Zach chuckled. "When Adam stepped in to assume leadership five years ago, it was only until a younger male took his place."

While the two of them talked, Theresa sat paralyzed, hyperventilating, in the grip of an anxiety attack. Perhaps sensing her distress, Zach's power spilled over Theresa, exerting a cooling influence. Some of the panic crushing her chest lessened.

Isabel sipped her milk through a straw. "Who's going to be the new pack leader?"

Zach puckered his mouth, staying ominously silent, and Theresa's worries returned with a vengeance. Within the pack's pecking order, every wolf-shifter held a ranking from Alpha to Omega. Sexy lawyer Robert Blane was the Beta, making him the second-highest-ranked wolf. Zach's title as Gamma placed him in the third-highest position within the hierarchy.

Isabel's gaze shifted from one adult to the other. Her eyes were wide. "What's wrong, Mama?"

"Nothing, sweetie." Theresa settled a reassuring hand on her daughter's arm, but her nervous gaze clung to Zach. She found herself assessing him in a whole new light. Did Zach aspire to be the next pack leader?

Unease churned in Theresa's gut. She enjoyed a close friendship with Zach and had ready access to him despite the differences in their ranks. If he became Alpha, that would change. His new responsibilities would consume all of his time, and, of course, he would have to take a mate. There were so many more appropriate females than her. Theresa stood to lose him completely. The prospect terrified her, causing her heart to ache within her breast.

"You didn't answer my question," Isabel said to Zach. "Who will be the next Wolf King—you or Mr. Blane? Would you have to fight each other?"

Theresa shuddered. Fights for dominance between male wolves almost always ended in death for the lower. The thought of Zach dying terrified her. Of course, she didn't want Robert, who she liked but didn't know as well, to come to harm either.

Zach set down his fork. "Most likely one of us, though I'm willing to bet that Charlaine could hold her own if she set her mind to it."

Envy burned through Theresa to hear Zach speak with such open admiration of Charlaine Gale, the pack's senior-ranked female wolf. Her shoulders tensed, and her face tightened into an unhappy mask.

"I thought you were content as Gamma," Theresa said.

Zach studied her from beneath a hooded gaze. "I have aspirations."

"But you're not well suited to—" Theresa cut herself short because she could hear how cranky and unsupportive she sounded. The last thing she wanted to do was to give Isabel the wrong idea. Her daughter had big ears and an even more expansive imagination.

"I'm not well suited to what?" Zach asked, deadly soft.

Theresa stuttered. "I-I mean, what about deadlines and book signings?"

Zach's eyes narrowed. "What about them?"

"It's just...." Theresa stumbled to a verbal halt. She felt like a hypocrite, hiding her selfish desires behind concerns for his career. In truth, she wanted to keep Zach all to herself. The prospect of losing him had her on edge.

Zach's brow rose. "Just what?"

"Nothing." Theresa hung her head.

"I think Zach would make a good pack leader," Isabel said.

Zach smiled at the girl. "Thank you for the show of support, pixie."

Theresa winced at the implicit accusation. Here, she presented herself as Zach's best friend, but she certainly wasn't acting like it.

She opened her mouth to say something, but then Zach gathered up all the dirty dishes and headed for the sink.

"You don't have to," Theresa said, also standing.

"Of course I do. You cooked. I'll do the dishes. Fair's fair."

Theresa picked up on the hurt in his voice. "Zach, I didn't mean...."

His eyes narrowed. "We're friends here, Theresa. I can handle you being honest with me."

"Mommy?" Isabel grabbed her hand.

"What is it, Isabel?" Theresa glanced down at her daughter, and Zach turned away to do the dishes. A thin sigh of regret escaped her lips.

"Is Daddy coming to see me today? I want to tell him about the new fairy in the garden."

"Your father's picking you up in an hour. Let's go pick out your outfit and do your hair, sweetie," she said. "We need to pack your overnight bag."

"Want to catch a movie this afternoon?" Zach asked over his shoulder. Their gazes met and caught.

"I have to work today," she said, failing to conceal the wistful note in her voice. She would have liked nothing better than to have an afternoon off to spend alone with Zach. Unfortunately, weekends were always the busiest time at the diner.

"Tomorrow?" he asked.

"I'm working tomorrow too," she said.

Zach's face remained expressionless. "I'll finish cleaning up and put everything away."

"Thank you, Zach."

Theresa cast a final glance over her shoulder, committing the vision of him to memory. Granted, he belonged to her only as a friend, but now, she stood to lose even that. In the years ahead, fond recollections might be all she had left.

That and heartbreak.

CHAPTER THREE

A craftsman-style house on a mountainside overlooking Iron Stone, Nevada – Sunday afternoon

The pristine page of Zach's word processor formed a literary desert on the computer screen. He started a sentence, reworded it, and reworked it again. Two cups of coffee later, he composed a second sentence, left it incomplete, and began the third. In the end, he deleted the entire paragraph and returned to staring at blankness.

The harder he tried to focus, the more uncomfortable he grew. Instead of concentrating on the plot, his vivid imagination tormented him with erotic visions of Theresa. In his dreams, he cupped the side of her face and bared his soul.

"I can't tell you how long I've wanted to kiss you," he whispered, stroking his thumb over her cheek. "How I've ached to taste you."

In his dreams, Theresa tossed her hair, amusement dancing in her dark gaze. "Is that so?"

"Hell yeah." A primal growl rolled from his throat.

She traced her upper lip with the tip of her tongue. "So, what's stopping you?"

"Nothing now."

Rough with savage desire, Zach pulled her into his arms, and Theresa clung to him without fear or shyness. Their lips met and merged. He probed the depths of her mouth with his tongue, savoring her surrender.

Theresa pressed against him. The fullness of her breasts crushed against his muscular chest, and their lower bodies bumped together. The friction made for such exquisite torture, and his cock throbbed inside his pants.

Maybe all this was a fool's dream, and he was a fool for dreaming. Despite the admission, Zach ached to his core with unfulfilled desires. He wanted Theresa to need him as much as he needed her, but only in his fantasies did she reach for him, wrapping her arms around his neck. A sweet, teasing temptress, she climbed him like a tree, locking her strong legs around his trunk. Through layers of clothing, they humped like horny teenagers, and it was glorious.

Abruptly, Zach became aware that he was physically uncomfortable. For starters, he was a lot hotter and sweatier than he should be, especially considering that he kept the air conditioning set to a cool sixty degrees. For another, his pants were so tight they hurt.

"Man, do I ever—as Americans say—need to get laid," he muttered aloud.

Leaning back in his office chair, Zach scanned the scene he'd just written. Before he finished the first page, his mouth had puckered. A sex scene—what utter rubbish! At this rate, the only career ahead of him might be as a romance novelist.

Aggravated, he saved and closed the document.

All excuses aside, Zach heaved a heavy sigh. No matter how hard he tried, he couldn't resist the urge to analyze his non-existent romance with Theresa. After years of working diligently to earn her trust, Zach had almost resigned himself to permanent placement in the friend zone.

Then *BAM* yesterday happened. An erotic foot rub and mixed signals.

Never in his life had Zach been so simultaneously confused and frustrated. Why had

Theresa initiated the sexual overture if she never meant to follow through? She wanted him. He was sure of it. The unmistakable aroma of arousal had surrounded her like a spicy fragrance. But then she had cut and run, and Zach was left wondering what he'd done wrong.

A one-woman wolf at heart, Zach had stayed faithful to Theresa since the day they'd met. The first time he'd laid eyes on her, he'd recognized her as his soul mate. Back then, however, she'd been fearful and wary, especially of men, and who could blame her given the pack's traumatic history? So Zach set out to win her confidence, to prove himself worthy of her trust.

He just hadn't expected it to take years.

Bollocks, but he missed sex. He didn't know how much longer he could wait for Theresa to make up her mind. This whole hot-cold thing was killing him. Did she want to remain simply friends? Or would she finally muster the courage to claim him as a lover and partner?

His gut released a loud gurgle. The sound vaguely resembled the complaints of a bridge troll in a goat famine. Zach glanced down at his abdomen with a faint grin then stole a glance at the clock. It was already past one.

Break time.

Zach surged to his feet, almost knocking over

the office chair in his haste. He headed for the kitchen, enjoying the smoothness of the hardwood floor beneath his bare feet. The refrigerator offered slim pickings, however, only beer and sausage. It wasn't precisely a feast fit for a wolf, but at least the air here was cooler.

He sniffed the sausages, gagging at the stench of rotten meat. *Nope.* The links went straight into the trash.

Restlessness drove him to prowl the confines of his house. Once again, his mind returned to Theresa, conjuring an acute longing for both the woman *and* her cooking. The culinary recollections got his mouth to watering and his stomach to growling.

He rechecked the time—one-thirty in the afternoon—and heaved a regretful sigh. Theresa's shift at the local greasy spoon didn't end until five. It would be hours before he could seek her out, but even so, there could be no homecooked meals, no matter how hungry the wolf.

"Banish the thought, mate," Zach lectured himself. "No one wants to put in a full day on her feet only to have to turn around and serve some selfish prick."

The reprimand helped him cool his heels, but it also put a thought in his head. He snapped his fingers, and the angel on his shoulder suggested, "Maybe I should cook for her? But what?"

Zach knew darn well that he was hardly a gourmet chef. If not burning the meal was the objective, then steak was the obvious answer. As a rule, wolves liked their ribeyes so rare that they had to stand guard over the salad.

Mulling it over, Zach entered the master bedroom. He trucked on through, shedding his clothing along the way. A twist of the handle turned the master bathroom shower on full blast. He didn't allow the water to warm up. Drawing a bracing breath, he stepped directly into the spray. The icy jet sluiced across his skin.

"Crikey!" he exclaimed but forced himself to stay put. Blue balls were just what the doctor ordered to cure his overheated libido.

It worked for all of a minute. Then, the water got hot... and so did he.

Zach's cock sprang to full attention, jutting from his body at a proud angle. His physical predicament left him in a painful state of arousal.

"Bugger." Well, there was yet another obvious solution. Grabbing for a bar of soap, he lathered his hands and adopted a wide stance. Suds seeped between his fingers to the tile floor. Discarding the bar, Zach wrapped his slick hand about his shaft, stroking the length.

His imagination put Theresa right back on her knees before him, only this time she was naked. The dark-haired beauty knelt with her head tilted back to expose her lovely throat. Dark eyes gleamed up at him from beneath long lashes. She had full, round breasts tipped in the prettiest, perkiest nipples he'd ever seen, and her bosom heaved with lusty panting. Her lips parted in a slight smile, revealing a glint of shining white teeth. The set of her posture conveyed submission, but he wasn't a fool. Despite her innate shyness, Theresa was not a maiden who lacked experience. The gleam in her gaze told him that she understood *precisely* how her feminine wiles drove him wild.

Theresa licked her lips, and Zach just about lost it.

"What do you think, pet? Do you like what you see?" He tugged on his erection. His blood surged, and his balls swelled, heavy between his thighs.

From beneath lowered lashes, Theresa studied his raging hard-on. Giggling, she teased him with excessive admiration. "Oh, my. Your cock is *verrry* impressive."

Zach chuckled. "Even in my imagination, you're a mean woman."

"Why, sir, whatever do you mean?" Theresa slid her hands across his athletic thighs. The sharp points of her fingernails dug into his skin, pressing into rock-solid muscle. With a tug, she urged him to come closer.

Zach sank into a deep squat that left his leg muscles burning. He braced his back against the wall for support. Piping hot water blasted across his skin, running in swift rivulets over his sculpted physique. Thick steam made it hard to breathe. A low rumble trembled in his throat, audible over the shower spray. It'd been far too long since a woman had touched him so intimately.

An eternity.

Theresa stroked his arse next, kneading his buttocks. The fullness of her breasts, round and voluptuous, brushed against his thighs. Her face came close enough to his jutting cock that he imagined he felt the stir of her breath despite the rainshower. His erection throbbed strong and proud.

"Do you like this?" She cupped his balls, cradling the weight in her palms.

"I quite like that." Zach swallowed convulsively and shut his eyes in delicious anticipation. Every beat of his heart sent the blood surging into his dick. The pressure built until he feared he would burst at the stroke of a feather.

"How about this?" She flicked the tip of her tongue along inside of his thigh, and a violent tremor traversed his entire body.

"Hell yes," he all but shouted.

"No swearing, mister, or this blow job is over."

Hastily, Zach reformed his wicked ways. "Gods, yes. I love that."

With a husky laugh, his enchantress peppered kisses across the sensitive skin of his groin. Zach kept his fingers loosely tangled in her silky tresses while Theresa freely explored his lower half. Her hands roamed his hard thighs, and then she reached for his arse. She dug her fingernails into his muscular buttocks hard enough to hurt, delicious pain in sharp contrast to the unbearable pleasure.

A moan just about tore him in half, and Zach bucked his hips. "Stop teasing. Suck me now."

"Your wish is my command." Theresa's hot mouth enveloped one of his balls. She sucked the heavy sac, ratcheting his need to even greater heights. The whole while, the vixen meticulously avoided touching his cock. Zach's head fell forward, and the trembling in his throat intensified into a full rumble.

Theresa coaxed him to the verge of completion, only to deny him at the last second. With a final lick on his scrotum, she leaned back to gaze up at him. "Do you like it rough, Zach?"

Zach snarled like the wolf lurking beneath his skin. He tightened his grip on Theresa's curly black hair. "Yeah, I love it rough."

"Should I make you beg?" Theresa's suggestive whisper sent a bolt of lightning through his rugged physique.

"Enough," he rasped. "No more teasing, love. I'm going to fuck your mouth. Open."

Sweetly submissive, she tipped her head back, parting her lips. "I'm all yours."

The erotic sight of her just about proved his undoing. With a guttural groan, Zach eased the thick head of his cock past her pretty lips, pressing into her cheek pocket.

From there, Theresa teased and tormented him with her wickedly clever mouth. She stroked her slick tongue along his length then scraped her pearly teeth over his hypersensitive skin. Gentle and then rough, just as he'd requested. The treatment elicited divine sensations, a rollercoaster ride alternating between pleasure and pain.

Zach's chest labored as though he'd run a marathon. He panted to catch his breath enough to speak. "Ease up a second, love."

Theresa gazed up at him, curiosity in her eyes. Her mouth grew still on his cock, yet she continued to caress his balls with a featherlight touch that proved tremendously distracting.

A tormented chuckle shook Zach. "I want to come in your mouth."

Skin glistening from the hot spray of the shower,

Theresa answered with a rhythmic rumbling that originated in her chest like the purring of a great cat. Zach took the sound as a sign of permission.

Coming unraveled, Zach plunged his dick into her eager mouth. He rocked his hips, slowly at first but with escalating urgency. His restraint dangled from the barest thread of reason.

Theresa gripped his thighs with both hands. With a husky moan, she pulled him closer, accepting more of his shaft, and dragged her lips and teeth along his length.

They settled into a natural rhythm with plenty of give-and-take, a playful competition of tug-o-war. However, Zach recognized this was a contest he couldn't win.

Determined to break his self-control, Theresa sucked lighter then firmer, toying with him. She produced throaty little sounds of encouragement while devouring his cock with feral greed.

Red hazed Zach's vision. He thrust harder and faster. Deeper. Then, Zach's cockhead struck the back of Theresa's throat, and she stretched her lips around the thick base of his penis. His brain shut down, and he could hold back no longer.

Zach threw back his head and shouted at the top of his lungs. His heart hammered, and his chest heaved. The muscles of his abdomen clenched, and his balls tightened. The orgasm ripped through his body like an earthquake. He came in Theresa's hot mouth, howling with all the might of his wolf.

The vestiges of the wet dream faded—Theresa disappeared like a ghost— leaving him alone once more.

Zach leaned against the tile wall of the shower in exhaustion. Water poured across his skin, washing away the evidence of his arousal. Running his hands through his hair, he bowed his head in a state of near despair.

CHAPTER FOUR

The Hunter residence – two p.m.

The knock of an unexpected caller pounded on the front door.

Zach padded barefoot through the cavernous rooms of his craftsman-style home. High vaulted ceilings made the house expensive to heat in the winter and difficult to cool in the summer, but the spectacular view of the rugged wilderness more than made up for the inefficiencies. He liked the isolation, too. Reaching his residence involved a treacherous drive along a single-lane road. It tended to discourage all but the most determined visitors.

The Wolf King of the Iron Stone Pack certainly fit the bill.

The front door swung open to reveal Adam Teller on the front porch. The pack leader had silver hair, a handlebar mustache, and a blocky stature. Beneath his bespoke suit, he was heavyset, but solid muscle lay beneath the fat.

Three members of the king's guard stood about ten feet back. The squad of elite soldiers acted as the alpha's enforcers and protectors. They existed outside of the pack's rank structure and answered only to Adam.

"Good afternoon." Adam touched the brim of his white cowboy hat trimmed with braided black horsehair.

Zach took care to hide his surprise. "Good afternoon, sir. What brings you up to my side of the mountain?"

"No need to be so formal, Zach. At least, not while we're alone. Call me Adam."

"Adam," Zach said with a forced smile.

As much as he disliked the Alpha, he understood that the grizzled werewolf was tough and wily, a formidable opponent. Teller commanded Zach's sense of caution, if not his approval.

"I'm sorry to disturb you at home. We need to talk." Adam's drawl held a distinct undercurrent of tension.

Zach suspected the apology came only for the appearance of good manners but lacked sincerity. The Alpha wasn't the sort to concern himself with the convenience of others.

"Would you like to come inside?" Zach stared past Adam to the bodyguards flanking him to either side.

Adam turned to address his enforcers. "Wait in the car. I'd like to speak with Zach in private."

The guards gave curt nods and departed.

Zach swung the door wider and stepped back. "Come in."

"Thanks." Adam crossed the threshold inside and removed his cowboy hat.

Zach shut the door, but he refrained from offering to take the hat. Adam never relinquished control of anything that belonged to him. The male werewolves squared off across from one another. Zach folded his arms and leaned against the doorframe.

"What brings you by, Adam?" Zach asked.

"Pack business, the sort that requires discussion and a good stiff drink." Adam straightened his tie. His tailored suit was midnight blue over a pressed white shirt, and his detailed cowboy boots shone from meticulous polishing.

"Let's move into the study," Zach said.

Adam inclined his head, and Zach took the lead.

Neither man spoke again until they reached his office. First thing, Zach headed to the bar. Though a Scotch man himself, he kept an expensive Kentucky whiskey on hand for his American guests.

"Bourbon?"

"Please." Adam settled in a leather armchair and set his hat on his thigh.

Zach poured two fingers into each tumbler. He passed one to Adam and then took a seat opposite the Alpha.

Adam held the glass up in a mock salute. "Thank you."

"Sure."

They sat and regarded one another without speaking.

Zach finally broke the silence. "What's on your mind, Adam?"

"Word has gotten around that I'm thinking about retiring. It's causing a stir."

"That's not surprising."

"I'm calling a pack meeting Monday night to make the official announcement. At that time, I'll set out the rules for determining succession. Course, I reckon it'll come down to you and Robert. No one else is dominant enough to be a real contender."

"What about Charlaine?" Zach asked.

Adam snorted and dismissed the suggestion with a shake of his head. He downed his whiskey and set the glass aside. "Charlaine is a scrapper, but we both know that a woman doesn't have what it takes to lead a pack. No, sir. It's you or Robert."

"Have you spoken to Robert?"

"Not yet, but I will. I wanted to talk to you first."

"Why?" The word, already short, came out clipped.

Adam's eyes narrowed. "What's wrong, Zach? Did I hit a nerve with Charlaine?"

"I think a dominant female could be the pack leader." Zach's gaze never wavered, making it clear he would not submit or be intimidated. Unwavering defiance was as good as a verbal challenge if Adam chose to accept.

Technically, Zach was way out of line. Only Robert, the Beta, had the right to challenge the Alpha to a fight.

Zach had never been one to play by the rules.

Adam stared back, and the tension in the room escalated. Anger flickered in his eyes before he regained his self-control. Then, he sat back and slapped his knee. His laughter boomed. "You had me going for a minute there! I swear, I can't tell when you're pullin' my leg, Zachery."

Zach offered a thin smile. There were times when his reputation as a prankster came back to bite him in the arse, but the matter wasn't worth pursuing. He made the deliberate decision to allow Adam to mistake his meaning. "I guess I have one hell of a poker face," he said grimly.

"That you do. That you do." Adam leaned forward with a conspiratorial smile that implied they were just a pair of good ol' boys shooting the shit. "Now, as I said, it'll come down to you and Robert. I won't state this in public 'cause I can't appear to have a favorite, but just between you and me, my money is on you to win."

Zach worked to hide his disapproval. "Thank you," he said in a curt tone.

Adam sat straighter. "You're surprised. I can tell."

"Robert is your second," Zach said, reaching for misdirection to cover his intense disapproval before the man intuited more. His deference to the Alpha was grudging at best, and it was only his respect for pack tradition that forced him to check his disdain.

With time—and a spot of luck—they would be rid of Adam soon enough.

"Robert is arrogant," Adam said. "He's a good enough enforcer, but he lacks the level head necessary to be a king. He's unsuitable. There's no polite way of putting it."

Translation: a black man wasn't smart enough or strong enough to stand in Adam Teller's boots. Never mind that Robert Blane held two advanced degrees and was considered one of the sharpest attorneys in the state.

A hundred impolite ways of expressing his opinion crossed Zach's mind, but he bit his tongue. He didn't want to kill Adam in a challenge simply because the man was an ignorant bigot. Besides, that honor should go to Robert, if the Beta wolf chose to take matters into his claws.

Zach pressed his lips into a flat line. "I hear what you're saying."

Adam nodded, seemingly confident that he had Zach's support. "This pack is damaged, maybe irrevocably. Zanatos and his enforcers destroyed the spiritual bond that should unite the wolves of Iron Stone. I presume you know what all that went down?"

Zach chose his words with precision. "Zanatos and his enforcers were executed."

The Alpha's nostrils flared as he exhaled. "But do you know the ugly details?"

"It was before my time, but yeah, I've heard the stories," Zach said. "Zanatos encouraged infighting and exploitation. The dominants were constantly at each other's throats, while weaker wolves were abused."

"Eventually, a child was murdered, and then the Wolf God was forced to step in," Adam said. "Our liege had Zanatos and his enforcers killed, and then he sent me here to clean up the mess."

Zach scratched his chin, wondering why they were discussing old history. Rather than ask outright, he preferred to bide his time. Adam would show his hand and get to the point eventually.

Adam continued, "As I'm sure you're well aware, you and Robert were chosen to help stabilize the pack."

Leaning back, Zach propped his long legs on the leather ottoman. His relaxed posture belied the tension within his lean frame. "I understood the implications when I accepted the invitation."

"The Wolf God selected Robert without consulting me, and I've had to work with him these last five years, but I've had enough." Adam's mouth curled in contempt. "I'm through wasting time trying to fix this shipwreck of a pack."

The man's scorn for the people under his care turned Zach's stomach, but he kept his feelings under wraps, being careful not to let anything show. He relied on misdirection again. "I've heard of new packs forging a fresh connection but never a dissolved pack forging a new bond."

"This is the problem my successor will inherit. Becky and I are ready to retire and head home to Alexandria."

None of this was news to Zach, but rehashing

old issues clued him to where the conversation was heading. "I take it that rekindling the pack's magic will be the determining factor for your successor?"

Adam flashed a cold smile, showing teeth. "You're as sharp as a tack, Zach. I'll make the announcement Monday night."

"I understand."

The leather armchair creaked as the Alpha shifted his bulk to stand. "In the end, a fight for rank is almost inevitable. I hope you're prepared to kill Robert. A pack leader can't be perceived as weak."

Cold iron settled in Zach's gut. "I'll do whatever is in the best interests of the pack."

Adam tilted his head and settled his hat atop his crown. "I'm glad we understand one another."

"We're clear," Zach said in a flat voice.

Then and there, he vowed this matter wouldn't end with him and Robert killing each other. Call it a wild hunch, but Zach was ready to bet that the Beta wolf would agree. They should take any action necessary to ensure that neither of them died by the other's hands.

Zach rose to escort his guest to the door. "Thanks for dropping in to visit, Adam. It was informative."

Adam tipped his hat. "Always a pleasure."

CHAPTER FIVE

The Russo residence – Sunday afternoon

After an exhausting day at work, Theresa drove across town to pick up Isabel from her father's house. On the way home, they swung by the market store because the pantry was bare. An hour and a half later, it was a huge relief to make it home finally.

Theresa stood on the porch with a bag of groceries balanced on her hip. She dug one-handed through her purse, trying to find her keys. "Did you have a good time with your father, Izzy?"

Isabel bounced impatiently on her the balls of her feet while she waited. "Yeah, it was okay," she said in the manner of bored five-year-olds. "We went to the park. Tammy is going to have a baby."

Floored with surprise that her ex-husband's second wife was pregnant, Theresa fumbled and almost dropped the keys. It took a few seconds before she recovered her senses enough to unlock the front door.

"When did they tell you that Tammy's having a baby?" She tried hard to keep an even tone even though her feelings about her ex were anything but pleasant.

"At the park," Isabel said with an indifferent shrug. She dropped her backpack on the floor and sprinted down the hallway toward the kitchen. "Mama, I'm going to take my fairy friends some honey!"

"No more than a teaspoon!" Theresa's lips curved in an indulgent smile. Her daughter's imaginary friends consumed an entire honey bear every month.

Thoughtfully, she stared after her child and gave a philosophical shrug. If Isabel wasn't upset about the news of the impending sibling, then Theresa had no reason to be concerned. She had gotten over Antonio long before Isabel had even been born.

"Do we have any white bread?" Isabel's voice floated from the kitchen, along with the sound of cabinet doors being opened and closed.

"I just bought wheat bread. It's healthier for you."

"Fairies don't like wheat." Isabel slammed the pantry with a thud. She headed for the backyard, clutching the honey bear.

The phone rang, and Theresa answered it. "Hello?"

"Theresa?" Zach purred in her ear, and her pulse jumped with excitement at the sound of his voice.

"Hi, Zach." Theresa moved into the kitchen and set the groceries on the table. She hooked a chair with her foot and dropped into it, releasing a tired sigh. Her feet ached from hours of waitressing. She still wore her white and green uniform.

"Rough day, love?"

"No more grueling than a typical ten-hour Sunday. Isabel and I just got home from the market."

"How were tips?"

"Tips were good, so I'm happy. Did you get any writing done?"

He grunted. "My house is cleaner than it's been in months."

Theresa smothered a snort of laughter. This counted as the first time they'd spoken since their tiff on Saturday morning. She had started to worry, but to her relief, though, Zach sounded cheerful.

"Zach," she said, "you're never going to get past

this if you don't sit down and write. You've said it yourself time and again the secret to breaking writer's block is ass in chair time."

A beat passed before he responded. "Adam is calling a pack meeting Monday night."

Theresa sighed. Fine, he didn't want a lecture. "I have to work Monday night."

"Can you trade shifts with one of the other girls?"

"I'll ask Anne. I took her shift last week, so maybe I can take her day shift. No, that won't work either. My mother has a doctor's appointment in Reno on Monday morning, and she'll be gone until three or four. I have no one to pick up Isabel from school."

"What about her father?" Zach said with plenty of sarcasm.

Theresa winced because she hated making excuses for her ex-husband. "You know Antonio has to work."

"Work so he can renege on paying child support, which is the only parental responsibility the lazy sod has ever assumed in his life."

Theresa sucked in a breath, not wanting to have this argument again. "I should go."

"Theresa, wait." Zach's tone turned apologetic. "Look, I'm sorry. I'm sick of listening to you defend him."

Tears stung her eyes. "I know, but he is Isabel's father. I can't bash him within her hearing, no matter how badly he behaves."

"I understand." There was a pause. "Why don't I pick up Isabel from school tomorrow? She gets out at two-thirty?"

Surprised, Theresa fell silent for a moment. "Are you sure? Don't you need to write?"

"Write what? I'm stuck, remember?" he asked with a snort. "How long will your mum be gone?"

Theresa bit her lower lip. "Maybe two hours?"

"Sure, I can manage a five-year-old for two hours. I'll take Isabel to the ice cream parlor and then over to Main Street Park. It'll be fun."

"Zach, I don't know what to say. Thank you."

"You're welcome," he said.

The warmth returned to his voice, and Theresa wanted to wrap herself in those dulcet tones, to close her eyes and forget all of her worries and fears. Zach's steady presence in her life made things bearable whenever she felt overwhelmed. His strength always got her through the hard times, but she wanted far more than just friendship with him. She longed to be his lover, to be a family, to have his children.

"Theresa, can I come over tonight?"

Theresa tensed up. "Why? What's wrong?"

"Nothing's wrong. I'd just like to see you." His

mellow baritone conveyed a sensual current, smoky desire, and intense longing, so electric her entire body tingled in response.

Her hopeful heart skipped a beat. She could not refuse attention from Zach. With a nervous hand, she tugged at her collar and sniffed her blouse, which stank of grease and sweat. *Gross.*

"I'm still wearing my uniform," she said. "Give me a half hour to shower and change."

"A half hour then."

They said their goodbyes.

Theresa called out the back door, "Isabel?"

No reply.

She repeated her daughter's name two more times and then ventured out into the fenced backyard. "Isabel?"

"Back here, Mama."

Theresa found her tiny daughter tucked in the far corner of the yard beneath a sugar maple. Isabel sat in the dirt amongst fuchsia snapdragons and golden daisies. An army of fairy miniatures scattered throughout the flowers. The plastic playthings lay on their sides, and honey was everywhere. The child had stickiness all over her hands and sundress.

Theresa groaned. "Oh, Isabel, I told you no more than a teaspoon."

"It wasn't me, Mama. The new fairy didn't want to share. He grabbed the honey, and it spilled everywhere." Isabel's brown eyes filled with tears-on-command at the suggestion that she might be in trouble.

Theresa sighed and disposed of the ruined bear in a garbage can. She bent to lift Isabel free of the mess. "The ants will eat well tonight. Let's take you inside and get you cleaned up, shall we? Zach is coming over to visit."

"Cool!" Isabel's face lit like houses on fire, and then she scrunched her nose. "You should shower, Mama."

"Gee, thanks." Theresa laughed.

A hard knock on the front door punctuated Zach's arrival. Theresa hurried to answer it, but Isabel beat her there. The little girl grabbed the handle even as her mother advised caution.

"Isabel, you can't just open the door without looking."

"It's Zach." Isabel jerked the door open. "See?"

"That doesn't change the fact that—"

Zach finished her sentence. "You shouldn't answer the door without finding out who it is first."

Isabel pouted and held out her arms. "Hi, Zach."

"Hello to you, too." Zach dropped to one knee and opened his arm to accept the child's hug. In his other, he held a brown paper grocery sack that crunched against his chest.

"I have a new dress." Isabel twirled so the skirt of her yellow sundress flared about her like the petals of a flower.

"Pixie, you're as pretty as a picture."

"Thank you. Isn't Mama pretty too?"

"Isabel!" Theresa started to fold her arms to cover herself then stopped. Hiding defeated the point of dressing up for Zach, but she hoped her efforts to impress him weren't obvious. She wore a white cotton sundress that flattered her tanned complexion and emphasized her curves without being too fancy.

Zach grinned, showing teeth in an excellent impression of the Big Bad Wolf. "Your mama looks good enough to eat."

"Oh, you, stop." Theresa hid her embarrassment while Isabel's curious gaze flickered between the two adults.

"It's nice to know that I rated new dresses from both of my girls." Zach's smile softened, but his eyes lingered on Theresa's low-cut bodice.

The hunger in his stare brought a flush to her skin. Her heart pulsated to a staccato beat. Theresa sucked in a sharp breath that left her light-headed. Her gaze snared on those delicious male lips. It wasn't fair what the man could do to her with just a look. Kissing fantasies filled her head, a desire never far from her thoughts. His mouth was all she could think about, and she loved to daydream about how he would feel and taste.

She had no idea what had gotten into Zach to bring his blatant masculinity to bear on her. He must have plenty of girlfriends, and she couldn't envision him living the monk life. To be fair, he never brought other women around Theresa or her daughter. Before that fateful foot-washing incident, he had always treated Theresa like a platonic friend. He cracked jokes but not of a sexual nature and certainly not in front of Isabel.

"What's in the bag?" Theresa asked, seeking a diversion from the sizzling sexual tension crackling in the air.

"I brought over some ribeyes and potatoes and one of those salads in a bag. Oh, and a good cabernet sauvignon. I thought I'd cook for you." Zach's blue eyes were oh-so-serious, indicating that more was going on than he was saying.

But what?

Dry-mouthed, she asked, "Did I hear that right? *You* want to prepare dinner for *us*?"

Zach jutted his jaw and stated with great deliberation, "I believe that is how courtship works."

Whoa. Theresa staggered in pure surprise at his

bold declaration. From ancient times, male wolves had wooed their prospective mates with food gifts to prove their prowess as hunters. Back then, it might have been as simple as a dead rabbit laid at her feet. Today, it entailed a trip to the butcher, although the sentiment was the same.

"What's courtship, mama?" Isabel tugged on Theresa's skirt.

Too tongue-tied to talk, Theresa glanced down into her daughter's puzzled face. Theresa imagined her expression resembled the proverbial deer-in-headlights. Fortunately, Zach rode to the rescue with a ready answer.

"Courtship is when I cook dinner for you and your mum," he said with a twinkle in his eyes.

Theresa knew him too well to miss the seriousness underlying his mood. The potency of his basal scent—a heady mixture of aggression and arousal—vanquished any lingering doubts she might have harbored.

For a frightening second, Theresa thought Zach meant to create a scene in front of Isabel. Did he expect her to decide whether to accept or reject him now? *As in, right this instance?* Fear paralyzed her and also self-recrimination. Zach was everything she had ever wanted. How could she throw that away?

Coward that she was, Theresa arched her brow

and went straight to skepticism. "Zach, you hate cooking."

Zach frowned. Displeasure accentuated the sharpness of his angular features, and his cheekbones could've cut glass. He dragged his tongue over his lips, and then his entire demeanor changed to clownishness. To blink was to miss it. He offered Isabel a goofy grin. "I do know how to make mac 'n' cheese, you know."

Isabel giggled. "Zach only makes the gross orange stuff from the box. Not homemade like yours, Mama."

"Hey, I resemble that remark!" Zach took a stab at Isabel's side with his finger.

It sent the girl straight into a giggling attack. While they horsed around, however, Zach never lost his undercurrent of seriousness. He watched Theresa with a knowing gaze that perceived far too much for her peace of mind.

"Why don't you let me make dinner?" Theresa's motivations for offering to cook did more than ensure a palatable meal. It put them back on comfortable footing. She could continue to pretend that his gift of food meant nothing out of the ordinary so long as he chose to allow it.

No confrontations, no hard decisions.

"Are you sure?" Zach asked in a tight voice, surly but grudgingly cooperative. *For now.*

"Oh, I'm sure." She headed for the kitchen. "Besides, it'd be a shame to allow beautiful ribeyes to get charred."

"Hey, I'm not that bad a cook." Grumbling playfully, he accompanied her into the kitchen.

Food preparation, however, failed to hold Isabel's interest.

"I'm going to watch TV." Isabel headed into the small family room. A minute later, lively music blasted on the television.

Zach set the groceries on the counter and unpacked the food. His mood remained somber. Theresa was curious, but she preferred not to press him. The man would share his thoughts when he was ready. For now, she concentrated on preparing dinner.

"Are baked potatoes okay?" she asked.

"Baked potatoes sound fabulous. I'll set the table."

"Great, thank you." Theresa carried the potatoes to the sink and dumped them into a colander. She dropped the scrub brush a moment later when Zach brushed against her elbow. The proximity of his powerful body sent a jolt of awareness coursing through her. She gasped and glanced up to find him standing right beside her. Her upper arm brushed against his breastbone.

The smile on his mouth told her that this was no

accident. "Has the landlord fixed the faucet yet?" Zach asked.

"Uhh." She gurgled, failing to formulate a coherent thought, let alone a sentence.

"Was that a yes or a no?" he teased with a throaty chuckle.

Theresa trembled when he lightly stroked his fingertip from the side of her throat down to her shoulder. His hands were large and powerful, callused across the palms and edges because he often performed mechanical tasks, but he had the graceful fingers of an artist. His short nails were always blunt and clean. She'd spent hours daydreaming about having him touch her like this, and the fantasy didn't even come close to the fabulous reality.

Water gushed from the faucet in a steady stream, swirling down the drain. She groped for the dropped vegetable brush. Zach slid in even closer, so his face drew alongside hers. His closeness raised gooseflesh on her arms, and his heat radiated across her skin.

Zach's breath blew across the sensitive side of her throat. The teasing caress stirred a delicious aching between her thighs. Her imagination flooded her mind with wickedly naughty images of their bodies entwined. Alas, his persistent inquiries disrupted her reverie again.

"Theresa, is the faucet fixed yet?"

"N-no. It's still leaking. I keep a bucket under the sink." Theresa hit the faucet handle and shut the water off. She ducked beneath his arm.

Zach observed her escape with an amused expression on his handsome face. He cocked his head like a predator scenting prey. Of course, it was in a wolf's nature to relish a good hunt, so his reaction came as no surprise. What baffled her was why she seemed to be on Zachary Hunter's radar all of a sudden.

"I'll take a look at it. Wrench still in the garage?"

Relief suffused her. "Would you like me to get it?"

"I can find the tools," he said with a level stare.

She flushed, torn between confusion and frustration. Of course, Zach knew where to locate the toolbox in the garage. The man performed all of her maintenance. Without him, the roof would have fallen around their ears ages ago, no thanks to her miser of a landlord.

"Back in a sec," Zach said. He didn't strike her as being angry, merely determined and energetic.

The back door shut, leaving Theresa staring after him.

"What the hell has gotten into you, Zach?" Theresa asked after he was out of hearing range. Maybe she waited until he left because she wasn't ready for the answer. The corners of her mouth curled down, and she exhaled heavily.

There was a whole lot of banging and clanging involved in the final dinner prep, a reflection of her inner turmoil. Self-recrimination ate at her. After years of longing for Zach's attention, what had she done the second he paid it to her? She had frozen up and rejected him.

Zach returned with the toolbox. Theresa watched with a pensive gaze as he opened the cabinet to access the plumbing beneath the sink. "You ought to complain, Theresa. That lazy sod of a landlord never repairs anything around here."

She mustered a weak smile. "If I complain too much, he might decide to raise my rent. Then, Isabel and I would have to move back in with my mother."

"I like your mum."

Theresa laughed. "And my mother adores you."

He snorted. "Not so you'd notice. The woman never says more than two words to me."

"Nonsense. My mom thinks you're the cat's meow."

"What about you?" he asked with a cocky grin.

Theresa snickered. "You know I don't like cats."

"Touché." Zach tipped an imaginary hat, and Theresa breathed easier. He lay on his back under the sink, so his voice became muffled. "Did you speak with your mum about me picking up Isabel on Monday?"

Awestruck, Theresa grabbed the rare opportunity to ogle Zach's fantastic physique without any chance of being caught. The contours of his six-pack abs were visible beneath his shirt. His blue jeans were form-fitting in all the right ways. Skintight denim cupped the impressive bulge at his crotch. Heat pooled between her thighs, and her fingers itched to rip open that row of three buttons. She yearned to cradle his swollen shaft in her hands, to taste the salt of his skin on her tongue.

"Are you still there, love?"Zach asked, prodding her from under the sink.

Theresa gulped and nodded. "I've called the school principal and Isabel's teacher to let them know you'll be picking her up. My mom said to tell you that she'll meet you at the park by five at the latest. Does that work for you?"

"Sounds good. I think I can survive a couple of hours alone with the munchkin." Zach clanked around under the sink a bit more and then grunted. "Well, there's your problem."

"Can you fix it?"

He scoffed. "Am I not a debonair hero?"

"Of course, but no one said anything about you being Mr. Fixit."

"Oh, you wound me." His hand pantomimed an injury to his heart.

"You're such a ham."

"You're going to eat those words when I fix this leak."

She laughed. "I'd rather eat this steak."

"I'm all for that, love."

Theresa stepped over his long legs. She continued to make dinner while Zach clanked and cursed his way through the repair. They traded a few snarky remarks regarding his plumbing skills, but eventually, he slid out from beneath the sink.

Zach flashed a triumphant grin and rolled to his feet with a smooth motion. "There you go. As good as new."

"My hero. What would I do without you?" Theresa fluttered her eyelashes and held her hands together, mimicking a grateful maiden.

Zach arched his brow. "Hire a plumber?"

Theresa shooed him. "Go wash up. I'll call Isabel."

"Yes, ma'am." He went easily enough, heading down the hallway to the downstairs bathroom.

Theresa strolled into the small family room, where Isabel sat on the couch watching cartoons in front of the television.

"Sweetie, dinner time. Turn off the TV."

Isabel slid from the sofa and did as instructed. "Is Zach staying for dinner?"

"Of course." She waited until Isabel passed in front of her and then followed. "Why wouldn't he?"

"No reason." Isabel stopped to gaze up at her mother. "Is Zach your boyfriend now, Mama?"

Theresa's jaw dropped. *Out of the mouths of babes.* Confusion tumbled through her mind—denial or confirmation. What should she say?

She cleared her throat. "No, baby, we're not dating. Why do you ask?"

"Because he acts like your boyfriend, but you don't ever kiss him. Daddy kisses Tammy all the time."

Isabel's penetrating gaze sent Theresa mentally scrambling. On impulse, she crafted a lie, a little white one, to direct her daughter away from the sensitive topic. "Zach and Mommy are just friends, Isabel. I don't think of Zach like that."

A slight movement behind Theresa alerted her to Zach's presence. Without looking, she knew he'd heard. She immediately wished for a takeback. Too late. Zach pinned her with a direct stare that darned near broke her heart. Theresa wanted to stammer an apology, but she couldn't speak a word. Not in front of Isabel. The poor girl was already confused enough.

"Come on, pixie," Zach said in a quiet voice.

"Let's go get some of that delicious food your mum made and talk about what we're going to do tomorrow after school."

Turning to the side, Zach slid past them into the room. He moved with lithe grace while avoiding even accidental physical contact. Theresa couldn't see his face, but her throat closed, and a hand crushed her heart.

Distracted, Isabel followed him into the kitchen. The child chattered up a storm, enjoying the attention of her favorite audience.

Theresa remained rooted in the hallway. *Damn, damn, damn.* Zach possessed excellent vocal control, but she knew him too well.

She'd hurt his feelings.

CHAPTER SIX

Zach stared down the table in a determined effort to make eye contact, but it appeared that Theresa was ignoring him. She picked at her food and paid attention to Isabel but otherwise avoided speaking to him unless spoken to.

Frustration had his teeth on edge. Bollocks, his casual flirting seemed to have backfired. Instead of persuading Theresa to loosen up, his overtures had driven the she-wolf into full retreat. She hadn't been so closed off to him since they'd first met. He had waited years for Theresa to come to him, but the changing political climate of the pack made that a luxury he could no longer afford.

Attempting a recovery, Zach shoved his exasperation aside and focused his attention on

Isabel. The child possessed none of her mother's innate shyness. He chose the one topic sure to get her going. "How are your fairy friends doing?"

Isabel perked up. A bright smile lit her face. "There's a new fairy in the garden."

"Is there now?" Zach regarded the girl with renewed interest. New characters seldom joined the troupe of Isabel's imaginary friends.

"Yep." Isabel speared a piece of steak with her fork but only took a nibble.

Theresa leaned forward and pinned her daughter with The Look. "Isabel, stop playing with your food and eat, please."

"What's she called?" Zach slowed the pace of his dining to match the women. As a bachelor, he tended to eat at whatever speed suited him. A delicious, home-cooked meal and a full moon less than a week in the offing magnified his hunger.

"He," Isabel said. "The new fairy is a boy, and his name is Talyn Drake."

Zach's brow rose. "Drake means dragon."

Theresa jerked her face toward him. *Finally,* he had her attention.

"Really?" Isabel asked with big eyes.

He nodded. "Really."

"Does this Talyn look like a dragon?" Theresa directed the question to her daughter.

"Sorta." Isabel held up her hands, palms twelve inches apart. "He looks like a dragon, but he's tiny."

"Is he nice?" Zach asked because the character of the girl's imaginary friend struck him as more important than the dimensions.

"Sometimes, he's mean and makes messes and hogs all of the honey," said Isabel. "Nikki doesn't like him."

Nikki, a bright yellow flower fairy with wings like a daffodil, was Isabel's best friend.

"This Talyn sounds like a tosser." Zach took a sip of his water and turned his bold gaze toward Theresa once again. She looked gorgeous, with her dark hair curling about her face and shoulders. Summer had darkened her complexion to a warm golden brown.

"If he's mean, then why do you play with him?" Theresa asked.

"Sometimes, he's nice, but other times, he's toothy and...." Isabel trailed off, frowning. "What's that word, Zach?"

"Greasy?"

"No."

"Greedy?"

"Nuh-uh." Isabel shook her head, fluttering her small hands. "He's toothy..."

"Expand on what you mean. Toothy as in a wolf or toothy as in a shark?" Zach bared his teeth for

Theresa's sake. His sweet little she-wolf looked good enough to eat.

Right then, Theresa stole a nervous glance up. When she caught him staring at her, she flushed and dropped her gaze. The musky scent of her arousal wafted to his nostrils, and he breathed deep to confirm the aroma. If nothing else, he derived satisfaction from the knowledge that she desired him as much as he wanted her.

Like *hell*, she didn't find him attractive. What lies.

Isabel thought it over and then answered, "Like a crocodile, I think."

Smirking, Zach returned his attention to the girl. "Unctuous?"

"What-uous?" Isabel struggled to wrap her mouth around the strange word.

"It means he wants something from you, pixie."

Isabel beamed. "That's it! Ut-uous."

"Unc-tu-ous." Zach enunciated every syllable with care.

"Unctuous." Satisfied, Isabel whipped around to face her mother. "Mama, I'm full. Can I please be excused?"

"You barely touched your food." Theresa sighed. However, her tone conveyed consent.

Isabel slipped from her chair.

"Wash your hands!" Theresa called after her daughter.

The child disappeared from the kitchen, dark hair bouncing.

Theresa inspected Isabel's plate. "At least she ate her meat."

"She's a growing pup," he said with the right inflection to convey his amusement. "Be glad. Growing up, one of my cousins declared herself a vegetarian when she turned ten."

Theresa laughed, and her eyes searched his face, maybe trying to decide if he were joking. "Oh, no. That must have been very aggravating for her parents."

"Laura's mother and father despaired of her becoming a proper wolf." Zach chuckled at his recollection of the childhood memory. "However, it was a different matter for her brother, Charles, and I. We had a grand old time teasing her at every opportunity. Charles had Laura convinced that she'd wind up becoming an herbivore-shifter. Perhaps a cow or a wererabbit. Her nickname became Bunny—behind our parents' backs, of course."

"Oh, no!" Theresa laughed so hard she held her sides. Tears shone brightly in her eyes. "You're terrible. That poor child!"

"Don't feel too sorry for her. She hit as hard as

any boy, *and* she got even." Zach made a show of rubbing his jaw.

Still laughing, Theresa reached out and caught his hand. He held fast to her fingers, pleased that humor had overcome the discomfort between them. Comedy was an old standby Zach often used to put her at ease. She seemed relaxed again, but he remained stressed out and on edge. With pack politics being what they were, he needed to penetrate Theresa's defenses and gain her complete trust. Quickly.

"What happened to her?" Theresa asked.

With an effort, he tried to set aside all distractions and focus. "To who?"

Theresa's brow rose. "To Laura. Who else?"

"Oh." He wiped his mouth with his napkin then stacked his silverware on his plate. "Laura grew up to be a wolf-shifter after all. She attended Oxford, graduated at the top of her class, and became a journalist."

"Is she still a vegetarian?"

He chuckled. "No, Laura got over that silliness."

Theresa tightened her grip. She gazed at him with wide, luminous eyes as if seeking reassurance and comfort. Zach had begun to suspect that maybe he'd played the nice guy for too long because it was coming back to bite him in the arse. He made the mistake of inhaling, and the alluring perfume of her pheromones flooded his nostrils. It was more than he could stand. The pent-up sexual tension had him ready to start howling at the moon.

"Zach, about what I said to Isabel," Theresa said in a voice riddled with aching discomfort, "what you overheard... I never meant to imply that you're unattractive."

So, the shy she-wolf believed his ego was that fragile? A quick grin crossed his face, and he stifled a laugh. Ever the ham, he adopted an expression of patent relief. "Thank goodness for that. I was starting to feel like an ugly duckling."

Her cheeks reddened. "I just don't want Isabel getting her hopes up or the notion that something might happen."

"Something like this?"

Zach surged to his feet and pulled Theresa toward him across the small table. Gently, he gripped her shoulders with both hands. Just before their lips met, he felt the gasp of her breath and the heat of her skin. He captured her mouth in a kiss.

A soft moan emanated from the back of her throat. Without hesitation, Theresa yielded and opened to him. He feathered his tongue across her upper lip before encountering the smoothness of her front teeth. The mingled scents of her sweat and arousal permeated the air. His sensitive hearing tracked the racing beat of her heart and the erratic rhythm of her respiration. More than anything, he wanted to strip away the bodice of her sundress, exposing her full breasts. He hungered to stroke her silken thighs and to taste the honeyed flesh of her sex.

In his mind's eye, her pussy was sweet and swollen and sensitive, wet and aching for him. The wolf's primal instincts urged Zach to strike fast and close for the kill. *She's mine now.* Common sense provided the discipline he needed to hold that beast at bay.

Go easy. Don't scare her. He kept the pressure light and tender, seductive rather than assertive. She tasted smoky and spicy, like peppercorns and paprika, not as he had imagined but so much better. Heavenly.

Under the persuasive stroke of his tongue, she parted her lips wider. Welcoming his advances, she was yielding ever more. The longer he exercised restraint, the more frantic she grew. Zach sensed the exact moment when the tables turned, and Theresa became the aggressor.

Fed up with being denied, Theresa growled from the back of her throat. She seized fistfuls of his shirt and hauled him closer with a she-wolf's strength. Their mouths crashed together, and her tongue thrust boldly past his lips.

Then, Isabel called out from the other room. "Mama! I want to watch a movie."

The ill-timed intrusion doused Zach's ardor more effectively than a bucket of ice water. He released Theresa and stepped back. They stared at each other like shellshocked survivors of a mind-blowing event.

An alluring siren, Theresa hid behind a curtain of ebony tresses. She wore a shy smile and a charming blush. Her tongue wet her swollen lips, and when she said his name, it sounded like a strangled plea.

"Zach?"

Zach looked straight into her eyes. He sought to ease her uncertainties with steady confidence. "Don't count me out so easily, love."

Theresa stammered. "I-I don't understand."

"Mama!"

"Just a minute, Isabel. You need to be patient." Theresa cast an irritated glance in the direction of her demanding daughter.

As much as he adored the little ankle biter, for once, Zach could've done without Isabel's presence, but the child came first.

"We can talk later, love, after Isabel's gone to bed." With a sigh, he glanced down at the table, still cluttered with dirty dishes, and picked up his plate. "Now, let's get this mess cleaned up, shall we?"

"Great idea!" Theresa seized the opportunity and stacked dirty dishes.

Zach observed her retreat with a touch of amusement but made no move to follow. The worst thing he could do would be to crowd her. Now that he'd made his point, he should give her space.

"Are we watching that animated movie about wolves?" Zach asked while they cleaned up.

"I'm afraid it's a bit of a chick flick. It's a wolf love story."

Zach chuckled. "What's not to love about wolves?"

CHAPTER SEVEN

The loveseat in the family room wasn't big enough to accommodate two adults and a child, so—to Theresa's vexation—she and Zach wound up sitting with Isabel wedged between them. Despite her best efforts to enjoy the movie, Theresa just couldn't get comfortable. She was hot. Sweaty.

Achy in places she couldn't touch. At least, not in the present company. However, Zach would probably be thrilled to volunteer as a masseuse if she asked. The titillating speculation left Theresa squirming and blushing.

"Are you okay, pet?" Zach asked in a voice that smirked.

Jerk. Theresa called him other not-nice names in

the privacy of her thoughts. Aloud, she answered, "I'm fine."

She winced. To her ears, she sounded incredibly bitchy, and Zach's soft chuckle only served to confirm her suspicions.

She was in a lousy temper. To be fair, though, not all the tension singing through her body was owed to sexual frustration. Frankly, she had put in a long day at work. Her neck and shoulders were cramped, and her feet hurt like nobody's business.

Zach had better not get too smug over those stolen kisses if he knew what was good for him.

Oblivious to his peril, Zach pulled a dating maneuver as old as time—or at least one that had been around since the invention of movie theaters, anyway. Big, loud yawn... *Now reach for the sky*.

Predictably, his overhead stretch ended with his long arm draped across the back of the loveseat. By nefarious design, Zach brushed the back of her neck. His caress sent tingles down her spine, and she shivered.

For a second, Theresa couldn't decide how to react. Initially, she gave serious consideration to dealing a sharp smack to his paw. Then, he stroked her nape again with his fingertips, fleeting and flirtatious, demonstrating the same restraint that he'd shown in the kitchen.

Stealing a sneak peek, Theresa verified that Isabel hadn't noticed anything amiss. The girl was enthralled in the story while downing fistfuls of popcorn.

Zach leaned back, and their gazes locked. He mouthed, "Up to you," and he returned his attention to the screen.

Torn, Theresa gnawed her lower lip. She wrestled with her inner demons and took a good hard look at the facts. A) Zach was trying, despite all the mixed signals she kept sending. B) He had made himself vulnerable, which was more than she'd ever risked. C) If she kept rejecting him, he would undoubtedly stop. D) She didn't want him to stop.

E) Was there an E?

F) Theresa wanted Zach in her life—and her bed —with the whole of her heart.

Firmly decided, Theresa reached up, catching Zach's wrist in a blind grab. He stiffened slightly but yielded when she positioned the "V" of his hand over the juncture of her neck and shoulder. His splayed fingers and thumb were in an ideal position for a neck massage.

Theresa patted his arm gently to communicate, "Rub."

A snickering-hiss escaped Zach, but he proved himself pliable. His fingers tested the tension in her neck, probing and stroking. Seeing by touch, he located the worst of the knots and dug in hard. Pain hit in a wave. Theresa damn near passed out from the initial onslaught. She gritted her teeth and hung on for dear life. Positive thoughts helped. *Labor was worse, and then there was the time I had my wisdom teeth removed.* The massage *hurt so good* that a strangled groan rumbled forth.

The saving grace was that her bout of lusty panty-moaning just happened to coincide with a noisy action sequence. Timely animation and loud sound effects saved Theresa from being awarded a Bad Mother of the Year trophy.

The longer Zach rubbed her sore muscles, the harder it became to stay still and quiet. His touch stirred erotic urges that left her wet and whimpering. She envisioned deeds that they couldn't hope to act on while Isabel sat between them.

Naughty list stuff.

At the same time, she felt so far out of her comfort zone it wasn't even funny. Zach's determination to redefine their familiar dynamic had also upended her entire world. Theresa had no idea how to react. It left her as jumpy as a long-tailed cat in a room full of rocking chairs.

What should she say? What should she do?

Surely Zach must be aware that she, Theresa Russo, was a respectable single mother. She didn't sleep around. Heck, she didn't even fool around. So, what were Zach's intentions? Theresa couldn't help but wonder, yet she understood that it was way too soon to ask.

They hadn't even made it to second base. Or had they?

It'd been so long since she'd last had sex, Theresa wasn't even sure what second base involved anymore. Slyly, she slipped her phone from her pocket and typed "second base" one-handed.

The search results returned *Second base – variously means tongue kissing, breast groping, or outside the clothes genital contact. Third base – hands down the pants.*

Theresa blanched. Shit. Now, she felt old.

Ultimately, Zach's masterful fingers distracted her from the ultimate humiliation. Mmm. She sank into ecstasy. By the time the movie credits rolled, Theresa was more relaxed than a jellyfish and hornier than a twelve-point buck.

Yet for all that tranquility, she all but bounded out of her seat. The ninety-minute animation officially qualified as the longest movie of her entire life. With unconstrained enthusiasm, she crowed, "Bedtime!"

Immediately, predictably, Isabel argued, "Mama... I don't want to go to bed. I'm not tired."

"Isabel, you have school tomorrow. I don't want to hear it." To emphasize her point, Theresa seized the remote and turned off the television with a punch of the button.

True to form, Isabel offered the obligatory protests, weaving a list of demands ranging from a glass of water to a story to multiple kisses goodnight. Theresa eased out of her daughter's bedroom a full half-hour later, shutting the door behind her.

Squaring her shoulders, she headed downstairs. Time to face the music.

CHAPTER EIGHT

Theresa found Zach looking larger than life in her tiny kitchen. The sight of the handsome male werewolf stopped her in her tracks. He appeared so out of place, polished and elegant, against the backdrop of battered cabinetry and peeling linoleum.

The bottle of red wine sat uncorked on the countertop. Zach welcomed her with a smile and offered her one of the two poured wine glasses. "Do you like Pinot Noir?"

"I don't know, so I guess we'll find out." She accepted, regarding him nervously. "Thank you."

Zach spun and straddled a chair. "You're welcome. Is the rascal in bed?"

Theresa sat facing him. "She's tucked in. Fingers crossed she stays there."

"Kids are a lot of work." Zach chuckled, sounding amused rather than put off.

"Does that bother you?" The demand burst past her lips before she could stop herself. Inwardly, she cringed, but then she braced herself for his reply.

Zach studied her from beneath a hooded brow. "I'm not a fool, love. I understand how much of your time and energy is devoted to Isabel."

She exhaled. "I wasn't implying anything, and yes, I know you know. We've been friends for years now. But..."

"But?" Zach quirked his brow.

"But to a bachelor...."

"Such as myself?" he teased, and she smiled.

"Such as yourself, the responsibility must seem overwhelming."

He cleared his throat with a rumbling grumble. "In the interests of total honesty, yeah, parental responsibility is intimidating."

"Oh." Theresa's shoulders sank.

His admission depressed her because she wanted to envision a future where Zach became her husband and Isabel's father. She longed for the stability of a loving relationship with a mate who respected and cherished her. She wanted Isabel to grow up in a home with a real family instead of being the solitary child of a single mother.

"That doesn't mean it'd be too much for me to handle," Zach said, sounding fiercely defensive.

Theresa latched onto that slim hope and perked up. "Of course not, but I imagine that it doesn't help that you were an only child."

"I always wanted brothers and sisters," Zach said, "but my mum had trouble conceiving. She went through three miscarriages before they had me."

Theresa blinked. The admission caught her by surprise because Zach guarded his privacy. He seldom spoke of intimate matters. She knew that his mother still lived in England, but his father had been killed in an accident two years before.

The corners of her mouth turned down with sympathy. "Both of your parents were shifters, right?"

"Right," he said then added, "at least I always knew that I'd be one also when I hit adolescence."

When both parents were werewolves, a child had the security of knowing that they would grow up to be a shifter. However, when only one parent was a wolf-shifter, there were no guarantees. Theresa envied the certainty Zach had enjoyed throughout his childhood. For herself, her father had been a werewolf, but her mother was human. She hadn't known she'd inherited her father's shape-changing gifts until she'd turned twelve and experienced the transformation into a wolf for the first time.

"I was the opposite," Theresa said with a wry smile. "Mom and Dad didn't have any trouble conceiving, and they wanted a large family. There are six of us, yet I was the only one who grew up to become a wolf-shifter. Our house was crowded, and we never had enough food. But we loved each other, and we were happy. My parents loved each other and stayed together until my dad passed away. I wouldn't change a thing about my childhood."

Staring into the glass, Zach swirled his wine. The rich burgundy liquid captured the light. "All werewolves face the same dilemma. Mating with a human means that you might only have normal offspring."

"Is that such a bad thing?" Theresa asked, sharper than intended.

He glanced up in surprise. "Of course not. I only mentioned it because the other choice—mating with another shifter—means risking no children. After all, our breed has such low fertility."

"For men, that's not entirely true."

Zach arched his brow.

"Men can always spread their wild oats," Theresa said, struggling to cool her tone, "but not women."

"Right, my apologies. That was a stupid thing to

say." Zach shifted, clearly uncomfortable. He never sounded more civil than when he was angry.

Fighting to control her wolf, Theresa stared at the ground. "I'm sorry I snapped at you. You're only saying what's true, and if it weren't for promiscuous males siring children, our kind would have long since gone extinct."

"That doesn't make it right."

Deliberately, Theresa raised her glowing gaze. "Doesn't it? How many dominant males have used 'propagating the species' as a justification for sleeping around?"

Zach glowered. His jaw was iron set. "Not me."

A flood of bitter tears stung her eyes. She fought to choke her grief back. "I didn't mean you."

Rigidness defined Zach's stance. He exhaled slowly and heavily. "Getting back to where we started, I'm not afraid of responsibility."

"I swear I wasn't talking about you, Zach. My emotions got the better of me. I'm sorry. Maybe you should leave."

A long, uncomfortable silence lingered, and so did Zach. "Do you want me to go?" he asked quietly.

She gulped, attempting to clear the mass lodged in her throat. "No. I want you here. With me. But if you do choose to stay, you have to understand... I'm not okay."

"I understand."

"Zach, I have issues."

"I get it," he huffed.

"Do you? I'm messed up."

"I'm here—for you and Isabel," he stated with a flat forcefulness that finally convinced her he meant business. She stopped challenging his conviction because to continue meant insulting his honor.

She nodded to signal her acceptance and then polished off her wine. Zach lifted the bottle, offering more, but Theresa held up her hand. "No, thank you. One is more than enough."

Zach sloshed red wine into his glass. His serious expression gave her pause because she sensed they were entering dangerous territory. "Theresa, did you have Isabel right out of high school?"

Theresa verbally stumbled. "Why do you ask? You've never pried before—"

"It's not my intention to pry."

"I'm sorry. That's not what I meant."

Zach exploded. "Will you bloody well stop apologizing for everything? If I'm pissing you off, if I'm out of line, say so!"

Theresa blinked and stared. To her shock, she reached a fantastic discovery, a realization that brought a smile to her lips. "I'm not afraid of you, Zachery Hunter."

Zach gnashed his teeth on empty air. "Bloody excellent. At least I've done one thing right."

"More than one thing. Zach, you're my best friend," she said, taking his hand in hers. She stroked his knuckles with her thumb, gathering her courage for what had to come next. "You took the first step by sharing your past. I want to do the same, but this isn't easy for me."

In every sense that mattered, he offered rock-solid support. "I'm listening."

She drew a deep breath and began, "I was already pregnant with Isabel when I graduated from high school. Antonio and I got married right away. Being a mother has defined every aspect of my adult life."

He cocked his head. "Do you regret Isabel?"

Theresa choked up, and tears filled her dark eyes. "Oh, no. I love Isabel. She's my whole world. Don't get me wrong. It's just... I do have regrets. I had a solid GPA and a full scholarship to the University of Las Vegas. I wanted to be a nurse."

"Why didn't you?"

Theresa shook her head. She had a past full of nothing but regrets and excuses. "I had a baby to take care of."

"Your mother and both of your sisters live here in the area. I can't believe your family wouldn't have helped."

Theresa trembled. The humiliation was too much. She wanted to crawl away rather than endure his censure, but it was better to own the shame of her past.

"Antonio forbade it," she said, "and Zanatos backed him up."

"Bloody hell!" Zach shot to his feet, clenching his fists. The action shoved his chair against the wall. "That soddin' bastard! I should kill him."

Theresa cringed, but she also rose. "Antonio was dominant to me at the time. I had to obey."

Zach's entire demeanor gentled when he looked at her. "I wasn't blaming you, love. The last thing I want is you afraid of me."

She'd already said it once, but it seemed to bear repeating. "You don't scare me."

"But you're shaking." Tentatively he rubbed his palms over her shoulders, and she calmed beneath his soothing touch. His support helped her continue.

"Not because of anything you did. Because of how much I feel. It's overwhelming." After a pause, she nodded to herself. "I want to explain how Antonio and I came to be divorced, but I can't do that without talking about the past. I know it will make you angry when I tell you my history."

Zach stilled, and his breathing grew shallow. "Go on. You can tell me anything."

Tightness constricted her chest. "Promise me you won't get angry."

He hesitated and shook his head. "I can't promise I won't become angry, Theresa. I can't turn my emotions on and off like that."

"I get that, but I'm still worried about what you might do."

With a visible effort, Zach composed himself. He donned stoicism like a suit of armor. "Go ahead and say what you need to say. I promise to remain calm. We'll sort out the consequences later."

Theresa hesitated, still worried about how he'd react, but the man had given his word, and she had to trust him. "Normally, our kind doesn't divorce because we mate for life."

Zach tilted his chin to indicate his agreement. "I admit I've wondered what happened to your mate bond with Antonio."

Clenching her teeth, Theresa forced out the terrible truth. "Antonio is the father of my child, but I never *chose* him as my lifemate. I only married him because I was pregnant."

"I see," he said, but his tone indicated that he didn't understand.

"I was seventeen when I got pregnant. Antonio was a year older than me. He was a senior and a linebacker on the varsity football team." She snorted with disgust. "It makes me ill now to recall how starstruck I was back then. How could I have been so stupid?"

"It's not stupid to have a crush. You were young, and you made a mistake. Cut yourself some slack, all right?" He offered her a gentle smile.

She sniffled and nodded. "The point is, I was overwhelmed when Antonio asked me to prom. At the time, I was the pack's Omega."

Throughout a wolf's life, their rank rose and fell based on numerous factors. The Omega was the lowest-ranked member of any werewolf pack, often the weakest and youngest, sometimes the eldest and most infirm. Zach, the son of two dominant wolves, couldn't hope to understand what it meant to be powerless.

"Did you want to refuse him?" Zach asked.

Murderous intensity glinted within his wolf's gaze. His face was a granite mask, but muscles rippled beneath his skin. Never before had she glimpsed so much of his beast, and it thrilled her to no end.

"No, I accepted Antonio's invitation. I was a teenage girl. I wanted the pretty dress, the corsage, to dance beneath colored lights to sappy music. I wanted the attention...."

"You wanted to be treated like a princess."

Theresa blinked, and tears trekked along her cheeks. "My mistake was choosing a real toad instead of a prince. The whole thing left me with some serious trust issues."

"You can trust me, love. I pray with all my heart that you believe that."

She scrubbed her cheek with the back of her hand. "I know I can, Zach. It's not you that I doubt."

He scowled. "Who then?"

"Me. Always me." Theresa laid her hand over her heart.

"Theresa, you have no reason to be ashamed," he said softly. "You're a great mum, and you hold a full-time job. You have every reason to be proud of what you've accomplished."

He understood her far better than she had ever imagined, and she wished for the self-confidence to feel pride instead of shame. She glanced down at her white-knuckled fists. Her stomach churned, and she tasted bile in the back of her throat.

"There's more," she said, hating every word that passed her lips. "You haven't heard the worst of it yet."

CHAPTER NINE

Theresa held her breath, torn apart by anxiety, while she awaited Zach's reaction to her rather dramatic announcement. A part of her felt silly about turning the whole thing into such a production, but she honestly didn't know how else to go about it. The tricky topic was profoundly personal and painful, and she was terrified.

Zach tilted his head, watching her from beneath a hooded gaze. After a delay, he caught her hands in his own and bent to kiss her knuckles. His lips were warm and firm against her skin.

"Say whatever you need to say, love. I'm here for you."

Leaning back, Theresa filled her lungs with air.

She gathered her courage and spat it out. "Antonio hit me while I was pregnant."

Deadly tension coalesced in the atmosphere even though Zach remained immobile. He didn't even twitch a muscle. Only his eyes changed. Arctic blue, his wolf stared out of his face. Primordial energy coursed through his body.

"Are you quite certain you don't want me to kill Antonio?" Zach asked in a voice encrusted icy rime.

"No," Theresa stated flatly. "I dealt with Antonio myself years ago. If you retaliated against him now, you'd undermine my standing within the pack. I would lose what little respect I command. I'm telling you this, so you'll understand what I've endured getting where I am. I don't need a knight in shining armor. I've already rescued myself. Are we clear?"

"Crystal, but so we're on the same page, consider it a standing offer. If you want your bastard of an ex dead, give the word." A wide grin split Zach's face.

A furious flush swept over her throat and face. Zach's bloodthirsty offer ran contrary to everything Theresa had accomplished on her own, yet somehow, his protectiveness thoroughly pleased her inner she-wolf.

Theresa huffed, rolling her eyes. "I'll let you know. Now, can I tell you the rest of the story, so we're not here all night?"

"I'm all ears." Zach gestured broadly.

Nodding, she continued, "Antonio is an alcoholic, although he's been sober for the last three years. He swore when we got married that he'd clean up his act—do right by our baby and me. For a couple of months, he kept his promises, too. He stopped drinking and showed up to work on time and sober. But then one night Antonio slipped up following a football party."

"What did he do?" Zach demanded.

She cleared her throat. "It was the big sports bowl. Antonio had started in on the beers, and his friends kept egging him on. He claimed he'd only had a couple, but the reality is that he drank way too much. Then, his team lost. After his buddies went home...."

"He hit you," Zach said, reaching the correct conclusion.

Rekindled anger blazed in her heart even though the incident was years past. "I was still pregnant and almost due. He punched me in the face and knocked me to the ground. I lay there stunned for a moment, thinking about how he might hurt the baby, and then I lost my temper. For the first time in my entire life, I got so angry that I had no control over my actions."

"Maternal instinct," Zach drawled with savage

satisfaction. "That's something I wish I could have seen with my own two eyes."

She shook her head. "No, I never want to be like that again. I climbed to my feet, and when he tried to hit me again, I punched him so hard that I broke his nose. I hit him, and I kept hitting him until I'd beaten him senseless. Then, I picked him up and threw him out of the house into the snow. The next day, I packed up and moved in with my mother. I never looked back."

"Bollocks," Zach cursed. Sorrow tinged his voice. "No wonder you're afraid of men."

Theresa burst to her feet, and Zach also surged upright. Unhesitating, she flung her arms around his waist and pressed her face to his chest. Beneath her touch, his muscular physique was thrumming with tension. She clung to him, trembling from the sheer force of her emotions, which had nothing to do with fear.

Tentatively, Zach enclosed her in his arms.

"You're a good man, Zachary Hunter. I've already said it more than once, but I'll keep repeating it until you believe me—I'm not afraid of you."

The truth of her words *finally* seemed to get through to the stubborn man. Zach cupped her chin in his hand and lifted her face to look up at him. Their gazes locked. His dilated pupils eclipsed the whites of his eyes. He stroked her shoulders, and his aura surrounded her like a fortress.

"You're shaking." His husky baritone dropped several octaves, layered with concern and desire. Undoubtedly, the scent of her arousal reached his nostrils because his body also hardened. The steely length of his arousal pressed against her stomach through their clothing.

"Zach, Zach," Theresa gasped and pleaded his name. "Kiss me. Please."

His lips brushed against hers, soft and then softer still. Theresa closed her eyes, enraptured by the feel of him. He tasted hot and earthy with the intoxicating hint of red wine. Her heart beat faster, throbbing in her breast, and every breath set her bosom to heaving. She might have suffocated for lack of air, and yet she longed only for the kiss to go on forever.

Zach broke off, murmuring, "Theresa, we should stop or I should go."

Urgency arose from her core. Theresa whimpered and clung to him, thwarting his attempts to withdraw. "No. Why?"

"I have to be sure that you understand that you have the right to refuse me," Zach grated out with immense difficulty, obviously struggling to retain mastery of his wolf.

Scowling, she regarded him with exasperation. "Does it *feel* like I'm refusing you?"

"You told Isabel you only feel friendship for me, but I scent your desire when I'm near." He ran the back of his hand across her cheek in a featherlight touch.

Theresa leaned into his caress. "We've known each other for years. Before now, you never gave any sign you wanted more than friendship. How are *you* the confused one?"

He flashed a wry grin. "Your point."

"What I said to Isabel...." She trailed off awkwardly and dropped her gaze. "I didn't mean it."

"Theresa, if I were to put you into a position where you felt compelled to submit... Hell, I couldn't live with myself."

"How about you start by explaining what prompted this unexpected courtship all of a sudden?" Theresa asked.

Zach worked his jaw like he wanted to say something, but then he shook his head. "I can't. It's too dangerous. I'm sorry."

"Don't patronize me," Theresa cried out, her pitch hiking with exasperation. "It feels like you're making decisions for both of us without consulting me."

Anger sparked in his gaze. "I wouldn't do that to you. I'm asking you to believe me when I tell you that pack politics are about to take a dangerous turn. Trust that I only want to keep you and Isabel safe."

"When you put it that way," she said, exhaling slowly. "Okay, I'll go along with what you think is best—for now."

"Thank you." Zach offered her a sexy smile. "For the record, I've always been attracted to you, Theresa Russo. I was just waiting for the right time."

"And the right time is now?" Theresa narrowed her eyes, attempting to discern his hidden secrets; however, she couldn't penetrate his defenses. Zach had a masterful poker face. In many ways, he was her polar opposite. She always wore her heart on her sleeve.

"The right time is now," he assured her with disturbing severity.

Theresa spoke without hesitation. "I trust you."

"Show me," he demanded.

No, dared.

Theresa wasn't sure what he wanted, but an impulse took hold of her. She seized the front of his shirt and hauled him to her. As a werewolf, her strength was considerable, and her aggression caught them both unprepared.

Zach yielded without the slightest resistance. He

surged against her, and their bodies collided with jarring force.

Theresa stood on tiptoe, sliding her hands across his muscular chest, and locked her arms around his neck. She claimed his mouth in a passionate kiss far rougher than anything they'd shared before. Bruised lips and scraping teeth characterized the fierce embrace. When they broke apart, they were both as worked up as if they'd been sparring.

Theresa demanded, "Was that clear enough?"

"Clear as day." Zach's wolfish grin would have brought Red Riding Hood to her knees. "It's becoming clear to me how I fell into your elaborate seduction, what with dinner and the wine."

"Oh, you!" Snickering, Theresa landed a light punch on Zach's chest, but she thanked her lucky stars for his unfailing ability to restore their comfort zone with his goofy jokes.

Eventually, their laughter died away.

"I'd like to follow this through and see where it goes, Theresa," Zach said. "May I have permission to court you?"

"Yes, I'd like that." A hot flush stained her cheeks. She dropped her eyes and beamed, bursting with joy because he was offering her everything she'd ever wanted.

A part of her was afraid to examine the gift too

closely. Of course, sooner or later, he would have to explain, but for the time being, she was content.

"Splendid." He sounded ecstatic.

Theresa fought to keep a level head on her shoulders. "What do you have in mind? Don't you have to go to Chicago on Tuesday for a book signing?"

"I'll only be gone for two days," he said. "I'll be home Thursday night for the full moon. How about I take you and Isabel on a picnic to Colton's Meadow next Saturday?"

She frowned faintly. "Don't you play golf with Robert on Saturday mornings?"

Zach grinned to show teeth. "We're only playing nine holes. I should be done by noon."

Theresa loved the fact that he was making an effort to include her daughter in their courtship. "A picnic sounds wonderful. Isabel will love it. What would you like me to pack for lunch?"

He arched his brow. "I'll take care of lunch. Proper courtship means that I need to show I can provide for you. I'm not taking the chance that you're going to play love 'em and leave 'em with me over a technicality, woman."

She laughed with delight. "That custom is as old as time and twice as silly."

Zach plied her mouth with a kiss so soft and

sweet it left her aching for more, "So call me old-fashioned."

Smiling, she threw up her hands. "Fine, you win! It's a date. You pack lunch. Just make sure there's chicken or turkey. Isabel won't eat ham."

"Right. No ham."

At the front door, Zach bid her goodnight and goodbye with a long, slow, deep wet kiss. Their open mouths melded, and their tongues stroked together like the act of lovemaking, a penetrating and thorough exploration. It left her breathless and light-headed.

Zach backed away with an insufferable smirk on his face. "Tell Isabel I'll meet her after school tomorrow."

"I'll let her know."

After she locked up, Theresa bounded up the stairs and down the hallway. She jumped into bed, causing the down comforter to billow beneath her. With a sleepy smile on her lips, she hugged a pillow and sank into dreamy bliss.

CHAPTER TEN

Kindergarten corral of the Iron Stone Elementary School - Monday afternoon

Zach showed up fifteen minutes early to pick up Isabel because he preferred to wait over the possibility of being tardy. He stood outside the fenced playground with the other parents, mostly women, who had assembled in groups of twos and threes. Pine trees ringed the grounds, providing shade for a variety of smaller bushes.

The school's release bell sounded, and a swarm of small people poured from the building. Zach spotted Isabel waiting with her teacher and headed toward them.

"Hi, I'm Zachary Hunter," he said, offering Isabel's young female teacher a friendly smile.

"Ms. Spaulding," she said, shaking his hand. "It's a pleasure to meet you. Isabel, do you have all your things?"

"Yes, Ms. Spaulding." Isabel gathered up a pink and white kitty-covered lunchbox and matching rolling backpack. "Hi, Zach."

Zach took Isabel's hand and led her toward the parking lot. "I didn't realize you are such a fan of cats."

Isabel tilted her head to stare up at him. "Fairies hate cats. Even if Mama let me have a kitten, I couldn't keep it because my friends wouldn't like it." She hugged her backpack, adding, "But I make a special expectation for this kitty."

"Exception," Zach corrected. He settled Isabel into the child booster seat Theresa had given him and got her seatbelt fastened.

Isabel frowned. "What?"

"Never mind."

"I don't like it when you talk to me like I'm a little kid." Isabel had long ago mastered the art of the petulant pout.

"Izzy, love, you *are* a little kid."

"Zach, you promised to stop."

He sighed. "All right. You make a special exception. Not an expectation."

"What's the difference?" she queried in confusion.

"An exception occurs when something doesn't conform to a general rule. An expectation is something that is anticipated."

"Okay, I get it."

Zach parted his lips. "Do you?"

"Uh-huh. I love ice cream except for Rocky Road because it's yucky. And I'm expecting an ice cream cone with great anticipation," Isabel said, and Zach busted out laughing.

"Well played, pixie."

The drive from Isabel's elementary school to the ice cream parlor took less than ten minutes. The child filled up the time with animated chatter, topics ranging from her favorite color of green to the superiority of chocolate pudding over vanilla.

"Without a doubt, chocolate is vastly superior. Which reminds me, have you eaten lunch?" Zach asked.

Isabel scoffed. "We eat at school."

He frowned, following her into the ice cream parlor. "Well, how am I supposed to know that? And what's with the attitude? You don't talk like this around your mum."

The girl considered him with big eyes. "Mama would ground me. You won't."

Zach chuckled. "Won't or can't?"

He received no answer because Isabel only had eyes for candy bins stacked high with every sugary treat imaginable. He attempted to herd Isabel past the confectionary section of the store, but, in the end, he bought her a half-pound of mixed hard candies in addition to a cotton candy-flavored ice cream cone.

"I don't know how you can eat that," Zach muttered, eyeing her ice cream with disgust. The neon pink-and-blue swirl drew his imagination to toxic nuclear waste.

"It's my favorite. Chocolate is boring." Isabel cast a pointed glance at his cone.

"Except when we're discussing pudding," Zach said with plenty of snark. "Speak for yourself, munchkin. Chocolate happens to be my favorite. It's a classic."

"Borrring." Isabel rolled her eyes. "Chocolate's only better because they don't make cotton candy pudding."

"As you said."

They moved outside with their ice cream to enjoy the warm afternoon sun. The late summer heat melted the ice cream quickly, making it perfect for licking. The grassy areas of Main Street Park were an oasis of green beneath patches of pine trees. A children's playground straddled the north end.

They sat on a park bench to eat, and Isabel swung her feet back and forth.

"Do fairies like ice cream?" Zach asked.

Isabel frowned. "I don't know."

"I thought you knew everything there is to know about the Fae."

She looked at him in that disquieting way of children and lunatics. "No one believes me. Not even Mama."

"Adults are skeptical of what they can't see with their own eyes," Zach explained. "Most grownups don't believe in fairies."

Isabel giggled. "Most grownups don't believe in werewolves, but we are werewolves."

He snorted. "Your logic is impeccable, pixie. You must never tell non-shifter adults what you are, but even if you do, they probably won't believe you anyway."

"Because we hide," Isabel said.

Zach nodded. "Because we hide."

"Like the fairies."

"Like the fairies," he agreed.

Isabel tossed her half-eaten cone into a trash can. "I'm full."

"Me too." Zach ate the point of his cone and disposed of the wrapper.

Isabel made a beeline for the swings. Zach

diligently followed, prepared to push for all he was worth. He enjoyed the brief, albeit temporary, respite from her relentless curiosity.

Would his son or daughter with Theresa be as intelligent as Isabel? Zach's straying imagination took him on an unexpected turn into the realm of possibility. It wasn't the first time he'd thought about having a family, but before, it had always been an abstract concept. Now, he envisioned Theresa round with his child, and it pleased him beyond words.

"My fairy friend, Nikki, says that it's okay for me to talk about fairies because the grownups won't ever believe me," Isabel said.

"I believe you." Zach gave a big push that sent her swing higher.

As she swung back, Isabel shot him a dubious glance. "Really?"

"I live in my imagination, so I know what you mean. My characters talk to me too."

The conversation continued as a back and forth exchange that kept rhythm with the swinging.

"What do they say?" Isabel asked.

He flashed a wry smile. "Right now, not a whole lot."

"But they're still in your imagination," Isabel stressed her point. "My friends aren't."

"They seem real to me."

"That's not the same." Isabel pouted but pursued it no further. "Have you figured out who killed the taxi driver yet?"

He grunted. "I think so." Then, he added, "No, I've no bloody idea."

"I think the murderer was his wife."

Zach stared at the girl's dark mane of hair as it lifted from her shoulders. He waited until she swung back and asked, "How do you figure?"

"Because it's always the wife or husband. You told me so yourself. It was the wife in your last book, *Abandon All Hope*."

Zach groaned. "Isabel, please tell me you're not reading my books."

"No, but Mama reads them, and you talk to me about them all the time. Mama wants Inspector Anders to fall in love with the pretty lady from the place where they take the dead people."

"The morgue," Zach said. "Theresa and most of my female readers seem to want those two to get together."

"Zach!" A familiar voice called out his name from across the park.

Zach turned to find Mary Esposito hurrying down the sidewalk toward them. She was a lovely woman, an older version of Theresa, with gray hair and wire-frame glasses perched on the end of her nose.

"Good afternoon, Mrs. Esposito."

"Nana!" Isabel jumped off the swing, landing confidently on both feet, and flew into her grandmother's arms.

"Izzy, my little love bug! How are you? Let me see you."

"You're an hour early," Zach said, checking his watch.

"My doctor's appointment let out early. Has Izzy been good for you?" Mary regarded Zach with the sort of motherly approval that set his ears burning.

"An angel," Zach said.

Isabel promptly launched into a long-winded, furiously paced account of their afternoon together. The adults waited patiently until the girl wore herself out.

"Thank you so much for watching my Izzy. Do you need to be going?" Mary asked.

"I should," he said. "I haven't written a word since yesterday, and I still need to pack. My plane leaves tomorrow at seven."

"Bye, Zach," Isabel said, waving her hand.

"I'll see you when I get back, pixie."

"Bring me a present?"

"Promise." He crossed his heart.

On returning to his car, Zach dug out his phone and launched the voice-recording app he used for note keeping. He suspected his ears were bright red as he spoke into the device. "Make sure the killer is not the wife."

CHAPTER ELEVEN

Hollow Hill Acres ranch on the outskirts of Iron Stone Valley, Sierra Nevada mountains – Monday evening

Theresa didn't care for political events, especially ones where the stratification between social classes was so apparent that no one bothered trying to hide it.

The entire pack had gathered in the living room of Adam and Becky Teller's spacious home for the Alpha's special meeting. The higher-ranked wolves assembled on a mint green couch and matching armchairs. Rows of folding card table chairs were set up for the remainder of the pack.

The seating arrangement sent a clear message—higher-ups here, lowers there.

"Theresa, over here!" Ambra Russo, Antonio's fraternal twin, waved at Theresa from across the room. Ambra was a beautiful woman with chestnut hair and manicured nails. Her outfit and shoes were stylish and tasteful, reflecting the high-end clothing boutique where she worked.

Antonio and his wife, Tammy, were seated with Ambra. Theresa had nothing personal against either woman, but she preferred to sit alone rather than get stuck near her ex-husband.

"One minute," Theresa called to Ambra, holding up her index finger. She detoured past the concession table as an excuse to delay the inevitable. From across the room, she gazed with longing at the empty chair beside Zach.

The pack organized itself roughly, though not rigidly, according to hierarchy in any social setting. Real-world terms, only the uppity-ups got to lounge on the tacky mint furniture. It looked about as comfortable as it was ugly. Theresa consoled herself with the thought that she probably wasn't missing all that much anyway.

Zach looked downright miserable.

A deep male voice rumbled in her ear, "You should march over there and stake your claim."

"Excuse me?" Startled from her reverie, Theresa

whirled around only to discover that the intrusive male was standing directly behind her.

And not just any man, but Robert Blane, the pack's Beta wolf.

Robert outranked everyone except Adam. The outrageously handsome black man had short, neat hair and chocolate-brown eyes. A trimmed mustache and beard covered his square jaw. He wore a charcoal gray suit tailored to his physique. And, *oh my God,* what an impressive figure he cut—tall as a tower and ripped like a god.

"I said you should stake your claim." Robert grasped Theresa's shoulders with his huge hands, steadying her even though she was in no danger of going over.

Going down, maybe. Speculatively, Theresa raked him with her gaze. *Those trousers don't stand a chance against my claws.*

A hot second after the scandalous thought crossed her mind, Theresa almost died of embarrassment. But the scorch sweeping her skin was nothing compared to the heat in her molten core.

What the hell has gotten into me? Why am I so horny?

Uncertainly, she dragged the tip of her tongue over her lower lip.

Robert tracked the motion with predatory

intensity. The potent scent of male pheromones permeated the air. There wasn't a she-wolf alive with a functional nose who would've doubted this man's virility.

Theresa cleared her throat. "That mint-awful seat is meant for *you*. Not me."

"Me? But you're so much lovelier," Robert said.

The blatant flattery left her blushing, and his smile widened to Big Bad proportions. *Oh, my, Mr. Attorney, what big teeth you have.*

"Zach is saving you a place, just like he always does." Theresa squared her shoulders, savoring the heft of Robert's hands. Naughtily, she wondered about how his palms would feel cupping her breasts or massaging between her thighs.

"You could sit with us." He quirked his brow while his stare hugged her curves.

"There's only one chair," she said primly.

"My lap is free," Robert suggested with a wicked smile. Surprisingly, he lightened the pressure by adding, "And so is Zach's. Lady's choice."

"Let me guess, you're fine either way?" Theresa gripped his wrists and raised his hands.

To her relief, he respected her wishes and withdrew; however, she couldn't help but notice how they both expelled regretful sighs.

"That's how I roll." Robert shrugged.

His tone held a mysterious message that Theresa didn't fully comprehend. She could only guess as to his true meaning, but the longings of her fertile imagination proved more than sufficient to set her blood on fire.

Oh, so tempting.

But common sense dictated that the time had come to exit the danger zone. Besides, Theresa already had enough on her romantic plate.

Worriedly, she glanced toward Zach only to catch him watching them. Her heart throbbed in her throat until she realized he wasn't angry. Zach's regard held speculation but not a hint of jealousy.

Interesting.

Theresa turned, gesturing past Robert. "Please pass me a water?"

She enjoyed the satisfaction of seeing the masterful Beta wolf momentarily perplexed. Finally, he reached back, snagged a bottle, and offered it to her. Theresa accepted and turned around. She retreated a stride, but then a dangerous impulse brought her to a halt.

"*I* decide who *I* straddle," she cast over her shoulder.

Robert quaked with husky laughter. "Yes, ma'am. I respect that."

"Good."

Resigned to her ex's unpleasant company,

Theresa made her way to where Ambra sat with Antonio and Tammy.

Ambra rose and greeted her warmly. "Theresa! Long time no see. How have you been?"

Theresa plastered on a toothpaste smile. "I've been well, thank you. And you?"

"Good." Ambra raised a delicate brow and grinned. "For a second there, I would have sworn that you intended to go sit with the dominant wolves."

"Don't be silly." Theresa flushed. *Sit on, maybe.*

"Theresa." Antonio wore a white Henley and indigo blue jeans tucked into cowboy boots. Although he was only a year older than Theresa, his hairline was already receding. Once, his dark good looks had impressed her, but now, she held the man in contempt.

"Antonio." Theresa gave him a curt nod.

"Have you heard the news?" Ambra dropped her voice to a hushed whisper and leaned forward with the eager expression of one in possession of a choice piece of gossip.

"What news?" Theresa had no talent for deception. Her face gave her away every time.

"Word is, Adam is going to retire. Robert is the logical choice to become Alpha, but Antonio doesn't think Zach will let him have it without a fight."

Theresa's abdomen cramped painfully. Just the

thought of Robert and Zach fighting for leadership scared her to death. Luckily, the meeting was called to order, saving her from weighing in on the discussion.

Oh, the irony, saved from politics by more politics.

CHAPTER TWELVE

Silence fell when Adam took the podium.

The atmosphere grew soupy with anxiety. Theresa had always been sensitive to the pack's mood, although her empathy sometimes failed when she focused on specific individuals. Now, she perceived the nervousness spreading through the pack's collective aura as swirls of sickly-colored energy, rather like vomit in a bowl.

"Howdy all. Thanks for coming," Adam drawled in his rolling accent. The alpha allowed the audience to offer a round of greetings in return before he continued, "Now, I know rumors have been spreading, and folks are getting worked up, so I'm going to speak my piece. Then, I'll take questions."

The Alpha paused.

"When I came to this community five years ago," Adam resumed, "I did so at the request of our Wolf God. Those of you who were members then know this pack was in a sorry state. Those who weren't here have heard the stories. Dominant wolves abused weaker members. Mates and children were mistreated or outright killed. Zanatos destroyed the pack bond, the foundation of our unity. Zanatos broke our people's most sacred laws. For those crimes, he was executed."

A stir moved through the pack, and Theresa shivered. The Alpha's speech was stirring trouble, unearthing long-buried memories of pain and suffering. Fear and anger seized the crowd.

"When I assumed leadership, I vowed things would get better, and I have kept my promises," Adam said. "The pack has been stable for years now. We're ready for a change of leadership. Becky and I"—he nodded to acknowledge his wife—"want to return home so we can spend more time with our family. I am ready to step down."

A roar of protests rang out, and violent emotions ran rampant through the pack. Theresa gripped the seat of her chair, riding out the psychic assault like a storm. Without the steady presence of the dominant wolves, there would have been chaos.

Adam raised his hands, commanding them to remain calm. "Settle down. Now. I understand how difficult this is, but I'm leaving you in competent hands. Robert Blane and Zachary Hunter are both fine, strong men."

"Who will be the new Alpha?" Theresa's voice rang out. Her boldness earned her glances, but no one was more surprised with her audacity than she herself.

Adam pinned Theresa with a look that made her skin crawl. "Excellent question, little lady. Logically, it's going to come down to a competition between the two strongest males to determine who will be the next Wolf King."

Everyone turned to stare at Robert and Zach, including Theresa. It amazed her that they'd endured the alpha's grandstanding without protest. Only then did she notice how the two men were standing shoulder-to-shoulder, arms crossed, presenting a unified front. The message was clear. They were a team, not rivals.

Theresa smiled and clasped her hands. Warmth welled in her heart. She wanted to cheer, especially when Adam noticed.

The Alpha scowled ferociously, and a tic worked in his jaw. "When I first met Robert Blane," Adam said, "I thought to myself, 'Now this, this is a wolf to contend with.' Since then, everything I've learned about Robert has proven me right."

"Thank you," Robert said evenly.

The room hung on a beat.

Adam glared at Zach. "When I first found out that they were sending an Englishman, I figured he'd be a fancy-pants sissy-boy, all tea and biscuits."

Pockets of coarse catcalls erupted but faded fast. Zach stiffened and clenched his fists. Tension sang in the air.

Theresa silently lent Zach all her strength, urging, *Don't fall for it, my love. You're smarter than this.*

Zach relaxed. "You've got me pegged, old man. I do love my tea and biscuits."

People broke into loud laughter, and their relief was palpable. Adam's complexion darkened redder than a brick outhouse. The dangerous smile on his face gave Theresa chills.

"Classic Zach," Adam drawled, "always ready with a snappy comeback. You'd better learn to watch your tongue when you become pack leader, Mr. Hunter."

When, not if.

Theresa wasn't the only one who noticed Adam's choice of words. The awful apprehension came crashing back over the pack.

Into the dead zone he had wrought, Adam announced, "Normally, the candidates for the Wolf King fight to the death. However, this pack has seen more than enough violence, which leaves me with a dilemma. Fortunately, my wife, who is as smart as she is lovely, proposed a solution. Now, I'm going to let Becky do the tellin', seein' as how this is her brainchild."

Adam took his seat, sipping a shot glass of whisky.

Becky Teller strode to the podium. The older woman radiated confidence that bordered on arrogance. "Good evening."

"Good evening," a round of greetings sprang from the pack. Theresa found herself chorusing right along with everyone else.

Becky flashed an aging beauty queen smile. "Adam is feeling shy about saying it, so I'll go right ahead. As all you single ladies undoubtedly know, both of these fine gentlemen are bachelors." She nodded to Robert and Zach.

Women giggled, but Theresa shared in none of their titillations. If anything, she felt the exact opposite, filling with dread. Whatever was coming, it couldn't be good.

"Every Wolf King must have a Wolf Queen," Becky said. "Therefore, Adam has determined that Robert and Zachery will compete for a mate from within the pack. The man who claims the highest-ranked she-wolf—"

"*I object.*"

Charlaine Gale rose from where she sat with the other dominant wolves at the front of the room. At six feet tall, the beautiful black woman wielded authority like a queen. A proven warrior, she possessed the strength and the skill to defend her position as Delta, the fourth highest-ranked wolf in the Iron Stone Pack.

Dead quiet engulfed the room.

On her pedestal, Becky scowled, but even that obnoxious woman didn't dare argue with Charlaine Gale.

Unable to resist, Theresa stole a glance at Adam out of the corner of her eye. The Wolf King smirked, nursing his whiskey.

Charlaine delayed until the pack's restlessness faded, and she commanded everyone's attention. She dismissed Becky with a sneer and speared Adam with a flinty stare. "The last time I checked, *I'm* the highest-ranked she-wolf," Charlaine continued. "Aside from the fact that Robert is my cousin, no one—*but no one*—is turning me into a Goddamn trophy. I will rip off the balls and feed them to any man that says otherwise."

In a show of power, Charlaine shifted her hands to claws. The crunching of bones carried to the far reaches of the room, and every dominant wolf erupted from their seats.

Every dominant wolf, that was, *except* Adam.

To her eternal shame, Theresa shrank in her seat. Despite her cowardice, admiration for

Charlaine overwhelmed her. Theresa couldn't help thinking, *I want to be that brave and confident.*

Charlaine glowered at her cousin. "Do we have a problem, Cuz?"

Robert offered a slow smile, raising his hands. "No, ma'am."

Before Charlaine had a chance to turn her head, Zach echoed, "No, ma'am. My mum raised me to respect women." A beat, then he flashed a goofy smile. "If Mum ever heard otherwise, she'd board the first flight out 'n geld me herself."

Laughter erupted throughout the room, breaking the awful tension. Theresa faked amusement, but she could not escape the dread coiled about her like a snake. The sense of doom intensified when Adam set his shot glass aside and reared.

An immediate hush fell.

Adam bared his teeth, addressing Charlaine. "You've made your point. Your wishes will be respected, as will those of any she-wolf who refuses to participate. For the official record, you *are* declining the honor of becoming our next Wolf Queen. Is that correct, Ms. Gale?"

A swirling sensation spun in Theresa's gut. *Oh, no. This whole thing was a setup designed to exclude Charlaine from the competition. Adam is evil.*

From the granite mask that settled over

Charlaine's expression, she grasped precisely how the Wolf King had manipulated the situation. Regardless, steel threaded her voice. "I understand, and I officially decline the honor."

Adam beamed like a spotlight. "Well, then, in the interests of fairness, I officially declare this competition open to all single *and* fertile she-wolves in the pack. Let's call it a free-for-all. At least, until I declare otherwise."

Excitement broke out among the rank and file. Every queen bee and wannabee was buzzing, all except for Charlaine and Theresa. Across the room, the two women traded a long, knowing look.

"Becky, my pumpkin," Adam drawled, bowing out. "The floor is yours."

The Alpha's subordinate mate glowered with all the bitterness of crabapples. Then, Becky rallied. She plastered a massive grin on her face and proclaimed, "Ladies, put your red dresses on. It looks like we have a mating game!"

CHAPTER THIRTEEN

A mating game—what the hell? Theresa fumed in outrage even as excitement exploded throughout the room. People surged to their feet. Their raised voices combined to create a roar. All around, activity whirled like a hurricane.

At the eye of the storm, Theresa sat rock-still. Her chest ached like a punch to the heart. She pressed a hand to her mouth to silence her instinctive protest. *No. Zach belongs to me. Mine all mine.* Every other she-wolf had better keep her paws off—*or else.*

Yet, even as she wrestled to keep her temper under control, Theresa couldn't help but wonder if Zach had been aware of the Alpha's plans. She didn't want to believe Zach would ever agree to such a cold-blooded scheme, but sneaky-awful doubts assailed her, especially when she recalled how secretive he'd been lately.

Theresa craned her neck, scanning the crowd. She finally located Zach lounging on the couch, as calm as could be despite the surrounding turmoil. Her blood turned to ice because he appeared utterly unfazed.

Against her will, Theresa leaped to the inevitable conclusion. Oh, God, Zach *had* known all about this demeaning mating game.

Suddenly, she couldn't breathe. She had to get out of here *now*.

Using the cover of the surrounding commotion, Theresa made a beeline for the nearest exit, a glass slider that led to a redwood deck at the rear of the house. She burst into the crisp night and pulled the door closed behind her.

An almost full moon hung in the clear sky against a backdrop of black velvet and shining stars. The wilderness came right up to the edge of the deck. Theresa seized the wooden railing with both hands. Sides heaving, she leaned out and gulped the refreshing air into her lungs.

Theresa's head hurt, and unshed tears stung her eyes. She found it unbelievable—*no, unthinkable*—that Zach might've cooperated with the Alpha's machinations. In a cringe-worthy fashion, she found herself questioning everything romantic that had transpired between them. Had Zach's spontaneous courtship been genuine or yet another of his pranks?

Rational or not, Theresa felt utterly betrayed. For the sake of fairness, however, she also acknowledged that Zach was entitled to an opportunity to explain himself. She owed him—and herself—that chance.

Without warning, the patio door slid open, and noise spilled from inside the house.

Theresa stiffened and jerked around to confront the intruders. Sourness filled her mouth, and her stomach sank when she recognized the two women who stepped onto the deck. *Great, just when I thought things couldn't get any worse, here comes MegaBitch and her minion.*

Debra Yeller stood as tall as most men, only a couple inches under six feet, and had an athletic build and curly red hair. Her cousin and companion, Simone Sovony, was six inches shorter and had dark brown hair cut into a page boy style. Both of the other she-wolves outranked Theresa—although not by much—and they used their power at every opportunity to make her life miserable.

Short of jumping the railing and fleeing into the woods, Theresa had no way of avoiding them, so she opted to stand her ground. Besides, she was sick and tired of being a coward. Squaring her shoulders,

Theresa strove to pull herself together before the pair noticed her.

"Who would you rather have, Simone? Because I'll tell you, I'd take either of them in a heartbeat." Debra produced an exaggerated purr from the back of her throat.

Simone laughed. "Deb, you're such a slut. Why, I bet you'd do either of them—or both of them at the same time. Anytime, anywhere, any position—"

"Shut up, bitch." Debra swatted at her cousin. Still laughing, she looked up and spotted Theresa. Then, Debra's expression turned ugly. She jabbed Simone with her elbow. "Look what we have here—the pack's biggest loser."

Simone sneered. "Yeah, it's Too Pathetic to Keep A Man Russo."

Theresa lifted her chin. "What, are we still in high school? Sad if that's the best you can do. Now, excuse me." Head high, she attempted to march past them, but Debra blocked her path.

"Have you been crying, Theresa?" Debra asked, scenting the air.

Simone also sniffed, following her cousin's lead. "She's probably heartbroken because Zach's going to choose a mate, and I can guarantee it won't be her. Everyone knows she's got the most pathetic crush on him."

Debra's eyes lit with glee, and she seized on the

suggestion. "Is that it, Theresa? Poor pitiful thing. No male wolf will touch you because you're damaged goods. No one wants Antonio's sloppy seconds."

Theresa saw red. Before she knew what hit her, her wolf surged to the fore. A low growl rumbled in her throat, and her gaze cast a crimson glow. "You should be careful," she gritted out, but neither woman heard or respected the warning.

"In fact," Simone said, "the only reason any male could want her is 'cause she has whelped a pup."

Motion behind the two women caught Theresa's attention. She glanced past them and spotted Zach standing directly behind her tormentors. The male wolf loomed like a terrible menace.

Theresa suspected that both Debra and Simone would've cut and run if they'd gotten a good look at Zach's face. His expression was murderous.

Simone kept talking, but her words faded from Theresa's awareness like the buzzing of a fly. They had an audience. The entire pack was eavesdropping. The commotion within the house faded away, and the quiet atmosphere thrummed with bloodthirsty anticipation.

Zach raised one eyebrow—a question? No, the severe cast of his features conveyed a clear challenge. She could hear his voice, his crisp English accent demanding, "How much more shit are you going to eat, love?"

Frankly, Theresa was fed up and beyond. Puckering her mouth, she glared at Debra, who finally reached the end of her trite monologue.

"I'll make this simple for you," Debra said, oblivious to their audience. "I forbid you to go anywhere near Zach or Robert. Disobey me, and I'll rip your throat out. Got it?"

"That means you need to learn your place, bitch." Simone struck Theresa with an open-handed slap across the cheek.

Theresa's head snapped to the side. She retaliated on instinct.

"Eat this." Theresa's fist flew and flattened Simone's nose. Bones crunched, blood spurted. The blow laid Simone out flat on her back.

Stunned silence followed. Crickets chirped.

Even Theresa was surprised. Zach had insisted on teaching her the ins and outs of self-defense, and she'd gone along with it for years, if for no other reason than she latched onto any excuse to touch him. For the official record, this was the first time she'd put her self-defense skills to the test.

Apparently, she had a mighty fine teacher.

"Hot damn," Theresa declared, grinning. "That felt good." She stepped on Simone's throat and leaned over. Theresa bored holes in the brunette's skull with her glare. "Submit, or I'll kill you."

Simone swallowed convulsively and turned her face to the side, a gesture of submission and surrender. Honor required that Theresa accept.

Honor satisfied, Theresa rounded on the megabitch. She bared her teeth and growled. "You were right about one thing, Debbie," Theresa stated loud and clear so her voice would carry to the far reaches of the pack. "My fertility is a proven fact. I got pregnant the first time I was ever with a man. I have given birth to a healthy child, and my daughter *will* become a wolf. My future children will be healthy and shifters. Robert or Zach would be lucky to be chosen by me."

She allowed that declaration to echo, to sink into the pack consciousness.

Then, Theresa leaned into Debra and inhaled a long, slow, deep breath. "Whereas you're infertile, bitch."

Debra sputtered. "L-liar! I'm fertile."

"You're as fertile as a dustbowl, Debra Yeller," Theresa snarled. "Half the males in the pack have fucked you, and you're still childless. No matter how many times you get plowed, you'll always be a barren field."

Crass laughter rippled through the ranks of the pack.

Scenting blood, Theresa closed for the kill. "You don't ovulate. Everyone with a nose knows it, even if no one says it to your face because you're a bitch and a bully."

Debra and Theresa locked stares.

Seething with fury, Theresa growled from the depths of her soul, a warning to the other she-wolf that she was about to get her heart ripped out.

Debra refused to drop her gaze. Debra refused to submit.

Faced with no other choice, Theresa shouted loud enough for her voice to carry for miles, "Debra Yeller, I challenge you to combat to the death!"

CHAPTER FOURTEEN

Electrifying enthusiasm careened through Zach. All that energy demanded a physical outlet. He wanted to run to shout to shift to howl. It took everything he had not to erupt into a one-man cheering squad for Theresa. Spectating from the sidelines proved equally problematic, especially since he desired nothing more than to leap to his lady's defense. Pack law forbade him—or anyone else—from interfering in a just challenge. The she-wolves had to settle the matter between themselves.

The thought served as a sharp reminder to Zach that his duties as a dominant wolf included policing the pack. He pivoted and confronted an unruly mob drawn by the confrontation on the deck. Bloodlust permeated the atmosphere. The werewolves rumbled with a booming commotion, growling and snarling. They pushed and shoved, competing for access to the deck. If things turned violent, it could spark a frenzy—and Zach alone blocked their path.

The odds against him left a sour taste in Zach's mouth. He adopted a solid stance, drew a deep breath, and opened his mouth, but he never got off a word or a warning.

"Stop it right now! You should all be ashamed of yourselves—acting like a bunch of animals." Glaring and scolding, Theresa descended on the quarrelsome wolves like fury. She embodied the essence of maternal authority.

Zach was left with his jaw hanging, and he wasn't the only one confounded.

Theresa marched straight up to Darryl Berg, one of the rabble-rousers leading the mob. The male werewolf had a full head and shoulders plus a hundred pounds on Theresa.

"Ashamed. Do you hear me, Darryl Jason Berg?" Theresa glowered up at the man. "Your poor mother June—may she rest in peace—would be horrified if she could see you now."

"You're not my mom! Don't tell me what to do." Darryl bared his teeth and snarled full in Theresa's face. He raised his fist.

A jolt of fear kicked Zach into action. He

lunged, but the cold lump in his gut told him he wouldn't reach Theresa in time.

Zach never fully understood what happened next.

Psychic energy whirled around Theresa, invisible but palpable. It raised the tiny hairs all over Zach's skin. From their reactions, others must have felt it also because people backed away.

"Don't you *dare* threaten me or any other woman for that matter!" Gold flashed in Theresa's gaze, and she dropped a psychic lash that knocked Darryl flat on his back.

Zach pulled up, halting mid-lunge. All around, shock held the mob in a paralyzing grip. No one moved or spoke except for Theresa.

She addressed the pack with a kind smile, looking her fellow wolves in the eyes. "If there's one thing we desperately need, it's a pack mother. Iron Stone is our home. We're a family. It's time we started acting like one. Don't you all agree?"

"Yes, ma'am," everyone chorused, including Zach.

A miracle happened then.

The potent psychic energy Theresa commanded poured forth in a wave of warmth and belonging. Homecoming. Zach had never experienced anything so wonderous. He smiled and laughed while he surfed the breaking crest. The magic engulfed and included every wolf present, knitting them together into a unified whole.

A newly formed pack bond was born, and the wolves of Iron Stone once again became a genuine pack.

"What in tarnation is going on here?" Adam bulldozed his way through the crowd until he reached the front. The Alpha quickly assessed the scene and then turned to Zach. "Hunter, did you do this?"

At a loss for words, Zach shook his head and pointed. Theresa narrowed her eyes and frowned at being signaled out. Zach felt the heat of her disapproval like a burn. He winced and mouthed, "Sorry."

"Hot damn!" Whooping, Adam smacked Zach on the back, almost knocking him off his feet. The Alpha glowed with excitement. "Well, smack my ass and call me Sally. Who'd have thought that this little filly would be the key to healing the pack?"

"*Me.* I've always believed in her," Zach muttered. He held his fists at his sides, suppressing the impulse to destroy Adam. How dare he treat Theresa with such blatant disrespect?

Following their alpha's lead, the pack joined in the rowdy celebration. Theresa got hugged, pawed, and jostled. She looked downright miserable with all the attention. Zach longed to whisk her away, but he didn't have the right to decide that for her.

Glancing around, Zach located Robert and Charlaine nearby. Both dominant wolves were already utilizing the new pack bond to make their presence felt. Zach figured he'd better get with the program quick or find himself eating dust.

"Hey!" a female voice shrieked at a grating pitch.

Heads turned. Another hush fell. The sliding glass door remained wide open so that the entire pack could witness the developing confrontation.

Debra Yeller strutted around the stage, demanding attention. "What about me?"

Theresa rounded on her rival. "What about you, Debbie?"

Debra rested her fists on her hips. "Theresa Russo, you're so out of line."

"You still haven't answered my challenge," Theresa said.

"What challenge?" Debra sneered, craning her head. "I don't see any challengers."

"Then I'll repeat it, so everyone hears. Debra Yeller, I challenge you to combat," Theresa snarled. "Answer me!"

Moonlight bathed Theresa. A sheen glistened on her skin, and wisps of black hair clung to her skin. Her chest heaved with the demanding rhythm of her panting. A crimson glow emanated from her gaze, and her parted lips revealed sharp canines.

She was magnificent. Once again, Zach's pants were three sizes too small.

"You can't do that!" Seeking support, Debra turned toward the pack. "She can't do that. I outrank her by far!"

Zach tensed and shifted to a ready stance, prepared to intercept any susceptible idiots who responded to Debra's pleading. Sure enough, three lower-ranked males stirred in response to her cries. The she-wolf had not come by her reputation as promiscuous on accident.

"Carl, tell this bitch to back off." Debra's gaze settled on her boyfriend Carl Reynolds, a burly man with more muscles than brains. As a wolf, he had mange.

Carl stomped toward Theresa. "You heard her, bitch. Back off."

The pack parted to allow Carl to approach the spot where Debra and Theresa had faced off.

Adam lazily watched the drama unfold. The Wolf King wore a smirk.

The bastard is enjoying himself. Coldly furious, Zach blocked Carl's path and speared him with a flinty stare. "You back off, or I'll put you in the ground. *Bitch.*"

Coarse laughter rolled through the pack ranks.

Humiliation stained Carl's face, but he lowered his head, signaling his submission. "Debra says it's not a valid challenge seeing as how she has two ranks on Theresa," Carl protested, studying his feet.

"The validity of the challenge is Adam's call." Charlaine stepped onto the deck.

Zach acknowledged her show of support with a tight smile, and Charlaine tipped her chin in return.

"Thank you, Char, and that's the right of it," Adam said in his slow drawl. He surveyed the situation, scanning the assembled wolves with cool detachment. The last sign of belligerence vanished from the pack.

"I'm sorry for speaking out of turn, Alpha."

Adam adjusted his cowboy hat to sit higher. "You're dismissed, Mr. Reynolds."

Carl bowed his head and retreated.

The Alpha stopped him with a harsh word. "Reynolds."

"Yes, sir," Carl replied without turning.

"If you ever threaten a woman or child again, I'll have you branded a coward and expelled from this pack. Understood?"

"Yes, Alpha." Carl fled as if he sensed the sear of Zach's gaze boring holes in his back. Smart move for a dummy.

Wrestling with his wolf's primal instincts, Zach quelled the urge to give chase. He hungered to rip out Carl Reynold's throat with his fangs, but revenge would have to wait.

With a curt nod, Adam regarded Debra and Theresa. The two women were the focus of attention. Simone crouched on the ground, occupying a far corner of the deck. Zach and Charlaine stood guard at the entryway to the family room. Zach sensed Robert somewhere inside the house, shepherding the more far-flung members of the pack.

Right then, Zach respected Robert more than ever. It spoke well of the Beta wolf that he put the welfare of lesser wolves before any need to be at the center of the action.

Adam's piercing gaze landed on Theresa. "What's your take on this, Miss Russo?"

Theresa held her head high and glanced at Simone. "Debra is trying to worm her way out of having to fight me," Theresa said. "Simone submitted to me. By our laws, I now hold her rank in the pack."

"Simone, did you submit to Theresa?" Adam stepped closer, towering over the trembling she-wolf who crouched at his feet.

Debra opened her mouth to interrupt.

Adam turned on her. A warning growl rumbled from his throat. "Speak out of turn, and I'll have you punished."

Dropping her gaze, Debra submitted with a frightened whimper.

Simone curled into a ball and sobbed.

"She submitted," Theresa insisted, sounding thoroughly frustrated. She crossed her arms and then uncrossed them before resuming a rigid stance.

The scent of her unease left Zach roiling with aggression. This whole thing had left him spoiling for a fight. He also felt an acute need to comfort Theresa but couldn't until they settled the matter.

Adam addressed the room at large. "Did anyone witness the altercation?"

"I did," Zach said.

"I saw it too," Charlaine said.

"No offense, Hunter, but you're hardly an unbiased witness," Adam said.

"Not a problem." Zach's statement came out clipped, but he acknowledged the necessity of impartiality. The laws existed for good reasons.

"Charlaine, by your account, what happened?" Adam asked.

Charlaine stepped onto the center of the deck. She gestured from Simone to Debra. "These two bitches—"

"Language, please." Despite the reprimand, a smile tugged at Adam's mouth.

Charlaine rolled her eyes. "Fine. I saw Theresa go outside alone. A while later, these two fine ladies," her inclusive gesture indicated Debra and Simone, and laughter rolled through the pack, "also stepped out onto the deck and initiated a confrontation. Insults were traded, and then, right after Zach showed up, things got nasty."

"Who struck the first blow?" Adam asked.

"That one." Charlaine leveled her finger at Simone. "She slapped Theresa, so Theresa floored her. Then, Simone submitted, and Theresa challenged Debra." The Delta wolf crossed her arms and gave a sharp nod. "That's what I saw. You can make of it what you want, but by my word, the challenge is valid."

Adam considered and then addressed Debra. "Do you have anything to add?"

"No, other than this bitch insulted my fertility. I should be well within my rights to kill her." Debra spat at Theresa's feet.

The pack reacted to Debra's blatant disrespect with snarling anger.

Disgust twisted Adam's face.

Zach's lips curled back, revealing his canines.

The entire pack vibrated with hostility, expressing their fury with a synchronized growl. Adam brought them under control. The Wolf King's power ebbed and flowed over the whole of the house, commanding all.

Zach weathered the psychic assault like a storm.

He clung to his defenses, resisting the pervasive influence of the Alpha.

"Regardless of the insult offered, I can't have a fertile female with a child at home endangering her life in a dominance battle," Adam said. "The fight will last until dominance is established and no longer. This is not a fight to the death. Am I clear?"

Theresa's head dipped in acknowledgment.

"I understand," Debra said, but her attitude reeked of defiance.

Zach didn't trust Debra Yeller to honor the fight's outcome, but unfortunately, he had no say in the matter.

"I declare the challenge to be valid," Adam called out loud enough that his voice carried to every member of the pack. "The fight shall take place tonight in the forest clearing alongside Foxtail Creek. This pack meeting is concluded."

The meeting adjourned, everyone went their separate ways. The communal aura fragmented into lesser pieces, but the pack bond held despite the chaos—the force that unified all wolves of Iron Stone.

At the first opportunity, Zach approached Theresa. He waited until they were alone on the deck. He closed the glass slider, and then he wrapped his arm around her waist. She remained rigid in his embrace.

"Theresa," Zach said, frowning slightly. "Are you okay, love?"

Theresa glared up at him. The ice in her dark eyes shocked him to his soul. She drew away, shrugging off his touch. "I'm fine."

He frowned, not understanding her rejection. "I'm proud of you, Theresa. Standing up to those two women took courage."

Theresa growled in his face. "Do you think I give a damn whether you approve of me, Zachery Hunter? Because I couldn't care less."

Zach jerked if she'd struck out at him with physical violence.

CHAPTER FIFTEEN

Shit kept coming in an onslaught, and just when Theresa thought it was over, life heaped on one more thing. Her heart ached within her chest, and with every beat, the pressure built. Now that the confrontation with Debra and Simone had passed, she recalled Zach's betrayal.

It hurt so much to be close to him, to hear him speaking words of praise, and to know that she didn't dare believe a word he said. The courage he had inspired evaporated, leaving her mired in mistrust.

After everything she'd just endured, it would probably have been for the best if she'd gotten some space to clear her head before confronting Zach. Unfortunately, Theresa had enjoyed no such opportunity. When Zach had strutted up, acting as if nothing were wrong, was it any wonder that she'd lost her temper?

Maybe so. Zach pinned her with such hurt in his soulful gaze that *she* felt terrible.

"Why are you snapping at me?" he asked.

Theresa fumed. "Can any man be *this* clueless?"

"Evidently, I am this oblivious, so why don't you break it down for me?" Zach snapped in his crisp English accent. As always, he projected calm and polished composure, whereas she was a total mess.

Theresa's throat hurt. She blinked, fighting the tears that threatened to spill down her cheeks. She refused to cry in front of him, so she shoved all her ugly emotions down deep. Her dry throat tightened, and she blinked to stop tears. She would *not* cry.

Taking a deep breath, she squared her shoulders. "Don't think I'm fighting to impress you, Zach," she said, tone sharp. "Nothing could be further from the truth."

A pained expression pinched Zach's handsome face. He stared at her in silence and then touched his fingertip to her chin, lifting her face. Their gazes met. "What is that supposed to mean?" Zach asked in a tone rife with confusion.

Theresa's conviction faltered. Had she misjudged the situation? Was she mistreating Zach? Perhaps this whole mating game fiasco had sprung from some colossal misunderstanding, but no. She must stop doubting herself.

"You heard me, Zachary Hunter." Theresa narrowed her eyes and leaned forward, toe to toe, risking everything. "Did you think it was funny, coming on to me right before Adam put you on the market for every single woman in the pack?"

"Bollocks," Zach said, a soft exclamation. He blinked, and his eyes rounded like he hadn't expected her to be angry. Theresa wasn't foolish enough to misinterpret the expression of surprise for one of fear.

"Is this one of your jokes?" Her finger struck his chest with surprising force, thumping his breastbone.

"Excuse me?" Zach sounded more British than ever. He always got polite right before he became truly dangerous.

His reaction caused Theresa to have severe doubts about her interpretation of what had happened. She frowned, staring hard into his implacable eyes, attempting to understand what went on in that mysterious male mind. Could he be so clueless? Or had she misunderstood? Was her heart such a mystery to him? She shook her head and looked away to hide her tears.

Zach's hand caught the back of Theresa's head, tangling his fingers in her hair. He pulled her toward him, and Theresa made a sound of protest but didn't resist. Oh, no, his strength eclipsed her own. His power shone like the sun, and she basked within his incredible warmth. His mouth covered hers, rough and rugged. He took and did not give, and his anger spilled across her skin, causing it to itch and burn. Theresa opened her mouth, heart, and soul.

The sliding glass door to the patio opened. Charlaine asked, "What's going on out here? Oh!"

Zach released Theresa as suddenly as he'd claimed her. With a snarl, he spun away. The sharp scent of his anger lingered in the air. Theresa scrubbed tears and faced the intruder. Charlaine peered out across the threshold.

An awkward silence settled.

"Hey, you," Theresa said, raising her hand.

"Yeah, hey." Charlaine stepped out onto the deck. "Theresa, you're expected to fight Debra in less than an hour. That bitch is bigger than you and ten times meaner. I thought maybe I could offer a few quick pointers."

"Thanks, Charlaine." Theresa sighed.

The lost opportunity was like sand slipping through her fingers, and she resented the Delta wolf's intrusion no matter how well-intended. Zach so seldom suffered such a loss of control, and Theresa had waited years. Now, that the moment was gone, and only vast uncertainty remained.

"I've spent three years training Theresa for this fight," Zach said. "She's ready."

Astonished, Theresa spun, and he met her stare with steady confidence. She reached the only plausible conclusion fast—he meant their regular self-defense training sessions.

"You said you wanted me to be able to defend myself."

Zach smiled slowly. "And so you can. I also wanted you to be prepared to take any female in this pack when the time came."

"Oh." Theresa wrung her hands, torn between anxiety and anger. *How could I have been such a fool?* She couldn't bring herself to believe that Zach had been manipulating her all along. Yet there was no denying it, especially with Zach confessing to it.

Charlaine snorted. "Ha. Maybe I should be watching my back instead of looking out for you."

Theresa slapped a hand to her mouth. "Oh, no, Char! Please don't think that!"

The Delta she-wolf laughed. "Relax, Theresa. I was only kidding."

"Char, will you help Theresa through the change?" Zach asked. "It's three nights until the full moon."

Heartsick, Theresa lowered her eyes. Dominant wolves had little or no difficulty embracing their beasts any time of the month, but most werewolves needed help when the moon wasn't full. Zach always acted as Theresa's principal, channeling the power necessary for her to shift. Apparently, she'd angered him so much that he refused to take on the burden for her.

"Of course," Charlaine said.

"I have something to discuss with Adam." Zach crossed the deck in a few long strides and reached for the door.

"Zach?"

Against her will, Theresa had called to him. She was furious with him, but he owed her an explanation at the very least and an apology.

Zach stopped, spine ramrod straight, and glanced back over his shoulder. With his face cast in shadow, Theresa found his expression unreadable, but she sensed his contained anger. His lashes swept his cheeks as he shut his eyes for a second, and when he opened them again, his implacable demeanor had not softened in the least. He continued inside without another word.

Theresa's stomach churned, and she struggled to retain a grip on her emotions. She curbed the impulse to chase after him, to shout her anger and demand his attention. Debra didn't matter. The bitch was insignificant, a bully, and a loser.

Charlaine's hand on her shoulder brought

Theresa back to herself. She blinked and looked at the Delta wolf.

"Let him go," Charlaine said. "He needs to blow off steam, and you need to get your head in the game, especially if you want to keep it."

Theresa nodded. "Right. Sorry. I guess I need to undress."

Charlaine's dark eyes gleamed in the dim light. "Before we go any further, I need to ask. Are you pregnant?"

Theresa looked at her in astonishment. "What? No! Why do you ask?"

Charlaine shook her head. "No reason. I was just wondering. Of course, you're aware that you can't risk yourself in a dominance battle if you are pregnant. If you even suspect that you might be carrying a child, that's reason enough to back out of the fight. Choose a champion to fight on your behalf."

Abruptly, Theresa understood. Her surprise deepened to confusion. She and Charlaine weren't enemies, but they were not exactly friends either. They were little more than strangers who happened to be members of the same pack.

"Oh. Are you offering to be my champion?" Theresa asked to be sure.

Charlaine flashed a feral grin. "I'd love nothing better than an excuse to whip Debra Yeller's ass."

Theresa chuckled. "I'm sorry. I'm not pregnant. There's not even a chance."

"Damn." Charlaine snapped her fingers. Her manner implied easy-come, easy-go, but Theresa saw the disappointment in the Delta's eyes. "Well, I guess you'll be fighting your own battles then."

Theresa smiled. "Guess so. Sorry."

"Don't worry about it," Charlaine said. "It'll be hard watching you fight, but if Zach can manage it, then so can I. Okay, go ahead and take off your clothes. Let's get this over with before Adam sends someone looking for us."

Theresa undressed with haste. She removed her top then kicked off her shoes to shimmy out of her blue jeans. "Why would it be hard for you to watch me fight?"

"Let's just put it this way. As a dominant, it's tough standing by while others fight, especially adorable little mommy wolves. Your daughter is just darling."

Theresa heard Charlaine's envy upon mention of Isabel. Her stomach twisted into a knot. "I'm not that sweet," she said, blushing.

Charlaine laughed. "And the sky ain't blue."

"Where do you know Isabel from?"

"I teach fourth grade at the elementary school." Charlaine frowned. "What's wrong?"

Theresa crossed her arms over her breasts. Her

bra and panties covered as much as any bikini, but still, she felt exposed. Her figure wasn't the source of her shame.

"It just occurred to me that I must have hurt the feelings of every woman in the pack who's had trouble conceiving. I feel like a wretch."

"Well, don't." Unexpectedly, Charlaine hugged her.

Following a pause due to surprise, Theresa returned the other woman's embrace. She shed no tears but pressed her face into the crook of Charlaine's throat and accepted the comfort offered.

"I'm sorry," Theresa said. "I wasn't trying to make anyone feel bad."

"I want children," Charlaine said. Her voice sounded tight, and she squeezed Theresa hard. She spoke in the manner of one unaccustomed to intimacy. "But I haven't tried and failed to conceive. I just haven't tried."

Startled, Theresa drew back a bit. "Why not? If I went solely based on scent, I'd guess you're fertile."

"Do you think? I've never met anyone who claimed to be able to identify fertility with their nose." Charlaine studied Theresa with a mixed expression—both hopeful and wary at once.

Theresa shrugged. "I'm not making any promises, but that's what my gut is telling me. If I'm wrong, then I'll apologize, but you definitely should be using birth control if you're not ready to become a mother yet."

Charlaine snorted. "Thanks, I'll keep that in mind."

Theresa smiled. "At the risk of being nosy, why haven't you challenged Zach or Robert for rank? Don't you want to be alpha?"

"Now, I'm imaging the look on Adam's face if a she-wolf contested for leadership of the pack!" Charlaine rocked back on her heels, roaring with laughter.

Theresa giggled so hard she grew short of breath. "He'd have kittens!"

At long last, Charlaine stopped laughing and urged her along. "Aren't you little Miss Dynamite? Come on, get out of those underthings, and let's get you changed. I can't wait to watch you hand that bitch her ass."

Theresa shed her bra and panties. She endured Charlaine's quick appraisal of her body with quiet pride. While she wasn't model thin or athletic, she had no reason to be ashamed. Her figure harkened more to Venus de Milo—generous breasts, trim waist, and full hips. Her ass was tight and round. Her legs provided most of her height.

"Take my hands," Charlaine said, offering both

of hers, which were already partially transformed to wolf claws.

"How do you do that? I'd give anything to be able to change at will."

Grasping the Delta's hands, Theresa bowed her head and breathed deep from her chest. It took an effort to channel the rush of nervous energy and anticipation that made her want to pace the floor.

"It takes practice. Nurture your wolf."

The summoning came then, flowing from Charlaine and into Theresa. The dominant wolf called forth her beast, and energy flowed across Theresa's skin, signaling the start of her transformation.

Theresa whimpered and then cried out as the painful change remodeled her body from human to wolf. Bones snapped, repositioned, and then mended. Muscles thickened, and fur sprang up across her entire body, bursting through her skin. Her teeth grew to sharp points, and the flat of her face pushed into a muzzle. A tail grew from the extension of her spine.

Afterward, Theresa lay on her side panting, her head in Charlaine's lap while the pain lessened. Charlaine remained human. Even her hands had reverted to normal.

Charlaine proved to be a good dominant. She offered everything Theresa could have wanted or needed, except Charlaine wasn't Zach. Theresa felt his absence as an emptiness inside her that only he could fill. Without meaning to, she whimpered.

"It's okay," Charlaine said, stroking Theresa's head. "You're okay."

Theresa lifted her head, feeling the pain receding and her strength returning. She climbed to her feet and turned to perform a quick inspection of her body. Her nose followed her tail. Thick red and black fur greeted her gaze. As a wolf, Theresa measured five feet in length from nose to tail.

Charlaine stood. "Are you ready?"

Gazing up at the dominant, Theresa barked in affirmation.

"Let's go." Charlaine led the way through the patio door and into the house.

CHAPTER SIXTEEN

Fury drove Zach's every step. He performed a thorough search of the house and located Adam in the kitchen. Becky and the Alpha's enforcers were also present. When Zach entered, everyone looked up, and their conversation ceased.

"Adam, can I have a word with you?" Zach asked.

"Sure thing, Zach," Adam said, pushing out his chair. "I've been expecting you. Let's step into my study."

Adam's enforcers started to rise, but Zach stopped them with a glare. "Alone."

"Wait here," Adam said to his guards, and then he led the way from the kitchen down a long hallway to the downstairs office.

Zach followed and held his tongue, jaw clenched in grim silence until Adam shut the mahogany door. The Alpha strode the length of the room, stopping near his massive desk.

"Have a seat," Adam said, indicating a leather recliner.

"I'll stand," Zach said, tone clipped.

Adam smiled and crossed his arms. "Fair enough. I can see that something has got your tail over the line, son. Go ahead and tell me what's eatin' at you then."

Son. The smug bastard had the nerve to call him "son." Zach's mouth twisted at the corner, and cold fury crashed over him, but he contained it with all of his willpower. Complete calm settled over him, a blanket of ice, which enabled him to put everything into perspective.

"You put us out there to the females of the pack without telling me," Zach said. "You showed me up in front of Theresa on purpose."

Adam chuckled. "Nah, Zach, you've misunderstood. It was just a bit of misdirection. I wanted everyone's attention focused on romance. The competition isn't important. My goal is to restore the pack's bond and hand off leadership to a competent successor, namely you."

Zach opened his mouth to speak but cut off what he'd been about to say. He stared at Adam, realizing that he'd underestimated the Alpha. He needed to rethink his assumptions, or they would lose the war before the battle even began.

The silence played to Adam's great weakness—the man loved the sound of his own voice. The Alpha allowed no opportunity to talk to pass untaken. "Your little filly will get over it. Buy her some flowers and make sure she knows who's in charge."

With a great effort, Zach retained a tight rein on his anger. "What exactly did you hope to gain then by making that declaration?"

A gleam entered Adam's eyes, lending him a wily air that served to reinforce Zach's sense of caution even further. "I'll admit I had my doubts about you after our last meeting. I wanted to gauge whether you'd talked to Robert behind my back."

"I see."

Zach's sense of cautiousness redoubled since he'd fully intended to warn Robert about Adam's intentions. Before Theresa's confrontation with Debra had distracted him, he had planned to speak with the Beta wolf after the pack meeting. Adam would turn on Zach if the Alpha suspected betrayal. There were other males further down the pack's hierarchy that could be potential successors.

Adam slapped Zach on the shoulder. "Don't look so grim. It was obvious from the look on Blane's face that you didn't warn him. You've proven your loyalty, Zach. Now, I suggest you take advantage of the distraction I've provided. Use the opportunity to formulate your strategy."

"I'll do that." Zach would've sooner bitten off his tongue than say thank you.

He left before he lost control of his temper.

Needing to be alone until he cooled down, Zach headed outside. He exited via the side door of the house and burst into the calm night air. Heart pounding, blood burning, he was about to burst. Restlessness drove Zach deeper into the woods, and he instinctively plunged into the deepest, darkest woods.

Adam's scheming made him furious. The Alpha had started trying to include him in dirty politics and made him a part of racist bigotry. He tolerated Adam's bullshit to a certain point, but Isabel and Theresa were off-limits. It infuriated him that Adam's machinations had led Theresa to believe that Zach's courtship was nothing more than an effin' joke.

A roar began in Zach's throat and rumbled his entire chest, issuing as a primal challenge to the night. From the largest predator down to the timid prey, every creature great and small trembled in fear. Then, a hush fell, and even the crickets ceased chirping. The patchwork night—a collage of greens and grays—promised sanctuary.

Zach turned his blind rage on the first thing to cross his path—a towering pine with thick branches. He dug his claws into the wide trunk, gouging slashes in the bark. Then, growling, he pitted his strength against the tree, channeling his aggression. Above, branches shook, and a shower of needles and pinecones rained down.

For a long moment, the tree held its own, providing Zach with an opportunity to work out his frustration. Instead, energy flowed across his skin, and the change to wolf threatened the very foundations of his control. He shoved harder, assaulting the tree with all of his strength, and inevitably, something snapped. With a mighty crack, the trunk tilted over and fell with a resounding crash. Roots tore free from the earth, turning up dirt clods, rocks, and a wealth of insect life.

Zach leaped back to avoid the protruding root system, which destroyed the ground under his feet. He landed well clear of the mess and remained in place until the last echo died away. However, his energy remained high, so he kept his wolf on a short leash because his control was tenuous at best.

After an indeterminate time, a single flame flared to life, igniting the tip of a cigarette.

Rumbling a warning, Zach turned his head in the

direction of the intruder. His sides heaved, and his nostrils flared as he drank in the aroma of nicotine. The underlying scent was that of his rival and friend. The flame of the lighter illuminated a male's face in profile: Robert Blane.

"Damn, man, you sure showed that tree who's boss." Robert gave a throaty chuckle that diffused the tension.

"Yeah, well..." Zach rolled his shoulders in a shrug. Not his most eloquent retort, but it demonstrated that he retained enough self-control for speech.

Robert puffed on his cigarette.

With a valiant effort, Zach deliberately slowed his breathing, imposing calm. Then, as his composure restored, his humanity returned. Snapping and popping, he transformed to fully human while Robert watched.

Afterward, the male wolves faced off. The air crackled with hair-trigger tension, violence waiting to be unleashed. Zach had height in his favor, but Robert outweighed Zach by a good twenty pounds. Solid muscle, Blane had the stature of a comic book superhero. Contemplating his rival, Zach thought, *Crickey, I should work out more.*

The tip of the cigarette burned brighter as Robert sucked smoke. "You've imagined how it would go down, haven't you?"

Without asking, Zach took the other man's meaning. "Yeah, sure I have."

Robert grinned, gripping the filter between his teeth. "Who do you think would win?"

Zach snorted and wiped the sweat from his brow with his forearm. "No matter who wins, we both lose. No matter what, I refuse to fight for the pleasure of that inbred shitkicker."

Robert threw back his head and roared with laughter. He clasped Zach's shoulder. "Ain't that the truth. Peace, brother."

"Peace, brother." Zach covered the other man's hand, and then they broke apart, now at ease with one another.

"Want a smoke?" Robert held up the pack.

Tempted, Zach hesitated. "I quit."

"It's not like we can die of lung cancer," Robert said, tone dry and to the point.

Werewolves were immune to most diseases and illnesses. The leading causes of death among wolf-shifters were violence, accidents, or suicide. A rare few succumbed to old age.

"Theresa hates the smell," Zach finally confessed.

Robert rolled his eyes. "Man, that woman has you whipped, and you're not even properly mated yet."

Yet. No challenge, matter of fact.

Yeah, I'm a jackass. Zach vanquished his testosterone-inspired suspicions. *What the hell,* he figured with a mental shrug. He was already in hot water with his lady, so he might as well go all in.

"Yeah, sure," Zach said, gesturing. "Thanks."

"Look who's living dangerously." Robert shook a cigarette loose from the carton.

"You're one to talk." Zach extended the cigarette. "Got a light?"

"Yup." Robert struck a flame, and Zach bent to light up. He puffed until the cigarette got going, and then he straightened. Almost immediately, the balm of the nicotine soothed his nerves.

They shared a peaceful, puffing silence. The ritual of smoking accomplished its purpose. He once again felt in control and no longer possessed a compelling desire to destroy everything in his path. Still, it felt odd.

Zach wondered if his friendship with Robert could withstand the test of pack rivalries. Exactly how much was three years of Sunday golf worth when push came to shove?

Robert cleared his throat. "What did you when you said I'm one to talk?"

Zach winced. "Yeah, sorry, mate. I didn't mean anything by it."

"What the hell is *that* supposed to mean?"

Robert ground out the butt of his cigarette beneath his heel and rounded for a confrontation.

Shit. Zach also ground his butt out. He pivoted, raising open hands. "Nothing. I experimented in college, too. We're all good."

Violence smoldered in Robert's regard. "Bullshit."

"No bullshit. I mean what I say," Zach said, crossing his heart. "You and I, we've spent the last three years of our lives building up this pack together. It's ours. Let's not allow prejudice and politics to destroy what we've accomplished."

Stone-faced, Robert stared. "What exactly do you think you know? State it out loud just so we're clear."

Zach sighed. "*Fine.* Cards on the table. You're attracted to men as well as women."

Robert opened his mouth.

"Don't think I haven't noticed you checking out my arse," Zach said. "Not that I blame you. At the risk of sounding vain, my arse is bloody well sublime."

Surprise slackened Robert's face, and then he snapped his mouth shut. It was quiet for a highly long time. Then, all of a sudden, he busted his gut with explosive laughter. "Sorry, man," Robert gasped, gripping Zach's bicep. "I assumed the worst."

Vastly relieved, Zach rested his palm on his friend's shoulder. "As they say, never judge a book by its cover."

They laughed until the awkwardness bled out.

Somber again, Robert said, "You could use that to get me disqualified from this competition."

"But I won't," Zach said in clipped reply. "It wouldn't be fair or right. Besides, who you shag is no one's business but your own."

Robert's brow drew tight, and his lips compressed. "Adam would use it to throw me out of the pack."

"Adam is a right bastard."

"Yeah."

Zach hesitated, but curiosity got the better of him. "You want to be alpha."

Robert tilted his head. "Of course."

"An alpha has to have a mate. Potential successors..." Zach shrugged, doing his best to remain neutral.

Robert twisted his face before he shrugged. "I swing both ways. Siring a child won't be a problem. I love women."

"Ah." With a shrug, Zach let the topic drop. Far be it from him to cast stones.

The silence that followed was more comfortable than any they'd shared before. Zach still harbored doubts, but he wanted to believe that he and Robert shared a trustworthy and fast friendship.

"Do you think this thing will survive what's to come?" Robert asked, demonstrating an uncanny insight that left Zach wondering if the newly forged pack bond was to blame.

"Are you reading my mind?"

"Maybe." Robert flashed a faint smile.

"Well, stop it." Zach pondered and then reached his decision. To deserve trust, he had to earn trust. "I won't do Adam's dirty work, so yeah, this thing had better survive. But, there's something you should know...."

Robert arched his thick brow. "Oh? What's that?"

Zach exhaled slowly. "Adam came to see me Sunday afternoon. He said that he favors me as his successor. Adam made it clear that he intends for me to kill you."

"Motherfucker, I knew it." Robert formed a fist with his hand and turned in a circle as if searching for something to strike. He ran his hand through his hair to channel his violent impulses into something more constructive. "That sonofabitch."

"He's racist."

"Yeah, I know." Robert stared into the darkness. "I know."

Zach cocked his head. "Are you going to challenge him? You're within your rights."

Robert smiled, white teeth flashing and eyes glowing within the darkness. "It would serve that bastard right, but no. The pack looks to Adam as their savior. After all, he rescued them from Zanatos. If I kill him, then I'm the bad guy, and Adam still wins."

"My thoughts exactly."

Robert released a breath in an audible exhalation. "I need to think, figure out what to do. Damn. Thanks, man."

They shook on it. Satisfaction surged through Zach because his gamble had paid off. Trusting Robert was the right choice. The Beta wolf had the cunning and discipline necessary to make a reasoned decision. Maybe, working together, they could figure out a way to outsmart Adam Teller.

"Zach..." Robert said and then hesitated.

Zach sensed the unspoken question. "Go on. Ask."

"In all this time, I never once got the impression you wanted the leadership of the pack."

"I came from London for the opportunity to be among this pack's dominant wolves."

"You've never challenged me."

"Adam invited me to join six months after you as Gamma. The objective was to restore the pack to normalcy. Infighting among the dominants would only detract from that goal."

"That's it?" Robert looked and sounded more than skeptical. "You never challenged me because it was for the good of the pack?"

Moonlight and shadow played across Robert's face, and Zach was left guessing. He regarded the other werewolf with renewed suspicion. "What the bloody hell do you want me to say? Why should I have to justify not trying to kill you? I thought we were friends."

Robert held up his hands, palms out. "Shit, Zach. Calm down. No one knows you or your motives all that well. You play it too close to the chest."

"That's my way."

"Look, I'm sorry," Robert said. "I didn't mean to piss you off. I just wanted to understand your motivations. Now, I have my answer. You're in it for the good of the pack. Fair enough. I feel the same."

"Damn it." Zach clenched his teeth. He started to walk away but then stopped. "Sorry, mate. I bit your head off over nothing."

"No, I'm sorry. I should've known better than to press you when your woman is about to go rounds with Debra."

Zach's mouth flattened to a grim line. He did not correct the other man's mistaken assumption about him and Theresa being lovers. He wasn't a fool.

"Theresa is going to hand that bitch her arse," Zach boasted.

"You sound confident."

Zach's lips twisted into a cold smile. "Oh, I am."

Robert nodded. "That's one fight I'd hate to miss. Let's get down to the creek."

CHAPTER SEVENTEEN

A pregnant moon hung in the sky, three nights shy of being full. Every member of the pack shared intense excitement to be outside beneath luna's silver light. The Harvest Moon would awaken their beasts, summoning every werewolf to shed their human skins. Only three nights until wolves roamed free through the alpine forests.

Moving along on all fours, Theresa walked beside Charlaine. They headed down the slope to where the pack gathered just north of Foxtail Creek. The chosen spot was a forest clearing, a peaceful meadow ringed by a natural fence of pine trees upon a carpet of needles and dry summer grasses. A mosaic of browns and greens composed the landscape of fall. Crickets sang counterpoint to the bubbling stream to create a nighttime concerto.

The pack gathered there, congregating in twos and threes, speaking in hushed voices. People turned as Theresa passed and reached out to press curious fingers into her fur. They murmured words of encouragement for the upcoming fight and patted the top of her head. The outpouring of support and affection surprised her, and the unexpected attention left her stunned. She accepted their help and soaked up the warm approval. Her fur moved in joyous ripples beneath the petting hands.

Across the clearing, Debra waited with Simone and Carl Reynolds. Debra's supporters were few and formed a loose ring about her, as if hesitant to stand too close to the female wolf. Debra's popularity had its foundation in promiscuity and bullying, traits that inspired sunny day loyalty. Her way harkened to the dark days of the pack when might made right, and tyranny came before justice.

Theresa's confidence stumbled now that the time for violence had arrived. The anger that had driven her to challenge Debra wasn't her natural predisposition. She was a mother and a protector but not a fighter. Her gentle wolf provided her with plenty of nurturing instinct but not primal aggression.

Charlaine dropped to one knee beside Theresa.

The Delta buried her hands in Theresa's ruff, threading her fingers through the thick fur. "Debra fights like a dog," she warned. "She's going to come right at you and go straight for your throat. She's bigger than you, but you can use that to your advantage. Keep moving, and stay out of her reach, okay?"

Theresa barked to indicate her understanding. She pressed her side against Charlaine, accepting the dominant female's tacit support. Theresa grasped the imperative nature of the conflict. She must win. Losing entailed a considerable loss of face and would leave her and her daughter vulnerable to Debra's predations. More than that, it was long past time that someone stood up to the bullying female.

Without speaking, Charlaine surrendered her hold on Theresa and moved a short distance away. The sound of footfalls caught Theresa's attention, and she glanced sideways to discover Zach standing beside her. Robert wasn't far behind him, watching with an implacable expression.

Zach knelt and placed his hands on her shoulders. Her heart leaped at his touch, but she hardened it against him. His manipulation was not forgotten or forgiven. When he pulled her toward him, she resisted and dug in her paws, but his strength eclipsed hers. Ultimately, she submitted to his examination, dropping her gaze and enduring it in sullen silence.

Zach cupped her muzzle and forced Theresa's head up so he could look her straight in the eyes. "I understand that you're angry with me, love, but this isn't the time or place. Put that anger aside unless you can use it in this fight. Remember what I've taught you, and you'll win this without breaking a sweat."

Theresa's jaws parted in a snarl. She flashed her teeth and jerked her head free of his grasp. Stiff-legged, she pranced away, making a show of her defiance. If he wanted attitude, then she could offer it up in spades.

Zach threw back his head and laughed. "Adam! Let's get this show underway, shall we?"

From the other side of the field, Adam tilted his hat in acknowledgment. Then, the Alpha advanced to the center of the clearing. He spoke loud enough for all those assembled to hear. "The rules are simple. This is a fight to establish dominance and rank. Debra Yeller is the defender. Theresa Russo is the challenger. Seeing as how this fight involves a fertile female with a pup, it will not be a fight to the death."

The pack stirred, but Adam did not invite questions or comments. Lifting his hands, he gestured both women forward. Theresa advanced to the specified starting position approximately thirty feet across from Debra.

Theresa trembled in the grip of excitement, every fiber primed for action. She stared at her opponent and found no fear or hesitance in the other female's gaze. As a wolf, Debra had a mottled coat with a black head and face. Dark brown and gray fur dappled the rest of her body, coloring like an Australian shepherd. She stood several inches taller than Theresa in the shoulder with a long body, rangy legs, and close to a hundred and sixty pounds of lean muscle.

Debra snarled low in the throat, lips curled back to reveal a flash of yellowed canines dripping saliva. Her ears laid flat against her skull. She held her bristling tail angled low.

Theresa answered with a warning growl, causing her throat to rumble, revealing her teeth. She summoned and projected confidence, drawing on the lessons Zach had taught her to appear imposing.

"Begin." Adam waved his arm and vacated the arena with a quick bound.

Debra rushed straight in without any regard for precision in her first strike. Theresa remained poised and held her ground, resisting the urge to succumb to reckless abandon. She waited until the last moment, until she felt the heat of Debra's huffing breath, and sidestepped the charge. The dappled wolf struck at empty air with her snapping jaws and then howled her frustration.

Debra performed a sharp turn and gathered speed. She came at Theresa again and employed the same head-on tactic. As the other wolf snarled past, Theresa's head jerked to the side, and she delivered a bite to her opponent's shoulder. Her sharp teeth grazed fur and skin, opening a six-inch gash.

Debra yowled, part pain, part surprise, and twisted away. Theresa's jaws snapped shut on empty air as she took another bite. The glancing injury drew a small amount of blood, but it gave her wolf a taste, and she wanted more.

The entire pack ringed them, watching with eerie intensity.

Debra whirled about and charged. Theresa sidestepped, but at the last moment, Debra changed course and drove straight into her. The collision brought them smashing together, shoulder to shoulder. Theresa landed on her side in the dirt, and Debra jumped atop her.

Theresa twisted around and took a bite at her opponent's front leg. With a snarl, Debra lunged to block her, and their fangs clanked as daggers. Locked together, the female wolves wrestled for the upper hand. They rolled across the dry grass, stopping near the edge of the arena.

The gathered audience retreated several feet,

creating a bulge in the circle. Shouts of excitement and aggression arose from the pack.

Debra's next lunge came within seconds. The dappled wolf rushed Theresa in a whirlwind of snapping teeth and angry snarls. They went over and rolled. Debra came out on top and sprang at her opponent's throat. Theresa dodged but didn't get out of the way fast enough. Debra's fangs slashed open a deep cut on Theresa's shoulder. An agonized yelp tore from her.

The pack howled with bloodthirstiness.

Debra lunged, and Theresa parried. Their snapping jaws clashed like the deadliest of blades. Theresa rolled away. Blood dripped from her muzzle. The saltiness left her hungering for more.

Staggering to her feet, Theresa rounded and caught a glimpse of her shoulder. Blood saturated her fur, turning it a deeper shade of red. She circled, watching for an opening in her opponent's defenses. Debra also scrambled upright, but her strength was faltering. Theresa's hit-and-run tactics paid off, frustrating the larger she-wolf.

Driven to snarling frustration, Debra sprang again. Theresa performed a quick sidestep, relying on her smaller size and superior speed to evade her opponent. She repeated the maneuver repeatedly, conserving her strength while Debra expended her energy in an all-out assault.

Debra's mouth frothed with the passion of her rage. Thick strands of saliva mixed with blood hung like streamers from her jaws, and her maddened howls continued to rise in volume and ferocity. Her attacks grew predictable. She performed one full-frontal assault after another and did not consider strategic concerns. Theresa fell into a rhythm—dodge to safety, deliver a quick nip or scratch to her opponent's sides and withers, and then retreat.

Theresa judged Debra to be tiring and growing clumsier. Then, she saw her opportunity. Debra dropped her shoulder as she passed and failed to move her hindquarters. Theresa seized the opening and delivered a bite that slashed open the other female's shoulder from the blade to the top of her front leg. Blood oozing from the injury, Debra staggered, and the pack roared with renewed intensity.

The female wolves circled one another, ears laid back and heads held low. Their glowing eyes gleamed in the darkness, the only source of light aside from the silvery moonshine.

Debra made a final desperate rush. Adopting a tactic Zach had taught her, Theresa sidestepped and brought her head in from the side. She aimed low, and instead of going for Debra's protected throat, her jaws closed on her opponent's front leg. A loud, stomach-curdling crunch announced the breakage of a bone.

Debra yowled in pain and plowed to a halt, standing on three legs. Her broken limb dangled uselessly beneath her.

With a howl, the pack surged as one, sending up the primal call of predators scenting blood. The strict and abiding law of pack hierarchy held them back. If Theresa's prey had been elk or moose instead of another female wolf, then every werewolf present would have participated in the kill.

Theresa moved safely away and circled again, employing her nimble speed. Balanced precariously on three legs, Debra spun, struggling to face her opponent.

Debra's strength continued to flag, and at last, Theresa spied an opening. She rushed from the side and slammed her shoulder into Debra. The blow knocked Debra off her feet and onto her side. Snarling, Theresa continued her charge, going straight for the throat.

Theresa's jaws closed on Debra's thick throat, and she pinned the wolf to the ground. Her teeth broke the skin, and she tasted blood, but she refrained from making the kill. Instead, her jaws closed like a steel trap but held steady, going no deeper.

Debra whimpered.

Blood flooded Theresa's mouth. Hot. Delicious. She yearned to rip out her rival's throat, but murder wasn't her way. Victory tasted sweeter than vengeance. Theresa contented herself with the knowledge that she had won.

The dominant males rushed onto the field. Zach's strong, familiar hands closed about Theresa's jaws and pulled them open. With an excited whimper, Theresa submitted to him and released her stranglehold on Debra. Robert bent and hauled the other female away, removing her from the arena.

Adam's voice boomed over the din. "I officially declare Theresa Russo to be the winner. Her rank is now Sigma, and she will be treated with the respect and authority she is due. I'm giving our combatants an hour to recover, and then I want the meeting to reconvene back at the house at midnight. Now, let's give the victor our congratulations."

The pack went wild.

CHAPTER EIGHTEEN

Cheering wildly, dozens of members of the Iron Stone wolf pack closed around Theresa.

Her body ached from several minor injuries, but she didn't feel the pain thanks to the exaltation of victory. Hands stroked her fur. Voices murmured praise and reassurance.

Again, that amazing thing happened. The pack's long-dead magic came to life, and it flowed through her and into everyone. Her courage provided the stimulus that brought them closer, and she held them all together. She felt their emotions as if they were her own. Theresa knew who to trust and who to fear. More than just approval percolated within the other members, and, as much as she basked in the glow of winning, she was mindful of the risks. Upsetting the pack's hierarchy had consequences. Higher-ranked members would now view her as a threat. Lower ranked would regard her with jealousy.

Charlaine materialized out of the crowd and approached them. She knelt to inspect Theresa's injuries. Her scolding hands shooed Zach and everyone else out of the way. "Let me see."

"Whatever you say, doc," Zach said with just the right note of sarcasm, but he aided in clearing the other members of the pack aside so Charlaine could conduct her examination in peace.

"Let me get a look at you, sweetie." Charlaine pried open Theresa's jaws with gentle hands, inspected the cuts on her muzzle and gums, and then moved on to her shoulder injury. The Delta wolf's intimate touch made her self-conscious, and her awareness of Zach's unwavering gaze on her made the antsy feeling worse.

"Everything okay?" Zach glanced to his left when Robert appeared at his side.

"Yes, all of her wounds are minor, and she's already begun to regenerate," Charlaine said, directing her words over her shoulder to him. "Debra got the worst of it by a long shot."

Theresa tilted her head and gave an inquisitive ruff.

Zach interpreted. "She wants to know how Debra's doing."

Robert snorted. "Debra's right front leg is broken, clean through the humerus. She has various other scrapes, cuts, and contusions, but she'll heal as soon as she changes forms."

"Bitch got what was coming to her." Smirking, Charlaine exchanged a meaningful glance with her cousin.

"Sorry you couldn't be the one to do the giving?" Robert asked.

"Oh, you bet I am." Charlaine turned to Zach. "Time is wasting. Shall I take Theresa back up to the house and give her a hand shifting?"

"I've got it," Zach said in a tone that brooked no argument. Then, he softened his manner. "Thanks for your help tonight."

"No problem. Always happy to help," Charlaine said.

Theresa wagged her tail and nuzzled the other woman's hand with her nose.

Charlaine laughed. Then, she stood. "You're welcome too, Theresa, but I'd better go check on Debra."

"Char," Zach said.

"Zach?" Charlaine arched a brow.

"Make sure Debra understands her place. I don't want any further trouble from her."

"That goes without saying."

"Let's head back," Zach said to Theresa.

She bobbed her head to indicate her agreement. For the moment, her top priority was shifting to her human form and getting dressed. Her body ached thanks to a myriad of minor injuries, fueling her impatience. The transformation process might be rigorous, but it would also speed her natural regenerative ability.

They returned to the house and sought the deck where Theresa had left her clothing. With easy familiarity, Zach bent and settled his hands against her back. His energy flooded her, potent and primal, so very masculine. He stirred her desire, an ache deep within her loins. His wolf was so much stronger than her own that he threatened to eclipse her.

Theresa trembled on the verge of ecstasy and surrendered to him. She rolled over onto her side, and the change flowed over her as swift as water. Beneath his deft guidance, she experienced no pain or discomfort. As her flesh and bones transformed, the physical damage to her body healed. The change always repaired all but the most severe injuries, such as those caused by silver.

Afterward, Theresa lay on the floor, gasping for breath. It wasn't often she changed from human to wolf when the moon wasn't full.

Zach retrieved her clothing from the bench where she'd left them folded in a neat stack. He returned and knelt beside her once again, offering her a garment. He treated her with such tenderness and consideration that she felt guilty for questioning his integrity. However, the doubt did not leave her heart.

"Thank you." Theresa took her clothing, dressed, and then climbed to her feet. She looked up, down, and around—anywhere but at him.

"You're welcome."

Theresa retreated from him toward the house. She ignored him, reaching for the sliding glass door, but Zach beat her to it. He blocked her retreat.

She swallowed hard against a lump in her throat. "Zach, please."

"Please, what, Theresa?" His tone was sharp, angry, and intimate, layered with so many emotions that she couldn't discern every nuance.

She refused to meet his gaze for fear of what she might find there. The terror of losing him ruled her, and yet she had never really had him in the first place. She was so bewildered by the difficulty of separating reality from fantasy.

"Zach, now isn't the time."

"Well, when is the right time, Theresa? Tell me when, and I'll bloody well—"

"Oh, there you are!" Becky Teller appeared on

the other side of the glass door and reached for the handle. Theresa let go, and the other woman slid it open. The Alpha's petite mate flashed her toothpaste smile. "Land's sake," she said, "I've been searching everywhere for you two."

"We were right here," Zach said, sounding as grumpy as a honey badger.

A frown furrowed Becky's brow, and Theresa hastened to intervene. She took a stride forward and grasped the other woman's hand. "It's my fault, Becky. You know how painful it can be to change when the moon isn't full."

"No, I don't know," Becky said, glaring with open hate. As a human, the woman's status within the pack depended upon her mate's ability to defend his rank.

Theresa snapped her fingers. "Oh, that's right. I forgot."

"It's all right, honey. Bless. Your. Heart."

Well, I just made an enemy. Theresa mustered an innocent smile and donned an angelic expression, acquired from years of careful observation of a master manipulator at work. Isabel was like no other. "Thank you so much, Mrs. Teller."

"Of course, dear. I understand how difficult everything is for you. Now, the both of you had better come inside. Adam is waiting."

Theresa's eyes narrowed, and she started to snap

out a reply, but Zach inserted himself between the two women with surgical precision. "My apologies for being so rude," he said, so very smooth, so very British. "I do hope you'll forgive me for creating an imposition. I hate to think that I've abused your hospitality."

Predictably, Becky melted before the overwhelming male charm that he wielded with such tact. Her demeanor transformed to flirtatious. She laughed gayly, fanning her face with her hand. "Zach, you're never an imposition."

Disgusted, Theresa snorted and turned away. She understood Zach's powers of persuasion all too well, and it wasn't in her to be jealous of the older woman. Still, she refused to listen to the rest of their exchange. Thankfully, the trip inside was a short one, and then they stood in the living room where the pack had assembled once again at their Alpha's bidding.

The room buzzed with multiple conversations like the busy drone of a beehive. The pack's collective aura carried that same energy so that it danced with a montage of clashing colors. Almost immediately, those closest to her noted her arrival.

A hush fell, and heads turned.

Theresa took an involuntary step backward. Zach pressed his hand to the small of her back, preventing her retreat.

"Ah, here she is—the lady of the hour." Adam emerged from the crowd and claimed the spotlight. His considerable personal power commanded the audience, and everyone's attention focused on him.

Theresa stared at him with wide eyes, feeling like prey instead of predator, as he approached her with long strides. When Adam took her elbow, she cast one desperate glance over her shoulder to Zach.

"Be brave," Zach mouthed. "You've got this."

Right. Theresa lifted her chin and squared her shoulders.

"Don't worry, none. I don't bite," Adam said, rolling the words. He led her to the front of the room to face the pack, surveying those present while the suspense built. "I witnessed something miraculous tonight. We all did. Theresa has managed to accomplish an impressive feat. She's restored the pack's magic, something that's been missing going on five years now."

Jolts of approval and jealousy ran through the pack, chain lightning striking water, and Theresa suffered a profound shock. The open admiration left her embarrassed, and the disapproval made her cringe.

Theresa muttered a weak protest. "I don't think I can take credit."

Adam's forbidding stare shut her up. She fell

silent, too frightened to cross him and earn his wrath.

"Oh, I think you can and will take credit where credit is due. Your role in this pack is now far too vital to risk. From this point forward, you shall bear the title Heart of the Wolf."

Thundering applause arose from the pack because the Alpha expected it. Even those who resented her put their hands together for fear of angering Adam. Through it all, Theresa made an effort to close her hanging jaw. She glanced around in stunned silence, unable to process the newest development. Refusing such an honor was unthinkable, but she had a bad feeling in her gut.

The applause played out, and then Adam lifted his hands for silence. He rumbled deep in the throat. "In light of this new development, I am modifying my rules of succession. Seeing how Theresa has resurrected the pack's magic, I am convinced that she must become the mate of the next Alpha. The contest is now between Zachary and Robert. They will compete. Whoever Theresa chooses as her mate will be the next leader of this pack—our future Wolf King."

Disbelief caused her to stagger. The imprisoning cage of Adam's hands kept her upright.

Theresa whispered, "I don't want this."

"You'll keep quiet if you know what's good for

you," Adam hissed in Theresa's ear. "You, Miss Russo, are no Charlaine."

Theresa stiffened. She couldn't have been more shocked if Adam had physically struck her. Her first instinct was to tell Adam to go straight to hell. The right to choose her lifemate belonged to her alone. Not even the Alpha got a say.

Anger resonated through her entire being, but a healthy sense of fear kept her silent. Theresa had lived through Zanatos's fascist rule in the days when the Alpha's word was law, and disobedience carried a death sentence.

Supposedly, the pack politics had changed, but deep down, Theresa clung to her cynicism. If she openly defied Adam, how would he retaliate? The Alpha wielded the authority necessary to banish Theresa from the pack and separate her from Isabel. Of course, Zach would try to protect them, but what chance did he stand alone before the might of the Alpha and his enforcers?

Adam flexed his grip on Theresa's shoulders. His basal scent soured with displeasure. "Now, what do you suppose those three are up to?"

The rhetorical question required no answer, but it piqued Theresa's curiosity. She followed the Alpha's stare to where Charlaine, Robert, and Zach had pulled together. Their huddled conversation was quiet and intense. It ended, and Charlaine stepped forward. The Delta wolf commanded attention through the pack bond.

An uneasy hush fell.

"I have an annoucement," Charlaine declared. "I'm speaking for Robert and Zach as well as myself here."

"This should be interesting. Speak your piece." Adam glowered like the sun, obviously annoyed over Charlaine's bold defiance, but at least he removed his hands from Theresa's person.

Theresa stepped away from Adam immediately. The Alpha's touch left her feeling dirty. She wanted nothing more than to rush into a hot shower.

"Theresa Russo is worthy of becoming our pack's Wolf Queen." Charlaine tipped her chin to Theresa in a show of respect. A flush of pleasure swept across Theresa.

"Thank you." Theresa mustered a smile, but she couldn't bring herself to look directly at Robert or Zach. The two men were good friends, and she hated that they might be forced to fight, especially over her.

"Leaving only the matter of a queen's consent." Charlaine's confidence exerted sway over the entire pack. They bowed before her. "Theresa Russo, do you accept the honor of becoming our future pack mom?"

Theresa couldn't believe it. Charlaine must be a

secret magician because she'd just performed the equivalent of spinning straw into gold. A mating game was demeaning, but this felt empowering, like an opportunity to do good. Theresa still wasn't sure she was excellent queen material, but she figured what the heck? Even on her worst day, she could do a better job of looking out for the pack's best interests than someone like Donna.

Besides, Theresa had rekindled the pack's magic when no one else could. That had to count for something, right? In her heart, she believed the wolves of Iron Stone needed new leadership to flourish. Adam and Becky had to go. Last but not least, this would allow Theresa to devise a workaround so Robert and Zach wouldn't wind up dueling to the death.

"Thank you, Charlaine." Theresa smiled in gratitude.

Charlaine nodded.

"For the good of the pack, I accept this honor," Theresa said in a strong, steady voice, "and I promise to always—*always*—act with the best interests of the pack in my heart."

CHAPTER NINETEEN

The moment the meeting broke up, Robert and Zach rushed to Theresa. She disliked the appearance of being claimed by her prospective suitors like a trophy. On the other hand, the attention of the pack's two most eligible bachelors sure as heck beat being a wallflower.

"If you don't mind," Zach said to Adam, "we're here to collect our future bride-to-be."

Adam smiled like a snake oil salesman. "Of course not."

Zach linked elbows with Theresa to her right, and Robert took her left side. Like an honor guard with their queen in the middle, the men whisked her off. The pack's scrutiny followed them as they passed through the house. Every step of the way, her knees threatened to give out, and her chest felt ready to burst from the pressure. She wouldn't have made it without their support.

By some miracle, she held it together until they made it outside. In the cool night air, she sagged in relief and breathed deeply. By unspoken consent, they made their way to Theresa's car, where the three of them formed a tight circle.

Robert broke the brittle silence. "Fuck," he said at long last. "Zach, you were right. The Alpha is determined to see us fight to the death. He's managed to find the one thing that's guaranteed to bring you to the field."

"Adam's a manipulative bastard. That's for certain." Zach stole a sideways glance at Theresa.

Theresa's gaze volleyed between the two men. Their grim expressions did nothing to alleviate her apprehension. "But you won't fight?" she demanded. "Because you're friends."

Neither male answered. The stillness stretched and grew uncomfortable.

"I don't suppose you've changed your mind about challenging Adam," Zach said to Robert.

Robert remained silent for a time, considering, and then shook his head. "It would cause too much damage to the pack. We need to find some other way."

A quick grin twisted Zach's lips. "Would you like to stand down?"

Robert snorted and chuckled. "No. Would you?"

"Not if it means surrendering my woman." Zach's tone possessed an underlying vein of steel and permitted no room for misunderstanding.

Theresa's heart leaped in her chest, and she darted a glance at his face. The severity of his expression terrified her, but his presumption made her furious. She glared. "I'm not your woman, Zachary Hunter."

Zach frowned and spoke with a warning note in his voice. "Theresa."

"Don't." She leveled her finger at him. "Don't you dare!"

"Maybe we'll wind up killing each other after all," Robert said.

The ominous observation sliced through Theresa's anger like a molten blade against a wall of ice. Abruptly, all emotion deserted her, leaving her empty and exhausted.

Zach also fell silent for a moment, and then he sighed. "I'm going to take Theresa home," he said. "We'll have this out another time."

"That's probably for the best." Robert cuffed Zach's arm. "Get some rest, man."

"You too," Zach said. They waited until the other man departed, and then he escorted Theresa to her car and opened the door. "Do you want me to drive you home?"

She licked her lips, torn between accepting his offer and needing to assert control over her life. Robert's final words echoed through her mind, a lingering torment. Would they fight over her? She understood the greater goal—to become Alpha—yet, with one sweeping edict, Adam had made her synonymous with attaining the goal of leadership.

"No," she said. "Thank you."

She tried to get past him, but he refused to move. "Theresa, tonight you accused me of coming on to you as some sort of cruel joke. I'm bloody well not letting you leave until we discuss this."

Theresa's gut churned, pushing acid to the back of her throat, and she wanted to puke. There was no denying Zach, and she owed him an opportunity to explain his actions. She licked her lips and asked him point-blank, "Zach, did you know about this mating game contest before you came on to me?"

His jaw clenched. "No, I didn't."

Theresa's anger welled up inside her with nowhere to go. Tears flooded her eyes because she wanted so badly to believe him, but distrust made that impossible. She doubted him and herself. Most of all, she questioned her value.

She crossed her arms over her breasts. "You can't be surprised, then, that I find your motives suspect. We've been friends, just friends, all these years. Am I supposed to believe that you just happened to discover your attraction to me just days before Adam concocted this scheme?"

Zach exhaled hard, and his nostrils flared. His anger spilled into the ambient aura, bright and burning with intensity. Seconds elapsed before he regained control once again. The aura cleared, leaving behind an ice-cold atmosphere, lacking their usual affection and warmth.

"I knew Adam intended to retire and choose his successor soon," he said. "I told you as much on Saturday."

Her heart ached, on the verge of breaking. "So you admit it wasn't a coincidence?"

"It wasn't a coincidence," Zach said. "My timing was deliberate."

Her eyes filled with tears, and her throat closed. "That's what I was afraid of."

Zach put his finger under her chin and forced her to look up. His bright blue eyes glittered. "Just to be crystal clear," he said, "tell me exactly what you suspect me of, Theresa. I've never given you a single reason to fear me. I expect you to respect that if nothing else."

Theresa blinked, and her vision cleared. "I'm not afraid of you," she said. "I never have been."

"Well, there's that at least." He sounded bitter, full of tightly controlled anger.

Theresa hesitated. She moistened her dry lips with the tip of her tongue.

"Go on," he said.

She nodded. "Fine. I'd like to know whether you courted me because you thought I'd be an easy conquest or because I can produce healthy children."

Zach gave no immediate response, but his entire expression altered. His eyes hardened until they resembled sapphires set in a stone mask. He withdrew his hand from her chin. "How can you think something like that of me, Theresa? I thought we were friends. Worse, how can you set such a poor value on yourself?"

"Maybe I wouldn't have these doubts if you'd been honest with me right from the start," Theresa said, her tone soft but steadfast. She looked Zach right in the eye and refused to back down. She didn't care if he was upset because she was every bit as angry.

He opened his mouth, obviously struggling for words. His brow furrowed, and his head ducked as he bit off whatever he'd been about to say. She expected sarcasm or withdrawal, whatever obfuscation best suited the moment. Zach never showed his hand to anyone, not even her, and he wasn't likely to start now.

Abruptly, Zach's demeanor solidified into one of resolution. His big hands reached out and grasped her shoulders, and he hauled her to him. A squeak of surprise escaped Theresa just before his mouth descended and claimed her lips in a kiss. Rough, passionate, demanding. His skin felt hot and dry, and she tilted back her head to grant him better access. She clung to his arms with both hands, digging her nails into his muscular biceps.

Her lips parted, and his tongue thrust deep into the moist recesses of her mouth. He tasted of nicotine, and she realized with a burst of shock that he'd been smoking. The taste didn't repel her as she might have expected because the heat and spiciness of his mouth blended with the smokiness, creating a rich flavor. Pure Zach.

His tongue delved deeper, stroking the slick surface of her teeth, and then caressed the roof of her mouth. It was nothing like the last kisses they had shared, lacking both in playfulness and gentleness. Instead, he communicated anger and need. He crushed her soft curves against his chest so that the friction rubbed her erect nipples, and she whimpered, wanting to experience his hands cupping her full breasts. The intensity of the embrace left her breathless, and her weak legs threatened to collapse from beneath her.

As suddenly as it had begun, the kiss ended. Zach set her away from him, back on her feet, and then released his hold on her shoulders. He looked at her, obviously waiting, expecting her to say something.

Theresa produced a slight whimper, unable to formulate words. Her fingers crept to brush her bruised lips, and she ached for his touch.

The kiss tasted like goodbye.

"Take care, Theresa," Zach said in a voice frozen, devoid of emotion. He stepped away from her and walked to his car.

In disbelief, Thereasa watched as Zach drove away. The whole while, she fought tears of confusion and loss as her world crumbled about her. Had she just lost her best friend?

CHAPTER TWENTY

Kindergarten corral of the Iron Stone Elementary School - Tuesday afternoon

Theresa arrived early to pick Isabel up from school. She waited with the other mothers who cast speculative glances in her direction. Their hushed whispers behind raised hands were not her imagination. She seemed to be the subject of their gossip, and yet she couldn't fathom why. Since this was Isabel's first year in primary school, so Theresa didn't know most of the other mothers very well. Their reaction worried her and left her wondering what she had done wrong.

"Don't take it personally." A short woman with

curly red hair stepped forward and flashed a smile so that her cheeks dimpled. "They're just dying to know more about that man of yours who picked up your daughter from school yesterday. He was gorgeous and a famous author to boot. It's pricked the curiosity of every red-blooded woman in town."

"Oh." Theresa stared at the impertinent woman. "He's not mine. We're just friends."

The mention of Zach caused her heartache. By now, his plane would have landed in Chicago, and he would have checked into his hotel room. The poor man would be alone in a city full of beautiful women. Opportunities would abound, and who could blame him for seeking solace? An angry green-eyed monster gnawed at her insides at the thought of him in the arms of another woman. Violent self-recrimination plagued her. What had she done? He was all she had ever wanted. Why had she rejected him?

"Well, that's something you should fix right away." A mischievous light shone in the redhead's eyes.

Right away, Theresa decided she liked this nosy little woman. "I'm working on it," she said with a sheepish smile and offered her hand. "Theresa Russo. My daughter is Isabel."

"I'm Martha Wilson. My daughter is Madison."

The women shook hands and made small talk

until the bell rang. Theresa walked away from the encounter feeling oddly optimistic. Maybe she had made a new friend. She joined the other moms at the gate to the kindergarten yard and waited while the playground filled with children excited to be free.

Isabel appeared, carrying her backpack. "Hi, Mom!"

"Hi, sweetie. How was your day?"

Before Isabel replied, Ms. Spaulding, Isabel's teacher, motioned Theresa aside. "Mrs. Russo, could I speak with you for a moment?"

"Of course." Theresa cast a worried glance at her daughter. Isabel wore a pensive expression. "It's Ms. Russo, please. I'm divorced."

"Of course. I'm sorry. Isabel, why don't you go onto the playground and give me a moment alone with your mother?" Ms. Spaulding asked.

"Yes, Ms. Spaulding." Isabel tilted her head back and gazed at them with knowing eyes. She looked to her mother for permission.

"Go ahead and play." Theresa watched while Isabel turned toward the swing set and broke into a skipping run. She waited until her daughter was out of earshot. "Is everything okay, Ms. Spaulding?"

The young teacher crossed her arms. Theresa scented discomfort and embarrassment emanating from the other woman. "Isabel is a wonderful child. She's bright and imaginative..."

"But?" Theresa suspected she knew what was coming.

"She's just a little too imaginative," Ms. Spaulding said. "Isabel constantly talks about her imaginary fairy friends, so much so that I'm afraid it's becoming a distraction in the classroom."

Theresa closed her eyes and sighed then opened them. "I'm sorry. We had the same issue last year in preschool. I'll speak with her about it."

The teacher's face reflected her relief. "Thank you. I do appreciate it."

Theresa nodded and walked out onto the playground to collect her daughter. Isabel sat on a swing by herself, rocking slowly back and forth. Isabel was always alone, even in a crowd of other children, and it made Theresa sad. She wasn't sure what to do to help her daughter make friends. Isabel lived in her imagination and clung to her fairy friends with stubborn tenacity.

"Am I in trouble?" she asked with a worried frown.

"No, sweetie, you're not in trouble, but we do need to talk when we get home."

Isabel pouted. "That's what I was afraid of."

"Don't frown, sweetie." A smile curved Theresa's lips. She took Isabel's hand, and they started toward the gate. Halfway there, a woman's voice caught her attention.

"Theresa, hi!"

Theresa turned and spotted Charlaine standing on the other side of the fenced-off kindergarten playground. She wore the orange safety vest of a teacher on yard duty and stood at the gate, directing the flow of children and parents.

Theresa mustered a nervous smile. Together, she and Isabel walked over to greet Charlaine. She felt a little uncomfortable due to the difference in their ranks within the pack, but Charlaine's assistance the night before had done a great deal to alleviate her uncertainty.

"Hello, Ms. Gale," Isabel said.

"Hello, Isabel, you look pretty today," Charlaine said. "Hello, Theresa."

"Hi, Char," Theresa said. "Beautiful day, isn't it?"

"Yes, it is."

They conversed, mostly small talk, and passed a few minutes. Theresa enjoyed the social interaction more than she'd expected. After a few minutes, the crowd thinned, and then the playground was empty.

Acting on impulse, Theresa grasped Charlaine's fingers. "I never said thank you for your help last night, so thank you."

Charlaine's brow shot up, but she permitted the contact. She squeezed Theresa's hand in return and then released it. "You're welcome. So, do you two have any big plans today?"

"We're going shopping over in Sparks," Theresa said. "Isabel has outgrown her shoes. Again."

"I want big kid shoes with lights and laces," Isabel said with a disdainful glance at her strap-fastened athletic shoes.

"I hear rhinestones are all the rage." Charlaine kept a straight face, but her dark eyes danced with laughter.

Isabel frowned. "Only if they're pink or red. My favorite color is red."

"Mine too," Charlaine said.

Theresa hesitated and gathered her courage. "Char, are you free? It'd be nice to have company."

Isabel, bless her little heart, jumped on the idea. "Oh, please! Come with us! It'll be so much fun."

Surprise crossed Charlaine's face but only for a second. She considered and consented with a slow smile. "I think I'd like that. Shall we take one car?"

"I parked around the corner on Ray Street," Theresa said, indicating the direction to her vehicle.

Charlaine checked her watch and then removed the orange safety vest. "I'm right here in the parking lot. Let's take my car."

Theresa glanced down and hid a smile behind her hand, pretending to scratch her nose. Dominant wolves always wanted to drive. They had such control issues.

"I saw that." Charlaine shot her a quick smile and sideways glance.

A backdrop of voices engaged in hushed conversations created a slight din, but Zach had no trouble following what his companion was saying. Her voice had a sultry resonance that made him believe she would be a fantastic singer. She was pleasant to listen to and even easier on the eyes. However, the tiresome harping didn't sit well, and his annoyance grew with each passing second.

At long last, she took a break from talking to solicit his opinion. "Mr. Hunter, what do you think?"

Blue eyes narrowed. Zach peered over the rim of his wine glass. The gorgeous redhead had a model's ideal figure—tall, svelte, and leggy. He sighed and slugged his wine without regard for the rich bouquet that demanded sipping for sincere appreciation.

"I'm sorry, Miss Dawson," he said. "Could you please repeat that?"

Irritation crossed Danielle's face. She obviously knew he'd been paying attention and understood everything she'd said. He figured he owed her one last chance to come to her senses and retract her erroneous stance.

No such luck.

"I said," she gritted out, "that I don't buy Wesley's actions in chapter twelve. Frankly, I feel it's out of character for him to shoot McTavish, especially considering how long they've been friends."

She kept talking, but Zach wasn't listening. He polished off his wine and motioned to the waiter even though their food had not yet arrived. "Check, please."

Miss Dawson sputtered. "Mr. Hunter, you could at least hear me out. My concerns as your editor—"

"Junior editor," Zach snapped. "And I only agreed to meet with you as a favor to Suzie while Sam is out with an emergency appendectomy. If we're frank, it isn't your place to tell me what is or is not in character for Wesley. He's my creation, and it's because of that betrayed friendship that he must shoot McTavish. Now, if you'll excuse me."

Danielle colored a delicate shade of pink. "Mr. Hunter, I'm aware some writers don't take criticism well, but really, I'm trying to help you."

Zach stood and intercepted the check before the waiter had a chance to set it on the table. "Thank you so much for that."

"Mr. Hunter!" Danielle shot to her feet.

"Miss Dawson." Zach swung on the young woman.

He met her gaze and summoned his power, allowing her to perceive enough of the wolf lurking within to stop her in her tracks. Stop she did. Her pale complexion blanched, and she shook in her expensive high heels.

Zach continued with his outburst. "I did not come here to receive a lecture on the canonical doings of Wesley Anders from you. This conversation is over."

The tiresome redhead took a step back. Zach accepted her expression of fear and astonishment as a gesture of submission and reached for his wallet. He withdrew a credit card and forked it over to the waiter for payment. "I'll contact Suzie in the morning so that you will not have the chance to make this mistake again. Good day, Miss Dawson."

As he watched, Danielle Dawson's green eyes filled with tears, and her lower lip trembled. However, he refused to take pity on the foolish woman. It might have been her misfortune to cross him while he was already in a foul mood, but damn it! She'd been asking for it, and he had curbed the sharper edge of his tongue.

Zach jerked his credit card from the waiting server, took his leave, and caught a taxi back to his hotel room. The early fall Chicago evening was quite lovely, but he remained too preoccupied to enjoy it. His entire day, from the early morning flight with the associated delays in security and takeoff to the four-hour book signing, had been crap. Danielle Dawson had been the last straw.

Bollocks, it was past time he finally took the plunge and went indie.

CHAPTER TWENTY-ONE

Back at his hotel, Zach set down his keys and wallet on the dresser. He kicked off his leather shoes and dropped his coat over an armchair. His unknotted tie hung draped over his shoulders. To relieve the suffocating heat he was suffering, Zach seized his dress shirt at the collar and ripped open the row of buttons. Coolness washed over his skin.

Better. Much better.

Zach investigated the mini bar, opened a bottle of Scotch, and dumped the contents over ice. Glass in hand, he sank into one of the rectangular hotel chairs and fished his cell phone from his pocket. He had no missed calls, but the voicemail message symbol showed on the top of the screen.

Zach took a sip of his Scotch and sat back,

putting up his feet on the edge of the queen-size bed. He considered the phone, deliberating on the potential identity of the sender. There were a small handful of friends who might call him. The trouble was, he would be in an even worse mood if it weren't Theresa.

His phone had been silent all afternoon while he'd attended events and meetings. Now, he was stuck staring at his phone with a mixture of dread and anticipation. The suspense was killing him. Making the decision, he checked his incoming call log. For the first time that day, he smiled to see that it was from Theresa.

He dialed his voicemail and listened to Theresa's soft voice, full of uncertainty. "Zach, are you still mad? Call me."

The timestamp read 8:45 p.m. The phone's clock showed that it was now 8:58 p.m. Isabel would be asleep, and Theresa would be winding down before going to bed.

Zach set aside the glass and used the touch screen to pull up his directory. He selected Theresa's number from the top of the list. The house phone rang once before she picked up.

"Hello?" Theresa said with a breathy quality.

His insides warmed at the sound of it. He longed to hear her sultry voice sigh his name, crooning and whimpering with the intensity of her desire. He wanted to taste her lips and feel those luscious curves writhing beneath him. He needed her to complete him.

"Theresa?" Zach's smile infused her name with effusive joy. "I thought you were angry with me, love."

She hesitated, and he envisioned her front teeth biting into her lower lip. "I'm not angry with you. Just with myself."

Zach snorted. "Why? This is on me. I managed to balls up everything."

Theresa laughed. "How's Chicago?"

"Eh," Zach said, but it was an unfair characterization of the city. "It's lovely. The weather is perfect."

"I miss you," Theresa said on a melancholy note.

"I miss you, too." Abruptly, everything felt okay, but he knew it to be an illusion that couldn't last. There wasn't enough trust between them.

"We miss you," she said, amending her first statement. "Isabel said to remind you about her present."

Zach chuckled, and his hand reached for the bag bearing the exclusive toy store logo. He pulled out the stuffed pony he'd purchased for inspection. "I have it right here. I hope Isabel still likes horses."

Theresa giggled. "Isabel is a girl. Of course, she likes horses."

"That's good because I couldn't find a stuffed fairy."

"Isabel has every fairy toy ever made. I'm sure she's going to love it."

Zach slipped the toy back into the bag. On an optimistic impulse, he had made a second purchase —a wrapped box filled with tissue paper containing an expensive peignoir and lace panties. It was a piece reminiscent of the glory days of Hollywood, a sheer Georgette robe. He possessed a vivid imagination and could envision how the white silk would look against her warm brown skin.

Zach realized he'd gotten hard and had to adjust his pants, so his rigid cock wasn't crushed. He cleared his throat. "Theresa?"

"Hmm?"

"Are you still angry with me, love?"

Theresa drew in a sharp breath. "I... I don't know," she said. "I think I was more hurt than angry."

"You don't trust me." The harsh statement slipped past his lips despite his reluctance to speak his conclusion out loud. Saying it aloud made the damning fact all that much more real. However, more than one person had accused him recently of being tight-lipped. He owed it to Theresa to try to communicate.

She protested. "That's not true! We've been

through this already. I know you'll never hurt Isabel or me."

He exhaled. "You trust that I'm not violent, yet you don't trust me with your heart."

He had her.

She stumbled over the words. "Zach, I-I..."

"At least respect me enough to admit it."

Her breathing stuttered on a wet exhalation. She sounded close to tears, and his chest ached for the hurt she must be enduring.

It was a long time before she spoke again. "It's not you, Zach. It's me. I don't trust *my* judgment. *My* worth."

"Because of Antonio," he said, thinking for the millionth time that he should have killed that slimeball ages ago. He couldn't undo the harm the bastard had done, but there was something to be said for some old-fashioned vengeance.

"Because of Antonio," she said, "but also because of me. I've made bad choices, and I just don't see why..."

"Why?" He kept his tone gentle, but the prompt carried command.

"Why would someone like you be attracted to someone like me?" she whispered.

Tightness constricted Zach's chest. He hurt for her and with her. Right then, Zach would have given anything to be able to take her into his arms and prove to her just how very attractive he found her. Violent emotions tested the limits of his control, but discipline softened his response.

"Theresa, I've wanted you since the first time I laid eyes on you," Zach said. "I've waited years for you to trust me enough so I could act on it."

She drew in a sharp breath. "My God. I've been waiting for you to say something—to notice me—and this whole time you were waiting for me? We've failed because I was afraid."

"We haven't failed." He allowed power to touch his voice so she would feel the strength of his resolve. "I refuse to fail. I won't give up on you, on us."

She hiccupped, and he suspected she was crying. His throat hurt from the dryness, but what was important was that he sensed her responding to his confidence.

"Be patient with me, Zach, please. I just need time."

He exhaled so quickly his nostrils flared. "I'll be as patient as I can, Theresa, but time is running out. I don't have the words to explain, and I'm not sure I want to try on the phone."

Theresa gave a shaky laugh. "That's funny, coming from you. You always know what to say, how to say it."

Zach snorted and shook his head. "Not always.

Look, can you trust me enough to believe that my attraction to you has nothing to do with Adam's competition? If it makes you feel better, then we can wait it out."

His response must not have been what she was expecting because she gave an awkward laugh. She fell silent, and he danced on pins and needles, waiting for her response. Finally, she asked, "You'd give up being Alpha for me?"

He exhaled. "Yes, in a heartbeat."

Her voice hitched. "Zach—"

"Theresa, have I ever lied to you?"

Impatience crept into her voice. "Zach, you're not letting me get a word in edgewise."

"Sorry." He put a lid on it and waited for her.

"Are you going to let me talk?" Theresa adopted her official voice of maternal authority.

Zach grinned like mad. "Yes, ma'am."

"It really wouldn't be an act of trust if I made you give something up to prove yourself, would it? If you want to be Alpha that much, then you should keep courting me."

Zach shut his eyes. An odd feeling filled him, akin to revelation, affirming his choice of Theresa as the woman meant to become his mate. Not that he'd ever really doubted it, but the last three years had been an exercise in patience and faith.

"I won't let you down again, Theresa. I promise."

"You'd better not, Zach." The vulnerability in her voice wrenched his heart.

"I won't. I'm going to take care of you, love."

The emotional drain of the moment exhausted him, and they both lapsed into silence.

Theresa recovered first and brought about a welcome change of subject. "How did your book signing go?"

"It went." Zach's tone expressed his weariness and his frustration. He talked about the event for a couple of minutes but didn't go into great detail. Still, it was good to move onto a less intense topic, and he sensed Theresa felt the same. "Afterward, I met with the junior editor the publisher assigned to replace Sam while he's out on medical leave."

"I take it that didn't go so well?" His sweet Theresa sounded both amused and sympathetic.

"It was a farce. The woman was twenty-four if she was a day. Fresh out of college, and she didn't know the first thing about publishing."

"Zach, I'm twenty-three." Theresa's tone turned sharp.

"Yes, but you're not an idiot," Zach said, running a hand through his hair. "Theresa, the woman had the nerve to tell me that Wesley can't shoot McTavish because it's not in character." He sprang to his feet, his outrage fueling a violent gesture of his arms.

Theresa gasped. "Wesley shot McTavish?"

"Yes." His brow knit, and confusion replaced his outrage.

Absently, Zach removed his cuff links and set them on the dresser. Then, he unbuttoned the remaining buttons on his shirt and shed the garment.

Theresa sputtered, "Oh, Zach, no. Wesley can't shoot McTavish! They're partners. They're like brothers. It wouldn't be right."

Zach hesitated but made no reply. The unexpectedness of Theresa's reaction threw him for a loop. He hadn't realized she was such a passionate McTavish fan.

"Did you kill him?" Theresa tipped her hand, and he caught the laughter in her voice lurking just beneath her exaggerated outrage. "Zach, please, not McTavish! Please! Anyone but McTavish!"

She made him see the ridiculousness of the situation. Sides cramping in stitches, Zach dropped onto the bed. He laughed until it hurt. Tears flooded his eyes, and he wiped them away with the backs of his fingers.

When at last he had enough air to speak, he gasped. "Am I that insufferable?"

Theresa's laughter lit him up. "Yes, but it's okay. I'm here to keep you real."

"I appreciate that," Zach said, the last chuckle

fading away. Abruptly, he felt so much better. His terrible tension dissipated, and the pain eased from his shoulders.

"Did you take that poor woman's head off?"

"No," he said then confessed, "Yes, but I exercised admirable restraint."

"Oh, Zach." Theresa sighed into the phone. The sound of her weight shifting atop fabric reached his ears. "What am I going to do with you?"

"I could offer all manner of suggestions." Zach's mouth went dry, and his voice had acquired a sultry tone, deliberately suggestive, a hint of the lewd.

"Oh, you. Stop!" She giggled with delight, and there was nothing in her attitude to make him believe she meant anything but the opposite.

His slacks had become tight in the crotch, so he unfastened the sliding tabs. As a rule, he went commando because it made undressing to shift forms easier, but he happened to be wearing black silk boxers under his suit. He shoved his boxers down to mid-thigh, and his aroused shaft sprang into his hand. His balls were swollen and tender, and the slightest pressure felt exquisite. He muffled a moan.

"Where are you, Theresa?"

"In bed."

"Tell me what you're wearing."

"Zach!" Theresa sounded scandalized, but he

also detected the note of intrigue in her voice. Her breathing grew rapid and uneven. "I'm wearing a white robe. I just got out of the shower."

"Is it silk?"

"No. You know I can't afford silk, silly. It's cotton."

His gaze flickered to the gift he'd bought her, and he licked his lips. He stroked his engorged member, fingers and thumb encircling the thickness. "Anything else?"

"What do you mean?"

"Do you have on panties?"

"You're bad!" Her muffled laughter did not disguise the sound of pillows being beaten and fluffed. "No. I'm not wearing panties."

"Is your hair wet?" In his imagination, the long strands of her hair tickled his thighs, and her hot breath caressed his skin.

"Yes, I just washed it."

Zach dropped onto the mattress and rolled to his back. Still massaging his erection, he stared up at the room's white textured ceiling. "I love your hair when you wear it down."

"You do?" Theresa sounded shy and pleased. She hesitated. "I'm untying my robe."

"You know I do. I love the way it's wavy and then corkscrews tumbling down your back. The ends are just long enough to reach the line delineating your arse."

"You sound like you've spent a lot of time thinking about that." Theresa's come-hither breathy tone invited him to continue, and he did so without hesitation.

"I have, love, constantly for the last three years. You have the sweetest, tightest arse I've ever laid eyes on, and I can't wait to pry apart your thighs and taste your pussy. I'm going to lick every lovely inch of your gorgeous cunny."

In his mind's eye, he held the enthralling vision of Theresa nude, and it required no effort to add sensory details to his fantasy. He could taste the salt of her skin, feel the hot flush of her flesh against his own, smell the musk of her arousal flooding his nostrils.

He heard the distinct rustle of bedding beneath her restless shifting. Theresa panted in the receiver, and she whimpered with need.

"Tell me what you're doing," he urged as he fisted his throbbing member with renewed vigor. A throaty moan tore from him.

Her breath caught on a hitch. After a brief hesitation, she said, "Massaging my breasts. Zach, what are we doing? I haven't ever done something like this."

"Shh, love, it's okay. We're just playing."

Theresa giggled. "Okay. Tell me what to do."

The coy invitation was almost his undoing, but he was determined not to lose control like a horny teenage boy. Zach pressed his ear to the phone and listened, intent upon hearing every delicious sound she produced. "Stroke your breasts gently in little circles. How do they feel?"

A short delay followed, and then her soft moan of pleasure. "Good," she said. "Firm, full... My nipples are hard."

Ah, fuck. Zach mouthed the words, taking great care not to speak them aloud. The last thing he wanted was to startle her out of the mood; however, his palm was too callused for the fantasy—the smoothness of Theresa's lips, the velvet of her tongue, and the heat of her mouth. Extending his arm, he reached toward the chair beside the bed and snagged a silk handkerchief out of the front pocket of his suit coat.

"Press a little harder. Pinch your nipples for me."

Theresa's gasp signaled her obedience. "I want..."

"Yes, tell me what you want."

Frantic for relief, Zach shook out the silk square and dropped it over his turgid member. He sucked down a strangled breath as he wrapped his long fingers around his cock and squeezed. The soft material cocooned him. It felt like heaven against his hot skin and created a funny tent that he would have found hilarious under different circumstances.

"I want you." Theresa punctuated her proclamation with a whimper. The soft rasp of skin on skin reached his straining ears.

"I want you, too, pet."

It was the ultimate statement of the obvious, but his brain wasn't fully functional. His capacity for reasoning was fading fast. His cock was engorged. His balls felt ready to burst, and every stroke of his hand felt like heaven.

"Slide your hands down, love. Stroke your stomach. Lower. Touch your pussy. Don't be quiet. I want to hear you."

"I am. I'm touching myself. I wish it were you," Theresa moaned.

"I'll be home in two days, love."

Theresa, his little beauty, gained most of her height from her long legs. Zach envisioned her slender fingers caressing her flat stomach and then reaching the dark curls at the apex of her thighs. His imagination wrapped those sexy limbs around his hips as he thrust and then pounded into her tight channel.

"I've fantasized about you so many times..."

Being the center of her sexy dreams surpassed his wildest hopes. "Tell me your favorite fantasy."

"I—" Theresa faltered, and the blush that he was sure covered her cheeks tinted her voice.

Zach stilled, becoming intent upon the unexpected intrigue.

"Theresa, tell me." Zach made it a command, infusing his voice with the authority of his dominant wolf. It was cheating, but he was too damn horny to care.

Stammering just a bit, Theresa obeyed. "I-I fantasize about being taken. Restrained."

His mouth watered. "Held down or tied up?"

"Both. Sometimes, I struggle, just a little, to pretend that I don't want it. You always force me to come over and over again." She whimpered and then moaned, a ragged cry of passion.

"Jesus."

His sight blurred even though the vision in his head remained crystal clear. The hand on his shaft moved faster, creating a slapping sound that echoed. It almost certainly carried over the phone.

"I'd like to be spanked," Theresa said.

"I'd love to spank you."

She laughed. "You're a bad man, Zachary Hunter."

"Don't you know it," he said, chuckling despite the cresting intensity of his need. Lust and laughter were the best combinations, a powerful aphrodisiac.

"Oh! I'm coming!" Theresa's voice dissolved into the sweet stutter of moans muffled against a pillow.

She didn't utter another coherent word other than to call out Zach's name, but he hung on every sound she made. His fertile imagination supplied the image of her face contorted with passion—eyes shut, teeth sunk into her lower lip. Her full breasts, nipples erect, full and quivering while she panted for breath. Her fingers buried to the third knuckle in her pussy, glistening moisture coating her hand, forming a sweet cream layer on her inner thighs.

Zach's balls contracted, and he came with a hard shudder that wracked his entire body. A thick stream of cum spurted from his cock, soaking the silken handkerchief. He squeezed tighter, deliberately inflicting enough pain to slow the spasms, wanting to draw out the glorious moment of release for as long as possible.

A howl rolled from the back of his throat, filling the confines of the hotel room with a wolf's untamed song. His orgasm continued to peak steadily, resulting in the most protracted climax of his life. Milky streams shot from his penis, gradually lessening in intensity until the pressure in his scrotum finally subsided.

Panting, he slid into warm drowsiness. Theresa's breathing provided a solid sense of comfort, almost as good as being able to hold her but not quite.

"You howled." Theresa giggled.

"Yeah. I'll be lucky if security doesn't come knocking, looking for a dog."

"Will you call me again tomorrow night?" Theresa asked with a wistful note in her voice.

Zach chuckled. "Love, you'll be lucky to get me off the phone at all."

CHAPTER TWENTY-TWO

Dream Chaser Cafe

"Theresa, you're late. Again." Viv Beeman, the diner owner, stood behind the cash register and did not look away from the till as she rang up a customer. Her voice had a raspy quality from too many years of smoking, and she wore her gray hair beneath a hair net. From her jowls to her barrel limbs, every part of her had the swollen look of an overstuffed sausage.

Theresa opened her mouth to argue the point. In actuality, she was seldom late. Indeed, it wasn't the way the obnoxious woman made it sound. Her tardiness that evening was the exception and not the rule. Her recalcitrance startled her, and she bit her sharp reply off before she spoke aloud. Instead, she forced out the apology required of her.

"Viv, I'm so sorry. It won't happen again."

Reaching back, Theresa struggled to tame the thick curls of her hair into a ponytail and secured it with a band. She felt bad about being late, but her mother hadn't picked up Isabel on time. When one person got delayed, it created an unfortunate domino effect.

"Table six is waiting for their food," Viv said with a sharp jerk of her head toward the customers in question. "Hurry up. Maggie's been covering your tables since five."

Theresa cast a glance at the clock. 5:10 p.m. She sighed and reached for an order pad and a pen. Then, she grabbed a tray and went to the kitchen window where the completed dishes waited.

"Hey, sweetie, don't let that cranky bitch get you down." Sam Smiley's easy grin greeted her from the other side of the window. The cook came by his name honestly. She'd never seen him project anything but a cheerful attitude.

"Thanks, Sam." Theresa grabbed the ticket for table six and loaded all of the dishes onto the tray. The order consisted of three blue plate specials—chicken fried steak with thick white gravy and garlic mashed potatoes. The Wednesday night menu always brought in bustling crowds of hungry locals. Without fail, the entire restaurant was packed with a line out the door.

She passed Maggie, another waitress, a woman in her forties with frazzled red hair and tired, hazel eyes.

"Hey," Theresa said to her co-worker. She flashed a smile. "Thanks for covering my tables."

"No worries, honey," Maggie said. "How's that little one of yours doing?"

"Isabel is good," Theresa said with quiet pride. "She's already reading chapter books."

"That child's a smart one."

Maggie passed Theresa, heading toward the heated counter. Meanwhile, Theresa went opposite, stepping into the dining room with a full tray balanced in her hand. Halfway to the table, her foot slipped on a patch of wet tile, and she almost fell. Thanks to her preternatural agility, she recovered her balance at the last second.

An impatient male customer raised his voice from a nearby table. "Hey, miss, can I get some ketchup?"

"Of course. Just give me a moment." Theresa made it another two paces before a customer turned to her with an angry expression.

"My order is wrong," he said, holding up the top bun of his hamburger so she could see the insides. "I asked for no mustard. This has mustard. I didn't want mustard."

"I'm sorry about that," Theresa said without missing a beat. She removed the plate from the table and placed it on her tray. "Give me just a minute, and I'll get you another with no mustard."

Three more steps, she arrived at table six, served their food, received a request for steak sauce, and then returned to the kitchen. She set the rejected hamburger with mustard on the counter and met Smiley's knowing gaze. "No mustard, please."

Ire touched his eyes, and Smiley eyeballed the rejected food. "Sweetie, that tag didn't say no mustard. I know what it said, and it didn't say no mustard."

Theresa offered an apologetic smile. "I know the customer didn't say no mustard when they were ordering. They still sent it back anyway. Please, no mustard?"

With a grumble, Smiley seized the plate, dumping the untouched food into the trash. He turned away to toss another patty on the grill. Theresa got what she needed from the condiment station and headed back onto the floor.

Her first few minutes set the tone for the entire evening. Over the next four hours, she got stiffed on tips three times and received more complaints than usual, all the while enduring Viv's passive-aggressive scrutiny and jibes.

After ten, the second shift was released from the silver mine, and hungry workers filled up the booths. Three human men arrived—Hal Smith and brothers, Joel and Ruddy Arneson. They had a reputation for being troublemakers known for their rowdy behavior and not keeping their hands to themselves.

Theresa traded a long look with Maggie. "It's my turn," Theresa said with a grimace.

Maggie frowned in return. "Those boys need a good talkin' to," she said. "I know Hal's mama, and she's a lovely woman, but her husband knocks her around somethin' awful. Her sons didn't learn respect growing up."

"Don't worry. I can handle them," Theresa said, squaring her shoulders. She gathered three menus, plastered on a bright smile, and headed toward the men who were waiting to be seated. She greeted them with more enthusiasm than she felt, delivering good old-fashioned customer service.

"Good evening. Welcome to Dream Chaser Cafe." She seated the three miners in a booth and endured their unskilled flirting with an unwavering smile, the whole time envisioning her body encased in a suit of armor. Everything they did slid right off. Nothing stuck.

The first time Hal pinched her butt, she ignored

him and removed her backside from his reach, but the insult riled her wolf in unexpected ways. It annoyed Theresa that the miner dared treat her in such a manner when she could put his arm in a sling.

As a predator, she always walked a fine line between balancing her two halves. Within the pack, she had gained status and power. Her packmates respected her now. However, humans viewed her as nothing more than a lowly waitress and a single mother, and they often treated her accordingly.

The second time Hal grabbed her ass, Theresa whirled and smacked his offending appendage, shooting him a glare. "Stop putting your hands where they're not welcome!"

"Hey, darlin', don't be like that." Hal spread his hands to demonstrate his innocence. He wore a big, toothy grin, making it clear how little he respected her warning.

"We gotta have a reason for comin' here, and it sure as hell ain't the food." Ruddy leered at her, and the three men shared a good laugh at her expense.

Their mockery fueled her irritation. With the full moon so close, her wolf was already in ascendance. It took minimal provocation to push her toward real anger.

She swung around with her hands clenched into fists. "I won't tell you again," Theresa said in a voice laced with threat.

The men laughed again at her warning, refusing to take her seriously.

Theresa frowned and made a point of turning her back on Hal, daring him to touch her again. Her actions were bold, but her newfound self-confidence allowed her to take unprecedented chances. She refused to be treated like a piece of meat to be pawed by whatever offending male perceived her as easy prey.

Hal surged to his feet and pawed her backside again, delivering a hard pinch intended to hurt. A low rumble erupted from Theresa's throat, and she spun on him. Acting on instinct, she drew her arm back and took a swing. She threw all of her strength into the punch and hit Hal square in the face.

The blow knocked Hal clean off his feet. He struck the back of the booth and slumped over with blood gushing from his mouth and nose. Ruddy bellowed in outrage and lumbered to his feet. Theresa seized his throat with her hand. His mouth gaped open, and he gasped for air.

"I am through putting up with your harassment," Theresa said, voice soft but deadly.

She met Ruddy's gaze and allowed her power to show. Her wolf peered out of her eyes. All color drained from his face, and he pissed his pants. The rank smell of urine filled the air.

Sneering, Theresa released her hold on him and

stepped back to avoid the puddle forming at his feet. He landed in a heap on the floor.

She turned toward the front of the restaurant, and dead silence confronted her. Abruptly, she became aware of their audience. Throughout the once busy restaurant, all activity had ceased. The customers, fearful and suspicious, stared at her with wide eyes and open mouths.

Flabby jaws hanging, Viv grabbed for the phone and called for the police. "It's an emergency. A man is hurt. No, no, send the cops. My waitress beat him up."

Crap.

Well aware that she'd messed up big time, Theresa walked away from the table, past all of the shocked customers, into the back. She gathered her possessions and went out front to wait for the cops. Theresa harbored no illusions that she still had a job at the diner. Not that she would miss it in the least. As Zach liked to point out, it was a crap position where the employees endured slave wages and toxic treatment.

I'll find another job. Even if I don't, unemployment isn't the end of the world. Theresa always had the option of moving in with Mary. Besides, the pack would never permit a mother and child to go hungry. It hurt her independence to admit it, but Zach would take care of her and Isabel if it came down to it. She had no doubt.

A much more pressing concern was the prospect of being arrested. Maybe she should have been panicking, but instead, she felt disconnected. She had assaulted not one but two men. She would be lucky if she didn't wind up in jail and her child in the custody of social services. Fortunately for her, the town sheriff also happened to be a member of the pack.

A short time later, two police cars parked in front of the diner with lights flashing but silent sirens. An ambulance pulled alongside, and a crowd of curious onlookers gathered just beyond the official vehicles. Sheriff Sly Mahoney talked to the three miners, making notes on a pad of paper.

"All right. That will be all for now," Sly said, flipping the pad closed. In his late twenties, the handsome lawman stood about five-eleven and boasted a strapping build. He held the title of Epsilon within the pack, fifth-ranked, after Charlaine, and his career in law enforcement made him a valuable and influential member.

The EMTs loaded up the ambulance, removing both Hal and Ruddy to the hospital for further treatment. Although uninjured, Joel accompanied them.

"Are they going to press charges?" Theresa asked

Sheriff Mahoney. She stood on the curb in front of the diner beside the lead police car, wringing her hands as she waited to learn her fate. Unshed tears stung her eyes, but she refused to cry, no matter how dire the circumstances.

"Theresa, I'm not going to arrest you," Sheriff Sly Mahoney said with a distinct note of reluctance in his voice. "Neither of those men wants to press charges. The embarrassment of standing up in a courthouse and admitting that a slip of a waitress put them in the hospital—not to mention what their wives would say—is too much."

Caution tempered her relief. Theresa's features twisted into a grimace. "But?"

His voice dropped so that only she could hear. "But Adam is going to have to be told that you've used your strength in front of humans."

Her expression grew grim, and her stomach churned. She dreaded the prospect of facing Adam more than all the lost jobs or jail time in the world. If he chose, the Alpha had the authority to banish her—to take away her child and kick her out of Iron Stone forever. His power was absolute. He could even condemn her to death. She doubted he would allow her newfound celebrity status to temper her punishment for endangering the entire pack.

Heart of the Wolf be damned.

Her fancy new title wasn't anything more than a

political ploy to rally the Iron Stone wolves to do his bidding. Her only hope lay in continuing to play along with Adam's plans. Once Robert or Zach seized control of the pack, then she would be safe.

"Don't worry, Theresa," he said with a reassuring smile. "You know Zach isn't going to let anything happen to you."

"Thank you, Sly," Theresa said with a grateful smile. The empathic pack bond connected them, allowing her to sense that his assurances were sincere. She could count Sly Mahoney as a friend. It served to reinforce her faith and loyalty to her pack. There was a Charlaine or an Ambra to counterbalance the good against the bad.

A ghost of a smile curved Sly's mouth. The sparkle in his eyes conveyed his approval. "Don't put any more men in the hospital, all right?"

"I'll try not to." She found it shocking that she'd put anyone there in the first place. Violence wasn't her way, and yet it seemed to have plagued her for the last week.

Casting a final glance at the departing ambulance, Theresa took a few tentative steps toward her employers. Along with a crowd of spectators, Viv and her husband Spencer huddled together near the entrance. They watched her approach with considerable unease, frightened rabbits before the wolf.

Viv's jowls trembled as she marshaled her outrage. "Theresa Russo, you're fired! Clear out your stuff, and don't bother coming back. We'll mail your last paycheck!"

Theresa closed her eyes. She felt like laughing hysterically but settled for a sigh of resignation. Some things were worth fighting for. There were other crappy jobs out there. Tomorrow, she would start looking, but for tonight, she wanted nothing more than to go home, soak in a hot bath, and cry herself to sleep.

She turned and left without saying a word.

A veil of clouds cloaked the bright moon, and a breeze blew through the valley. Theresa drove home with the windows rolled down so she could enjoy the lovely night. Isabel was spending the sleeping over at her grandmother's, so Theresa headed straight home. She parked in the driveway, locked the vehicle, and started for the front door. Her porch lighting fixture was busted, another item on the long list of requested fixes her landlord hadn't gotten to yet. Theresa relied on her wolf's nocturnal vision to navigate the dark sidewalk, moving with confidence until a stir of shadows caused her to stop in her tracks.

A hulking male figure stepped out of the darkness surrounding her front porch. For a crazy second, Theresa imagined that one of the men from the diner had followed her home. Then, the man's features resolved into Carl Reynolds's, Debra's boyfriend, dispelling her wild conjecture. A bolt of fear lanced through Theresa. Carl both outranked and outweighed her. She preferred to face three human men over a male werewolf.

She drew herself up, shoulders squared, spine straight, and held steady. She met his eyes with pure bravado and refused to demonstrate even a hint of submissive behavior. "Carl," she said. "What a surprise. Have you been lurking in my front bushes for long?"

He glared daggers at her. "Theresa, you and I are gonna talk about uppity bitches that don't know their place."

CHAPTER TWENTY-THREE

A hotel in Chicago, Illinois

As Zach entered the lobby of his hotel, a disturbing foreboding overcame him. His wolf rushed to the fore, roiling with aggression, and the instinctive desire to transform seized him. Although dozens of humans were nearby, he wanted nothing more than to shed his clothing and slide into his canine form.

Fear and panic plagued him, provoking his most primal instincts. The emotions were not his own, and it took him almost a minute to identify the external source. As he stepped into the elevator, he put his finger on it—Theresa. Her distress reached him across the miles, calling him to protect her, an impossible feat given the distance separating them. However, his aggression had no outlet.

Somehow, she had reached out to draw a significant amount of energy from him—enough to fuel a transformation or a fight, maybe both. Since they did not share a mate bond, it was a remarkable feat. He could cut her off any time he wanted, but such a thing was unthinkable. He remained open and allowed her to borrow from his power.

The elevator doors slid open, and it was, thankfully, empty. He could not have entered a small room full of humans without someone noticing the glow of his eyes or the elongation of his canines. Of course, the power draw was the primary reason for his slippery control. The energy ripped through his body, traveling across the surface of his skin, arousing his wolf.

Entering the empty elevator, Zach punched the button for his floor and pulled out his cell phone. He called Theresa's home number and listened while it rang and then went to the answering machine.

"You've reached Theresa and Isabel. Please leave a message."

Beep.

"Theresa, it's Zach. I know something's wrong.

Call me when you get this." He hit disconnect and stared at his phone in frustration.

He checked the time and saw that it was just after midnight in Nevada. Theresa should either still be at work or on her way home. Isabel would be spending the night with her grandmother, who would take her to school in the morning.

After a moment's consideration, he used his Internet browser to locate the phone number to Dream Chaser Cafe.

An abrupt-sounding man answered the phone. "Yeah?"

Zach wasted no time with niceties. "Is Theresa there? Theresa Russo?"

A weighted silence ensued. Then, the man said, "She's not available right now."

Click.

"Bloody hell." Zach exited the elevator and made his way to his room. He curbed his desire to throw the phone at the wall. As soon as he got home, he intended to buy Theresa a cell phone and to make her promise to carry it, her stubborn insistence about not accepting anything from him be damned.

He wracked his brain, trying to figure out what to do next. Thinking that Theresa's mother might know what was going on, he performed a directory search for her phone number. However, it turned up no public listing.

It took a real effort not to rip the door to his hotel room off its hinges. He slid the electronic key into the reader and entered the impersonal space. In his current frame of mind, it felt more like an enclosure, and he paced the length of the room with the pent-up energy of a caged tiger, yearning for the physical expression of his aggression. A chance to kill. An enemy to destroy. Only, there was nothing: no physical foe, no ready answers.

There were several people he could call. The trick was narrowing it down to the one person who wouldn't fail or betray him. Finally, Zach made a calculated decision, opened his phone again, and dialed his friend and rival. He sat there listening to the phone ring, thinking it was funny how a crisis showed a man who he trusted.

"Yeah?" Robert answered. A car engine purred in the background.

"It's Zach. I need your help."

Robert didn't hesitate. "Sure, man. What's up?"

"Theresa is in trouble, and I haven't been able to get hold of her. I'm still in Chicago."

Creaking leather and the rev of the engine indicated a downshift. Robert's voice retained the same calm precision that made him a deadly opponent in the courtroom. "What's happening? Do you have any specifics?"

"I don't know exactly, but I can tell that something's wrong." A growl of frustration rumbled in Zach's throat, and energy crawled across his skin. It required all of his willpower to maintain control. "I only know that she's upset, and she's drawing power from me."

"I can feel something, too, but I hadn't realized Theresa was the source," Robert said. "Do you know where she is?"

"She should be leaving work or on her way home." Zach supplied the diner's address and Theresa's work schedule.

The roar of the engine intensified as the car accelerated. "I'm down the street from her house. I'll check it out and call you back." Then, after a pause, Robert asked, "Would Isabel be with her?"

The prospect of Isabel being in danger set Zach even further on edge. He clenched his fist, almost crushing his phone. "No, she should be at her grandmother's house."

"Good." Robert's tone conveyed heartfelt relief.

"I'm heading to the airport." Zach grabbed his bag and shoveled his belongings into the duffle.

"Hang in there, man. I'll call you back as soon as I know what's up."

"Thanks, Robert."

"Sure thing. No problem." Robert hung up.

Zach shoved his phone into his pocket and crammed the last of his belongings into his bag. He yanked open the door to his hotel room and stormed out, but a sense of dread rode on his shoulders. No matter how fast he moved, it wouldn't be fast enough.

CHAPTER TWENTY-FOUR

Carl Reynolds stood dead center on Theresa's front walk, blocking her way into the house. Fists clenched, he bristled with malevolence but remained a man, not a wolf. Still, even without a wolf's claws and fangs, his strength was far greater than that of any human.

For precious seconds, Theresa panicked and froze in her tracks. The coil of fear held her imprisoned while he advanced on her. Carl towered over her, and she had to tilt her head back to gaze up at him. He reeked of booze and rage.

"You think you're so much better than the rest of us. Adam's fucking Heart of the Wolf." His mouth contorted into an ugly sneer, and his eyes glowed crimson. The ambient aura roiled like stormy seasons with the force of his rage and resentment.

At well past midnight, none of her neighbors were outside. Trembling from head to toe, she glanced around, but there was no help to be found. Probably for the best. An unarmed human could do nothing to help her and would certainly die if caught between two battling werewolves.

Her throat felt so tight it hurt, but she swallowed and found her voice. "I don't think I'm better than anyone, Carl."

His face turned ruddy. "Don't lie to me, bitch! It's past time someone put you in your place."

Ice formed in her gut, and dark emotions welled up in her soul. Anger. Revulsion. Those were words she'd heard before from Antonio, from others—the language of bullies. Whenever a weaker wolf demonstrated the slightest strength or achieved success, oppressors responded with violence and intimidation.

"You're making a serious mistake," Theresa said, infusing her voice with as much confidence as she could muster. "Who put you up to this? Debra?"

Rage suffused his face. "It was my idea."

"Seriously, didn't anyone ever warn you against letting your little brain make your decisions?"

A growl erupted from Carl's throat, and he lunged at her. Theresa ducked, and his beefy hands closed on empty air. Powerful but clumsy. He worked as a butcher, and his physique reflected the demanding nature of his job. Speed was on her side.

She whipped past him, heart racing and blood pounding. The heavy huff of his breathing filled her hearing, and she only made it to the first step before he caught hold of her ponytail. He yanked so hard that she cried out in both surprise and pain. When he wrenched her head back, she lost her balance and fell. She landed on her rump and scrambled to regain her footing, but he had turned her long tresses into a leash, limiting how far she could get from him.

"Zach is going to kill you," Theresa said, hissing between clenched teeth.

"Hunter is a thousand miles away in Chicago. I made sure he'd be out of the way before I came after you," Carl said with a chortle. He slapped her across the cheek while holding her hair. The blow turned her head, and a trickle of blood filled her mouth. "No one is coming to your rescue, cunt. You're all alone," he taunted, standing over her. "What do you have to say to that?"

Theresa kneeled with her head bowed, hair hanging in her face. The humiliation of being forced to crouch at Carl's feet burned in her center worse than fear. After all the years she'd spent working her nails to the bone to provide a home and a good life for Isabel, what right did this overblown bully have to take it all away?

None. Not a single *fucking* one.

Carl yanked on her hair and delivered a punishing kick to her thigh. "I asked you a question, bitch."

A surge of anger enhanced Theresa's strength. She balled her hands, Primal energy coursed across her skin as her wolf gained dominance. Breathing heavily, she threw back her head to glare. "It's eighteen-hundred miles, dipshit."

"What?" Carl bellowed.

"It's eighteen-hundred miles from here to Chicago." Theresa planted a gut punch in his solar plexus. It drove the wind from his lungs.

Carl doubled over and lost his grip on her hair. Holding his belly, he jeered, "So, you do have spirit. Good, 'cause I'm gonna love breaking—"

Theresa shut his mouth with her fist. The uppercut nailed Carl square on the chin. Blood-trained saliva sprayed, and he staggered.

"Nothing's getting broken," Theresa snarled. "Unless we count *you*."

"Bitch!" Carl sprang, flying through the air. He delivered a sweeping roundhouse punch that packed his total weight behind his knuckles. It shattered her cheekbone and knocked Theresa off her feet.

She hit the ground in a faceplant, skidding across

the wet grass. Talk about a messy facial. Still, lawn topped concrete any day. Spitting out vegetation, Theresa rolled onto her back, only to find a menacing shadow dropping toward her like a sledgehammer.

Heart throbbing, Theresa tucked her knees against her torso. When Carl descended, her soles planted against his chest. Her legs, muscles ablaze, bore the brunt of the burden, but her breasts got crushed. Pain brought stinging tears to her eyes.

Carl grabbed for her throat. "Bitch!"

"For F's sake, find a new insult."

With a guttural grunt, Theresa heaved his unwelcome bulk off with her legs. The sudden removal of his weight freed her to roll forward. Carl reeled backward into the front of her car. Metal shrieked when he smashed into the fender. A river of dollar signs for auto repairs clouded her vision.

She shot upright. An inferno blazed at Theresa's core. Mama Wolf parted her jaws. The howl that penetrated the night from the future queen of the Iron Stone Pack was heard three counties over—across state lines—well into California.

"Bastard! I need that car to go to work."

"You don't get it, do you? You're not going to go to work or anywhere else ever again." Carl hauled himself off the vehicle. He drew a silver knife from a belt sheath. The blade gleamed in the moonlight, and the toxicity wafted on the currents.

Silver killed werewolves, the most lethal substance known to wolf kind. The deadly threat upped the stakes to a life or death gamble, one Theresa aimed to win. Her senses sharped, and unexpected agony erupted as her hands transformed into claws. Bones crunched and reformed—all without the assistance of a dominant wolf.

"Where did you learn to do that?" Carl halted, considering her with newfound wariness. The scent of fear swirled about him. He smelled like prey.

A fundamental change upended Theresa's worldview. "You're afraid," she said with a high tone of astonishment and dawning realization, "of me."

"Am not," Carl denied, but a tremor ran through him. He hung back, holding up the knife like a shield.

"There's no point in lying. I can smell you." Theresa inhaled through her mouth, drawing the aroma deeper. A heady sense of empowerment left her giddy, but she clung to her common sense. Carl might not have claws, but he still had the physical advantages of size and strength.

Time to fix that.

The pack bond flowed through Theresa, and it sprang from a vast reservoir of untapped magic. She had sensed its potential before, but up until now, she'd shied away from tapping into it. No more. With a flick of her willpower, Theresa opened the flood gates. In truth, having never done it before, she hadn't known what to expect. Regardless, the reality caught her wholly unprepared. A deluge of energy rushed like a roaring river, and she struggled to keep from drowning.

Spiritually, Theresa connected to Zach, all his tremendous power at her disposal. Her heart thrummed like a war drum, and before she found the beat, another surge crashed over her head. Robert joined her in psychic communion. As relentless as a hurricane, the Beta wolf's magic poured into her.

On an extrasensory level, she felt all eyes upon them. The entire pack was watching.

A violent transformation wracked Theresa. It hit like a seizure. Excruciating. Convulsive. Blotches clouded her vision. She accidentally knicked her tongue. Blood pooled in her cheeks. In a hot second, her body ripped apart and reknit. She gained height and heft as her physical form contorted into a living tank. Her clothing tore along the seams, exposing the fur covering her skin. She halted the change halfway once she achieved the combat powerhouse of a wolfman.

Make that *wolfwoman*.

Carl yelped. He lunged, aiming the knife at her

heart. Theresa jumped backward. The point of the blade sliced open her shirt and left an extended cut on her chest. Steel gouged deepest into her breast. Night air gusted across her skin. Blood seeped from the sizzling wound.

It would leave a nasty scar.

An angry snarl rumbled in her throat. Theresa retaliated across Carl's lowered guard. As the silver knife entered its downswing, she swung her arms in a broad sweep. Her claws raked a path across his upper arms and chest, shredding both cloth and flesh.

Blood spurted, and Carl shouted at the top of his lungs. Twisting lower, Theresa clamped onto the forearm of his knife hand with her wolf's jaws. She sank her canines deep into his flesh. Heat splashed on her tongue, feeding her bloodlust. She locked her jaw and shook him violently.

The silver knife flew from Carl's hand. Snarling, he threw a roundhouse punch blow that nailed Theresa in the side of the head. A haze fogged her brain, and she lost her bite hold on Carl. He wrenched free and dove for the dropped knife.

The blare of a horn and the revving of a powerful engine shattered the night. The brilliant glare of headlights lit up the yard like a spotlight. Theresa didn't have time to react. She could only watch. The SUV jumped the curb, roaring into her front yard. It smashed full-speed into Carl, sending him flying. For an awful moment, it appeared the vehicle would plow through the front of her house, but then the driver hit the brakes.

Tires screeching, the SUV skidded to a halt. Carl crashed into the old-growth rose bushes lining the front of the bungalow. The briars had wicked-nasty thorns. Carl collapsed into a limp heap atop the shrubs.

In a surreal outtake, realty froze. Theresa cast a frantic glance around, looking for any signs of witnesses. So far, she hadn't noticed any of her neighbors emerge from their houses, but the entire fight couldn't have lasted much more than a minute. However, with the ruckus they were making, it wouldn't be long before someone saw them. Worst case scenario, the police arrived in response to a 911 call, and she got spotted in her half-wolf form.

"Theresa!" The SUV's front door burst open, and Robert Blane bounded from the driver's seat toward her.

"Robert!" Theresa greeted him with a wide smile. She'd never been so happy to see anyone, although a tiny part of her wished he'd arrived a minute later. Now, she would always wonder whether she could've defeated Carl on her own. As soon as the thought crossed her mind, she frowned and shook her head. Never mind, she was better off not knowing, especially since she didn't want to become a murderer.

"Are you injured?" Robert halted a yard away, respecting her space, for which she was darn grateful.

Aches and pains covered every inch of her body. Even her bruises had bruises, but Theresa put on a brave front. "Nothing that won't heal." Filled with sudden uncertainty, she crossed her arms below her breasts. "Carl attacked me."

"I'll deal with him," Robert said grimly, "but we need to get you inside before someone sees you like this. Where's Isabel?"

"She's with my mom. She's safe." Theresa thanked her lucky stars that her daughter hadn't been with her when Carl had attacked. It made her ill to think of how Isabel could have been hurt or even killed.

"Good. I'm glad to hear that." Robert offered the briefest smile, which vanished when he glanced at Carl. A crimson glow ignited in his gaze. With deadly intent, Robert bent to pick up the silver knife. He stalked over to Carl, still passed out in a heap. Robert raised the knife for a killing stroke.

Theresa took a shaky step toward them. "Robert, don't kill him."

Robert cast a glance over his shoulder. "Theresa, I don't want you to watch this. Please, go inside."

Theresa faltered before his steely gaze, but she had been through too much recently to obey without question. She stiffened her spine. "You can't just murder a man in cold blood."

Robert scowled. "He attacked a lower-ranked female without provocation. The penalty is death."

"Shouldn't that be for Adam to decide?"

Silence, and then Robert smiled slowly. "Damn, woman. You're taking this Wolf Queen business to heart, aren't you?"

A flush crept up her throat, making her grateful for the fur covering her skin. Theresa knew that Robert valued justice above all else, so she decided to appeal to his sense of honor. "Killing an unconscious man isn't justice. It's murder. You're too good of a person to sink to this level."

"I'm not half as good as you seem to think, and this bastard doesn't deserve to live," Robert said, slashing the air with the silver blade for emphasis.

"Maybe not, but I don't want his death on my conscience."

"Fair enough," he said, "though a merciful death now will be preferable to what Zach is going to do to him."

Theresa pursed her lips and considered Robert's statement. She knew he had the right of it. Zach would eviscerate Carl when he learned of the attack. His fury would be epic. She shuddered to contemplate it. With any luck, he could be reasoned with once it became clear that she'd suffered no permanent harm. Besides, she could only manage one problem at a time.

"Thank you," she said to Robert.

Just then, a neighbor's front porch light came on, and their front door cracked open. Theresa bolted for the side of the house. She crouched low, followed the hedge, and then jumped the six-foot fence surrounding her backyard with a deft standing leap.

The sound of Mrs. Homer's voice made her pause. The older woman sounded suspicious and fearful. "What's going on over there?"

"There's been a dog attack, ma'am," Robert said, sounding confident and reassuring at the same time. "This man's been bitten pretty bad. You might want to go inside. The animal is still running loose."

"My goodness, I'll do that right away," Mrs. Homer exclaimed. "Thank you so much. Have you called the police yet?"

"Not yet, but I'm about to," Robert said. "If you'd alert animal control, too, I'd appreciate it."

Theresa didn't catch any more of their conversation. Moving with all of her stealth, she made her way to the back door and recovered the spare key she kept hidden beneath the garden bench. After a frustrating minute of pain and tears, she managed to return her claws to hands well enough to manipulate the lock. She let herself in and crept into the front room, where she peered through the window. Her stomach dropped when she spotted the distinct flashing light of a police cruiser.

Hidden behind the curtains, she watched while cop cars and an ambulance congregated in her yard. Carl was taken away on a stretcher. Robert and Sheriff Mahoney formed a huddle, conversing intently.

"Damn it," Theresa muttered to herself. "Sheriff Mahoney looks pissed. He warned me not to put any more men in the hospital."

CHAPTER TWENTY-FIVE

Robert stood on the bungalow's front lawn, watching while the sheriff climbed into his patrol car. All the other law enforcement vehicles had already departed. Theresa had gone inside a while ago, and the last of the nosy neighbors had returned home. During the commotion surrounding Carl Reynold's arrest and removal, Robert had parked his SUV on the curb down the street.

Seated behind the wheel of his vehicle, Sheriff Sly Mahoney, a dominant werewolf and a member of the Iron Stone Pack, rolled down his window. From the thrust of the man's jaw, he had more on his mind than goodbye.

"Is there something I can help you with, Sly?"

Sly pursed his lips, then burst out, "Yeah. Are

you aware this was the second call *this evening* that I've responded to concerning Theresa Russo?"

"I wasn't," Robert said, hiding his surprise.

"There was an incident at the diner." Sly provided a quick recap of the confrontation involving the miners and Theresa. He wrapped up, "Neither incident was technically her fault."

A surge of protectiveness left Robert on edge. Without meaning to, he slapped on his professional lawyer demeanor. "Based on what you've told me, Theresa acted in self-defense. *Both* times."

Sly looked up and smiled. "Easy barrister. I only brought it up because these sorts of disturbances draw unwanted attention to the pack. We lucked out this time. The neighbors heard growling, but no one saw werewolves fighting. At least, no one who was willing to report it."

"I appreciate you bringing it up. Thank you, Sly."

"Yup. Have a nice night, whatever's left of it anyway."

"You, too." Robert waited until the sheriff's taillights vanished in the distance before he strolled to the bungalow's front porch. He took out his phone to check the time—three a.m. on the dot.

Right on cue, it rang. The screen identified the caller as Zachary Hunter.

Robert rubbed the aching muscles in the back of

his neck. He was dead tired and not up for dealing with any more drama. "No rest for the wicked," Robert muttered to himself and then swiped to accept the call. "Zach—"

"How is Theresa?" Zach demanded, clutching his phone to his ear as he plowed his way through the throngs of fellow travelers who seemed to exist for no other purpose than blocking his path. Pent-up aggression rolled off him in seismic tremors, and everyone with a healthy sense of self-preservation instinctively hurried to get out of his way.

All around, the Chicago airport bustled with the morning rush. Fluorescent lighting reflected on the white subway tiles, and a constant stream of announcements sounded from the staticky speaker system. The crowds were thick, and the waits were long, absolute torture for an agitated English werewolf desperate to return home.

"Theresa is fine," Robert replied into the phone. "A bit banged up, but she'll heal."

Relief surged through Zach, and the worst of the strain crushing him eased. "What about Isabel?"

"She's also fine and at her grandmother's house."

"Sorry about biting your head off," Zach said,

apologizing after the fact. "Theresa hasn't been answering her phone."

"Don't sweat it. I get it."

Still jogging, Zach followed the terminal signs leading to his destination. The exertion left him sounding winded. "Can I speak with her?"

"She's inside. I'm outside." Robert placed heavy emphasis on the otherwise innocent-sounding statement. "Do you want me to go inside?"

The implications crashed over Zach with the flattening force of a tsunami. Although he didn't yet possess the hard facts, he understood that Theresa had endured a brutal physical assault. She must be utterly traumatized.

When upset, wolves needed physical contact with their fellow wolves—intimacy. As concerned as Zach felt, he harbored severe reservations about entrusting Theresa to Robert's sole care. This damnable mating game could end before Zach ever set foot on that plane.

The silence stretched.

Robert grunted then asked, "Are you at the airport?"

"Yes. I'm catching the first available flight back." Zach had already checked in online with his air carrier, but there was no avoiding the inevitable—airport security.

The line progressed with agonizing slowness, inching toward the conveyer belt that whisked bags and shoes through the scanners. Nostrils flaring, Zach ground his teeth and hung onto his patience with both claws.

Robert provided a much-needed distraction from the agonizing wait. He related everything that had transpired in Iron Stone while Zach had been away. While he talked, Robert projected steady coolness through the pack bond.

A deadly calm took hold of Zach, far more dangerous than a fit of temper. He was determined to make the bastard who'd hurt Theresa pay, preferably with his miserable life. The focus of his rage had one target—Carl Reynolds.

Miraculously, Zach made it through security without inciting an incident. He retreated to an isolated corner where he dropped his bag to the dirty white tile floor and bent to put on his athletic shoes.

"I'm going to kill that shit stain," Zach said quietly.

Robert grunted. "I was going to do just that myself, but Theresa stopped me. She insisted that Reynolds has to be tried and judged before the pack."

"That's better than he deserves."

"I agree one hundred perfect." A pause, then Robert said, "Listen to me, man. The threat is over. Theresa is safe. Get a grip before you board that airplane. A berserk werewolf would be bad publicity."

Zach snorted. "I already have a publicist."

"Then consider this a word of friendly advice."

Zach's jaw worked. "Right. I'm calm."

"Are you?"

"Cucumbers."

"I've no clue what that means."

Zach tilted his head back, staring at the heavens through the skylights. "Thank you for protecting Theresa."

Robert chuckled. "Theresa pretty much took care of him herself. By the time I got there, he was ready to roll over and submit."

A slow smile spread on Zach's face. "My Theresa?"

"Your Theresa," Robert said with a chuckle. "She managed a partial shift on her own. It was the damnedest thing, Zach. She's making amazing progress."

"She's always had the latent talent. She just needed that push," Zach said, bursting with pride. He'd always believed in Theresa and sensed her immense hidden potential.

"The entire pack experienced her distress last

night. The fight has created a huge stir. It's going to take a while to calm everyone down."

An uneasy notion occurred to Zach, which left him worrying. "How is Theresa doing emotionally? She must be upset."

Robert hesitated then admitted heavily. "To be blunt, I don't know. She ran inside before the police arrived. That was a couple of hours ago."

"Will you check on her, please? Make sure she's okay."

"I figured you'd prefer I kept my distance." Robert's voice held a distinct undercurrent of tension. His defensiveness bled through the pack bond. His attitude was that of a man concerned with upholding friendship and integrity.

Zach found his friend's reaction oddly reassuring. It served as a much-needed reminder of all the reasons why he and Robert were mates in the first place. He exhaled deeply. "I don't want Theresa left alone. Will you stay with her?"

"You trust me?" Robert's pitch rose on a note of astonishment.

"Right now, you're the only one I do trust."

"Thanks, man. I'm honored."

The airport loudspeaker announced: "True Blue Flight 3453 is now boarding."

"My flight is boarding. I've got to go," Zach said. "Tell Theresa I'll be home soon."

"Zach, be damn sure you've got your wolf under control before you board that plane."

"I'm calm." Zach hung up before Robert could nag further. Nothing was keeping him from that flight—not hell or high water.

CHAPTER TWENTY-SIX

The aromatic scent of cooking bacon wafted up the stairs and roused Theresa from a sound sleep. She sniffed the air, stomach rumbling like a tiger's growl, and rolled from the bed. Throwing back the covers, she jumped out of bed. Her bare feet hit the floor with a light thud. In a hurry, she threw on a T-shirt and jeans. The prior evening's activities had left her starving, and she couldn't wait to put food in her belly.

A glance out the window revealed a sky gray with early morning and the red orb of the rising sun low in the eastern sky. That evening, the full moon would shine over Iron Stone, and already, she could hear the irresistible siren song of the wild serenading her, calling her to the forest. Tonight, she and the pack would become wolves and run beneath the canopy of pine trees, gliding across the wooded carpet of needles and dry grasses. They would sing to Mother Moon and hunt deer and hares. They would be home.

Before going downstairs, Theresa called her mother and confirmed that Isabel was all right. She spoke to Isabel for a couple of minutes and then said their goodbyes.

"I'll see you after school, Mama. I love you."

"I love you, too, baby," Theresa said, aware her voice sounded tearful despite her best efforts to remain calm. "Give the phone to Nana."

"I'll drop her at school this morning, just like we planned. Don't worry."

"I won't. Thanks, Mom." Theresa hung up.

Tantalizing smells emanated from downstairs, so Theresa followed her nose. In the kitchen, Robert and Charlaine were engaged in a quiet conversation. Charlaine sat perched on the edge of a barstool, munching a strip of bacon, while Robert cooked breakfast. He wore a fluffy white apron, zipping about the kitchen with surprising agility.

Charlaine noticed her first. "Theresa, you're finally up!"

Robert turned to face her. "Hey, how're you feeling?"

Theresa made a face. "Okay, I guess. I'm hungry enough to eat a horse. Not kidding."

Charlaine laughed and patted the other stool. "From what I've heard, you earned your appetite last night. Here, sit down and eat. Robert is the best breakfast chef this side of the Mississippi."

"Not that much of a boast anymore since we moved to Nevada," Robert said. "We have eggs, toast, and bacon, and coffee, and orange juice. What would you like?"

"All of that sounds fine."

Theresa frowned, embarrassed that they'd brought their food. Her cupboard would remain bare until she figured out how to pay the rent due on Friday. As much as she dreaded it, she would have to confront Antonio about the late child support he owed her.

After a moment of hesitation, she settled on the stool and accepted the plate of food that Robert handed her. She set it down in front of her, picked up a fork, and took an experimental jab at the scrambled eggs.

Robert watched her with thoughtful dark eyes and snickered. "Please, try a bite. I promise it won't kill you."

"It's not that. Everything smells delicious." She didn't want to offend him, so she dug in with gusto.

The food was fantastic, and she fell on it with the appetite of a hungry wolf.

"Does it meet with your approval?" Robert asked with a cheeky grin.

Theresa swallowed a large bite of food and nodded. "Delicious."

Charlaine laughed at her expression. "Didn't think he had it in him, did you?"

"Can I take the Fifth?" Theresa asked, cracking a joke, even though her thoughts had turned down a more serious path. She still had no explanation for why two of the pack's most dominant members were in her kitchen.

Charlaine dropped a reassuring pat on her shoulder. "What's wrong, Theresa?"

Theresa licked her lips. "Am I in trouble?"

Both dominant wolves regarded Theresa with surprise.

"Not at all," Robert said. "Why would you think that?"

"Last night, I caused quite a stir," Theresa said.

Charlaine slapped a hand to the countertop. "That's one hell of an understatement. You have the entire pack worked up."

Theresa winced and set down her fork. She believed Charlaine, even though she had no idea how such a thing could have happened. The events of the prior evening still held a dreamlike quality. No, make that nightmarish. It seemed reasonable that it must have something to do with the pack's newborn magic, but she had no idea how it linked to her.

Robert leaned forward. He had a compelling gaze, and she couldn't tear her eyes away. Immense power lurked behind that warm smile, a clear rival for Zach. She suspected she couldn't have judged the more dominant male even if they stood side-by-side before her.

"Theresa, the other night, you managed to awaken something in this pack that no dominant wolf has been able to do since the old leaders died," he said. "You connected every member from Alpha to Omega. Your courage inspired the empathy and sense of unity that binds a healthy pack together."

"Carl attacked me because I inspire fear and jealousy," she said, her voice sounding bitter despite her best effort to dismiss the emotion.

"There are always going to be people who react like that." Charlaine smoothed her hand along Theresa's arm. "The important thing is not to let them get to you because they are the minority."

Robert regarded Theresa with respect, which she found flattering. However, the cool calculation apparent in his demeanor frightened her. "Do you understand what it all means?" he asked.

Theresa shook her head. "Not a clue."

"It means you're a linchpin, Theresa," Charlaine said. "You have the potential to make this pack whole and healthy again."

She frowned in dismay. "What if I don't want to be a linchpin?"

"You may not have a choice," Robert said. "Without a linchpin, this pack will fall apart, and we'll be right back where we started—chaos."

Theresa looked away and picked up a slice of bacon from her plate. She devoured it in silence, unable to think of anything clever or appropriate to say.

Charlaine snorted. "Smooth, Cuz, real smooth."

"Guess my motivational speaking needs some work, huh?" Sounding chagrined, Robert turned back to the stove and removed the last of the bacon from the skillet. He shut off the burner and set about cleaning up the cooking area, carrying pans to the sink.

"You think?" Charlaine grinned and got up to help him by wiping down the countertop.

A vehicle turned into her driveway, and the engine shut off. A car door opened and shut. They all turned toward the sound. The ambient aura shifted with the addition of another wolf. Robert and Charlaine both grew alert.

For a second, Theresa panicked, thinking that it must be Adam. Tension gathered in her shoulders and throughout her back. Undoubtedly, the Alpha must have heard from the sheriff already. Was he so angry that he'd come to see her in person instead of summoning her to him?

But then, Theresa just *knew*. She stood, pushing out the chair. "It's Zach!" she exclaimed, jumping to her feet.

Charlaine shot her a look. "How can you tell?"

"I just can," Theresa said. Across the distance, even with walls between them, Theresa sensed his proximity through the pack bond.

"Theresa!" Zach called urgently from the front yard.

Zach and Theresa rushed together and met on the front porch. Taking a running leap, Theresa vaulted into the air and flew into his open arms with a strangled cry. She locked her hands behind his neck and grasped his hips with her knees, clinging to him. His arms came around her, supporting and imprisoning her.

"You had me worried sick, love." Zach kissed her full on the lips, rough and passionate, coaxing her mouth open so he could delve deeper. He wore his favorite beaten leather jacket that felt as soft as suede. It smelled rich and luxuriant, just like Zach.

Theresa lost herself in an erotic haze that defined her entire existence from the moment he touched her. He plundered her mouth, tasting her, taking her with a penetrating motion that mirrored the most primal act. His hard body pressed against hers, chest to chest, hip to hip. She clung to him with her legs, riding him, and their crotches rubbed together, creating exquisite sensations. Theresa whimpered her need into his mouth, and Zach moaned in lusty reply.

Robert cleared his throat. "Well..."

Charlaine's sultry chuckle intruded on Theresa's passion. "We should leave these lovebirds alone."

Suddenly self-conscious, Theresa released her hold on Zach and ended the kiss by pulling away. He opened his arms, and she slid down his body, landing on her feet. Flushing, she stared at the front of his shirt. An awkward silence settled over them.

Robert and Charlaine laughed at their obvious embarrassment, and the air thrummed with the newborn magic that bound all of them together into a cohesive unit. In just a week, all of the wolves of Iron Stone had progressed from a disjointed band to interconnected members of a big family. They were finally a proper pack.

Zach offered Robert his hand. "Thanks for your help, mate."

Robert grasped Zach's forearm. "Sure thing."

Theresa tilted her head, evaluating the two dominant males. Without intending to, she found herself comparing them with thinly veiled speculation. The men were an impressive pair, close to being an even match within an inch in height. Robert outweighed Zach, a mass difference based on twenty pounds of pure muscle that might make all the difference in a fight. While the Englishman had a black belt in martial arts, Robert came from a large pack known for their violent conflicts. He had to be familiar with a more down-and-dirty style of fighting.

Under her scrutiny, the males squared off. Their reaction was predictable and primal, maybe even inevitable. Their handshake broke. Zach narrowed his eyes, squared his shoulders, and his hands clenched into fists. The room roiled with the surge of power that flowed from him, so his aura swirled with red and ochre. Robert assumed a more defensive posture, but his body language was that of a dominant wolf. There was no doubt that he would respond with violence if Zach initiated a fight.

"Robert, this is wrong. Think about what you're about to do," Charlaine said, tone sharp. Her command cut through the tension and set everyone off-balance.

Theresa gasped in dismay, coming to her senses. Acting on impulse, she stepped between the men and grabbed hold of the ambient aura, exerting her presence as a cooling influence over the males. To her shock, it worked, and the aggressive fog thinned.

Reaching out, she placed a hand on Zach's chest. She caught his gaze and held it. "Stop, please. I don't want you fighting over me."

Robert took a step back. "I don't want to fight you, my friend. Theresa, no offense intended. You're a beautiful woman."

She flashed a genuine smile. "None taken."

Zach ran a hand through his hair. Beneath her touch, he relaxed, and his heartbeat slowed. "Sorry," he said, speaking to Robert. "I'm on edge."

"Not a problem," Robert said, retreating toward the door. "Come on, Char. Let's head home and grab some shut-eye."

"Sounds good to me, but I have to be at work in two hours," Charlaine said with a wry smile. Her hands brushed Theresa's shoulders. "Call me if you need anything, honey."

Theresa smiled. "I will. I promise. Thank you both for coming over."

The door closed behind them with a final thud, and Zach blew out a long breath. He glanced at her, and his expression shifted, betraying the turmoil in his thoughts. He looked torn between cracking a joke and saying something world-ending serious.

Theresa launched herself at him, and he caught her out of the air. His arms engulfed her, holding her safe, protecting her from all of the bad things in the world. He was her strength, her anchor, her shelter from the storm. With a stifled sob, Theresa buried her face against his chest. She didn't break down in tears, but she did emit a wet hiccup. Sniffling, she clung to him for a long time, taking comfort from the fact that he would be at her side no matter what bad thing happened next, and he held her in return.

He hooked an arm beneath her knees, and she settled her arms around his neck. Then, he carried her into the family room and sat down on the small loveseat with her on his lap. He arranged her so she sat facing him, and his hands stroked her long hair.

"Do you feel up to talking?"

She agreed with a quick jerk of her head. "Yes. I think so."

He pressed a soft kiss to her forehead. "Go ahead. I'm here for you."

※

"And that's pretty much everything," Theresa concluded her tale of the prior evening's events. It had taken the better part of an hour, but she had brought Zach up to speed. He knew everything about what had happened at the diner and the confrontation that followed with Carl. He had listened intently, interrupting with the occasional question, but otherwise gave her his undivided attention.

Throughout the conversation, their positions had shifted several times. At the moment, he lay stretched out across the loveseat with his head in her lap. The short couch wasn't long enough to accommodate his frame, so his legs dangled over the side.

Theresa combed her fingers through his blond hair, loving the silky texture, loving the intimacy even more. This was her daydream—them talking and touching. Together. She had other dreams as well, dark fantasies set against the backdrop of the bedroom, but also a wistful image of them spending time as a family—laughing and walking while Isabel played on a swing. When she dared indulge her heart's desire, a vision filled her mind of a baby with the bluest eyes cradled to her breast.

"I'm sorry, love. What an awful time you've had," Zach said. "Thank God you and Isabel are safe."

"Yes, I'm grateful Isabel wasn't with me last night."

Anger flashed in Zach's eyes, and his grim expression alluded to dark thoughts. He had not made a secret of the fact that he was unhappy that Carl yet lived. "The pack will meet tonight to judge Reynolds."

Theresa shared his discontent for different

reasons. She also faced judgment. As much as she might wish it, Adam would not forget about her infraction, showing her true strength to humans. Later. She would deal with it later. For the moment, she needed downtime to recover from the latest ordeal before she faced the next.

Determined to distract him, she reached out and laid a hand on his arm. "It'll be okay," she said in a soothing tone. "You'll see."

He grunted, and the stubborn set of his jaw remained, but he appeared mollified. "I wish I'd been here last night to protect you."

Her lips curved in a coy smile, and she fluttered her lashes at him. "My hero..."

"Right." His ironic grin played well with her playfulness. "From what I hear, you managed just fine without me."

"I was lucky," Theresa said, dropping her flirtatious façade.

Suddenly serious, she lost her smile and wrung her hands. The unresolved issue of Carl weighed on her. Adam and the other dominant males still might decide to kill him.

Zach sat up and captured her hands between his own. A light entered his eyes. Desire and pride shone with such intensity that her insides melted with pleasure. "You shifted on your own. I'm damn proud of you, Theresa."

"Oh, I don't know. It was mostly luck," she disagreed bashfully.

"Such bollocks." He said it with a grin, thus removing any sting from the words.

Pleased, Theresa scooted closer to him, so her toes touched his leg. In response, he reached down and drew her feet into his lap. His fingertips dug into her instep, creating a delicious sensation that caused her to shiver as he massaged her feet. They fell silent for a moment, him thoughtful, her rendered speechless by his touch.

Her thoughts drifted, and she spoke without thinking. "The worst of it is that I lost my job."

"Good riddance," Zach said. "Those bastards didn't treat you right."

Annoyance made her tense up. Her desperate finances were never far from her mind, and his easy dismissal of her job wasn't what she wanted to hear.

"That's easy for you to say, but not everyone is a bestselling author, Zach, or born rich."

His brow rose, and he stopped rubbing her feet. "Money isn't everything, Theresa."

"It is when you don't have any."

She hadn't meant to snap at him, to sound so accusing and envious, but the words just slipped out. There were times when she resented his privileged upbringing, even though the feelings of jealousy shamed her.

He frowned, but his eyes were kind, despite the sharpness of her tone. "Love, I'll give you however much you need."

Theresa's jaw set, and she climbed to her feet. "I'm not taking money from you, Zach. I've worked hard to be independent. I shouldn't lose everything because a couple of jerks couldn't keep their hands to themselves."

He remained seated, tilting his head to gaze up at her. "You're making too much of this, love. It was a crap job, in a crap diner, working for crap people. You'll do better. You are better."

Theresa's exasperation hit a new high. "Zach," she said, slow and soft, "I'd appreciate a little sympathy. I've got a child to think of. There's rent, utilities, food."

"If you won't accept my money, then move in with me."

Her jaw dropped, and her heart stopped before resuming with a staccato beat. She swallowed before recovering her voice. "I...I can't! Zachary Hunter, I have a six-year-old daughter. How would that look?"

Zach grinned. "Like you're having a passionate and torrid affair with me?"

Theresa aimed a finger at his chest. Her voice held a low note of warning. "I thought you wrote mysteries, not trashy romances."

"Ouch." He covered his heart with his hand, but

the smug smirk never left his lips. "I guess that's a 'no' to you being my kept woman, eh?"

"No would be correct."

Unable to hide her hurt feelings, she turned away. His cavalier attitude stung. Theresa wanted empathy and support, not blatant insensitivity and mockery. Sure, Zach was a jokester, but his humor had never been intentionally cruel. Before.

Zach remained silent for what must have been a full minute. Every second felt like a tiny eternity, dragging past, so she almost stopped breathing with the anticipation of what he would say next.

When at last he spoke, his accent emerged crisp and clipped. "You don't want me fighting to protect you or to prove my worth as your mate. You won't accept my protection from your ex-husband. You refused my financial assistance. It's starting to feel like there's no place for me in your life, Theresa."

She shuddered and blinked against hot tears. Her throat closed, and she had to shake her head to communicate the wrongness of what he'd just said.

It took longer than she liked to find her voice. "That's not true," she said, speaking so low she whispered the denial.

"Then what is true, love? Tell me, but I need to know what's going through that mysterious head of yours."

The very idea that he'd called her mysterious was

laughable. "Me? What about you? With your ambush attraction and your I-can't-explain-myself courtship?"

"Theresa, I realize my courtship caught you off-guard, but is it that much of a surprise? Three years—"

"Three years of platonic friendship, Zach. At first, when you started coming around, I hoped..." She flushed with acute embarrassment.

"I've been right here the whole time, waiting for you."

The implicit message left her stunned; however, there was no denying the truth. Zach had been there the whole time. Three years of friendship dates to movies and restaurants, picnics at the park with Isabel, summer evenings under the stars, Thanksgiving dinners, and Christmas mornings together. He maintained her car and fixed her leaky pipes. Zach was her best friend in the truest sense. She cried against his shoulder, and when she was down, he made her laugh.

Dry-mouthed, she faced him. "You're saying I only had to reach out and take what I wanted this whole time?"

Zach tipped his head in a slight nod.

Theresa felt like a fool, as if he'd played some vast, cruel joke at her expense. She crossed her arms and fought for a semblance of composure. "Tuesday,

I went shopping with Charlaine, and she told me you've chased off every other male that's even come near me. Is that true?"

His features worked with protest, but the truth of it was in his eyes. "Bloody hell, Theresa, you make it sound like I was marking my territory. I don't treat you like a possession. I respect you as a person."

"That's not an answer," she said. "What about Mark?"

His brow knit. "Who?"

"The pilot I dated two years ago," she said. "He took me out twice and then just stopped calling. At the time, I thought he was just another jerk. Did you have something to do with that?"

Zach's lips compressed, giving Theresa her answer.

"My God, Zach! You've got some nerve!" She threw up her hands. Keeping his attraction to her a secret for three years was one thing, but driving off other suitors behind her back was too much.

She'd had more than enough of his close-lipped behavior, which seemed to be at the root of every misunderstanding and disagreement they'd had. But, on some level, she was also to blame—her deep-seated insecurity and fear of losing her independence. It took two to tango.

"I'm going upstairs to take a shower," she said. The time alone would allow her to cool down.

She started for the stairs. Zach sprang into her path, moving with strength and grace. Purely masculine. Masterful. His earthy, musky aroma flooded her nostrils. An adrenaline rush left Theresa trembling with excitement and arousal.

"Theresa, you can fault me for having waited too long," he said, "but if I let you walk up those stairs, then I'm committing the same mistake twice. There are two sides to every story, and you're going to hear mine."

Zach advanced then, encroaching on her personal space, and his power blew across her skin, hot and dry like a desert storm. Head high, shoulders square, he adopted an authoritative stance. Theresa tilted her head back, assessing her options—advance or retreat. Without a doubt, she wasn't getting past him.

Their gazes locked, and Zach patiently awaited her decision. A snarl issued from her throat, and she bared her teeth in a display of aggression. Bristling, Theresa darted in, closing the inches separating them, and shot onto her tiptoes. Her fingers grasped the front of his shirt and then dug into the muscular wall of his chest for support.

In a real fight, he would have maintained a close guard on his throat, but courtship skirmishes required the male to take certain risks. Throat rumbling, she drove for his throat, and he took no defensive action. With the flash of teeth, she nipped the spot just below his ear. He growled deep in his chest, a lusty sound that reverberated. Nostrils flaring, she tasted his flesh and ran her tongue along the side of his throat to lap up the salty blood as his beard stubble abraded her tongue. Almost as soon as she tasted him, the small wound healed, thanks to his accelerated healing.

Just in case he wasn't paying attention, she bit him again, nipping his earlobe. This time, she took care not to break the skin, closing her teeth over the meaty tidbit of flesh. Theresa chomped once, twice, and then gave it a quick lick and a kiss. Zach shook with silent laughter, and they separated enough to allow their gazes to meet. His eyes, the brightest blue of sea or sky, shone with carefree humor. His arms closed about her, and she giggled as he swept her off her feet.

"Well played. Your feminine wiles have won this round."

Theresa laughed. "I submit, and you accuse me of deception. I'm wounded."

Zach snickered. "My arse. I take it you're listening?"

She ran her fingers up the front of his shirt until she reached the collar and then tightened the two sides of the V-neckline, tugging playfully. "I'm listening."

He took a seat and set her on his lap. Theresa scooted back so her bottom rested on a couch cushion. Her legs remained across the top of Zach's thighs. She fell against the throw pillows, gazing up at him, and he held her hand.

Silence reigned. Zach exhaled audibly.

"Zach?"

"Yeah?"

"Is it really that hard for you to put your feelings into words? Isn't this what you do for a living? Use words to express emotions?"

He snorted and gently squeezed her fingers. "I write crime novels, love. No one talks about their feelings but the bad guy."

Theresa laughed and shook her head. "Zach, do you remember last year when your father passed away?"

"Hard to forget."

"At the funeral, you talked about what a great guy he was and how you always knew you were loved because he never let a day pass without saying it."

The lines of his face contorted into a harsh mask of sorrow. Abruptly, he looked exhausted. "Great story, wasn't it? Not a dry eye in the house. Course, I made the whole thing up. The bastard never said it once my entire life, not even as he lay dying, but I made them believe it. I sold it."

"It was a great story, Zach. You always tell the best stories." Theresa met and held his eyes, staring soul deep. She hated reminding him of the painful event, but it was necessary to get her point across. "Afterward, I held you when you cried. Do you remember that, too?"

"I'll never forget." His gaze never wavered. He faced her without a hint of evasion or fear, comfortable with her knowing his feelings in the most intimate ways.

She wished that he would consistently demonstrate such openness with her. If only she could get past his aversion to emotional intimacy and then overcome her distrustful nature, maybe then all of their problems could be worked out.

"Zach, don't tell me any stories. You don't need to tell me stories. Just tell me the truth."

His jaw worked, and he nodded, obviously thinking it through. Wetting her lips, Theresa gave him the time he needed and didn't interrupt. He would come to her, or he wouldn't, but it had to be his choice.

"The first time I saw you at the market, I just knew. I felt you here." He placed his closed fist over his breast. "It was as if I felt my heart for the first time. I ached for you."

"Zach, we met at Adam's house." Theresa's blush burned her face. His confession pleased her so much she squelched the impulse to squirm. At the same time, it left her confused.

With a slight shake of his head, he flashed a wry smile. "I saw you, love. It was that corner market down the street from your house. Isabel was with you—pitching an absolute fit—and you had your hands full trying to manage her and the cart. You didn't even notice me watching."

"The terrible twos," she said with a surreal sense of disbelief. She didn't recall the specific incident, but it had been a common enough occurrence that she could envision it. "Isabel was a handful. I can't believe you saw that and didn't head in the opposite direction."

"She wasn't all that terrifying," Zach said with a quick grin. He squeezed her fingers, providing her with a rock-steady strength to cling to in her turmoil. "At the time, I assumed you already had a mate, or I'd have introduced myself right then and there."

Theresa winced, but she had no choice but to acknowledge the truth of the matter. The vast majority of wolves mated for life. It would have been logical for him to think her already committed to another man.

"That would've been a reasonable assumption," she said.

"I asked some discreet questions and found out about your ex-husband," he said. "By the time we were introduced, I knew I had to win you."

The boldness of his declaration shocked but also pleased her. She flushed and sat up straighter. "And yet, here we are three years later...."

"Theresa, you were so shy and uncertain then, especially around me. I knew you'd been abused under Zanatos's rule, and there was Isabel to consider, too."

"So you waited." The enormity of his investment in courting her began to sink in, but it was more than she could process—more than could be believed.

He inclined his head, a slight tip, eyes bright. "And so I waited."

"You didn't want me submitting," Theresa said and looked away. "You assumed I'd accept a dominant male even if I didn't want him."

Zach stiffened and held her hand hard enough to hurt. His mouth adopted a downward turn. "Bollocks. Don't twist it. I waited so you'd have time to get to know me. I wanted to earn your trust. More than anything, I had to be sure that you chose me because you wanted me."

Theresa pursed her lips in a thoughtful gesture.

"What changed? How did you go from waiting one day to initiating an active courtship right before this competition for pack leader?"

Zach's grip on her remained tight, allowing her to feel the strain his lean frame endured due to bunched and corded muscles. His lips compressed, and his jaws ground together. The tension between them soared. For a moment, she thought he would refuse to provide her with an answer once again. Then, he exhaled, releasing a pent-up breath.

"Adam came to see me Saturday afternoon," Zach said. "He told me that he intended to retire and that Robert and I would be in competition to become the new Alpha. There was nothing I hadn't known all along."

"But?" Theresa stroked a hand across his forearm, at least so far as his hold on her permitted. "I sense a big but. Is it because Robert is bisexual?"

Zach's brow shot up, and his mouth opened. "You know about Robert's orientation?"

His surprise forced a giggle from her. "Of course, I know. Robert spends as much time looking at men as he does women."

Zach snorted and shook his head. "Just keep what you know to yourself, love. Adam would use it as ammunition in his vendetta."

The deadly serious nature of his demeanor scared her. "What does Adam want from you?"

"Adam would rather I kill Robert than allow a black man to become the new leader." Zach spat the words out, giving voice to the ugly truth. The light in his eyes was murderous, and restrained violence defined his every move.

Theresa gasped and strained against his grip. This time, he let her go, and she pressed a hand to her throat in heartfelt disbelief. "Adam said that?"

"Yes, he did," Zach said, speaking as if he had something nasty in his mouth.

Theresa stared at him in shock. The pack's Alpha had saved them all from abusive leaders and had long been regarded as a hero. Her recent disillusionment with Adam aside, she still didn't want to believe such a thing could be true.

"I don't get it," she said. "We're not human. We're wolves. Discriminating against someone for the color of their skin is like holding the shade of their fur against them."

A sardonic smile twisted Zach's lips. "Believe me, pet, there are those of our kind so elitist and narrow-minded that they do just that. Frankly, love, I'd rather leave Nevada and head home to London than kill a man for such a reason."

She had no desire to undermine him, but particular inescapable possibilities needed to be addressed. "There's no guarantee that you'd win, Zach."

He continued to smile and met her eyes without wavering. "I know that, too. I have even less desire to die to please Adam Teller's purist ideals."

The dark colors and calm of his aura communicated the true nature of his resolve. She understood then where his thoughts were heading, and it chilled her to the bone. "You're thinking of leaving Iron Stone," Theresa said.

Zach nodded. "After I spoke with Adam, I knew my time for courting had run out. I fully intend to take you and Isabel with me if I'm forced to go."

Theresa sat in mute silence, attempting to process it, to make some sense of the news. She hurt for Zach, but with each passing second, an absolute certainty became increasingly evident.

"I can't leave, Zach," she said softly, staring at him with her heart in her eyes. "You can't leave either. We're all connected now to one another. Sure there are a few bad people, but there are many more good ones who need us. The pack magic binds us."

His grim expression, the tilt of his chin, the look in his eyes acknowledged the reality of what she said. "I won't go without you, Theresa."

"Maybe you and Robert won't have to fight," she said, grasping at straws, desperate to find some other solution to their dilemma.

Zach gave a slow, inevitable shake of his head. "Robert and I are both too dominant for this to have any other outcome. Even if we agree not to kill each other, instinct always takes over once combat starts. You saw what almost happened in the kitchen this morning."

She hugged Zach fiercely, absolutely terrified of losing him. "I refuse to believe the only solution is violence. We'll figure something out. We have to."

"All right. We'll figure something out," he agreed, but his voice lacked conviction. The poor man appeared exhausted with dark circles under his eyes and a wan complexion. The scruff on his jaw alluded to more than twenty-four hours since the last time he'd shaved. His haggard appearance reminded her that he'd traveled all night to be at her side. Robert had said it was a miracle Zach had made it through airport security without an incident.

"You look tired," she said.

"I'm shagged out."

She put a comforting hand on his arm, rubbing the bones in his wrist and then working her way up along the tense muscles in his shoulder. "You should get some sleep."

A low groan of pleasure rumbled in his throat, and he started to rise. "I'll head home and crash for a few hours."

She caught his hand and gripped his fingers. Her

heart beat faster, and she ached to her very core, longing for his touch. "Don't go."

Zach glanced back with an unspoken question on his face.

"You can sleep here," she said, maybe too fast. Heat swept her cheeks. "That is if you'd like to stay."

His wolfish grin and the suggestive gleam in his eyes made her flush hotter. His chuckle stirred her insides, and her breath hitched in her throat. "Love, that's an invitation that I can't refuse."

CHAPTER TWENTY-SEVEN

Zach had a nice view of Theresa's sweet, round arse as they mounted the stairs. He had an incredible hard-on, making his already tight pants unbearable. The seductive sway of her hips tempted him deeper into arousal.

"Did you get any sleep at all last night?" Theresa asked.

"Not much." He'd remained tense the entire flight from Chicago to Reno until his airplane had set down at the airport. The long drive home had further tried his patience. Only now that he was home did Zach feel like he could relax.

Theresa reached the top of the stairs and turned back to face him. Zach mustered a tired smile to reassure her, but his energy was at a low ebb, rendering his mind sluggish. He took the two final steps with one stride.

"Your eyes are pretty bloodshot." Theresa rose on her toes to close the distance between them. She pressed her palms to his scruffy cheeks and then pushed a stray lock of his blond hair away from his forehead.

"I'm knackered."

Zach closed his eyes, indulging the simple pleasure of being touched. He inhaled, drinking in her familiar scent, awakening the powerful spiritual connection between them so that his wolf spilled into hers and their auras ran together like wet paint on a canvas.

Her hands slid to his shoulders, and her fingertips dug into the taut muscles there, wringing a groan of pleasure from him. She pulled his face toward her and took his mouth in a lusty kiss. Then, her tongue parted his lips and rubbed against his teeth to the roof of his mouth. It woke him up faster than a sonic boom. Her boldness delighted him, and he submitted to her advances, eager to encourage her confidence.

Energy flowed between them—buzz and hum, burn and sting—and an adrenaline spike jolted Zach from his reverie. His eyelids lifted, catching a glimpse of Theresa's intent expression. Her eyes were closed, long lashes caressing her flawless skin.

She tasted like seduction and sin as she devoured his mouth, taking from him, claiming him with newfound confidence. She drew on his power with perfect impunity.

Any other wolf taking such liberties would have triggered an aggressive response, but she only drove him to an unsustainable height of arousal. Their courtship dance demanded such exchanges, increasing levels of intimacy until they chose to take the oath of mating together. Once mated, their wolves would be irrevocably bound together for life, to be parted only by death.

A rumble began in his throat and spread, creating a resonating vibration throughout his chest, communicating his sexual excitement. With a giggle, Theresa broke the kiss and turned her face into his throat. She pressed fluttering kisses along the underside of his jaw and then created a trail down the column of his neck.

With a huff, Zach tilted his head back to grant Theresa full access to his throat. She caught hold of his hands and backed, leading him toward the bedroom. When they passed the mirror in the hall, Zach glanced into the mirror, and his wolf stared back at him. His eyes were solid blue with slit black pupils, no whites showing, glowing within his face. The sight brought him up short, and he halted in his tracks, causing Theresa to whine in protest. She tugged at his arms, attempting to compel him to resume movement.

"My control is slipping," Zach said in a gruff voice.

"That's the plan." Theresa flashed a mischievous grin and writhed, so her full breasts pressed against his chest. Her nipples were erect buds, straining against the cotton of her shirt.

Zach sucked down a sharp breath, and his throat reverberated with a soft growl, which he modulated to a rough chuckle. "You saucy minx."

"Guilty as charged." She laughed and rubbed up against him again, rolling her hips so her mons bumped against his upper thighs, her stomach pressed to the prominent bulge in his pants.

"Keep that up, and I'm going to take you against this wall." He snarled the threat, provoking further giggles from her. He inhaled a deep breath, and the scent of her arousal flooded his nostrils. It was enough to drive him mad.

"Promises, promises." She fluttered her long lashes and dodged his attempt to scoop her into his arms. Her laughter taunted him, leading him onward, a siren's call, straight off the precipice into desire.

Playing the saucy temptress, Theresa evaded Zach's arms but by mere inches. His growl of frustration inspired her to put forth a burst of speed, racing toward the bedroom with him hot on her heels. He caught her in the entryway, and his mighty arms closed about her waist. Theresa shrieked when he yanked her off her feet and dropped her facedown down onto the bed.

"How long do we have until we need to get Isabel from school?" Zach asked. His hot breath huffed against the nape of her neck.

He encircled her waist with his arms, pressing his broad chest to her back, and her ass pushed against his groin. His burgeoning erection strained against the denim of his jeans, jutting against her buttocks. She shivered, titillated and yet nervous, so aroused that the sensitive flesh between her thighs ached.

"We should leave by two to find parking and be there on time." Theresa whimpered and bucked her hips, longing to feel him riding her, even if her only satisfaction came from dry humping him through their clothing.

He snickered. "Plenty of time then."

"Plenty of time for what?"

"You'll see," he said in a smug tone, insufferably so, but she did not mind. The man had her under his spell, and she was so very eager to please him.

She cried out in frustration when Zach lifted his torso, supporting his weight on his arms, and then she reached behind her back with grasping fingers, seeking to hold him to her.

He chuckled and evaded her hands. "One second, pet."

"I hate waiting." Theresa pouted and turned her head to the side so she could see him.

"You sound just like Isabel."

"Isabel doesn't like waiting either."

She watched from beneath hooded lids as he shrugged out of his jacket and set it aside on the nightstand. He hooked his fingers beneath the bottom of his shirt and pulled it over his head. She coveted his powerful body with her gaze. Dark blond hair covered the broad expanse of his chest, and corded steel muscles rippled beneath his tanned skin. His tight pants clung to his ass and long legs like a second skin.

A strand of blond hair flopped onto his forehead, and he flashed a crooked smile. With a quick puff, he blew the hair from his eye. His boyish grin touched her heart, creating a painful ache, reminding her how much she adored and valued him.

Uncertainty and doubt overshadowed her, causing Theresa to worry her lower lip with her teeth. She still had personal reservations. Were they about to ruin a good friendship? She couldn't stand to lose him if things didn't work out. So much at risk, so much to gain.

Twisting onto her side, she gazed up at him. "Zach, I'm not ready to commit to a mate bond yet," she said, wanting no misunderstandings between them.

Zach settled lightly on the bed beside her, moving with the dedicated grace and precision of a predator. His bulk took up most of her full-size mattress, a sharp reminder of how he dwarfed her. The hunger in his eyes made her insides melt. She felt so incredibly desirable beneath his admiring gaze.

He cocked his head and considered her for long enough that she stopped breathing for several seconds. "Let's be specific, shall we?" he asked eventually. "Sex seals the mate bond but only after we take the vow. You tell me what's allowed and what's not. I'll respect your limits."

Her face heated. Theresa exhaled and chose her words with care. The last thing she wanted was to hurt or offend him. "I want to make love with you, Zach. I'm just not ready to take a vow with you yet. We can consummate our relationship, but I want to use protection. Is that okay?"

"So, I can do this?" His hand slid across her flat stomach and covered her breast, teasing her with a light squeeze, so her heart leaped within her breast and heat pooled in her abdomen.

"Yes," she said in a strangled voice.

"And this?" He leaned forward, and the tip of his tongue flickered against her lips. "What if I want to lick and taste every delicious inch of your pussy? Can I do that too?"

"Yes," Theresa said as her core clenched in anticipation, drenching with wetness. "And yes, please."

His smile grew wider. "You're demanding sex without strings? Who am I to complain?"

Laughing, she touched his face with her fingers, tracing his high cheekbones. "So, you're not upset?"

"No. Why would I be?"

Zach moved forward, using his arm to support his upper body, and swooped to capture her mouth in a passionate kiss. Their lips met, smashed together, parted, and clung. The kiss modulated, growing softer, and Zach suckled her upper lip, grazing the tender flesh with his teeth, and then released her. He touched the middle of her back, brushing her dark hair aside. When he kissed the nape of her neck, the stubble of his beard scraped across her skin. Delicious tingles ran up and down her spine.

"You need to shave," she said, giggling even as

the folds of her sex heated and clenched, panties growing wet with proof of her arousal.

He kissed her, lips heavy, and his shoulder-length blond hair spilled to conceal one of his blue eyes. The other gleamed with deviltry. He rubbed his face against hers, so his scruff abraded the tender skin of her jaw and throat. "Don't you like my beard, love?"

"I like my men clean-shaven," Theresa drawled and smirked.

His brow rose, and his expression grew dangerous. "Man."

"Man?" she asked as if she didn't understand.

"You mean your clean-shaven man." Zach's open palm smacked her denim-clad ass.

Theresa jumped and squealed, giggling as she tried to escape, but he pinned her down with one lazy hand on the middle of her back. Those clever fingertips fluttered across her sides, tickling so that she dissolved into helpless laughter.

After several failed attempts at escape, Theresa gasped and surrendered. "You win. Man, man!"

"Damn straight," Zach said, laughing.

With a deft action, he hooked the bottom of her shirt and drew it over her head. Theresa cooperated, lifting so that the garment slid over her skin, leaving her bare to his gaze. She wore no bra. She settled face down on the mattress, luxuriating in the way her full breasts smashed against her chest and the sheets agitated her sensitive nipples.

He lowered his face to press a trail of butterfly kisses along the length of her spine. The rough stubble of his jaw created a startling contrast to the silken feel of his long hair as it trailed across her skin. He settled some of his weight atop her lower body, pinning her legs beneath his own.

"You're so beautiful, Theresa," Zach whispered, kissing her nape. "I've fantasized about you for so long."

She blinked and struggled to focus. After a second, her lust-addled mind brought his meaning into focus. Between them, they had years of mutual longing. A cold splash of shock hit her. Her heart thudded in her chest before missing a beat. She ached with love for him, so much so that her throat closed and her eyes filled with tears.

Zach stilled. No doubt, he had smelled her sorrow. "What's wrong?" he asked in a husky tone.

"Nothing," she lied, even though he would detect that also.

Belatedly, she realized that he must be aware of her feelings for him. The newly awakened pack bond had rendered her an open book. She wondered if she'd ever fooled him.

If only Zach were so easy to read. Thanks to his stoic nature, he maintained walls around his emotions, leaving her wondering if his affection for her went any more profound than friendship. Fortunately, Zach caressed her body with capable hands, distracting her from more serious thoughts.

Zach reached around her to cup her breast in his hands. His palm and spread fingers pressed to the underside, his fingertip tormenting her pebble-hard nipple. She whimpered and squirmed, enjoying his heaviness pinning her to the mattress. As his hands massaged her breasts, she endured each torturous second for the sake of the pleasure to be had in the next moment. In every way possible, she was his— his woman, his supplicant, his lover, his toy. However and whatever he required of her. At that moment, she existed solely for his pleasure.

The late morning sun bathed her bedroom in a cheerful light, which filtered in through a south-facing window past the blinds. Zach lifted his lower body, so he no longer had her pinned and knelt on the edge of the mattress, placing one knee between Theresa's legs. His denim-clad thigh created delicious pressure against her buttocks. She shivered and sighed, giddy with anticipation.

The mattress squeaked and shifted when he left the bed for a moment. Theresa stifled a cry of denial, and Zach immediately returned.

"I bought these for you in Chicago," he said.

"What is it?" she asked, insatiably curious.

Fabulous material touched her bare skin—smooth and wispy. Zach trailed it across her bareback and her spine from her shoulder blades to her ass. Oh, God. Theresa's pussy creamed, and she pressed her thighs tight together, trapping his leg between them. When they had masturbated on the phone, she'd never imagined Zach turning her fantasies into reality.

"Silk scarves," he said. "They're Italian."

She giggled and turned her face, catching a glimpse of his smirk. "You always get me the best presents."

"Do I?" Tartness flavored his reply. "I had figured that vacuum cleaner I got you last Christmas would land me in the doghouse for a month."

She laughed. "You always give me what I need. That vacuum cleaner was so much better than a bottle of perfume."

He snickered. "Would you like a mop this Christmas?"

Theresa laughed. "Don't test your luck, buddy."

"I can't seem to help myself with you, love."

"Are you going to do something with those scarves, or are we going to cuddle?" Theresa asked, rife with impatience.

Zach's soft snort resonated against the back of her neck where his lips visited a tender caress. The weight of his body covered her, pinning her against the mattress. His chest pressed against her back, his crotch to her ass, and his knees rested between her splayed legs.

"Zach?" she called, pleading and needing him to do more than tease her.

"Patience, pet," he said in a voice full of reverence. He made her feel like the center of his universe, a sense of specialness that left her overwhelmed.

He allowed the wispy silk to pool in the middle of her back. He retained a firm grip on her wrists, positioning her hands just above her buttocks. The intense vulnerability of the position set her to quaking with excitement, and more moisture soaked her panties and the insides of her thighs. Sweat coated her sensitized skin, beading upon her brow and her upper lip, causing her skin to itch most pleasingly. She squirmed and cried out when he blew out a breath across her back.

The muscles in her arms bunched, and she tested his strength, finding him to be unyielding. He looped a scarf around her wrists several times and secured it with a tight knot. Then, he used another to tie her elbows, a fantasy because had she desired to rip through the scarves, even steel restraints could not have held her, but she gave herself wholly to the game.

Bound. Helpless.

If any other man had attempted to put her in such a position, her instinct would have been to fight him, but she had perfect trust in Zach. The terrible danger excited her beyond bearing. He could do anything he wanted to her—use her for his pleasure or torment her beyond endurance.

"Did you miss me while I was gone, Theresa?"

"Yes, so much it hurt." With a sigh, she closed her eyes to experience every physical sensation without the distraction of sight.

"They say absence makes the heart grow fonder."

"Zach, you don't know how I've ached for you. Not just for these past few days. For years."

"The wanting becomes painful." From his tone, there was no mistaking that he understood her feelings. He knew.

The reminder of his duplicity riled Theresa up all over again. She squelched her ire in favor of looking to the future. Gentleness graced her nature, not spitefulness, and she would not be robbed of happiness due to an inability to forgive either him or herself.

Zach settled a scarf over her eyes, holding it against her temples with his agile fingers so the silk caressed her face. "Blindfold or no? It's your fantasy."

She hesitated but only for a second. "Yes, please."

Gently, he pulled the blindfold taut across her eyes and tied the ends of the scarf behind her head with a simple knot. Of course, she was strong enough to rip through a dozen such scarves, but she would not do so and ruin the mood. If anything, the tenuous nature of her restraints posed an incredible challenge to her self-discipline.

Zach rolled Theresa onto her side and tilted her head back to capture her lips in a deep kiss. His tongue thrust into her mouth and then withdrew, suggestively mimicking the motion of lovemaking. He tasted rich and salty.

Oh, his hands! His hands were those of a sculptor, working the clay of her flesh for the sole purpose of creating pleasure, and he did so with the skill of a master craftsman. He stroked her generous curves, evoking incredible sensations with his gentle touch. The rough calluses on his palms agitated her taut nipples.

With growing desperation, Theresa moaned into the depths of his mouth and writhed with need. The blindfold amplified every sensation so that Theresa remained acutely aware of each distinct smell and sound. Her nostrils flared, and she inhaled deeply, drinking in the musky scent of his arousal. In her mind's eye, she envisioned the proud length of his erection, and her mouth watered. Together, they created a delightful chorus of want and need: her panted gasps and moans, his deep breaths and growls, and the steady pulse of their racing heartbeats.

"Tell me what you want," Zach whispered against her mouth. He pressed his groin against her thigh, so she felt the heat of his arousal even through the denim. The musky male scent of testosterone and adrenaline flooded her flared nostrils. "Do you want my mouth on your breasts?"

A whimper of pure desire tore from her throat. "Yes, please. Lick me all over. Suck me. Bite me."

"With pleasure."

Zach lowered his mouth to her breast. His hot tongue laved her nipple while his hands stroked the flat planes of her stomach, stoking the fire burning between her thighs. His teasing evoked such acute need that she shuddered and panted. Her arms tensed, and she tested her bonds, causing the silk to tighten. She sucked in a deep breath and strove to remain calm, managing to relax her shoulders and arms.

"How do I taste?" Theresa demanded out of impatience with his thoroughness. She wanted him to hurry. She needed so much more.

"You're delicious," he whispered against her

skin, alternating kisses with light nips from his clever lips. "I want to devour you."

Her arousal spiked through her body, and she shuddered, panting harder. "Devour me," she begged. "Spread me open and take me."

"I'm going to claim you in every possible way." Zach's voice contained a sultry promise.

Without warning, he withdrew his mouth from her body.

The pain of denial caused Theresa to whimper and once again pull against her bonds. "No, please..."

He chuckled, a gruff sound of amusement that created a ripple upon her skin. "Patience, pet. Give me a chance to get my pants off."

The mattress shifted beneath his weight, and he eased off the bed to finish undressing. His shoes hit the floor in successive thuds. A shiver traveled the length of Theresa's spine at the unmistakable rustle of his jeans dropping. Her arousal spiked to an unbearable intensity.

Zach returned to the bed with lithe elegance. The mattress barely moved beneath his weight. He crouched over her, a hand positioned to either side of her torso. His body heated the air between them. His chest hair brushed across her smooth back, and her bound hands came into brief contact with his rigid member before he settled between her parted legs. His powerful arms encircled her, hands stroking her stomach before dipping to her waistband.

"Lift, love."

Obligingly, Theresa arched her hips to give him more space to maneuver. Zach caught hold of the top of her fly and gave a hard tug, popping the entire row of buttons. She sank her teeth into her lower lip. Her sex ached until she couldn't concentrate on anything else.

"Up." Zach landed a sharp smack on her buttock.

"Meanie." She bared her teeth in a playful snarl.

"You betcha," he said, sounding perfectly smug.

Huffing, she lifted so he could slide the jeans off her hips and down her slender thighs. With a final tug, he pulled them over her feet, leaving her clad only in snug black bikini briefs.

Behind her, he grew still, and she felt his gaze raking her helpless body. The sound of his breathing, deep and rhythmic, and hers, shallow and frantic, filled her hearing. His fingers found and traced the lace trim of her panties, following the curve of her buttock. Theresa tilted her pelvis toward him, craving the heat and pressure of his touch against her weeping core. She ached to feel his bold cock thrust into her, parting the tender folds of her pussy, plowing deep into her.

"Do you have a particular fetish, Zach?" Theresa asked, dropping her tone to a seductive caress. She squirmed on the mattress so that her hips and ass writhed with suggestive sway.

"You could call me something of an arse man." Zach's wicked chuckle exacerbated her desire, so she giggled and then groaned all at once.

"I might just call you an arse!" She was giggling until his even teeth sank into the smooth flesh of her butt cheek. Theresa yelped and bucked, scooting forward across the mattress in a futile attempt to evade his bite.

His husky chuckle caused delicious shivers along her spine, and he followed her, lightly biting her ass. He spread her ass cheeks with his big hands, exposing her private parts to the cool air of the room. The scorch of his gaze kept her body at a steady boil. She gasped and then groaned as his warm, wet tongue stroked the length of her ass crack, leaving a trail of hot saliva.

"Zach, please." Despite the blindfold, Theresa squeezed her eyes shut, and her core repeatedly clenched, sending tremors of pleasure and the hint of ecstasy throughout her body.

Zach grabbed a pillow from the top of the bed and dragged it to Theresa's hip. He slipped his hand between her stomach and the mattress, palm pressed flat against her abdomen. "Lift again, pet."

Obediently, Theresa raised her hips, arching her ass into the air, and Zach slid the pillow beneath her stomach.

Finally, finally, Zach hooked his fingers beneath the lacy trim of her panties and dragged a scrap of satin over her shapely bottom and down her long legs. Theresa emitted a single strained whimper, dying of want and need. Her body flexed, arms briefly straining against the silk scarf binding her wrists, but she kept her strength in check, so the restraints did not tear.

His raspy jaw caressed her buttock, and then she experienced the huff of hot breath upon her skin. The tip of his tongue flickered against the exposed lips of her pussy, creating sensations like sweet agony, and she bucked.

Zach's strong hands caught her ass, immobilizing her, making resistance futile. His tongue returned, lapping and licking, playing across the delicate outer folds of her labia. Theresa shook and wept when he at long last found her clit and flicked the small bud with tongue and then a finger.

"My, what a delectable arse. I wish you could see this as I do. Your perfect backside, the pink line leading to your rosebud, the lovely lips of your cunny." He nibbled at the back of her thigh. She yelped and jumped, causing Zach to chuckle and nip her again.

"Zach?" Theresa begged, unable to formulate a coherent plea. Instead, she put so much feeling into her voice, letting him know the depth of her desperation.

"My, but you're wet, love." With an impertinent chuckle, Zach penetrated her pussy with a single digit. His fingers skimmed her sex, exploring slick folds of flesh until covered in her cream.

Theresa gasped, and the walls of her vagina contracted around his finger, grasping him with all her strength. That finger thrust into her hard, and his tongue traveled an indecent path, tracing the smooth skin of the perineum to her tight rosette.

Beneath the blindfold, Theresa's eyes widened, and she bucked her hips. Only Zach's firm hold kept her from twisting and squirming to escape. His bold, inquisitive tongue followed, closing the gap.

Zach thrust his thick thumb into her pussy while stroking her clit. Unbelievable pleasure welled through, carrying her away. The rhythmic penetration brought her to the verge of climax. Right before she flew, however, he withdrew.

"Zach, why are you stopping?" Theresa asked with a whine of protest.

"Because I'm not through exploring yet," he said with a sultry chuckle. Then, he spread her ass cheeks, and his tongue persisted at naughtier pursuits, rimming the clenched ring of muscle.

"Zach!" Theresa writhed against the restraints. She pushed her hips toward him, begging with her body for release from the torment. So bad, so wrong, so delicious. She couldn't think, couldn't reason, couldn't do anything but feel as he took her on an unbelievable ride.

A growl of satisfaction rolled from his throat, amplifying the sensation within her lower body. Waves of heat rolled off his athletic body. The heavy huff of his breath and the racing pulse of his heart filled her ears. The thick scent of his arousal mingled with the spicy aroma of her desire. Even without sight, the montage of sensations overwhelmed her. The swift current of sexual energy carried her toward total abandon.

Somewhere in that jumble of erotic sensation, Zach finally hit the perfect combo. His finger fluttered against her clit. His thumb invaded her pussy. That teasing fingertip flickered about her nub as his long, supple tongue breached her bottom. For the first time in her life, she let go of all her inhibitions and embraced her sexual nature with open arms. Her pussy clenched, and her arousal crested. Wailing, she climaxed with a spasm, the muscles of her body seizing, vagina clenching about him. A burst of heat scalded her skin, and her mind crashed into a wall of excruciating pleasure originating from every nerve ending in her body.

Tears dampened her blindfold, and it took a long time before she could formulate words. "Oh, please," she begged. "Stop. Stop. No more. I can't bear it."

"Love, we're just getting started." Zach chuckled a deep rumble that created a delicious vibration throughout her lower body. Her flesh remained connected to him via fingers, teeth, and tongue.

Sexual energy crashed over her in a wave, warm and welcoming. "I don't think I can take anymore," she said, gasping.

"You're stronger than you think."

He communicated wickedness and sensual intent with a growl, creating anticipation in her loins as unbearable as his physical assault. Her pussy clenched yet again, taking Theresa through a sweet, slow climax.

"Come for me, Theresa. You're so beautiful. I want to see your pleasure."

With Zach's voice caressing her skin, she cried out as her pussy seized. Twitching and shivering, she rode out the series of explosions. The final spasms took her as a violent storm but tapered off gradually, a wave that washed her ashore and deposited her like a strand of seaweed. Her extremities tingled, and deep relaxation settled in her muscles. She sighed with deep satisfaction. Spent, Theresa rested face down upon the mattress, limp and lethargic, while her breathing calmed.

Zach's muscular body remained tense behind her. He untied the silk scarves, freed her arms, and rose from the bed in a single swift motion. She felt him leave the bed, muttering in frustration, "Where the bloody hell are my pants?"

Gathering her strength, Theresa reached for her blindfold and lifted the scarf from her eyes. She turned her head to the side and watched his frantic scramble to find his missing pants. "Over by the dresser," she said, smothering a grin.

"Right."

The word flowed off his tongue, and, quick as a light, he shot over to the dresser toward the missing pants. Toned muscles rippled beneath smooth skin as he moved with lithe precision, every motion graceful and deliberate despite his urgency. His broad shoulders and chest, trim waist and hips, tight ass, and long limbs were perfectly proportioned.

A beam of sunshine streamed through the bedroom window. In the light, Zach's shoulder-length hair glowed like a golden halo. Zach pawed through his pants frantically until he located the back pocket. He removed his wallet and extracted a single condom.

She gasped, exaggerating the sound. "Just one?"

"Hell," he grumbled beneath his breath. "Yeah, just one. Sorry."

She giggled and boosted her backside into the air, giving her butt a playful wiggle. "I guess we'll have to make it last."

With an expert motion, Zach rolled the condom onto his erect cock. "Keep it up, woman. Keep it up," he said in a tone of mock threat.

"Isn't that your job?" she asked as he approached the bed. She laughed as the mattress bent beneath his weight. She felt his heat against her back and buttocks, and then his big hands spanned her waist.

A growl rolled from his throat as he positioned her, lifting her hips, parting her legs with his knee. His thick cockhead brushed against the lips of her pussy, and her breath hitched. He rocked forward, parting her flesh and finding the entrance of her channel, and then sank into her with a slow, smooth motion.

"Ooohhh," Theresa wailed, eyes wide open.

Her fingers dug into the mattress, scratching the sheets with her nails. His cock felt thick and long. Amazing. Her pussy stretched until she was full to bursting. Energy coursed between them until the hairs on her arms stood on end, and her entire body vibrated in tune with the primal rhythm. His masterful touch reduced her to a quivering pool of need.

"Ah, you're so unbelievably wet. That's it, love."

Zach pumped his hips, rising and falling behind her so his member withdrew and then entered her pussy again. A slick sound accompanied the motion, exquisitely erotic as he cleaved her flesh, cutting into her with his rod.

Theresa whimpered and thrust back to meet him, loving the intrusion of his cock, savoring the slap of his balls against her clit. So many hours she had spent with her fingers buried in her sex, fantasizing about him, dreaming of this moment, and the reality far exceeded her wildest expectations.

His hand slipped between her stomach and the mattress then slid downward, so his long fingers caressed her mound. His finger pressed against her sex, the tip seeking her clit. He found and flicked that tiny erect nub of flesh with the decadent precision.

Without warning, a convulsion seized her pussy and spread outward in devastating tremors through her core, obliterating her sense of individuality. Her climax came easily, flowing across her skin like warm water, pouring into every nook and cranny of her body. Existence beyond her physical body ceased, and ecstasy overtook her as a devastating tsunami of pleasure. Blood roared in her ears, and her heart pounded against her ribcage, trying to escape.

Distantly, she heard Zach speaking words of encouragement. "That's it, love. That's it. Give yourself to me."

Gradually, the tremors dissipated, and she lay gasping upon the bed. Zach remained rigid behind her, holding his body upright so his weight did not crush her. His cock remained as stiff as steel, and it amazed her that his self-control had weathered the climatic convulsions of her pussy.

"Don't move, Theresa, or I'll lose it," Zach said in a voice rife with tension.

His tone assured her that he wasn't nearly as self-possessed as she'd thought. She became aware of his labored breathing and the tremors running through his limbs. Sweat coated his body and dribbled onto her back, ass, and thighs.

"I'll keep still," she promised, recognizing the precarious state of his self-control. She wondered why he denied his climax, but she had a patient nature.

Quickly enough, Zach satisfied her curiosity. He withdrew his dick entirely from her channel, wringing a soft moan of disappointment from her. Still, the head of his cock moved upward and repositioned against that tight ring of muscle, causing Theresa's eyes to widen. Disbelief and then the titillating shock of sexual taboo flowed through her. A tremor of nervousness passed through her body.

"Relax, love, and this will go easy. I want to know you like this, to claim you in every way possible, to make you mine. I won't hurt you. I promise." Zach's voice filled her ears. His fingers probed her pussy, gathering her moisture as a lubricant. His index finger eased into her ass, ever so gently. He sank to the first knuckle and then the second. "That's it." He whispered gentle encouragement. "Relax."

"Zach, I've never done this before," Theresa said, biting back the urge to squirm at the unfamiliar sensation. His touch felt right, naughty but amazingly erotic, the same as his tongue had earlier when he'd rimmed her.

"Love, I've been dying to sink my cock into your sweet arse since the day I met you," Zach gritted out, his tone conveying raw sexual frustration. His free hand spread, grasping her buttock, depressing the skin, and digging into the muscle beneath.

"When you said you were an ass man, I wasn't quite expecting this." Laughter shook her, thwarting her attempts to remain still.

The sharp click of his teeth snapping together served as his reply, conveying the limits of his need. Abruptly, another finger joined the first, both buried inside her ass to the third joint.

Theresa gasped and jumped at the extraordinary

feeling of fullness. She clenched and unclenched the muscles of her buttocks, making a conscious effort to release all of the tension in her body. Her pussy contracted, and cream gushed between her thighs. He thrust his hand against her, fucking her ass with his fingers, and she mewled in response.

"That's it. You're gorgeous."

His fingers withdrew, leaving her empty, but soon enough, his cock replaced his fingers. He positioned the thick head against her sphincter and breeched the ring of muscle. So much more significant than his fingers had been.

"Oh. Oh, my." Sobbing with desire, Theresa arched off the mattress to meet his advance.

His long, thick cock entered her inch by inch, an inexorable advance that ended when he filled her to bursting and his balls rested flush with her aching flesh.

Panting, they remained still while her body adjusted to having him inside her virgin passage. The forbidden nature of what they were doing added a razor's edge of thrill to the act. Her arousal peaked once again, causing tiny tremors to tug at her core, cascading toward yet another orgasm.

"Fuck, you're so tight. I'm not going to last," Zach said from between gritted teeth.

"Don't hold back. Fuck me, please. I need to feel you." She had never felt so full to the point of bursting, so thoroughly possessed. The mischief of it thrilled and excited her.

"Holy hell, love, you're as hot as fuck."

Without warning, Zach drew back, just a few inches, and then thrust. He rocked back again, further this time, and entered her harder. It wrung a cry of delighted pleasure from Theresa. Zach grunted and moaned, and she sensed the reverberation in his chest throughout her entire being and knew he needed to howl as much as he needed to come.

A white-hot blaze of ecstasy enveloped Theresa, and she threw back her head to release a low howl of pleasure. Behind her, Zach surged against her with short, hard thrusts. Sweat made his skin slick. His shouts rose in volume and ferociousness, the triumphant song of a dominant male wolf claiming his mate. Their bodies crashed together in violent union. They lost all control over their wolves. Her climax blindsided her, hitting without warning, sending her into a wild spin. Her pussy clenched, and every muscle in her body contracted.

"Theresa!" Zach shouted her name at the top of his lungs. His cry turned into a wolf's howl.

He bucked against her with hard, impatient lunges that caused their bodies to clash together. Against her mons, his balls tightened as he spilled his hot seed.

Afterward, he collapsed on top of her, crushing her beneath his weight. She mustered her strength and turned her head to the side. Her eyelid lifted in a lazy motion.

"Did you really only bring one condom?" she asked.

His mouth yawned open, a rumbling snore her only answer.

CHAPTER TWENTY-EIGHT

The shrill ring of her house phone nudged Theresa from her stupor. She opened her eyes and lifted her head from the pillow. Beside her, Zach stirred. Her lover lay atop her crisp white sheets in all of his naked glory. One eyelid crept to half-mast, and his jaws parted in a wide yawn.

Fighting a yawning attack, Theresa answered the phone. "Hello," she said into the receiver.

"Theresa, this is Becky Teller."

Theresa sat straight up in bed. "Becky," she said, struggling to sound casual. "What can I do for you?"

Zach's scent altered, adrenaline and aggression becoming more prominent, and he sat erect on the bed so that the mattress issued an audible creak.

Following the sound, a significant silence ensued before Becky spoke again.

"It sounds like you have company. Have you chosen a mate, dear?"

Theresa bit her lower lip and stared at Zach. "I'm making some very nice progress."

Becky produced a harrumph sound in the back of her throat. "I'm pleased to hear it, but that's not why I'm calling. Adam has called an emergency pack meeting. The pack is to assemble at Foxtail Creek before moonrise. I'm sure you know why."

"Yes, I know why." Theresa stiffened. *Bitch, please*.

"I expect you'll tell Zach," Becky said.

"I'll do that," Theresa said and hung up the phone without saying goodbye.

Zach cocked his head. "What did the queen bitch want?"

Theresa exhaled and felt the weight of the world settle on her shoulders. "The shit has hit the fan. It's time to face the music."

He frowned. "Those two idioms don't go well together, love."

She knelt and scooted across the bed to take a swat at his shoulders. He fended off her attack with his hands.

"Zach, you're an ass."

He flashed an unrepentant grin and captured her wrists. "Yeah, but I'm your ass."

The stupid declaration made her teary, and she sought to hide her embarrassment, averting her eyes.

He captured her chin and forced her to meet his gaze. "I'm not going to let anything bad happen to you, Theresa."

She believed that he would do his best to protect her, but would it be enough?

She forced a brave smile. "I know."

He flashed a quick grin and kissed her. "Good."

Wild, disconnected thoughts ran through her head, disrupting her sense of peace. Theresa inhaled a long breath, and then she blew the air out through her nostrils. Shifter blood ran hotter than human, but she shivered and crossed her arms across her chest, chilled to the core. The prospect of what was yet to come scared her to death.

Zach sat upright. His face contorted with concern. "What's wrong, love?"

Theresa bit her lower lip. "I'm afraid you and Robert are going to be forced to fight each other, and one of you will wind up dead."

He cocked his head and stared at her with thoughtful eyes. "Yeah, it's a possibility, but I'm doing my darndest to avoid it."

"I hope so," Theresa said in a prayerful tone. She grabbed hold of his hands to reinforce the empathic pack bond and because she wanted him to experience her sense of urgency. "I'm scared, Zach, because if Adam has his way, you might not have a choice."

Zach sighed, and the corners of his mouth tugged downward at the corners. "Look, Theresa, I don't want to fight Robert. Hell, I don't even really want—"

"Leadership of the pack," she said, finishing his sentence for him.

They stared at one another for a long time as if they'd both known for some time but had not wanted to admit it aloud. The truth, spoken aloud, carried myriad implications.

Zach's nostrils flared. "I want you," he said, "and I will fight for you, love. Have no doubt."

She closed her eyes, too tired to think, and sagged beneath the immense weight riding on her. When she opened them again, they felt too dry, and her mouth quivered with the effort not to twist into a sob. "That's the thing, Zach. I don't have any doubts. Not about you or your willingness to fight to keep me. I don't even have any doubts about us. At least, not big ones. Little ones, maybe, but I think that's normal."

"Why won't you seal the mate bond with me then?" Zach demanded with burgeoning impatience. His blue eyes held endless torment. The stoic mask he wore for the world had a crack, revealing his turbulent emotions.

Her breath hitched. It was the first and only time Zach had stated the words aloud. To speak of the mate bond—it was the language of lifetime commitment. Not the fleeting union of marriage that humans entered into, but the irrevocable joining of two wolves as a mated pair. Only the death of one or both partners could terminate a mate bond.

She chose her following words with care, aware that so much rode on what happened in the next few moments. "Because the second I seal the mate bond with you, then you become Alpha," she said, "and become the leader of the pack, a responsibility you don't even really want."

His lips compressed, a grim not-smile curving his mouth. "But Robert does," he said. "You think he wants it enough to fight and kill me. Is that what your magic has shown you, Theresa?"

She shook her head. "I don't know. Maybe. I'm not sure. The one thing I do know is he wants to lead more than anything else. When he's close, I can sense his ambition, his drive. I believe he has the best interests of the pack at heart, but...."

"Instinct is a powerful motivator," Zach said, nodding his understanding. "We're territorial creatures by nature and social ones as well. I admit I've always been something of a loner."

An involuntary chuckle escaped her. She pantomimed in surprise and disbelief, raising her hand to her throat. "Really? No. I'm shocked! Not you."

"Silence, wench." Zach also laughed, and some of the bowstring tension bled out of his body.

She caught his hand and his gaze and looked him straight in the eyes with unwavering devotion, so he could not doubt as to her sincerity. "I don't want you to have to fight your best friend, Zach. It's the only reason I haven't chosen yet."

"You're my best friend."

Her heart caught in her throat, aching as if a giant hand had closed on her chest. "Oh, Zach..."

He flashed a sardonic smile. "Don't get all sentimental on me, pet. We'll figure some way out of this mess."

Her breath caught on a hitch, and fear wrung her heart. Theresa clung to his hand, drawing on his solid strength for support. She offered him a brave smile. "I know we will," she said, burying her doubts down deep.

Zach had to park two blocks from the elementary school because of heavy traffic. In her rush, Theresa shoved the passenger door of the sports car open before he shut the engine off.

"We need to hurry. School lets out in ten minutes," Theresa said, scolding him to move faster with her arms.

"We've got plenty of time, love." Stepping onto the path, Zach settled his arm about Theresa, resting his hand upon the crook of her hip. He found shortening his gait to match his companion's stride to be a bit of a trick but well worth the satisfaction of having his lover close.

As they approached the kindergarten playground, he noticed heads turning in their direction and felt the pressure of prying eyes following their movement.

"Has everyone always got their noses in other people's business here?" he asked Theresa in a hushed whisper.

She glanced at him and grinned. "Yes, absolutely. You made a big impression with the other moms the day you picked up Isabel. I've never seen so much speculation. No one wanted to believe that we're just friends."

Zach huffed and adopted an expression of mild annoyance. "We're not just friends."

She laughed. "Yes, I know that, but—"

"We should give them something to talk about."

Without warning, he spun and pulled Theresa into his arms with a grand flourish. A startled cry escaped her, but she offered no resistance when he bent her backward and captured her lips in a marauding kiss. She clutched his biceps, holding tight as he plundered the sweet depths of her mouth. She tasted spicy and sinful, and the enticing scent of her arousal flooded his nostrils.

The watching eyes did not avert but instead intensified with avid interest. He heard gasps and whispered phrases, picking up on their jealousy and speculation. Secretly, he enjoyed the primitive act of claiming Theresa publicly, relishing the fact that she could no longer insist on calling him just a friend.

The clanging of the school bell interrupted their heated embrace, and they broke contact to stand a couple of feet apart. Zach faced her with an unrepentant smile. She tilted her head back to gaze up at him, looking pretty and delectable, sides heaving with exertion, lips bruised and rosy.

Her eyes narrowed, and she flashed her teeth. "Don't look so smug, mister," she said. "I'll get you for that."

"Promises, promises," Zach said, tone teasing. He waggled his eyebrows. "Take your best shot, pet. I'm looking forward to it."

Laughing, they joined hands and made their way

to the gate. Along with a group of other five-year-old children, Isabel emerged from her classroom and headed toward them.

The girl's face lit up, and she broke into a run. "Zach!"

Zach dropped to a crouch and opened his arms to catch her in a hug. "There's my girl. Did you miss me?"

Isabel grinned up at him. "Did you bring me a present?"

Zach frowned. "Is that a condition of you having missed me?"

"Maybe." Isabel pouted, turning down her lower lip. "How big is my present?"

He threw back his head and laughed, setting her back on her feet. "I suppose you'll have to wait and see. It's at your house."

Theresa reached down to hug her daughter hello. "Big things come in small packages, sweetheart."

Isabel's head tilted to the side. "What does that mean?"

"It means that small presents cost more," he said.

Theresa took her daughter's hand, and they started back to the car. He followed a pace behind mother and daughter, watching over them with marked protectiveness until they reached the vehicle. They buckled Isabel into the tiny backseat.

As he drove, Zach listened to Theresa and Isabel chat. He played with the radio, flipping channels until he located a station playing a rock and roll song he liked. He sang along with great enthusiasm, loud and off-key until the girls dissolved into hysterical giggles.

"What's that?" he said, affecting the coarse Cockney accent of London's East End. "Are you ladies laughing at me?"

Theresa pretended surprise, round eyes and mouth, hand fluttering before her throat. "No, never! Goodness, was that terrible sound you?"

"It was pretty scary," Isabel said, chiming in from the backseat.

"At first, I thought it might be a bull moose in love," Theresa said, "but then I realized no moose would commit such crimes against music."

Theresa and Isabel laughed all that much harder, giggling up a storm and prompting a good-natured grin to cross Zach's face. He quelled the impulse to join in and instead orchestrated an audible snort. "A man's car is his castle."

They reached Theresa's house, and he turned into the driveway. As the vehicle slowed, Theresa tensed up and uttered a soft groan followed by a barely audible curse. He followed her gaze and saw Avery Paunch, her landlord, standing on the front porch. The man watched them approach, arms crossed over his chest, body language shouting anger and hostility.

"It's the first of the month. Rent is due today," Theresa said in a low voice. She cast a worried glance over her shoulder at Isabel in the backseat.

"Does he always come 'round to collect in person?" Zach asked.

"Yes," Theresa said, spitting out the harsh word.

Zach took her hand, holding her fingers against his palm. "You're still short?"

Eyes bright, she nodded. "With everything that happened, I never got a chance to talk to Antonio."

She seemed overwhelmed, and his heart ached for her. Thanks to her stubborn pride, she could not even bring herself to ask him for help now. He stopped the car, put it into park, and shut off the engine.

Isabel squirmed about in the backseat, bouncing about with her youthful energy. "Mama, I want to get out."

"Be patient, honey." Theresa removed her hand from his grasp and reached for her purse.

Zach caught her elbow. "Theresa, let me take care of this for you."

She glanced up at him with tormented eyes, white teeth sunk into her lower lip. He read her anguish in those chocolate depths, the conflict between pride and trust. He stilled and waited for her decision.

At last, she nodded and smiled with gratitude. "Yes, please. Thank you, Zach."

"You're welcome, love."

Pleasure suffused his chest, spreading outward to warm every part of his being. Covering her rent for a month was not a big thing, but he knew it to be a huge gesture of trust on her part. It made him happy to be able to do something for her. He dropped a quick kiss onto her forehead and extracted his checkbook from the glove compartment.

Zach climbed from the vehicle and moved to intercept the landlord while Theresa helped Isabel from the backseat. He mounted the three steps to the front porch and approached Paunch. The landlord shuffled his feet, demonstrating uncertainty, but held his ground.

Paunch was a human who liked to intimidate those weaker and timider. Zach had always disliked him for being a bully and a coward, but Zach had kept his distance from the man at Theresa's request. That had finally changed.

Zach allowed his wolf to rise. Power touched his eyes and voice. He regarded the man with the same disgust one might bestow upon roadkill. "Mr. Paunch."

Confronted, Paunch cowed and fell back, retreating until his back hit the front door. His hands shook, as did his voice, and the scent of fear surrounded him. "Mr. Hunter," he said. "How can I help you?"

"A word with you if I might." Zach indicated the side yard with the tilt of his head. "In private."

The man swallowed, so his Adam's apple bobbed, but he moved to obey the command. They passed Theresa and Isabel on the stairs. Paunch greeted Theresa in a subdued tone. "Ms. Russo."

She paused for a second and regarded the landlord with open dislike. "Mr. Paunch."

As mother and daughter went inside, Zach caught Isabel's lilting voice. "Mama, where is Zach going?"

"He's taking care of us, sweetie," Theresa said before the front door clicked shut.

An extraordinary sense of pride filled Zach, convincing him further of the rightness of his choices. Theresa and Isabel were his to keep, to protect. His girls. He vowed to do anything necessary to protect them from danger, including killing or dying, if necessary.

As much as Theresa wanted to hear what Zach had to say to her landlord, she did not want Isabel exposed to such unpleasantness, so she closed the front door behind them. It was difficult for her to trust him to decide on her behalf, but she also acknowledged that it was an issue she needed to work on if she wanted their relationship to succeed.

Theresa glanced down at her daughter and found Isabel gazing at her with dark, thoughtful eyes. "Did you and Zach change your minds about dating, Mama?" Isabel asked.

"Would it be okay with you if we were dating, Izzy?"

Isabel stared a moment longer and then looked away. She started toward the kitchen. "Sure. I like Zach. Can I have a snack?"

Theresa blinked and then followed her daughter. Was it really that easy? "What do you want to eat?"

Isabel set down her pink backpack on the kitchen table and made a beeline for the pantry. "Cookies?"

"How about crackers and cheese?" Theresa asked, moving to the fridge.

"Can I have a cookie, too?"

"Just one. I want you to drink a glass of milk also."

"Okay."

Theresa placed the snack down in front of her daughter and then cleaned up while the child ate. "Do you have homework?"

"Not much." Isabel perched on a kitchen chair and watched her mother move about the kitchen. "Math and spelling, and I'm supposed to read for twenty minutes."

Theresa brought a glass to Isabel and schooled her expression to sternness. "Thirty."

Isabel's dark eyes lit up with laughter. "Twenty-five."

"Done," Theresa said, nodding her agreement. "It's a deal."

"Is everything a negotiation?" Zach asked with wry humor as he entered the kitchen through the front hallway. He walked with one hand behind his back.

"Of course. We're a family of master hagglers." Theresa turned to greet him with a smile.

"Do you have my present?" Isabel jumped to her feet.

Her daughter's bad manners made Theresa frown. "Isabel!"

Zach grinned and fluffed the girl's hair. "Did I say that I brought you a present?" he asked, feigning confusion. "Funny, I don't recall—"

"Zach! You're mean!" Isabel darted to the right

and attempted to race around him to see what he had behind his back.

With his superior speed, Zach evaded the girl, turning to face her to conceal his hand. Theresa caught a glimpse of a stuffed animal.

Isabel tried to gain the upper hand for a couple of minutes before she gave up. Panting, the girl crossed her arms over her chest and adopted an adorable pout. "Please, Zach, I've been good."

"I very much doubt that," Zach said in a cheeky reply, but he brought his hand from behind his back and surrendered a stuffed pony to the girl.

With a squeal of delight, Isabel took the toy from him, giving him a quick hug in the process. She held the pony up for closer examination. "Aww, she's so cute!"

Theresa moved closer to get a better look at the gift, and Zach reached out in an automatic gesture and wrapped his arm around her waist. "I'm guessing that it meets with your approval then, pixie?"

"She's perfect! Thank you so much!" Isabel rose on tippy-toe, reaching for him.

Zach bent to offer his cheek, accepting Isabel's kiss of thanks.

Theresa smiled. "Isabel, take your new toy upstairs and put it in your room until Nana arrives."

Isabel started to obey and then stopped in her tracks. "Tonight is the full moon," she said, staring at her mother with complete understanding in her dark eyes. "You're going out."

"I have to, sweetie. Tonight is the one night of the month when grownups must turn into wolves."

"I don't like it when you go out at night, Mama," Isabel said, clutching her stuffed pony. "I have bad dreams. Last night, you had to work late. Can't you stay home tonight?"

Theresa sighed. Guilt weighed heavily on her shoulders. More than anything, she wanted to make her daughter happy, but being a single mother put her under enormous pressure and conflicting demands.

"I'll be home tomorrow night, Isabel," she said at last. "I promise. We'll do something special. Maybe dinner out and a movie?"

Isabel's frown softened, and the peace offering appeared to satisfy her. "Can Zach come?"

"I wouldn't miss it for the world," he said. "Now run upstairs. I need to speak with your mum alone for a minute."

The child flew up the stairs.

Theresa waited until her daughter had gone before she cast the man beside her a sly glance. The question at the top of her mind burst from her lips. "What happened with the landlord?"

With his arm still hooked about her waist, Zach dropped into a kitchen chair and tugged her into his lap, all in one smooth motion. His mouth wound up pressed right next to her ear, and his smoky chuckle sent shivers along her spine.

"A repairman will be coming over on Monday to address all of your maintenance issues. He was going to send someone over sooner, but I wanted you to have enough time to assemble a list of everything that's not working."

Her eyes widened with comical astonishment. Her small hands pressed against his chest, rubbing the broad wall of muscle through his shirt. "Oh, my, but you are my hero," she said in a breathy voice. "Did you intimidate him into submission?"

"All I had to do was flash my teeth," Zach said with false modesty while he made a production out of preening under her ardent admiration.

"Goodness." Theresa fanned her face.

"There's more," he said, rumbling deep his throat.

Theresa gasped. "More? Do tell!"

"He's crediting you two weeks of rent for the inconveniences you've endured."

"Oh, wow, Mr. Paunch must have been beside himself. I would have loved to have seen his face."

"It was rather amusing."

"Did you enjoy yourself, Zach?"

He flashed a wolfish grin. "Oh, yes, immensely."

Laughing so hard it hurt, she pressed her face to his throat. His chuckling created a pleasant vibration throughout his chest, and his vitality, his sheer liveliness, soothed her ragged nerves. As silly as it was, his joking was what she needed to relieve the stress crushing her.

"Oh," she said, gasping for breath and wiping a tear from the corner of her eye. Reluctantly, she rose from Zach's lap. "My mom is due over in a half hour, so we can go to this meeting."

He tipped his head forward to acknowledge her words but remained quiet. Their silence was mutual and comfortable, the result of longtime familiarity and easy intimacy. Without being asked, Theresa fetched him a cup of black loose-leaf tea.

He wrapped his fingers around the mug and leaned forward to inhale the steam and the aromatic scent. Theresa took the seat next to him, close enough that their elbows touched.

"Zach, what are we going to do about Adam?"

Zach's rangy form remained relaxed except for an almost imperceptible tightening of his jaw. He grasped her hand and squeezed. "No matter what happens tonight, pet, I want you to know that I have your back. I won't allow anything bad to happen to you."

She mustered a brave smile and squeezed his hand in return. "I know you do."

"I've discussed it with Robert, and we want to avoid fighting one another."

"Thank God," she said, exhaling slowly.

"But it might be unavoidable," Zach said, destroying her short-lived relief.

"Do you have an agreement?" Theresa asked.

"Yeah," he said with such heaviness that she rocked back in her chair, balancing on two legs. Then, he sighed, and her chair thumped. "No, not really."

She swallowed the lump in her throat and licked her dry lips. "That's hardly reassuring, Zach."

"Sorry, love." He gazed at her with an apologetic grimace. "I'm unable to challenge Adam directly without fighting Robert first. Robert doesn't want to challenge Adam because he'd have to kill him. He wants to claim leadership of the pack without violence."

"That's admirable," Theresa said, crossing her arms tight over her breasts. "Can't Robert just concede rank to you? Once Adam is out of the way, and you're Alpha, you could swap again. Or something like that..."

A quick grin tugged at his lips. "You know it doesn't work like that, love. Maybe if one of us were old or infirm."

She released a long sigh. "If not killed in combat, the ousted Alpha must leave the pack," she said, quoting from canon law that governed their kind.

"Right," he said.

She stared at Zach, waiting for him to say something more, but he volunteered nothing else. "Zach, please don't take this the wrong way, but do you even want to be Alpha? Really? You're pretty much a loner other than for the time you spend with Isabel and me."

Zach huffed. "Robert and I golf every weekend."

Theresa nodded. "Of course, but being Alpha would quadruple your responsibilities to the pack. It would certainly take away from your writing."

Zach's expression grew increasingly dour with each passing second. She felt terrible about making such an issue out of it, but...

"Robert would make a better Alpha," Zach said with a casual shrug, but it was impossible to tell if he whether he felt insulted or upset. The man kept his cards close to his chest.

"I didn't want to hurt your feelings by saying it," Theresa said.

A reluctant smile tugged at his mouth, and he looked at her. "I'm not five, love."

She sighed. "We have a problem, then, don't we?"

"Absolutely." Zach's dark humor vanished, and he grew deadly serious. "Because the only way for Robert to become Alpha is for him to claim you as his mate, and I refuse to give you up—not for him, not for the good of the pack, not for anyone."

CHAPTER TWENTY-NINE

Meadow north of Foxtail Creek, Iron Stone Valley

Before the sunset on the evening of the full moon, the Iron Stone pack gathered in the meadow north of Foxtail Creek, located within a mile of Adam Teller's home. They arrived in twos and threes but crowded together at the center of the clearing. The twilight sky contained enough light to see by, and the moon was three hours from rising. The pack's voices filled the air, creating a moderate rumble that competed with the din of running water.

Theresa stood beside Zach, her arm linked with his elbow, waiting with tense anticipation for the meeting to be called to order. Robert and Charlaine watched from the other side of the clearing. The cousins projected a blended aura—solidarity, a team. It was no wonder that people often mistook them for a mated pair.

Although outwardly calm, Theresa's wolf roiled with pent-up aggression. She wanted to break free from the pack, to shed her human form and shift to a wolf, to run with the sky overhead and the forest at her feet.

"Easy, love," Zach said, running a gentle hand across her shoulders. He remained rock steady at her side, her oasis in the storm, and his incredible energy caressed her skin and calmed her jittery nerves.

She acknowledged him with a quick smile but made no reply. They had already discussed what might occur at the meeting. Theresa knew that Zach had her back, no matter what happened. His solid support gave her the courage to stand her ground before the Alpha.

Her fragile bravado served as the foundation for the rest of the pack to unite about her. The others assembled around her and Zach, auras pulling together and blending into a continuous whole, allowing all to experience the excellent connectivity. They flowed through and about Theresa—the Heart of the Wolf.

"Attention, everyone. Quiet down." Adam separated from the crowd, arms in the air, and moved to stand on the meadow's high ground about fifty feet north of the creek bank. His guard flanked him, occupying four evenly spaced points to either side.

The voices of the crowd rose in volume, and then, silence fell.

Adam lowered his hands and gestured toward the side of the clearing. "Bring him."

On cue, Sheriff Mahoney escorted Carl to stand before Adam and the rest of the pack. Silver chains bound the prisoner. Theresa glimpsed fresh blood on the restraints and winced, feeling pity for the man who had assaulted her. The sheriff shoved Carl down, so he knelt in the dirt before Adam.

Adam regarded Carl, gazing upon him with a killing look in his eyes. At great length, he bared his teeth in a silent snarl. His disgust for the other man was plain.

"Carl Reynolds," he growled, voice booming to carry to the assembled pack. "You stand accused of attacking a lower-ranked female without provocation. Do you have anything to say in your defense?"

Carl kept his gaze lowered in the timeless gesture of submission. "No, Alpha. I speak only to beg for mercy as I was led astray by a manipulative bitch."

Theresa scowled, and Zach's hand on her back tensed. He grew alert, ready to fight, and a collective murmur of displeasure passed through the rest of the pack. At the very periphery of the crowd, Debra Yeller skulked, reduced to pariah status.

"Debra's part in this has been noted, and she'll be sanctioned." Adam cast a dangerous glare toward Debra, who flinched in response. "However, that does not excuse or mitigate your crimes. The penalty for attacking a childbearing female is death."

Carl cringed, shoulders hunching and his arms contracting against his chest. His hollow terror traveled through the pack's ambient aura, engendering pangs of pity from some and ripples of anger in others.

"I beg for mercy," he groveled.

Marshaling her courage, Theresa took a deep breath. She held her head high and unlinked her arm from Zach's to step forward. She stopped before Adam, standing over Carl, and took care to keep her gaze averted so as not to challenge the Alpha's authority. Her action caused a stir within the pack, curiosity being the predominant emotion.

"Alpha," she said, keeping her head bowed to show respect, "may I speak?"

"This should be interesting," Adam said with a

sarcastic bite in his voice. She felt his gaze boring into her. "Very well, you have a right to confront your attacker. What do you have to say, Theresa?"

"I would like to ask that Carl be granted mercy," Theresa said in a quiet voice.

She sensed the pack's surprise, and a small handful of members reacted with disapproval. However, the support and approval she received far outweighed those negative feelings. More than that, respect emanated from specific individuals—Zach, Robert, Charlaine, and even Isabel's aunt, Ambra— and spread with quiet persistence.

Adam's narrow-eyed gaze signaled his displeasure, placing him with the vengeful minority within the pack. "What punishment do you suggest then?"

"Exile him from the Iron Stone Pack. I ask not for his sake but for the pack. The death of another member would hurt everyone," Theresa answered without hesitation. She had thought about what she should say before the meeting.

Even though Zach had argued in favor of Carl's death, he remained silent, supporting her decision before the pack. She traded a glance with him, silently thanking him, and he offered a grim smile in return. He might not like her decision, but he respected her right to make it.

"That's a magnanimous gesture," Adam said in a

way that implied it was not. He made a show of considering both her and the cowering Carl in turn.

A chill ran down Theresa's spine because she doubted that she would be granted the same clemency when her turn came to be judged. If not for Zach's steadfast presence, she would not have had the courage to stand up and speak on her assailant's behalf.

"All right," Adam said in an adamant tone that brooked no discussion or disagreement. "It's an admirable thing to show mercy, but the presence of a wolf known to have attacked the pack's most valuable breeding female is also intolerable."

Theresa winced and bit her tongue. Outrage at being labeled a broodmare caused her spine to stiffen, but she swiftly hid her anger. Adam had granted her request, but the Wolf King also needed to put Theresa in her place in front of the others. She hated it—she hated him—but she recognized the necessity of keeping her mouth shut.

"Carl will be branded and exiled to live out the remainder of his life as an outcast." Adam gestured for the man on his knees to be removed.

At the pronouncement, Carl cried out in a mixture of relief and agony. While his life had been spared, he had been condemned to an existence that many wolves regarded as worse than death. Outcast. A wolf without a pack.

The pack's four enforcers closed on Carl with lightning speed, seizing his limbs and holding him down. He screamed and bucked, but their combined strength far outstripped his desperate struggles.

Becky stepped forward, holding a black bag. She removed a tool the size of a fireplace poker, which had a steel grip but a pointed end made of pure silver—the branding iron. With great care, she offered her husband the handle, and he took it from her grasp.

The sight of the wicked implement caused Theresa to shudder. It had been more than three years since she had seen the branding iron used. Adam might be a despotic ruler, but he had never been excessively cruel or unfair about dealing with minor transgressions.

The enforcers tore open Carl's shirt, baring his chest, and Adam moved to stand over the prisoner. Holding the branding iron aloft, he pressed the silver tip to naked skin, and the air filled with the sickening scent of burned flesh.

From the moment that silver touched him, Carl writhed in agony, thrashing with all of his might so that it took all four enforcers to hold him down. Terrible screams tore from the man's throat as Adam carved the word OSTRAKON, Greek for outcast, across Carl's torso.

Stomach churning, Theresa turned from the

sight and closed her eyes. Zach's arms closed about her shoulders, and she pressed her face against the crook of his arm. He offered steady support, even though she knew that he watched the entire branding without flinching or looking away.

After a couple minutes, Carl's screams faded to blubbering, and the branding was finished.

"He is outcast—without name or honor," Adam announced in a harsh tone. "Remove this worthless scum from my sight."

Two of the Alpha's enforcers bent to seize his elbows, lifted Carl from the ground, and then carried him from the meadow. Theresa watched them go with a queasy roiling in her stomach and tried to content herself with the knowledge that she had done everything in her power to help him. Ultimately, he had gotten less than he had deserved.

"Debra Yeller." Still wielding the branding iron, Adam swung on the skulking woman. "Step forward and hear my judgment."

Debra's eyes grew huge and wild, and, for a moment, it seemed like she might bolt and run from the clearing. The muscles of her throat appeared to tighten as she swallowed, and finally, she took a shaky step toward the Alpha.

Taking long strides, Adam closed the distance between himself and the trembling she-wolf. He towered over her, more than a head and shoulder taller, and she shrank visibly, adopting a posture that made her appear even smaller. Her gaze remained fixed on the ground in submission.

"Debra, after you lost the challenge and your rank to Theresa, I declared the matter settled," Adam said with a sneer. His contempt for her rivaled what he had shown for Carl. "However, in defiance of my command, you have conspired against Theresa and resorted to duplicitous manipulation."

"I'm sorry, Alpha," Debra said, her voice and body quaking with fear.

"You shall share your lover's fate," Adam said. "You are to be branded and cast out of this pack, to live out the remainder of your miserable life in isolation. Since you are female, the branding will be done in private to spare the pack the trauma of witnessing your suffering."

A shriek tore from Debra's throat and then a litany of incoherent curses and pleas. Theresa winced in sympathy. She averted her gaze as another of the Alpha's enforcers removed the sobbing she-wolf from the clearing.

Adam passed the branding iron to Becky and gave his mate a sharp nod. Becky accepted the implement and dipped her head. The Alpha's mate would administer Debra's brand.

Becky departed, and Theresa gulped nervously.

Her turn had come.

Once Debra's voice faded away, Theresa looked up and squared her shoulders, facing Adam with quiet pride. She mustered her courage and met the Alpha's gaze, refusing to cower before him. Even if he condemned her to be branded and exiled, she resolved to keep her dignity. She would not beg or show weakness.

Through the pack bond, she sensed Zach's tension and the pack's confusion.

"Theresa, you've broken our laws and endangered this pack by using your strength in front of humans," Adam said.

"Yes, Alpha," Theresa said, and her voice remained steady.

Adam stared at her. His features set into a hard mask. Then, without warning, he smiled, and an admiring gleam entered his eyes. "You're a fine female, Theresa, too valuable to this pack as our future Alpha's mate and our Heart to be exiled or severely punished."

Despite her resolve, a wave of relief swept through her because the prospect of being exiled frightened her to death. Any other punishment, no matter how draconian, was preferable to being separated from her child.

"Why did you break our rules and beat up those men?" Adam asked. "I've heard Sheriff

Mahoney's explanation, but I'd like to hear your side."

Theresa swallowed and quelled the impulse to fidget. She took a second to compose her thoughts and then said, "Those men treated me with disrespect, and it made me angry."

Adam rolled his head in a nod. "You wanted to show them that they were inferior to you in every way."

Not exactly the way she would have put it.

Theresa kept her mouth shut and tipped her head to indicate her agreement. She appeared to have Adam's sympathy, and she couldn't risk alienating him for the sake of quibbling. Not with so much at stake.

"I understand that you drew power from Zach and managed a partial transformation on your own," Adam said, continuing his one-sided conversation.

"Yes, Alpha."

"Have you and Zach sealed the mate bond yet?"

She flushed so that her skin grew hot. The man's gall was unbelievable. He did not even pretend to respect her right to choose or substantiate Robert's worth. It took an act of willpower not to betray her anger.

"No, Alpha," she said, struggling for an even tone. "Not yet."

Her answer did not please Adam. He grunted

and frowned. "Don't take too long choosing, or you might find your options reduced."

The implied threat caused her to shudder. "I won't, Alpha."

Adam growled a rumble that cleared his throat and communicated his dominance to all within hearing range. Excitement surged through the pack, a combination of the full moon and the Alpha's aggression speaking to their inner beasts. More than one wolf tilted back their head to release a haunting howl.

Adam waited until the last wolf cry died away and then addressed the pack. "It is not a normal situation for a female with a pup to be without her mate's protection."

Even without stating it aloud, the pack sensed the Alpha's implied criticism. Antonio became the recipient of condemning glances and harsh whispers. He dropped his gaze and adopted an ashamed posture.

"Theresa's pheromones are enhanced because she is coming into heat," Adam said. "Her wolf recognizes that she is to be our new Alpha female, that she must mate with the most dominant male and bear his offspring, thus strengthening the pack and assuring his succession."

Theresa's jaw dropped, and her head twisted toward Zach. She stared at him in stunned silence, mouth hanging, wondering if it were true. Was she coming into heat?

From his stoic expression, she learned nothing. Damn the man, but he had one hell of a poker face. She wanted to shake her head and exclaim no. No way.

But no. When she considered the matter, she knew the truth of it. She had felt the changes taking place within her body, and it explained everything, from her high sex drive to her increased aggression.

"The men who assaulted her are not to blame, and we will not be seeking vengeance against them. It's only natural for them to have responded to her with sexual advances, the same as it is not her fault for having attracted trouble in the first place. Let it be known that I am forbidding any member of this pack to seek out those three men and take any action against them. It is a matter I now consider settled."

Theresa shifted and returned her gaze to Adam. She could not believe that the Alpha intended to let the matter go without so much as a verbal warning. There had to be more coming. She refused to let her guard down.

Zach stepped forward. "I'll see to Theresa's protection from this point forward."

Robert also raised his voice. "As will I."

"Good," Adam said. "Until she is properly mated

and with child—meaning she will no longer be in heat—I forbid Theresa to hold any more jobs that place her in contact with human males. Once she has chosen, then her new mate will provide for her."

Her jaw snapped shut, and her teeth gnashed together. Her anger rendered her speechless, which was just as well since she did not dare express her thoughts aloud. Stiff-necked, she bowed her head and allowed her long hair to slip over her face. In her outrage, something deep inside her wanted to demand that Zach challenge Adam on the spot and defend her against the outrageous directive.

Her heart thundered in her ears, and she sensed Zach through the pack bond. She felt his fury. He wanted to kill Adam also. The realization helped to cool her heated emotions so that the voice of reason could prevail. It took a valiant effort to swallow her pride, but after several deep breaths, she calmed and breathed easier.

As she had expected, the Alpha had devised a devious punishment, one designed to hit her where it hurt the most. He had taken away her prized independence and her ability to provide financially for herself and her daughter, leaving her reliant upon a man for support.

But the consequences could have been so much worse.

"Do you understand and accept my judgment, Theresa?" Adam asked.

"Yes, Alpha," Theresa said, though the words stuck in her craw.

Adam swung to face the gathered pack. "The meeting is officially adjourned. The moon will be up soon, and I'm planning on having one hell of a grand hunt tonight!"

The Alpha tilted back his head and released an ascendant howl that incited exuberance among the other members of the pack. Wolves bounded to his side, rollicking and wrestling beneath the canopy of pine trees, their anxiety, and angst forgotten in the heat of the moment.

Theresa retreated from her packmates and made her way to where Zach waited at the edge of the clearing. Charlaine and Robert stood with him. She slowed her steps as she approached the trio until Zach opened his arms. With a strangled sound, part angry cry, part sob, she rushed into the safety of his embrace. Her slender arms wrapped about his waist, and he held her tight.

Zach pressed his mouth to the top of her head. "I'm sorry, love. You wanted me to challenge him. I could feel it."

Robert stirred. "Hell, Zach, the challenge needs to come from me. You're not even in line to challenge Adam. He'd be within his rights to demand that you fight me first before you could fight him."

"Seems like the bastard will get what he wants eventually, no matter how he plays it."

Theresa's head jerked up, and she drew back from Zach to look at both men. "No, I won't have you two fighting. We agreed that we'd figure out some other way to handle this without anyone dying."

Charlaine snorted. "Once one of you replaces Adam, then you'll be able to return to work, Theresa."

Zach's blue eyes lit with laughter, and he grinned. "Oh, I don't know. Barefoot and pregnant has a certain appeal."

Theresa's fist struck his bicep. Not lightly. "Don't test me, mister."

He forced the grin from his face. "Yes, ma'am."

Charlaine's lovely face pulled into a grimace. "We'd better come up with some smart idea soon, or that bastard will win."

Abruptly, their laughter stopped.

Robert scowled, and his shoulders slumped. "It's time for me to challenge Adam," he said, shaking his head. "I'd have done so already, but I didn't want to come to power through more bloodshed."

Theresa's heart ached for him. "There must be

some other way," she said, grasping at empty air with her hands.

"Robert is right," Zach said, resting a supportive hand on his friend's shoulder. "One or both of us has to challenge him. It's the only way."

Theresa shook her head, unwilling to believe that violence was the answer. Unfortunately, the men seemed to agree, and she had no other viable suggestions.

"If either of you needs a second, then I'll stand up for you," Charlaine said in support of the two men.

"Thanks, Char," Robert said with a weary smile for his cousin.

Feeling outnumbered, Theresa sighed. "You can't do this tonight," she said at last. "The night of the full moon has to be the worst possible time for a challenge."

The full moon brought their wolves to the fore. The newly established connection between the wolves of the Iron Stone pack lacked both strength and endurance. Brittle tension existed within the pack bond, a disharmony that left Theresa deeply troubled. She feared that internal conflict between the most dominant members might destroy the tenuous unity.

"You're right. I'll make the challenge tomorrow," Robert said.

"Thank you," Theresa said. More than anything else, his wisdom and patience convinced her of his worthiness to become Alpha, solidifying her determination to support him.

"The moon's rising." Zach glanced heavenward, and everyone followed his gaze. To the west, the sky paled as the sun's rays faded. To the east, the moon's silver halo glowed just above the horizon.

"It's so beautiful." Theresa reached out and caught Zach's hand.

He returned her smile in an expression of shared happiness. The lunar song beckoned their wolves, an irresistible siren's call.

Usually, the pack retreated to deep wilderness, far from human habitations, for the one night of the month when the full moon rose. Under the silvery glow, within the pristine forests of the Sierra Nevada mountains, they were free to become wolves. The transformation brought freedom from the burdens of humanity, regarded as a time of rejoicing and celebration.

"Let's get moving," Char said, heading south toward the uninhabited forest where the pack would gather.

Robert followed swiftly on her heels, leaving Zach and Theresa to bring up the rear. Together, they walked hand in hand until the first moonbeams reached for them, the soft glow caressing bare skin.

"Whatcha thinking?" Zach asked in a low voice.

She forced a joking smile. "That it's too bad I can't just take both of you as a mate and have a male harem."

Zach's head jerked to the side, and he stared at her, an ah-ha expression of discovery on his face.

Alarm bells rang in Theresa's head. She knew that expression. It accompanied his mercurial and strange sense of humor. On the other hand, she feared he might have taken her seriously.

"Zach," she said. "I'm kidding. It was a joke."

Abruptly, he threw back his head and laughed, a joyous, booming sound that carried through the forest. He seized her arms and swung her around, off of the ground and up into his arms. "It was brilliant. That's what it was. Theresa, you're a genius!"

She squawked right before he planted a wet kiss on her lips. His enthusiasm proved contagious, and she found herself laughing too. "Zach, stop it! Knock it off, and tell me what you're going on about."

Grinning, he set her back on her feet. "No time now," he said, pulling off his shirt as the first ray of moonlight caressed his bare skin. "I'll explain tomorrow."

"You'd better!"

Hurriedly, Theresa stripped and set her clothing aside as she felt the change overtake her. A growl tore from her throat, and she bent forward as the pain of the transformation ripped through her.

Red fur erupted from her skin, and her teeth elongated to sharp points. Sinew pushed and pulled. Bones cracked and then reformed. Her face grew to a muzzle, her ears to points high atop her head, and she dropped to all fours, losing the ability to stand upright as her arms became legs.

Beside her, Zach also succumbed to the moon's call. A ferocious howl rose from him as he transformed. As a wolf, he had thick, dark gray guard fur that lay atop a white undercoat. Like most males, he weighed twice what she did.

Other wolves joined their chorus from the dense forest, blending their voices as every member howled with joy and vitality. Praise for the night.

Wolf song.

CHAPTER THIRTY

"Is this it?" Theresa asked early the following day, staring at the white one-story house with a manicured front lawn and towering pine trees along the property line.

"This is it." Zach parked his sports car along the curb in front of Robert Blane's sprawling ranch-style house. He shut off the engine and pocketed the keys.

Taking a breath, Theresa climbed from the vehicle and waited on the sidewalk while Zach circled to join her. The sun had risen hours before, and bright morning light illuminated the landscape. Theresa had arranged for her mother to drop Isabel at school and pick her up afterward.

She took a second to indulge her curiosity,

studying the slate paver walkway that led up to his front porch. Robert's SUV was parked in the driveway. A garden gnome peeked out from beneath a juniper bush. She attempted to envision the polished attorney standing in line at the hardware store with the gnome statue in his cart and suffered an epic failure of imagination.

Her reflections took a somewhat sad turn. Zach and Robert were opposites. Even the men's choices of private residence mirrored their respective relationships to the pack. Zach lived on the side of a mountain and chose to remain on the periphery of their social group. In contrast, Robert dwelled at the town center and occupied a central role in their small community.

Zach stepped onto the sidewalk and faced her with his arms held loosely at his sides. During the drive over, they had reached an agreement. Accord resonated between them, a single harmonious note reinforcing their unity.

"You ready?" Zach asked, watching her with wise blue eyes.

Theresa inhaled and nodded. She met his gaze, and her resolve solidified. She had doubts, but their answer seemed to offer the only possible violence-free solution.

"Yeah, I'm ready."

Zach took her hand and led her toward the

house, past the waist-high gate, and up the slate paver walkway to the front porch.

"Here goes nothing." Before she could change her mind, Theresa stabbed at the doorbell. She glanced over at Zach, mustering a smile for his benefit.

Zach tightened his grip on her elbow, expressing nonverbal support, and their auras meshed, presenting an integrated front. "Hang tight, love. Worst case scenario, he calls us crazy and kicks us out."

"I'm not sure that's the worst case," Theresa said, giving her dry lips a nervous wetting with the tip of her tongue.

She heard footsteps approaching the door and then the sound of the lock tumbling. The front door swung open to reveal Robert clad in a pair of skintight black leather pants and a white muscle shirt. A gold hoop earring hung from his right earlobe, giving him a rakish air, further reinforced when his white teeth flashed in a cheeky grin.

Robert's thick brow gave an inquisitive lift. "You look like two foxes in the henhouse. What's up? Or should I be afraid to ask?"

"Robert, can we come in? We have a proposal for you." Theresa stepped toward him, allowing her newfound ability as the Heart to unfurl, and took his hand. Her power flowed, uniting the three of them, evoking the pack bond. With practice, it became easier to do so.

"She means that more literally than you'd think, Robbie." Zach delivered the dry statement with perfect poise. His blue eyes never lost their sparkle.

Robert laughed and opened the door wider. "Come in."

Their host escorted them to a room best characterized as a man cave—large screen television attached to the wall, surround-sound speakers, black leather furniture, and a bar.

"Bottled water?" Robert asked, tugging open the fridge.

Theresa shook her head. "No, thanks."

"I'll take one." Zach extended his hand, and Robert passed him a bottle.

Theresa settled on a couch, and Zach sat beside her, so their thighs pressed together. Robert chose the chair opposite them. The Beta wolf sipped his water and faced them with remarkable intensity. Silence reigned for a long moment.

Zach's hand gave her knee an encouraging pat, and his power flowed across her skin, lending his support. Theresa sucked down a deep breath, gathered her courage, and looked Robert straight in the eyes.

"We want you to enter into the mate bond with

us," she said, bolstering the magic she used to unite with her fellow wolves.

Robert rocked back, and a surprised huff escaped him. His jaw dropped, hung, and then snapped shut with the audible clash of teeth. He stared at the two of them for a minute, studying their faces in turn, perhaps attempting to discern if it was supposed to be a joke. The atmosphere grew brittle and charged, but pack unity held.

"You're not kidding," Robert said at long last in a voice rife with disbelief.

"No, we're not," Theresa replied.

"Mate bonds between multiple partners are uncommon," Robert said, playing the devil's advocate.

"But not unheard of," Zach said, tone reasonable. "We'd be breaking with cultural taboo but not in a severe manner. Besides, as the pack's dominant wolves, who's to tell us we can't do whatever the hell we want?"

Robert set the water bottle down on the side table. He sat back and folded his hands, elbows resting on his knees. His brown eyes narrowed, and his face acquired the shrewd calculation that made him a topnotch attorney. "I presume it would be a strictly platonic arrangement?"

Theresa blushed so that her face and throat burned.

"Beyond whatever physical intimacy is necessary to seal the mate bond." Zach flashed a wolfish smile. "No offense, buddy, but you're not my type."

Robert's dark eyes flashed. "None taken. I prefer my men more submissive and prettier than your ugly mug."

As always, Theresa envied Zach's ability to defuse awkward situations with humor. A flush warmed her face, but she did her best to dispel her embarrassment and adopt his easy-going attitude. She touched his knee, an intimate caress, allowing her fingers to linger along the inside of his leg. "I think you're damn handsome. Not ugly at all."

He glanced sideways with a sly smile. "Thank you, pet."

Robert directed a skeptical stare toward Zach. "Do you honestly believe you could overcome your possessive instincts and share Theresa with me for even one night?"

Zach remained silent for a time, considering, before he replied, "Yeah, I do. So long as there's no doubt that she's mine for the rest of our lives. Theresa is my soul mate."

Tears welled in her eyes, and her throat seized so that it hurt to breathe. She swallowed with difficulty and glanced at her lover with a watery smile, unable to express the overwhelming ache in her chest.

"What makes you think you can curtail your innate aggression toward a competitor?"

Theresa huffed. "I think I can manage the two of you," she said quickly. A second later, she realized how imperious the boast sounded and flushed.

Robert glanced at her, at first startled but then with chagrined respect. "Look who's Alpha now."

Zach laughed so hard his sides shook. "We've created a monster."

Theresa stifled a giggle, which escaped and sounded strangled. "This would solve all of our problems," she said, addressing Robert. "If I can present you to Adam as my mate, then he'll have no choice but to honor the conditions he set and hand over leadership without bloodshed."

"There's no guarantee that bastard will behave in an honorable fashion," Robert said. "Intolerance and hatred are powerful motivators. I wouldn't put it past him to try and rescind his ruling."

"I wouldn't either," Zach said with a cold viciousness that sent chills down Theresa's spine. "If he does, then we'll force him to step down. He can't fight both of us and expect to live."

Robert nodded his agreement. "I've been holding off challenging him because I don't want to traumatize the pack, but I'd love to kill that bastard."

Theresa winced. "It won't come to that. His enforcers wouldn't permit it."

Zach snorted. "Love, you have so much more faith in people than I do."

"Not faith," Theresa said. "I believe that people will always act in their best interests. If the enforcers are perceived as corrupt, they stand to lose their position when Adam is ousted. His departure is inevitable. By his own words, he and Becky want to leave. If we do this right, it should be painful for him but easy for us."

"Presuming this works," Robert said, looking toward Zach. "You're content serving as my second?"

"Beta is plenty of responsibility for me. Anything else would cut into my writing and family time," Zach said, straightforward and honest in his demeanor. "Frankly, I don't want to be Alpha. The hours suck, and the pay is terrible."

Robert's mouth twisted into a sad smile. "I can't name a single thing I want more."

"It's yours," Zach said.

"Robert." Theresa leaned forward to catch his attention.

He looked at her, brow raised in silent query.

"If we do this, I want to be sure there would be no misunderstandings or regrets," she said. "A mating bond is forever. It means—"

"That I can't ever offer my heart and soul to another lover," Robert said, making it clear that he understood the implications. He exhaled long and slow, sighing as he breathed out. "And I'm okay with that because it's for the good of the pack."

Said aloud, it sounded so cold. So cruel. So lonely. Bisexual wolves, especially incredibly dominant leaders, guarded their secret closely or risked being ostracized or killed.

Theresa blinked back tears, hurting for him. Outwardly, Robert Blane had everything going for him—intelligence, physique, looks, a successful career, and financial prosperity. She had thought of him as self-contained and autonomous before but never so isolated.

Robert focused on her with clear eyes that seemed to burn holes deep into her soul. She squirmed beneath that gaze, nervous about what he might see in her.

"What about children?" he asked with the air of a seasoned negotiator getting down to the nitty-gritty.

Theresa traded a glance with Zach. He tipped his head toward her and remained silent.

Theresa turned back to Robert. "My offspring will be your potential successors," she said. "Including Isabel. I won't have her dismissed or overlooked because her father is a low-ranked jerk."

Robert chuckled. "Fair enough."

"I'm in heat so there's a good possibility that I'll conceive when we consummate the mate bond." Her bluntness caused Theresa's cheeks to heat, but she refused to look down or hide behind her hair as she would have once done. "Whether the child is yours or Zach's, I expect both of you to treat it the same. No favoritism."

Robert tilted his head to the side and regarded her with an unwavering stare. "This is likely the only opportunity I'll have to sire a child, so I'm grateful," he said in a quiet voice, demonstrating vulnerability that was at odds with his typical macho demeanor.

Theresa's throat tightened, and she hurt for him. The poor man had already sacrificed so much for the good of Iron Stone's wolves, and he would give even more, forever forgoing the opportunity to offer his heart and soul to his true love—should they ever meet. Her compassion spread through the pack bond, drawing both males into sync with her. The overwhelming ocean of grief threatened to drown her.

"Bloody hell. Enough with the chick flick already," Zach gritted out with frustration and stood. His powerful aura, threaded with the strength of resolution, created a rude splash like cold water across the face. "Are we in agreement?"

Robert's glance flickered toward Zach. A brief smile tugged at Robert's lips. "We agree."

Theresa grinned at Zach to avoid looking directly at Robert. Reality crashed over her, igniting the heat in her wolf and causing her core to spasm. Erotic anticipation fed her excitement, and she felt her pussy getting wet. She intended to enter into a lifelong commitment with not one but two stunning men. Afterward, she would have sex with both of them to seal the mate bond. Her arousal spread like a fever across her skin. She breathed faster, causing her bosom to heave beneath her thin cotton shirt. Desire trickled along the inside of her thigh, and her sweatiness had nothing to do with the room temperature.

An awkward silence fell around the room for a full minute as they regarded one another. Possibility danced through Theresa's mind in a stream of sensual visions, some quite graphic, others lurid, all intensely carnal. Without thought, she surged to her feet and moved away from Zach.

Robert stood also and shifted to the right until they were the same distance apart. As three points of a triangle, they faced one another. Theresa had once heard something about tripods being extremely stable. She wondered if it were true.

The air vibrated with tension. Breathe in, breathe out.

"Zach, Robert," Theresa said, voice tenuous at first but gaining strength, "my heart beats for you—with you—and from this moment forward, we shall hunt and fight as one in the face of all adversity. Our hearts are one."

The sacred words of the oath of the mating invoked potent magic. She looked to her right, passing the torch to Robert.

"Theresa, Zach, my heart beats for you—with you—and from this moment forward, we shall hunt and fight as one in the face of all adversity. Our hearts are one."

They both looked to Zach.

He cleared his throat, offered a toothy grin, and adopted a practiced stage pose. "I never know what to say at these things, but I'd like to thank you both for coming—"

A throw pillow smacked against his raised arm and tumbled to the floor. Theresa reached for another. Her throat rumbled with a growl of warning. "Zachary Hunter."

Zach's laughter died away, but his aura still sang with humor. "Theresa, Rob, my heart beats for you—with you—and from this moment forward, we shall hunt and fight as one in the face of all adversity. Our hearts are one."

In the physical world, nothing at all remarkable happened, but in the spiritual realm, lightning flashed. Thunder crashed. An earthquake tremored the ground beneath their feet. Three souls became one, meshed into a single unit lacking harmony and concordance, but as a whole, they were stronger than any one individual.

Gradually, the fireworks faded, but the mate bond remained, tying the three of them together. The connection manifested as an indestructible platinum thread, stretching between them to form a triangle. Inseparable till death.

Tension buzzed in the air, causing her skin to itch, and the urge to squirm grew overpowering. She licked dry lips and inhaled deeply, scenting the perfume of pheromones heavy in the room. The allure of her arousal filled her nostrils, robust with her fertility and readiness to mate.

Both men kept their gazes glued to her. The brush of their auras sizzled across her body in an electrifying storm. She huffed, concentrating on the males, and drank in the odor of their lust and aggression, thick and musky.

Primal need spiked her abdomen, causing her stomach muscles to contract and her core to clench in anticipation. Heat and wetness pooled between her thighs. As much as it embarrassed her, she owned her desire, aware that with just a bit more confidence, she would come to celebrate it.

"You initiate, Theresa," Robert said in a gruff voice.

Her gaze darted between Robert and Zach, appraising each male in turn. They were both big, buff, delicious. Hers. Zach had the most sensual lips and hands she'd ever seen on any man. Robert radiated enormous power, born of a combination of sheer willpower and physical prowess. She barely knew where to start or how.

The men watched her with hunger in their eyes, rampant bulges straining the front of their pants. She smelled their excitement, an intoxicating aroma, and their auras meshed in a seductive net about her, yet they remained still, waiting on her to make the first move.

Uncertainty spiraled through her mind. On the one hand, it felt right and natural to go to Zach first, but she worried that doing so would send the wrong message. If Robert felt shunned or excluded, this whole thing might fall apart.

Zach saved her. He cocked his head and flashed an arrogant grin. "Go on, love. I'll watch and wait for my turn."

She flushed but turned toward Robert. Dilated pupils eclipsed his irises. He held his muscular frame tense, poised for action, the stance of a true predator. Her nervous tongue darted across her lips, and his eyes followed the tiny movement.

The flesh along the backs of Robert's arms rippled, and his canine teeth elongated so the tips cut into the insides of his mouth. Adrenaline surged through his body until he felt ready to jump out of his skin, muscles bunched to the tightness of coiled springs. His wolf surfaced, threatening his already shaky self-control, requiring all of his willpower to remain human and wait until Theresa approached him.

She wore her thick hair long and loose, so the midnight silk formed a curtain of curls about her shoulders. The V-neckline of her top plunged toward generous cleavage, revealing tanned skin dusted with a light sheen of sweat. Her hourglass figure suggested fertility. Motherhood. Her waist formed a gentle indentation, and then her hips flared. The glove-like fit of her jeans molded about a curvy ass that just begged for a man's hands to cover and squeeze. He studied her womanly form with open admiration.

She took a step closer, and the aromatic cocktail of female arousal and the pheromones that accompanied ovulation hit him like a rocket to the crotch. Bitch in heat. His nostrils flared as he inhaled deeply and knew beyond a shadow of a doubt that Adam had been right at least about one thing. Theresa was in season. Her ascendance to

Alpha female came along with the biological imperative to mate.

"Nothing prepares you for something like this." Theresa halted inches from him so the combined heat of their bodies created a blast zone. A smile curved her lips as she tilted back her head to gaze into his face.

"Porn." Zach's amused voice, awash with laughter, floated from the other side of the room. "Porn prepares you for scenarios exactly like this."

Robert chuckled. "He's right."

"Damn, my education is woefully lacking," Theresa said.

She placed her palms flat on his chest and directed him toward the couch. Her amazing magic, the remarkable ability to unify individual wolves into a coherent whole, manifested as a swirl of raw energy that swept through the room. She drew power from him and Zach, causing the ambient aura to light with brilliant hues.

"We're only too happy to rectify that oversight." Robert stepped backward and sank onto the leather sectional.

Sitting caused his form-fitting leather pants to tighten across the lap, putting pressure on his cock and balls. The throbbing in his crotch echoed in his ears, but he deliberately kept his hands at his sides. Submitting went against his nature, but he recognized the necessity until the she-wolf reached her comfort zone.

"Good porn needs a soundtrack," Zach said, heading across the room toward the stereo system. He stopped to examine the long-playing records on the wall, flipping through one at a time. "Mind if I look through your vinyl?"

"Help yourself, seeing as how you already are, but you're not going to find any lame music in my collection," Robert said with a sour expression. A portion of his mind tracked the movements of the other male wolf, but most of his attention remained focused on Theresa.

"What? No chicka boom, bow-wows?"

"Zach." Theresa shot the Englishman a glance of reprimand.

"Sorry, love. Couldn't resist."

She straddled Robert's legs and settled atop his thighs, balanced lightly with her toes resting on the floor. Theresa placed her hands on his shoulders and leaned forward, claiming his lips in a soft kiss. Theresa tasted of honey and chamomile tea. The fullness of her bosom molded against his muscular chest, breasts flattened deliciously.

Her lips were plump and soft against his mouth, and the tip of her tongue flirted with his teeth, darting along the smooth surface of the top row. Her fingers dug into the firm muscle of his shoulders, kneading tense knots centered at the juncture of his neck and shoulder.

He moaned and settled his hands on the curve of her waist, fingers splayed to caress her sweet backside, thumbs brushing over her hipbones. As the kiss deepened, the stereo system activated with the distinctive sound of the needle being lowered onto a record. A moment later, the smoky strains of instrumental jazz music swelled to fill the entire house.

Theresa's hands dropped, and her fingers snagged the hem of his shirt, pulling it over his shoulders. He bowed his head and stretched his arms in a diving pose to ease the removal. With a grin, she wadded and tossed the garment to the side.

While Robert's OCD nature despised any sort of mess, he let the matter slide. He had way more important priorities—the press of her lips just below his ear, the flicker of her tongue, and the sharp nip of her teeth as she worked her way toward his pulse point. His eyes closed, and he tilted his head back, exposing the substantial column of his throat.

Theresa's hands massaged his pectorals, coaxing a ragged moan from him. He heard the soft pad of footsteps on the hardwood, so he lifted his head and saw Zach approaching from behind the she-wolf.

Robert's posture grew tense with the potential

threat, but then the other male wolf sank to his knees behind Theresa, an implicit granting of rank that helped dissipate the tension. Robert relaxed again, allowing his bunched muscles to ease.

Zach's hands settled on Theresa's waist, and he pressed his face against the side of her throat. "I love the way your hair smells."

"Robert, stop checking out Zach and pay attention to what I'm doing," Theresa said in a voice lilting with laughter. Her palm patted his crotch, causing his dick to twitch and throb within the confines of his skintight leather pants. She squeezed, not enough to hurt but enough so his balls felt ready to burst.

His breathing hitched, and his gaze jerked back to her. The feminine challenge glimmering in her dark eyes and the slight smirk on her lips excited him unbearably.

"You've got my attention," he said, trying and failing to achieve an even tone. "What are you going to do with it?"

"I want your pants off." Theresa unfastened his belt buckle and then undid the fly. Her insistent hands hooked the waistband. "Lift up."

Obligingly, Robert lifted his hips enough to allow her to remove the garment. With a hard tug, Theresa stripped his pants down his long legs. She struggled with his shoes and then discarded his clothing with a careless toss, leaving him clad in only a pair of red briefs. His full erection swelled the crotch, straining the stretchy material.

Theresa stared at his crotch, and her brow arched. "Oh, wow! You really should be starring in porno movies."

Robert gave a husky chuckle. "I considered becoming a porn star, but my calling is the law."

CHAPTER THIRTY-ONE

Theresa knelt before Robert. Zach crouched directly behind her with his hands beneath her shirt so his long fingers stroked her stomach. She knew both males were fully aroused from sight and scent, awaiting her bidding, ready to service her. Her aching pussy creamed at the prospect, causing her core to clench, heat and wetness pooling between her thighs.

"If you're already erect, I'm impressed. If you're not, then I'm scared," she teased, licking her lips in delicious anticipation.

Her admiring gaze swept his sublime physique. Her breath hitched at the sight of his intense masculinity. The man was pure eye candy. His muscle definition indicated that he worked with weights regularly. A thin dusting of hair coated his dark chest, but his arms and legs were furry. His abdominal muscles were compact and prominent, a toned six-pack rippling beneath his skin. Sweat covered his body.

Reaching out, she snagged Robert's briefs. He once again lifted his hips in cooperation. With undisguised impatience, she tugged them down his long legs. His cock sprang free from the confines, fully erect and jutting at an insistent angle. Iridescent beads of precum gathered on the mushroom-shaped head.

Robert snapped a handful of her dark hair and gave a gentle tug, pulling her toward him. His other hand adjusted the position of his engorged cock. He spread his knees wider to grant her access. "Open your pretty mouth. I want to see it wrapped around my cock."

"Go on, love," Zach urged his voice a velvet timbre in her ear. His warm breath caressed her cheek even as his fingers worked to unfasten the front buttons of her top. "Pay homage to our new Alpha."

"Mmm." The small cry of need escaped her in reaction to Zach's touch.

He eased the shirt off her shoulders and made short work of her bra, casting the two garments aside. Her full breasts swayed without the constricting undergarment, and her taut nipples brushed against the coarse hair of Robert's knees as she bent forward.

Loose tendrils of hair fell forward about Theresa's face. Her hair and then her lips touched Robert's stomach, causing the skin to jump, and she dusted a trail of kisses across his thighs. Her gentle hands cradled his scrotum, supporting the heaviness in her palms, shifting the fleshy mass to discover first one testis and then the other. Her tongue traced up and down the length of his shaft. She swirled a clockwise lick around the head, and then her lips pressed a kiss to the tip.

A tortured groan dragged from Robert's throat, and his head lolled back as his muscular body relaxed. He ceded control to her, allowing her to establish the pace. Having such a powerful male submit to her excited Theresa unbearably, and she relished her ability to exert such power over him.

Zach's lips suckled the side of her neck, exploring the flesh below her ears and to the juncture of her shoulder. His spread fingers cupped the underside of her breasts and sank into the firm flesh, massaging with a delicate alternating rhythm. The sensitive pads teased her nipples, agitating the already peaked buds. The length of his long body pressed against her back, his hard erection humping her ass through the denim of their jeans.

Theresa allowed her hands to switch positions, reaching deeper between Robert's legs to locate the smooth skin between his scrotum and anus. She circled the tight ring of muscle, eliciting a purr-like growl from him. His breathing grew labored. She flirted with the temptation to draw the blowjob out for a long time, to test the limits of Robert's discipline truly, but denying him meant denying herself, and Zach's mouth and hands promised endless delight.

Time to slay the dragon.

Using her lips to create a seal, mouth suctioning to form a vacuum, Theresa launched a determined assault upon Robert's vaunted self-control. Her head bobbed at a frantic pace, and her index finger breached his ass, applying steady pressure until she found his prostate.

A shout ripped from Robert's throat, and his entire body convulsed, limbs shuddering in violent reaction, ripples of muscle moving across his abdomen. Howling, he ejaculated cum that tasted salty and scalding hot in her mouth. She swallowed and kept sucking until his member softened before releasing him. He collapsed against the back of the couch.

Theresa sat back on her haunches, leaning against Zach's chest for support. His steady hands grasped her arms and turned her to face him. She tilted back her head to look up into his face, and their gazes locked. In his blue eyes, she saw equal parts devotion and desire. A playful smile curved his lips. Amazingly, Zach still wore all of his clothing, which made her acutely aware of her nudity from the waist up.

"Hi," she said, feeling more than a little self-conscious.

"Hi." Zach grinned, and then, his head dipped toward her. His nostrils flared as he inhaled, and his hands settled on her waist, gripping with firm pressure. "Fuck, you smell delicious. I want to eat you up."

"You're more than welcome to," Theresa said, giggling.

She captured his parted lips in a firm kiss, and her tongue probed his mouth, insistent and curious, exploring the depths beyond. He tasted like the essence of sin, damp heat, and zing, and she drank from him.

He groaned, almost a growl, and she heard the thunder of his heartbeat. He held her against his muscular chest. The embrace crushed her breasts flat, and friction with his shirt agitated her pebble-hard nipples. Only when her lungs felt ready to explode from the lack of air did she break the kiss to draw air into her starved lungs.

"Why are you still dressed?" she asked, reaching

for the front of his shirt. She snagged the hem and dragged it over his head.

She heard the leather cushion of the couch creak beneath Robert's weight and heard him shifting, perhaps to obtain a better view. She felt the heat of his gaze focused on them, and the eroticism served to heighten her desire.

"Got distracted by the peep show," Zach said with a cheeky smile. He bent to facilitate the removal of the garment, which pulled away to reveal a broad chest and washboard abs. He went on to remove his socks and shoes, leaving him clad in only jeans.

Theresa found herself drawing comparisons between the two males again despite her best efforts. Robert had a physical advantage in terms of pure muscle. In contrast to Robert's dusky complexion, Zach appeared paler, but he had more elegant hands. She thanked her lucky stars that there wasn't a vast difference between the sizes of their dicks. She hoped they didn't ever trot out rulers.

"Pet, do I even want to know what you're thinking?" Zach asked with a knowing look on his face.

"Probably not," she said with a wry grin. Her cheeks flushed, and her gaze darted to the side. "If you ask, I'm going to plead the Fifth."

"You can always come to me for legal advice," Robert said with a silky chuckle.

"We'd better be getting the friends-n-family discount." Theresa cast a quick grin over her shoulder.

Zach smiled, but then, a somber expression overtook his amusement. He traced the line of her jaw with one finger. The shining adoration in his eyes caused her breath to hitch, and her heart to skip before settling into a steady throb, beating only for him.

"What is it?" she whispered, riveted beneath the intensity of his gaze.

"I love you, Theresa," Zach said, bending to claim her mouth.

Stunned, delighted, she clung to him and poured everything she had, heart and soul, into the kiss. He made her feel so special, so incredibly desirable. She knew then that he had loved her for years. He might not have said it, but he had showed her with his actions.

Framing his face with her hands, Theresa ended the kiss and gazed into his eyes. "I love you, too, with all my heart. Make love to me, Zach."

"With pleasure." Zach tenderly tucked a stray lock of hair behind her ear. He glanced sideways, and his voice rose even though he did not look directly at Robert. "I must admit, I'd love to make love to you on a proper bed instead of the couch."

Chuckling, Robert eased to his feet. He took a moment to pull up his tight briefs. Then, he crossed the room with long strides, his tight ass and powerful thigh muscles bunching with each step, a smooth play beneath his dark skin.

"This way, Captain Obvious," he tossed over his shoulder. "You know, if someone had warned me today would start with a threesome, I'd have gotten out the silk sheets."

With a sultry laugh, Theresa glanced back to make sure Zach followed them. With a smile, the Englishman brushed against her back. His heat radiated along every inch of her body from head to toe, and his hand pressed gently into the small of her back, urging her forward. She drew a breath and hurried her steps, gaining confidence as they passed through a long hallway, leading toward the back of the house.

Robert opened the door to the master suite and flipped on the light switch, illuminating a huge room sparsely appointed with modern furnishings. A massive platform bed sat centered beneath a bay window. Wooden blinds provided a degree of privacy. A black leather armchair beneath a floor lamp occupied one corner of the room. The only other furniture in the room was the mahogany dresser and armoire.

Robert slowed as he approached the bed and dropped sideways onto the surface. He said nothing, but his gaze remained fixed on them, intent and interested.

Being watched was an incredible turn-on. Zach's hand remained upon the small of her back and sent electric currents through her entire body. Through the mate bond, Theresa experienced his deep desire and adoration for her. When she reached the foot of the bed, she turned toward him just as he caught her wrist, pulling her closer.

Theresa sprung into the air. Their chests collided, and Zach's strong arms caught her. He held her suspended, feet dangling. With a teasing snarl, Theresa bared her teeth and nipped at his throat. She wrapped her arms about his neck and her legs about his hips, gripping him with her thighs. Her sharp teeth nicked his skin, so the salty blood teased her tongue.

"Feisty," Zach murmured even as she dragged his head down to claim his mouth. His entire body was ripped from the corded muscles of his arms, his broad shoulders and thick chest, the enticing protrusion in the front of his pants.

Mouths joined, Zach lowered Theresa onto the bed. The memory foam mattress barely created a discernible movement as their combined weight hit the surface. He felt Robert settle parallel to them, about three feet distant.

Zach propped up his torso with his arms while Theresa fumbled with the front of his pants. Her quick, clumsy attempts to undo the top button of his jeans ratcheted his arousal even higher. A growl trembled in his throat as she finally let loose a snarl of frustration and ripped through the denim to get at the cock underneath.

The crunch of breaking bones startled Zach. He glanced down to see Theresa's hands shift enough to grow razor-sharp tips. A startled yelp escaped him as her claws nicked the skin of his abdomen, light scratches that bled and healed in a blink. The slight sting fed his arousal, taking him over the edge of reason into primal aggression.

"Sorry. I need your cock," Theresa said, wearing an oh-so-fake angelic face.

His snarl choked, modulating to a chuckle. "Love, you're going to get my cock shoved all of the way up your pussy."

"If you're lucky, she might even notice." Robert tossed the zinger from his resting spot.

Zach shot the other male a narrow-eyed glance, promising retribution at a later time, but the Beta wolf only laughed. Theresa's enticing giggle lured his attention back to the nubile she-wolf. He willed his hands to claws and ripped through the denim of her blue jeans.

A feminine shriek and more laughter greeted his assault on her clothing, but the aggravating layer of material was gone. His chest connected with her voluptuous breasts, and their lower abs slapped together with a sharp smack. His dick thrust between her thighs, and the head skied across slick folds that coated his length. His balls swung as a heavy pendulum against her buttocks.

Using his arms to perform a pushup, he leveraged his lower body to position the head of his cock at the entrance of her pussy. Theresa's hands settled on his hips. She stared deeply into his eyes. Through the mate bond, her want and need of him, warm and inviting, pulled him down into the heat of her embrace.

Theresa tilted her head so her curtain of dark hair flowed down her shoulders and back in an ebony waterfall. She released a sultry moan, and her breath hitched. "Oh! Oh, my...I need to be fucked. I need to feel you inside of me."

Her erotic plea caused Zach's balls to tighten. The pungent scent of female arousal punched him in the gut. "Slide your hand between our bodies. Let me feel your hand on my cock."

Her lips curved in a smile of feminine mystery, but she complied and reached between their bodies, caressing his abs. The sound of slippery skin on skin reached his ears, and he realized she was pleasuring herself. Groaning, he envisioned her fingers, glistening with her juices, investigating every crevasse of her pussy, flicking against her clit. Then, her gentle hand, soft and glossy, closed on his dick.

A soft moan vibrated through his throat and chest, and his erection jerked as she tightened her grip. He experienced every pulse of his heart in the thick vein along the underside of his shaft. Her fingertips brushed his balls, and she circled the base of his cock, guiding the head to the entrance of her sex.

He breached the folds of her pussy and slid deep into her core, possessing her in the most intimate way. Just like their first time together, it blew his wildest dreams out of the water. In his fantasies, he'd loved her for years, listening to her moan and whimper until she exploded with a scream of pleasure. Slick and wet, tight and hot, she matched each thrust of his hips, wailing every time he withdrew and welcoming him home with a breathy sigh.

Muscles standing in bold relief against his skin, he eased all of the ways out of her, withdrawing inch by inch until only the head of his cock pressed against her entrance.

Theresa thrashed on the mattress, writhing with her need. Moaning, she dug her fingernails into his shoulders and tightened her legs about his waist.

He held on as long as he could and slammed his entire cock into her pussy with a single thrust. She wailed, and her limbs squeezed him, exerting enough strength to break the spine of an ordinary man. Her core convulsed about him so hard that a white haze blinded him. His balls clenched. He hit a violent orgasm. A shout tore from his lungs as he fell into ecstasy.

Robbed of his strength, Zach rolled to the side, collapsing to the mattress, sides heaving. For a couple of minutes, only the sounds of their labored breathing filled the room, subsiding to an even cadence. His heavy eyelids slid shut, and sweet lethargy seized him. His tired mind slipped toward slumber.

His mates. It sounded so unbelievable that Robert had to repeat it over and over. For about a half hour, Robert watched *his mates* nap beside one another on his bed in his home. Their breathing remained steady and shallow, indicating sleep. The very concept left him ecstatic and confused. A few hours ago, such a thing would never even have occurred to him as possible.

His gaze fell on Theresa's flushed face. A soft glow emanated from her skin. She smelled like motherhood, comfort, home, and desire. Her lips appeared swollen from being kissed, and the memory of her hot little mouth wrapped around his cock got him hard all over again.

In a couple of hours, this strange, wonderful new thing would end. Zach and Theresa would always be together, making love, maybe marrying. Robert planned to claim leadership of the pack, but the three-way mate bond that facilitated his peaceful ascension also guaranteed him a lifetime of loneliness. He envied their relationship but knew it was not for him. Destiny meant for him to always be on the outside looking in.

Wallowing made no sense and wasn't in his nature. He wanted to create memories to be hoarded in the years to come when times got tough.

Easing across the mattress, Robert laid a light hand on Theresa's upper arm, caressing her smooth skin. After a second, she stirred, and her eyelids lifted. For a second, confusion filled her dark eyes, and then, a sleepy smile curved her lips.

"Hi." She lifted her head, shoving her hair from her face.

"Hi yourself." His hand stroked along her back, fingertips tracing the length of her spine. His gaze followed the same path, admiring her lovely backside. By tilting his head back just a bit, he obtained an unobstructed view of Theresa's pussy and anal rosette. Between her perfectly rounded ass cheeks, the smooth crease led his eyes to her tight knot and then the swollen folds of her sex, visibly dripping with her juices.

He sat and lifted her from the mattress. He settled her on his lap astride his thighs. She gripped his shoulders, whimpering as his erection pressed against her flat belly.

"That's it, baby," Robert said. "Talk to me." He reached between their bodies, seeking her pussy. He found her sex to be scalding hot and dripping with juices.

"I'm so wet," Theresa said, moaning as he thrust his middle finger into her core, loving the way the taut muscles of her toned body grabbed hold of him. His dick surged in anticipation. "I need you inside me. Please."

"You're begging pretty now, but I want to hear you so wild with need you're incoherent," Robert said, easing his digit from her and then fucking back into her.

The action caused her eyes to flash with anger, full of pride and challenge. She rolled her hips and banged toward him insistently, causing him to throw back his head and laugh. Only the unexpected shift of the mattress startled him. He glanced over and saw Zach easing toward them.

Zach pressed against Theresa's back, eliciting a surprised gasp from her. She squeaked and glanced over her shoulder, eyes wide with surprise. "Zach," she said in a voice warm with welcome.

"I thought you intended to sit out the quarter?" Robert asked, a teasing challenge implicit within the question. The proximity of another male wolf so close to his throat inspired paranoia, especially given the presence of a naked she-wolf between them.

"Sorry, mate. I can't sit this one out. I want to play too," Zach said, reaching around to cup Theresa's full breasts, one in either palm. He found her plump nipples and rolled the nubs of flesh between his fingers.

Zach's blue eyes met Robert's searching gaze. The Brit arched his brow and rolled both shoulders in a casual shrug. He flashed a wolf's grin, lips pulled wide, teeth gleaming.

Robert grunted, unsure of how to respond. Zach's decision to join them surprised him, although he hid his reaction behind a calm mask. Through a conscious effort, he forced his wolf to relax, accepting Zach's right to be so close because they had exchanged the most sacred of vows. The presence of the mate bond helped, muting aggression and channeling the energy into desire.

Zach released Theresa's breasts and slid his hands across her shoulders to her back, disappearing from Robert's sight. Taking his cue from the other male, he slid his hands along the outsides of her legs, stroking upward toward the juncture of her thighs.

With a breathy moan, Theresa tilted her head back, exposing the slender column of her throat, sending her hair tumbling across her shoulders in ebony disarray. Her eyes shut, so that thick lashes lay upon her cheeks and her lips, bruised from Zach's kisses, parted to reveal the white gleam of teeth. She brimmed with the health and vitality of a healthy bitch in heat, eager to be bred.

Fucking gorgeous.

Feeling devilish, Robert cocked one eyebrow in challenge. "Are you sure you know what you're doing, Zach? Maybe you should watch and learn from a pro," he said, tone provocative even as he shifted his position on the mattress to make more room for the other man.

"Shut the fuck up," Zach said without any heat.

Robert tilted back his head and laughed, experiencing an unexpected rush of pleasure. The coil of tension in his gut unraveled.

"Both of you, hush," Theresa said, showing her teeth in an aggressive she-wolf smile. She placed a quick nip upon Zach's throat, leaving a mark without drawing blood.

The Brit chuckled. "Better give me something to do with my mouth then, pet."

"With pleasure."

Theresa twisted her torso to reach for Zach. Her arms circled his neck, pulling him down for an open-mouthed kiss. Their lips clung, and tongues coupled, flaring nostrils producing labored huffs. Her hips rocked toward Robert, her pussy painting fluids across his cock and thighs.

Watching the pair devour each other caused Robert to draw a sharp breath. The psychic connection binding them vibrated with energy, creating a thrumming on a gut level. Through the bond, he also sensed the profound love Zach and Theresa shared, soul-deep.

A burst of envy shot through Robert, briefly dampening his enthusiasm, but he shoved the insecurity down deep. Still, at his core, he ached with loneliness for the soul mate he would never have to call his own. It was the price to be paid, the cost of becoming Alpha without the stigma of bloodshed. He hoped the sacrifice proved worthwhile.

Their kiss broke, and Theresa turned to face Robert once again. She remained upright, straddling his thighs. With a demanding rock of her hips, she arched toward him, causing her mound to bang against the head of his dick. Theresa snaked her arms around his neck, drawing his lips down to her hungry mouth.

His cock ached to feel the tight crush of muscle gripping every inch of his length. His scrotum throbbed, threatening to explode. Intent, he plundered Theresa's mouth, exploring her smooth teeth and the moist recesses. She tasted like sin.

The kiss only broke to allow them to gasp for breath.

"Fuck me, please," Theresa said, pleading. Dark locks fell into her face, obscuring her features. Her skin shone with a high sheen.

"Sweetheart, I'm only too happy to oblige," Robert said with a sultry chuckle.

His hand rose to brush the strands from her face, but she captured his wrist. She drew his hand to her face and sucked the first digit of his middle finger into her hot little mouth, causing an explosive tightening of his balls. Blood roared in his head, and Robert curbed the impulse to tilt back his head and howl.

"Theresa, you're so bloody gorgeous." Zach's voice intruded on Robert's fever, drawing his attention to the other man.

Appreciatively, Robert allowed his gaze to roam Zach's body, appreciating his masculine beauty with the sensibilities of a true connoisseur. In truth, Zach wasn't his type, being too fair, too dominant, and too large, but he possessed an undeniable symmetry. More than that, Robert respected the other man for his intelligence and discretion.

Robert stroked Theresa's smooth stomach, explored the sweet indentation of her waist, and then followed the swell of her hips. His fingertips brushed the downy soft patch at the top of her mound. Her skin jumped as muscles clenched. A wet moan issued from her mouth, and she pressed against him, begging for more.

The earthy creature between the men appeared too caught up in the deluge of attention, male hands and mouths caressing her body, to be concerned with anything but her own pleasure. She tried to say something, but the words turned into incoherent babble as Robert's fingers found and stroked the sensitive nub between her thighs, coaxing her clit to readiness until it was pebble-hard. Her cream coated his fingers, dripping like warm honey.

Robert's stomach clenched, and his cock strained toward her body, hard as a steel rod. The alluring scent of her pussy flooded his nostrils, aggravating his arousal to an almost unbearable intensity. Only when Zach's hands came into contact with his chest did Robert give the other man his attention. Surprised, he arched his brow.

Zach extended his index finger and drew a circle counterclockwise in the air. He mouthed, "Turn her around."

Robert gave a sharp single nod and slipped his fingers from her pussy. She moaned in protest, but he settled his hands on her waist and lifted, turning her so she faced Zach. Robert scooted so he sat on the mattress with his knees at the edge. His dick protruded outward, aimed toward her center like a compass needle pointing north. Pearls of moisture beaded the slit across his cockhead.

Zach moved off the mattress, standing facing the bed with his penis jutting straight out from his body. He caught Theresa's dark hair in his hands, threading the long strands through his fingers and gently drew her face toward him. She emitted a throaty groan. Zach crouched to capture Theresa's lips in a kiss. The scent of her intense arousal coated the air, a thick musk, and moisture dripped from her pussy, dribbling across Robert's thighs.

Maneuvering her carefully, Robert positioned the head of his cock against the swollen lips of Theresa's sex and lowered her onto him, inch by inch, probing her pussy. He encountered heat and wetness, so much that he glided right in, sheathing his shaft in her silken depths. A growl trembled in his throat, and his penetration wrung a sobbing moan from her.

Physical and spiritual perfection united them. So fucking glorious. Bright, pure love flowed between Theresa and Zach, and Robert perceived a brief glimpse into something beautiful, something real. The sense of belonging following a lifetime of always being outside looking in nearly reduced him to tears. Desperation filled him, and he buried the feeling down deep, hid it well, determined not to ruin the moment by reaching for what he could not have.

As she sank onto Robert's thick dick, Theresa clutched at Zach's arms for support, digging into the corded muscles of his forearms with desperate fingers. As hot and bothered as she was, as eager as she was to be fucked, nothing could have prepared her for the reality of his cock advancing into her pussy, parting the tender folds of flesh.

With more than half his length inside of her, she wanted to shout and quake, begging him to stop while pleading for more. Her rational mind protested in a weak voice, reminding her that she hardly knew Robert, yet her wolf accepted him as one of her two mates. Conflict tore her apart—wrong, right—and overruling it all was her need.

Gasping, she tipped her head back, and her

eyelids dropped to hood her vision. At the same time, Zach's blond head dipped, and his hands pushed apart her thighs. For a second, Theresa failed to discern his intent, and then she experienced the flow of his hot breath upon her pussy, and she understood.

Behind her, Robert rocked his hips and buried his length within her completely, so the weight of his balls pressed against her sex. He slid his hands from her waist to cradle her breasts. His fingers caressed her areolas, agitating her pert nipples. His cock filled her, stretching her vagina until she felt full to bursting. She heard a guttural moan and knew that the sound hadn't come from Robert.

Zach.

His questing tongue caressed her sex, tasting the slick coating of juices flowing from her core. He used two fingers to spread the outer lips of her entrance, and then he lapped up her cream, consuming her honey as if she were a delicious dessert. The probing of his tongue, stroking inner folds, sliding back to where Robert filled her, sent her entire being careening. She gasped and reached for Zach, burying her hands in the long silk of his blond hair. She arched toward Zach's mouth, begging for more, her action eliciting a groan from Robert.

Robert's voice intruded on her reverie. "Theresa, are you all right? I want to go slow—"

Her eyes popped open, and she cut him off. "Don't go slow," she said. "Next time. Now, I want fast. Hard."

Zach obliged her begging, flicking his tongue against her clit, creating an unbelievably erotic sensation. Theresa moaned, almost howling, so close to coming. So fucking close. She wanted it. She needed it more than anything. Her desperation drove her to set a driving rhythm. Theresa rocked her hips toward his mouth, and Robert lurched into motion behind her, pounding into her with long, smooth strokes. His cock withdrew to the tip, leaving her wanting, then drove home until buried to the hilt.

"Harder," Theresa said, panting. "Faster."

Robert responded to her command. He withdrew from her pussy and thrust into her again, setting a rough, hurried rhythm. The man possessed a staggering amount of power, and he used it to fuck her, ramming into her, and she gloried in every rough stroke, vocalizing her intense and increasing pleasure.

"That's it, love. Come. I want to see you fly apart," Zach said, tormenting her clit with the whisper-soft touch of his fingertip.

She started to snarl a reply, but the blood rushed

in her ears, and she lost her ability to verbalize. The first spasm hit, and a cataclysmic quaking originated in her core, spreading outward in violent tremors. She shouted her pleasure at the top of her lungs, and Robert's voice echoed in her ears. His fingers crushed her breasts, and his cock and balls clenched with an orgasm she felt deep in her vagina as he pumped his seed into her.

The pleasure faded, and she sprawled in a boneless heap against Robert. Their bodies were slick with sweat. His chest rose and fell rhythmically. She pressed her ear against his heart, finding comfort in its intense beating.

From in front of her, strong hands lifted her from the bed, causing her eyes to pop open in surprise. Theresa hung limply in Zach's grip, staring up into his handsome face. Her mind remained blank, but one word formed. "What?" she asked.

"My turn, love," Zach said, gathering her into his arms. His erect member pressed eagerly into her buttocks, a persistent reminder that one of her mates remained unsatisfied.

"Oh," Theresa said with a dawning sense of oh, wow.

Did she even have the energy to survive another bout? Would she even be able to stand afterward? And by the time Zach achieved satisfaction, Robert should have recovered.

Good lord! She bit her lower lip and clung to his muscular chest. Better question—would she still be alive in a few hours?

"We're going to use your shower, mate," Zach said, addressing his words to Robert.

"Make yourself at home," Robert said. He remained supine upon the bed, not moving an inch.

Zach snickered. "Oh, we intend to," he tossed over his shoulder, carrying Theresa toward the attached master bathroom.

CHAPTER THIRTY-TWO

Having received her promised movie and Mommy-and-me time, Isabel had contentedly gone to bed following a couple of stories. Theresa made her way downstairs.

Time to face the music. She paused outside the family room to compose herself, but there was no unraveling the impossibly complicated knot of emotions that entangled her. She strolled into her family room, where Zach and Robert waited. Robert took up most of the loveseat with his considerable bulk. He smiled but said nothing, keeping his own counsel. His tense posture mirrored the restless energy ringing throughout his aura.

"It's time we put our house in order." Robert

pushed to his feet as if driven to move at any cost. He paced the length of the small room.

Theresa stepped out of his way, coming to a stop beside Zach. She glanced at his fingers, which hung suspended above the keyboard. She could almost see the river of words rushing through his head. He chased the wording of a sentence, tossing various phrasings through his thoughts, and then made his choice. His fingers flew again.

Robert waited and watched, expecting a response.

Theresa's finger poked his bicep. "Zach!"

He stopped typing and glanced up. "Sorry. I finally broke through my writer's block."

"That much is obvious," Theresa said with an arched brow.

Robert rolled his eyes heavenward. Unspoken words—*This is why I should be Alpha*— traversed his aura and then crossed the bond.

Theresa heard the words as clearly as if he'd said them aloud. Her astonishment rang as clear as a bell. Robert's realization and surprise followed a second later.

"We already agreed you'd make a better Alpha," Zach said with biting sarcasm. He looked up, and his blue eyes flashed. "No need to be an arse about it."

"Zach!" Theresa gasped and reached for his hand, clutching it between her own. "We heard his thoughts. Doesn't that surprise you at all?"

Zach offered a relaxed smile. His British accent grew rather pronounced. "Not really," he said. "In the last week, you have restored the pack's magic and ascended to the rank of Alpha female. Everything else seems rather mundane in comparison."

Robert's rich laughter filled the room. "All right then," he said, clapping in amusement. "I suppose that's something else we'll learn to deal with."

Zach closed his laptop. "For the record, I concur. We need to put our house in order. Tonight. Gather the pack and make the announcement. We need to remove Adam from his throne."

Both males radiated tension. The rising tide swept Theresa along, filling her with excitement. Her eagerness for the coming confrontation shocked her to the core, yet there was no denying her desire to knock Adam Teller from the top of his hill.

"My mother will be here in ten minutes to watch Isabel. I'll make the call," Theresa said. "I can't wait to tell that bitch, Becky Teller, that her reign is over."

Zach threw back his head, roaring with laughter,

and slapped his thigh. A second later, Robert joined in. Theresa smiled, grinned, and did her best not to blush.

"Well said." Zach chuckled. "Well said."

CHAPTER THIRTY-THREE

A meadow near Foxtail Creek in the Iron Stone Valley

At Theresa's request, the whole of the Iron Stone wolf pack had gathered in the meadow beside Foxtail Creek. She had chosen the location because of its special significance as the place where their pack bond had been reborn.

"I feel like we're in some old black-and-white Western gunfight at the O.K. Corral," Theresa said, pitching her voice low, although any one of the many wolves milling about them was close enough to eavesdrop.

"I call dibs on being Doc Holiday." Zach's mouth tugged into a closed-lip smile, but his facial muscles remained rigid, betraying the tension he carried in the taut lines of his long frame. His gaze moved through the crowd, searching faces and watching for threats.

"Why would you want to be one of the villains?" Robert asked from her other side. He stood apart, even though the unbreakable threads of the mate bond stretched between the three of them. Theresa sensed the Beta wolf's sheer determination through that connection.

"I think my definition of villain and yours may differ," Zach replied with perfect equanimity. He touched Theresa's elbow and indicated his watch. "Adam is late."

"He's coming," Theresa said, folding her arms across her chest. "I spoke with Becky."

"Villain isn't a debatable term," Robert said. "It means bad guy, plain and simple."

Zach snorted. "That's rich coming from an attorney—"

"Every accused party is entitled to legal representation..."

Theresa sighed and turned away from the men. *Her mates.* Even in her thoughts, the concept sounded strange, foreign, but that was not nearly as weird as the prospect of making their new relationship public through formal presentation to the pack.

The air vibrated with expectation. Every member of the pack felt the excitement. The mood swept the wolves on a rising tide of anticipation and intense curiosity. They all knew why they had gathered.

The old Alpha would cede his throne to the new king.

"At least no one's quaking in fear at the prospect of new leadership," Zach said dryly.

At the far side of the clearing, a tremendous force tremored the pack's communal link. Everyone turned toward the far side of the clearing where the trailhead led to the road.

"Adam's here," Theresa drawled.

"About bloody time."

Adam strode to the center of the field. Becky walked at his right side, and his enforcers formed a tight ring about them. Their entourage stopped five paces opposite Theresa and her mates. The rest of the pack crowded in closer, forming a half-circle about the threesome. Adam's sharp eyes settled on their little trio, and Theresa's skin crawled under his penetrating glare. She doubted that he appreciated her choice of venue.

"Evening, folks," Adam drawled with a broad smile that showed plenty of teeth. "Thank you all for gathering, especially on the night after the full moon. I understand that it's hard on folks, getting away from their families and friends two nights in a row. However, it seems that Theresa has an important announcement to make, so I'll turn the forum over to her."

The subtle dig caused the corners of her mouth to tug down, but Theresa refused to show weakness or doubt. Zach stood at her side, a steady source of support, and Robert had her back. All eyes were on them, full of curiosity and speculation. The pack sensed something was up with the three of them. She perceived the magic as a tangled mass of threads, each connecting an individual wolf to the whole, while she stood at the center of it all.

Taking a deep breath, she walked to the center of the circle. She cleared her throat and held her hands at her sides, elbows bent, fighting the impulse to fidget.

"Thank you for coming tonight," Theresa said. "I appreciate everyone's patience while I chose on a mate. It was a difficult decision, especially with so much riding on it. Both Robert and Zach are good men, and either of them would make an excellent pack leader."

Theresa turned her head to look at Zach and smiled warmly. "As I'm sure everyone knows, Zach has been my best friend since he arrived in Iron

Stone three years ago. He's fixed just about every appliance at my place. Isabel and I would have drowned a long time ago if it weren't for him."

The crowd burst into laughter. Speculative gazes turned toward Zach, and the audience's anxiety levels rose because they knew that a fight would inevitably follow if she had chosen him over Robert.

Theresa directed her gaze toward Robert. She met and held his eyes, bold and not fearful in her appreciation because of the sexually confident woman she had grown to become, thanks in part to him.

"I owe Robert my thanks and my eternal gratitude. When Carl Reynolds attacked me, he came to my rescue. He's a courageous, capable man, and he's willing to sacrifice everything for this pack." Theresa licked her lips, determined to remind the pack of Adam's promise. "As you all recall, Adam intends to step down and bequeath the position of Alpha to the man, to the mate, of my choosing."

The pack rumbled with intense excitement, and energy crackled in the atmosphere. Charlaine stood out from the crowd, apart from the other wolves, boldly claiming her place in the world. Theresa met her friend's gaze, and support flowed from the black woman to her. She felt that much better knowing the Gamma had her back.

Becky Teller frowned. Her cheeks reddened with impatience. "Enough grandstanding, Theresa. Tell us who you've picked already."

A smirk formed on Theresa's lips, and she stared straight at Becky. Her confidence rose and, with it, a deep sense of satisfaction. Glancing over her shoulder, she extended both of her arms toward Robert and Zach, beckoning them. The men stepped forward, coming to stand beside her, one to either side. Zach took her right hand, Robert her left.

When physical contact occurred between them, their mate bond flared to life, bright and brilliant for all to see. Together, they formed a triumvirate— more potent together than individually.

"I've chosen them both," Theresa announced, confirming with words what the pack already perceived. "The three of us have entered into a mate bond together. Robert will be our new Alpha and Zach his Beta."

Profound silence fell across the meadow. Everyone watched Robert, Theresa, and Zach with hope and terror in their hearts.

Fury suffused Adam's formidable body, and his stance grew rigid. He shifted his hands to claws. "You cannot have two mates. You must choose between them," he said in a dangerous voice.

Their joined hands fell apart as the men released

their grip on her. Robert advanced a pace, and Zach did the same. Theresa lunged and grabbed hold of Robert's bicep.

"Wait, please, wait," Theresa cried, well aware that she had no hope of restraining Robert. She wanted to speak before he issued a formal challenge, and the situation turned to violence.

He glanced at her and hesitated. She witnessed the conflict taking place in his head, and then he tilted his chin in a gesture of surrender.

"Some Alpha he would be. See how he obeys a mere female," Adam said with a sneer.

Theresa stiffened and squared her shoulders. "A smart male listens to his mate when it is appropriate to do so. That makes him wise, not weak."

"You cheated." Adam huffed in anger, and his influence flowed across the landscape, causing the weaker pack members to cower. She experienced the force of his personality, buffered as if a mighty wind had struck her, but the triumvirate kept her anchored.

"I did not cheat," Theresa said. "There is nothing in our laws forbidding three wolves from entering into a mate bond, so we took the oath together."

"Unless all three of you have had sex—together —it isn't invalid," Becky declared with an ah-ha note in her voice.

A smug smile curved Theresa's mouth. "I assure you we've had plenty the sex."

Becky gasped in righteous indignation, aiming her finger at Theresa. "How dare you, you whore!"

"You're one to speak, bitch," Theresa said, glaring at the older women with narrowed eyes.

"Enough with this travesty. I won't have disobedience in my pack!" Adam started toward Theresa with murder in his eyes, but Robert stepped between them.

"This isn't your pack anymore," Robert declared. "It's mine now."

Zach joined Robert at his side, so the two men presented a united front. "I'm backing Robert," Zach said. "Adam, I suggest you see this as an opportunity to retire as you wanted."

Adam shot and addressed his head enforcer. "Jax, I do believe we're going to have to put down an uprising within the pack."

The pack's tension skyrocketed. Many of the weaker members whimpered and retreated, but the stronger wolves started to choose sides. Sammy Turner walked to Adam. Charlaine joined with Zach and Robert. Methodically, the pack that Theresa had united and nurtured was breaking apart. The opposing factions faced off on the verge of a bloody civil war.

"I have to put a stop to this." Theresa strode

forward, but Zach caught her elbow. His expression held intense concern.

"Theresa, it's too dangerous."

"Please, let me go." She covered his hand with her own, offering what she hoped was a reassuring smile. "This is something I have to do."

Zach searched her face, and then he stepped back. "You've got this, my love."

The undecided members of the pack had dwindled to a handful. Theresa dashed into the middle of the field. As she ran, she extended her awareness out into the pack bond of her creation. To her perception, their collective aura appeared as a complicated, ever-changing spiderweb. She surfed the shifting currents, mapping the network of personal relationships and loyalty to determine the strongest commitments and identify the weakest links. Static shock hit her when she discovered that those closest to Adam—his enforcers—detested their leader. It opened a world of possibilities.

Theresa slid to a halt near the alpha's guards. The five men looked at her as if she were crazy. She didn't care so long as they kept from attacking.

Panting, Theresa s greeted the captain, an athletic man with a Marine Corps tattoo on his shoulder. "Hi, there."

The captain smiled faintly. "Hello. Can I help you?"

"I think maybe you can. What's your name?"

He regarded her warily. "Jax Dawson, ma'am."

"And do you know who I am?"

"You're the Wolf Queen of the Iron Stone Pack."

"Good," Theresa said with a predatory smile. She stole a glance over her shoulder. The great Alpha debate was still raging. While she watched, two of Adam's supporters deserted to Robert's side.

"You'd think a man his age would know better than to argue with a lawyer," Jax said.

Theresa laughed. "Jax, let's have a chat."

Theresa latched onto his forearm as if for a stroll through the park. Jax held his arm steady, and like a chowder of curious cats, the other enforcers trailed along. She led them away, deliberately relieving Adam of his veteran soldiers.

"A chat about what?" Jax asked.

"Why are you and your men supporting that racist douchebag?"

Jax halted abruptly. "Are you questing our loyalty?"

Oops. All five of the enforcers were bristling. Theresa sent a wave of cooling energy over them just as she'd observed the other dominants do countless times. It was a breeze.

"Not at all," she assured them. "I'm trying to understand your motives."

"Our unit was assigned to Iron Stone to protect the Wolf King," one of the enforcers volunteered.

Theresa smiled at her unexpected ally, a tall blond with green eyes. "Thank you..."

"Seth."

"Thank you, Seth. And who sent you here?"

"The Wolf God sent us," Jax admitted.

"That sounds like quite an honor."

Under her fawning admiration, the enforcers preened and puffed with pride. Even Jax's ears turned pink.

"It's a huge honor," Seth said, blushing.

"I feel so much safer knowing that such big strong warriors are here protecting my mates, my daughter, and I," Theresa gushed, laying it on thick. Surprised understanding crossed Jax's expression, but she kept going. "As the Wolf Queen of the Iron Stone Pack, I promise that your unit will be well-treated and appreciated."

"Dawson," Adam bellowed. "What the hell are you doing talking to that bitch? Get over here."

The enforcers stiffened, and the spicy scent of anger permeated the air.

Seth and the other men looked to their leader. "Jax, it's your call. What do you want to do?"

Conflict warred on Jax's face.

Deadly soft, Theresa said, "None of you have to tolerate further abuse."

"Enforcers," Adam hollered, "you will obey."

"Thank you, ma'am," Jax said, bowing his head. "This chat has been enlightening."

The captain led his unit to the field. The pack had split unevenly, with a two-thirds majority gathered behind Robert.

Heart in her throat, Theresa watched as Jax approached Adam—and then marched past the old alpha. She exhaled and grinned, giddy with disbelief. "It worked. Thank you, God."

The captain and his men sank to bended knee before Robert.

Jax led their pledge, "All hail the Wolf King!"

It started an exodus. Adam Teller stood there with his jaw hanging while his followers deserted him. A beet-red flush suffused the former alpha. Abruptly, he glanced around and noticed that he was all alone except for Becky. Suddenly, the former alpha turned tail and ran, abandoning his wife.

Adam beat a hasty retreat, shouting threats over his shoulder. "You've won for now, but I'll be back!"

Becky transitioned from shock to outrage with a huff. She jogged after the husband, yelling, "Adam Teller, I want a divorce!"

The whole pack lined up to watch Adam go.

A male presence approached Theresa from behind, and she recognized Zach by scent and aura. He wrapped his arms around her, and she sank against him. Chuckling, he quipped, "They're just like cartoon villains."

"Let's hope that's the last we ever see of them," Theresa said fervently.

"I don't know how you did it, Theresa, but you're brilliant," Charlaine said. "Respect."

They fist-bumped.

With laughter and tears, the wolves of the Iron Stone Pack gathered to crown their new sovereigns. Robert collected the psychic threads of each member and forged an indestructible bond.

"We are pack," he said, arms raised, palms extended. "We are wolves, and I am your Alpha."

Their joy ran in rivers. Wolves came to Robert with their heads bowed in submission. They eagerly reached out to touch their new king. Hands stroked Theresa's arms and back. Surprise jolted her, replaced by warm pleasure when she realized that they were paying tribute to her also—their Alpha female.

Beaming, Theresa allowed her gaze to roam possessively over the splendid males who were her mates.

"It's good to be Wolf Queen, huh?" Charlaine teased.

"It does have a nice ring to it," Theresa said.

The women joined hands.

"Are we okay?" Theresa asked Charlaine. "With me being Alpha?"

Charlaine grinned. "We're good. You're what this pack needs, Theresa. As cheesy as it sounds, you are our Heart."

"Yeah, that sounds pretty cheesy," Theresa agreed, opening her arms wide. She trembled with nervousness then joy when Charlaine stepped into her embrace. The two women hugged long and hard. Now, they were sisters.

"You'd better take good care of my cousin," Charlaine warned when they separated. "Robert is the smartest, dumbest man you'll ever meet, but he has a good heart. He deserves all the happiness."

The other woman was teasing, but Theresa wound up inwardly cringing. Guilt plagued her, and it was all she could do to smile and bite her tongue. What, she wondered, would Charlaine say if she knew about their secret bargain that left Robert out in the cold?

One thing was for sure. It wouldn't be pretty.

CHAPTER THIRTY-FOUR

His mates were in trouble.

Instincts ruled. Zach rolled out of bed and hit the ground, gearing up for a confrontation. His muscles rippled and strained against his skin, and thick fur covered his body. Searing pain ripped through him as he underwent the swiftest transformation that he'd ever experienced to his wolfman form. Combat-ready werewolf, he had the works—fangs and claws and a tail—before he awakened enough to gather his senses.

The distress of his mates flooded the mate bond. Theresa's anguish, in particular, carried like a shout. Robert's sorrow was less assertive but still problematic. The source of their upset remained a mystery, but Zach would do whatever was necessary to protect them.

"Theresa?" he called softly through a mouthful of canines even though he knew she wasn't present. The glow of his gaze lit the darkroom.

The time on his phone was 2:46 a.m. Hours before, he and Theresa had fallen asleep in each other's arms, but the room was empty except for him. For a man who'd spent his entire adult life as a bachelor until now, he found it alarming how much it upset him to wake up alone.

Isabel was spending the weekend with her grandmother.

A gust of wind whisked in the mingled aroma of rain and pine trees and blasted through the room, and only then did he realize the sliding glass door was open. The drapes flapped noisily. Zach turned, inhaling a deep breath to fill his lungs, and he caught Theresa's familiar scent on the current. His long claws scraped across the wood floor as he padded closer, and he spotted his mate standing out on the balcony.

Pure relief washed through him. His pulse subsided to normal, and some of the tension bled from his taut frame. Zach reverted to his human form and pulled on a pair of pajama bottoms. However, no matter how hard he tried, he could not shake the feeling that something was seriously wrong. Without bothering to put on a shirt or shoes, he hastened to join Theresa on the balcony.

The weather in the Sierra Nevada mountains was moody all year round. Outside, a summer storm brewed in the night sky. Gray clouds blocked the light from the moon and stars, and a blistering-cold gale swept through the valley off the mountaintops. The wind was wet with the promise of rain. The cold seldom bothered Zach, yet the persistent sense of unease caused tiny hairs to prickle all over his body.

Zach paused on the threshold to admire the stunning vision his mate presented. Theresa stood with her back to him, her elbows resting atop the railing. The diaphanous folds of her floor-length nightgown billowed about her feminine figure, and her long hair whipped wildly in the wind. To his rather poetical aesthetic, she appeared as lovely and mysterious as a Gothic heroine. Her beauty left him dazzled and distracted.

He halted right behind her, not touching but essentially breathing down the back of her neck. When she refused to turn around or otherwise acknowledge him, Zach's uneasiness redoubled. Knots cramped his gut. There was no way she could have missed his approach, which meant she ignored him on purpose.

Up close, the love of his life smelled like grief

and misery. Overcome with concern, he brushed her shoulder and cleared his throat. "Theresa, my love, what's wrong?"

At last, Theresa spun to face him. Lifting her face, she squared her shoulders. Zach's heart wrenched when he saw the tears glistening in her eyes.

"My whole life," she said, "I thought I wasn't good enough. But, in the last month, I've discovered self-confidence, earned respect and adoration of the pack."

"What am I, chopped liver?" Zach complained before he could stop himself. Even after his mate had lectured him long and hard that sarcasm often made relationship matters worse, he still reverted to his old ways. "Sorry," he said immediately. "Bad habits are hard to break."

She gave a broken laugh, and tears flowed down her cheeks. "You're so much better than chopped liver. You're my best friend, the man I've secretly loved for years, the man of my dreams."

"I love you, too. If everything's so bloody wonderful, then why are you crying?"

He opened his arms, offering shelter from the storm. She stepped straight into his embrace, looping her arms around his waist, and rested her face on his pec.

"Because of this..." Theresa opened the mate bond to him.

Devastating isolation and depression detonated between them. The brunt of the blast knocked Zach off balance. He staggered and would have fallen except she saved him. Theresa supported him until he recovered his strength.

"Is that..." he gasped, unable to complete the sentence.

"Yes." She gave a tiny nod against his chest. "That's Robert."

"Fuck me," Zach said. Even though he preferred not to curse in front of his mate, he couldn't help himself. "Excuse my French."

"It's okay." She hugged him harder about the waist. "There are times when you have to swear."

"That's the truth," he agreed, glad for the easy out.

Her tone grew sterner. "Don't let me catch you using language like that in front of Isabel, or you'll be wrapping your mouth around a bar of soap."

"Yes, ma'am." He hesitated then ventured, "So, it seems Robert got the short end of the shaft, eh?"

"He's despondent, and who can blame him? Here I am, supposed to be the Heart of the Pack. Yet, I've condemned our Alpha to a lifetime of isolation and unhappiness," Theresa said with such severity that Zach wound up hanging his head in shame over having been so cavalier.

Crickey, they needed do something about this mess fast before they all wound up wallowing in misery.

"We have to fix this," he said.

"What?" Theresa jerked away to gaze into his face. "How are we supposed to make this mess right? We made our choices. It was for the good of the pack, but never in a million years did I suspect that Robert would be the one to pay. It's awful, and I don't know if I can live with myself."

Zach spoke without hesitation. "Then, let's not live with it. Let's fix it."

Theresa gasped. Her eyes widened with amazement, glowing with hope. She trembled in his arms. "Are you saying..."

Zach believed that words had power and must never be misused. He understood the total magnitude of what he was suggesting, so he stopped to give the matter serious thought. Even then, his contemplation lasted mere seconds.

"Yeah, I'm saying to hell with it. We've already broken with convention by creating a three-way mate bond. Why not do what's right to make all of us happy?"

"Zach..." A beautiful smile spread on Theresa's

face. She glowed with such happiness that it almost killed him to interrupt.

Still, he had to ask, "What about Isabel?"

Theresa giggled. "Oh, Isabel will be fine just so long as she can keep her fairy garden, and I suspect having new brothers and sisters will go a long way toward making her happy, but are you sure? Once we make the offer, there are no takebacks."

The prospect of children filled him with overwhelming joy. Zach's grin widened until it threatened to split his face. Irrepressible optimism swelled through him. "Absolutely, one hundred percent."

They leaned in until their mouths met. The simple caress of lips on lips qualified as the most extraordinary thing Zach had ever felt. Lightning flashed between them. She moaned from her throat, and he answered with a guttural groan. Their mouths merged, melting molten magma, but they shared a mutual understanding—they needed their third to be truly complete.

"Let's go claim our mate."

CHAPTER THIRTY-FIVE

Hard knocking on the front door of his house tore Robert from a deeply troubled sleep. Robert exploded off the mattress, planting squarely on his feet. Thanks to the persistent mate bond, he identified his late-night callers as Zach and Theresa. Their agitation flooded Robert's mind with a sense of urgency that propelled him to action.

He would do anything necessary to protect his mates. But first, clothing.

With sleep still in his eyes, he groped blindly for something to wear. His boxers were the first thing that came to hand. Good enough. After some fumbling, he managed to get his legs into the correct holes, and the elastic waistband snapped into place.

Out front, Zach pounded hard enough to rattle the door on its hinges. "Hey, Robert! Wake up!"

"I'm coming. Hold on."

Robert abandoned all thoughts of pants and rushed into the hallway. From his bedroom to the entryway was the longest, shortest trip of his entire life. Along the way, he envisioned a dozen different scenarios to explain what could have brought Zach and Theresa to his front porch at three in the morning — none of them good. Most likely, Adam Teller had done something underhanded and malicious.

Nearing the door, Robert detected muted voices on the other side. Zach and Theresa were talking. Robert paused with his hand on the deadbolt, tilting his head to listen.

"Maybe it was a bad idea coming here in the middle of the night."

"It's the right move," Zach replied. "Trust yourself."

Robert threw the deadbolt in a swift motion and yanked the door open, revealing his unexpected visitors. To his immense relief, Zach and Theresa appeared disheveled, but neither of them was injured. Ironically, they both gave starts of surprise at being caught unaware in the middle of an argument.

"Well, this is getting to be something of a habit

with you two," Robert said into the awkward lull that followed.

With each passing moment, his sense of urgency eased, but his concern increased. His curious gaze shifted between his tongue-tied mates. Although adequately clothed, the potent scent of pheromones clung to them. They'd had sex recently. Jealousy cramped his gut, and he shoved the emotion down deep to hide it. The last thing he wanted was to pick a fight with Zach.

Finally, Theresa cleared her throat. "Can we come inside? Please."

"Certainly." Robert stepped back, pulling the door wider to make room.

Theresa entered first. As she passed, the she-wolf brushed up against his side with an easy intimacy. She was still in heat, and the spicy aroma of her arousal damn near proved his undoing. He had to suppress the urge to take her in his arms and kiss her passionately.

His cock pitched an impressive tent, leading Robert to regret his decision to forgo pants. Right about then, baggy sweats would've provided some much-needed camouflage.

Motion in the periphery of his vision alerted Robert to Zach's approach. Reflexively, he turned to face the other male wolf, adopting a posture that protected his throat. The men's gazes locked as Zach crossed the threshold.

"Relax, brother." Zach clasped Robert's shoulder in passing.

Robert exhaled, releasing a horde of repressed tension. He shut the door and locked up.

They stepped into the front room, where they remained standing around the coffee table, ignoring the leather couch and matching armchairs. Robert crossed his arms over his chest, doing his level best to project an air of confidence, but he suspected that his inconvenient erection undermined his dignity.

"All right, what's going on?" Robert demanded with a grumpy snarl.

Zach and Theresa traded a long look loaded with meaning. He nodded, and she smiled.

Robert clenched his jaws, striving to stay stoic, but he was unsure how to react when Theresa moved closer. Her initial step was hesitant, but she gained confidence with every stride. By the time she reached him, the she-wolf was strolling along with a sexy sashay of her hips.

Anticipation fractured Robert's self-control to a million pieces. The entirety of his attention was riveted on her, his gorgeous mate. He had no idea when or even how, but Robert had fallen in love with Theresa at some point. It just about killed him that he couldn't caress or embrace her as he ached to do.

Forbidden fruit, buddy, he reminded himself sharply. *Hands off.*

Theresa stopped in front of Robert, gazing up with the sweetest adoration. It shocked him how desperately he wanted her love to be genuine. He stiffened when she grasped his wrists.

"Zach and I have been talking," she said, gently prying his arms away from his chest, "and we've decided we're not happy with our agreement."

Anger flared, and Robert bristled at the injustice of her statement. What the hell! He had already sacrificed his happiness for the good of the pack. What more did they expect from him?

"A deal is a deal," Robert said in his best lawyer voice. "You can't go changing the terms."

On the other side of the room, Zach snorted. "We say we can."

Theresa snapped her head around while still holding Robert's hands in her own. From his vantage point, he couldn't see her expression, but she managed to shut Zach up with a glare. "Zachery Hunter, you're not helping."

"Sorry," Zach apologized with the most unrepentant smile Robert had ever witnessed in all his years of practicing law.

Theresa nodded and returned her attention to

Robert. She tilted back her head, exposing the exquisite softness of her throat, and gently squeezed his fingers. "Robert, we're not happy because you're not happy."

Zach chimed in with his two cents. "We know that you're miserable. You're broadcasting through the bond."

Robert winced. "Sorry," he ground out. "I'll try to control it better."

"No, that's not good enough. We want you to be happy, too."

"What are you saying?" Robert demanded.

He knew what he wanted, but he was afraid to have hope. Years ago, he had faced down a furious Kodiak bear shifter. That confrontation had scared the life out of him, yet it paled in comparison to his terror now. He was shaking.

"Please, hear us out," she said.

Theresa tugged on Robert's arms, attempting to maneuver him to be seated. He resisted, but she persisted. Finally, he submitted because he worried that his legs would give out from under him. He sank onto the couch. It creaked beneath his bulk. The expensive leather smelled good but not a tenth as delicious as the she-wolf before him.

"Theresa?" Robert moaned her name.

His torment only worsened when she looped her arms around the back of his neck and straddled his thighs. Theresa pressed her breasts against his bare chest, and his erection got trapped between their bodies. Suddenly, the layers of fabric separating were an intolerable impediment. It took everything he had not to rip off her clothing and impale her on his cock.

"Robert, look at me," Theresa commanded.

He obeyed, and their gazes locked. Her mane of glossy, curly hair, damp from the rain, framed her face. Foxlike, she peered at him with a hooded gaze. Once so shy, she radiated an aura of self-assurance. Her smile was sassy and secure. She tugged at the back of his neck, and he bowed his head. Their mouths brushed in a kiss, both tender and scalding hot.

She tasted like forever.

Once they parted, Theresa stroked her palms over his broad torso, testing his firm skin and steel-hard muscles with her nails.

"We want you to be with us," Theresa whispered, speaking the words he'd longed to hear. "We love you, Robert. Would you please join us in handfasting and be our mate forever?"

Tightness closed his throat, and Robert couldn't speak. Tears stung his eyes and overflowed onto his cheeks. Theresa wiped the wetness away with her fingers. He glanced over her shoulder to where Zach had sprawled in the nearest armchair. The blond was watching them with avid interest, an unmistakable bulge straining against the front of his pants.

"Are you good with this?" Robert asked, meeting Zach's eyes.

Zach smirked. "It was my idea, brother. Just say yes, all right? Don't go making a sentimental scene."

Robert flashed a wide, wolf smile. Genuine happiness whelmed through him, lifting his spirits until he felt light enough to fly. "Yes," he said with fierce joy in his heart. "Always and forever."

EPILOGUE

A sudden but not unexpected pregnancy came as a sheer delight to the expectant mother *and* both fathers. However, the joyous news also forced Robert, Zach, and Theresa to confront their first relationship crisis—elaborate ceremony or elopement?

After a brief discussion, three of them sat down in the living room of Robert's residence and put it to a vote. Majority wins.

"I say we elope. Vegas is lovely this time of year." Zach already had his phone out, scrolling through hotels.

Theresa's spine stiffened like a ramrod. She pressed her lips together to silence a vehement protest involving fluent and unpardonable French.

The strength of her emotions left her floored. Up until that moment, she hadn't even realized how she felt.

For Theresa's first *unhappy* marriage, they had eloped. Then, she hadn't cared, but now, a proper wedding meant the world to her. She anticipated living happily ever after with her new family—Isabel, Robert, Zach, and their future children.

New beginnings deserved commemoration. Celebration. Theresa wanted it all—a fairytale wedding.

Ever savvy, Robert took one look at Theresa's expression and correctly deduced how the wind was blowing. Carefully, he said, "While eloping has its advantages...."

Zach nodded, and Theresa scowled.

Robert concluded, "I cannot help but feel that it would be unjust, not to mention unfair, of us to deny our pack the opportunity to witness the union of their leaders."

Zach frowned, and Theresa smiled.

Theresa clapped her hands together and talked fast. "Formal wedding it is, then. I want Ambra to help with my dress. Dahlias and Shasta lilies are still in bloom. I'll call florists in the morning." She stared at Robert and asked, "Can you arrange for a venue and someone to officiate?"

"Leave it to me. Also, I know a skilled jeweler

who can design our rings. If you want, I'll also contact caterers for quotes." Robert offered his trust-me smile.

"That would be wonderful. Thank you so much," Theresa said, beaming. "Do you have any preferences on the color theme?"

Zach puzzled his face and pursed his lips. "I like blue."

Theresa narrowed her eyes.

"Autumn hues are good," Robert said. "Any combination of orange or red and white, silver, or gold works for me."

"Perfect. Where's a notepad? I need to take notes!" Theresa rushed to throw on clothing.

"In the kitchen," Robert said. "The top drawer below the phone."

"You're an angel." Theresa flew to Robert, kissing him full on the lips before she raced off.

"Hey! What about me?" Zach bellowed, mortally wounded. After she left, he looked to Robert for guidance. "Where'd I balls up?"

"Blue flowers are rarer than hens' teeth, especially in fall," Robert said. "Before you ask, carnations can be dyed blue, but they make Isabel sneeze. Also, Dahlias are Theresa's favorite flower."

Zach facepalmed."How do you know this, and I don't?"

Robert smirked and stroked his mustache. "I graduated from Harvard Law school."

Zach sneered. "La-dee-da."

Out in the hallway, the sounds of Theresa's footfalls signaled her return approach.

Quickly, Robert said, "Offer to write the invitations and our vows. You'll be golden."

Zach glared. "I have writer's block."

"If you know what's good for you, better fix shit that fast. Get with the program, man."

Strolling and scribbling, Theresa burst into the bedroom. "Hey, I'm back."

Zach pulled the swiftest about-face that Robert had ever witnessed. "I want to help, too," he declared in his dulcet English accent. "I would be honored to write the invitations and our vows."

Glowing with pleasure, Theresa descended on Zach with praise and smooches. "That would be wonderful. Good boy. I love you. Are you sure?"

"It might strain my literary skills," Zach harrumphed, "but I'll power through."

"We'll need matching tuxes," Robert volunteered helpfully. "I'll bet Zach can handle that, too."

"Maybe." Zach flashed a ruthless grin. "Maybe not. It depends on what I find on the Widow Crawley's laundry line."

Then, to Robert's profound confusion, Theresa and Zach traded a long stare that ended with both of them grinning like madmen. Robert felt as if he'd missed something big. Hello?

Theresa leveled her finger at Zach. "So help me, I'd better be the only one wearing a dress on our wedding day."

Robert's bedroom - two weeks later

Zach wore a smirk—and nothing more—when he made the initial announcement of what would become his official designation within the pack. "Henceforth, I shall be known as the Wolf Pot and Pan, Knight."

Just prior, Theresa had taken a sip of iced tea. Now, she sputtered, blowing liquid out of her nose. "What? No."

"It's Cockney rhyming slang for a husband," Zach explained, ever so proud.

Theresa dried her face on her sleeve. Adamantly, she shook her head. "We can't put that on the wedding invitations."

Zach jutted his jaw. The gleam in his gaze embodied all the stubbornness of a bachelor whose days were numbered, determined to go out in a blaze of glory. "*You*," he told Theresa, "said I could choose my royal title, whatever I wanted. Robert, back me up here?"

The Wolf King was indisposed, rolling around on the floor in stitches; however, Robert managed to stop laughing long enough to gasp. "You did say that, Theresa. I heard you."

With a mighty huff, Theresa crossed her arms beneath her bosom. "Well, I didn't think you'd choose something absurd!"

Zach arched his brow. "Have we met? Zachery Hunter."

He offered his hand. She slapped it away.

"Fine. Whatever. It's your funeral. Mark my words, I'll have this engraved on your tombstone." Theresa pretended to fume—secretly hiding a smile —as she penned, "Husband #2, Royal Pot and Pan."

"Wolf Pot and Pan," Zach corrected, *"Knight."*

"You two are the cherry on my day." Snickering, Robert dragged himself back onto the bed.

"Zachary Hunter, you're not a real knight," Theresa shot back.

Zach craned his head. "Hey, Your Majesty..."

The Wolf King waved his invisible scepter. "By the power invested in me as the Wolf King, I, Robert Blane, do grant you, Zach Hunter, a knighthood."

Zach grinned, showing all his teeth. "Thanks, mate."

"Sure thing."

They high-fived.

"I'll knight both of you." Theresa rolled her eyes, but deep down, she wondered whether two husbands might prove more trouble than anticipated. She had better keep a sharp eye out to ensure they didn't get too cozy.

Their official wedding invitation read,

Howling mad? Absolutely.
Together, we invite you to celebrate the marriage of
THERESA RUSSO, HEART OF THE IRON STONE PACK
and
ROBERT BLANE, WOLF KING
and
ZACHARY HUNTER, WOLF POT AND PAN, KNIGHT

Meadow north of Foxtail Creek, Iron Stone Valley

Theresa's happiness on her wedding day surpassed her wildest fantasies.

On a perfect autumn afternoon, the rugged mountain range donned her fall colors. Leaves turned shades ranging from golden to claret against the eternal backdrop of evergreens. The whole of the Iron Stone Pack gathered along with family and friends for the outdoor event.

The wedding music played, and a drama unfolded in the bridal tent where Theresa and Charlaine lurked near the entrance. Both the bride and her maid of honor wore gorgeous gowns and clutched bouquets of Dahlias and Shasta lilies. Anxiously, they awaited the return of their spy.

"Do you see her yet?" Theresa demanded for about the tenth time in the last five minutes. She was a nervous wreck, fidgeting with the edge of her veil. Where, oh, where could her daughter be?

Charlaine held a tent flap open, peering out. Suddenly, she waved her hand and exclaimed, "Here she comes!"

In a burst of excitement, Theresa rushed closer.

Isabel raced toward them, a streak of red in her flower girl dress. She entered the tent and slid to a panting halt. "Mama, I'm back!"

"Well, don't keep us waiting," Charlaine said. "Report, missy."

"Zach *is* wearing a dress!" Isabel threw her arms wide.

Theresa's life flashed before her eyes. She

swayed, on the verge of swooning. "I'm going to wind up a widow before we're even properly married," she muttered. "The nerve of that man."

Charlaine leveled an intimidating school teacher stare. "Tell the truth."

Isabel smiled sweetly. "Just kidding."

The bride and her maid of honor sighed and sagged in relief.

"Robert and Zach are both wearing skirts," Isabel proclaimed for her grand reveal.

"I've had enough," Theresa scolded her daughter. "Wipe that smirk off your face right now, or you can forget being my flower girl."

Isabel groaned. "Oh, but, Mom..."

"No one believes little girls who cry wolf," Charlaine lectured sagely.

Right on cue, the opening strains of the bridal march tolled through the meadow.

Demonstrating military efficiency, Charlaine took command. "Here," she said, shoving the flower girl's basket filled with dark red rose petals into Isabel's hands. "Scatter a small handful every few feet just like we rehearsed. Don't drop them all at once."

"Geez, stop talking to me like I'm a baby." Isabel rolled her eyes. "I'm going to be six next month."

"Almost a teenager. Make Mommy proud." Tears

brimming in her eyes, Theresa kissed her daughter's cheek and sent Isabel on her way.

Charlaine lingered a little longer. "Are you sure you don't want me to escort you down the aisle? Last chance."

"I'm certain, but thank you." Theresa nodded with confidence.

She had chosen to walk the bridal path alone as a show of independence. If her father were still alive, it would've been a different story. However, as it stood, she firmly believed that the new Wolf Queen of the Iron Stone Pack needed to come to the grooms of her own accord.

Charlaine seized Theresa in a fierce hug. "See you on the other side," she said with bright eyes before heading off.

Alone, facing her destiny, Theresa drew a deep breath. "It's okay," she assured herself, trying to soothe her rattled nerves. "Izzy was only kidding."

Thus reassured, the Wolf Queen and Heart of the Iron Stone Pack embarked on her voyage into marriage with the two men she loved with all her heart. The Wolf God himself had honored and validated their union by agreeing to administer their vows. All of their friends and family had gathered to bear witness.

Poised at the top of the aisle, Theresa caught her first glimpse of her grooms waiting at the splendid outdoor altar. Her stride faltered. An outburst of laughter almost split her sides, and it took everything she had not to fall over.

Big and Bad and Bold—*sooo sexy*—Robert and Zach both wore formal wedding kilts.

Theresa marched down that aisle. Two-step, double time. She greeted her grooms with a killer smile. Despite her righteous ire, it required an act of willpower not to ogle their muscular bare legs.

Hot damn, but both male werewolves looked terrific in man-skirts.

"Zachery Hunter," she whispered, "I expect this sort of thing from you. But, Robert..." She speared the Wolf King with her gaze. "Seriously? You're not even Scotch."

Robert offered a shit-eating grin. "I lost a bet. In my defense, that shot was one-in-a-million."

"Are you telling me this is because of *golf*?" Theresa demanded

"Golf is the sport of kings. A king must be a man of his word," Zach intoned. "Honor is vital."

Robert nodded in sincere support of his fellow groom.

Theresa aimed her bridal bouquet like a weapon. "I'll deal with both of you—later."

"Yes, ma'am," both grooms chorused.

Charlaine snorted. "It's obvious who should be wearing the pants here."

The Wolf God cleared his throat, a deep rumbling. "Dearly Beloved, we are gathered here today to join these men and this woman in holy matrimony."

And they lived Happily Ever After—The End.

ALSO BY MELISSA SNARK

Captain Hook & the Pirates of Neverland

Hook: Dead to Rights

Hook: Dead Wrong

Hook: Death Wish

Loki's Wolves Universe

Ragnarök: Doom of the Gods Series

Valkyrie's Vengeance

Hunger Moon

Battle Cry

Wolf's Cross

Hunter's Mark

Fragile Gods

A Novel of the Fallen Angels

A Time to Reap

Sassafras Shifters

The Mating Game

Out Foxed

Ram Rugged

Bewitched Dragon Mates

That Old Black Magic Universe

Heart's Desired Mate Series

Love is the Law